Nobeca

Lloyd Nesling

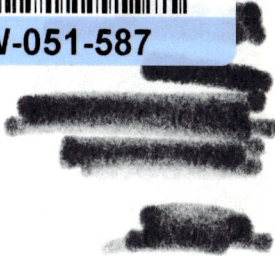

Matador
9 Priory Business Park,
Wistow Road, Kibworth Beauchamp,
Leicestershire. LE8 0RX
Tel: 0116 279 2299
Email: books@troubador.co.uk
Web: www.troubador.co.uk/matador
Twitter: @matadorbooks

ISBN 978 1788035 965

British Library Cataloguing in Publication Data.
A catalogue record for this book is available from the British Library.

Printed on FSC accredited paper
Printed and bound in Great Britain by 4edge Limited
Typeset in 11pt Minion Pro by Troubador Publishing Ltd, Leicester, UK

Matador is an imprint of Troubador Publishing Ltd

The author has used the real names of structures and hotels in the novel, with a few exceptions. For example, the Hotel Trabazon in Paris does not exist. Hotel Parisienne is completely fictional in this novel and should not be confused with any other hotel in Paris that may have a similar sounding name. Similarly, the terms Shropshire Police Headquarters and Shropshire Royal Infirmary are purely historical. Miles, gallons, kilometres and litres have been used depending on where the action is taking place.

Nobeca is entirely a work of fiction. The characters, incidents and dialogue are a product of the author's imagination and should not be interpreted as real events. Names of actual persons, living or dead, actual names, actual places and actual historical events in the public domain are incidental to the plot of the novel and are not intended to alter the wholly fictitious character of the book.

By the same author *(Norma Lloyd-Nesling)*

Season of the Long Grass
The Regis Connection'

For Tracey and Richard.
Looking forward to your next gourmet dinner.

PROLOGUE

Leningrad (St. Petersburg), 1970-1973

It happened when he was nineteen. The old woman wrapped in a shawl walking near the Wall sparked the memory of that terrible night. She looked so much like his mother, Irina. Images crowded his memory like scenes from a horror film. A drunken, slobbering woman, lips painted bright red. It was more than fifteen years ago, but he still remembered the metallic smell of her blood. He felt no remorse only a consuming anger and a hunger for revenge.

His stomach clenched when he thought about the abuse his mother had suffered at the hands of his father, Feliks; an arrogant, violent man with an insatiable sexual appetite. That night he had brought home a whore after drinking in his favourite haunt. Fuelled with vodka, they laughed and taunted Irina. She cowered in a corner, her face bruised and swollen from a recent beating.

Pasha snapped and went at his father with a kitchen knife, slashing in a frenzy of hatred. Terrified, he ran into the bedroom and bolted the door while Pasha turned on the woman. She was too drunk to fend him off. He stabbed her over and over again. Horrified, Irina screamed for him to stop, but nothing could stop him. All he could hear was mocking laughter. With the tip of his knife he carved the word 'whore' on the woman's forehead.

Panting with rage, he watched her writhing on the floor until her lifeblood drained away. Irina stood with her back against the bedroom door pleading with Pasha not to harm his father. Eventually, she managed to calm him enough to grab the knife. When Feliks finally emerged from the bedroom and saw the woman's blood-covered body, he panicked. Even more frightening was the hatred in his son's eyes. He tried to run to the door, but Pasha barred his way. Grabbing him by the throat, he lifted him off his feet and smashed him against the wall. He dropped to the ground, whimpering with fright.

Irina stared in disbelief at the woman's mutilated body, her mouth open in a silent scream. Pasha put his arms around her reassuringly and guided her to a chair. He had to get rid of the body. It wouldn't be an easy task with security police on the lookout for suspicious behaviour in the middle of the night.

Icily calm, Pasha avoided the sticky mess on the floor. Quickly, he stripped the bloody topcoat off the body and replaced it with a coat belonging to Feliks. Hundreds of workers wore similar garments so it would be hard to trace. He tied a woollen scarf around her head, covering her face. Nobody would think it suspicious on such a cold night.

Putting on a heavy overcoat and fur hat, he pulled down the earmuffs and fastened them over the lower part of his face. He hoisted his dazed father to his feet and slapped his face viciously from side to side. Wordlessly, Feliks obeyed his son's instructions and helped carry the murdered woman from their ground-floor apartment into the unlit road.

While Irina scrubbed the floor clean of blood, Feliks and

Pasha staggered along, pretending to be drunk. Supporting the body under each arm, they lurched along singing Red Army songs, to the amusement of drinkers emerging from the bars. When they reached the nearby Obvodny Canal, they pushed the body into the murky water.

Afraid to report his son to the police, in case he was implicated in the murder, Feliks went to work the following morning as though nothing had happened. That night the three of them sat down to supper. On the surface a normal family, but the urge to kill Feliks had triggered a violent hatred in his son he could not quell.

Feliks was so frightened he stopped drinking and kept his hands off Irina for months, but it didn't last. One night, he staggered through the door stinking drunk and gave her a savage beating. When Pasha arrived home from university he found her lying on the floor, her face covered in blood.

Feliks was in the kitchen bending over the open stove looking for his supper. Grabbing him by the hair Pasha pushed his head into the oven, straight into the sizzling stroganoff. Feliks tried to struggle, but he held him down until he felt his body go limp. A whimper behind him turned to a shriek. Irina was standing in the doorway screaming, her eyes wide with terror.

When the authorities turned up she was sitting in the middle of the floor babbling incoherently. The horror of her husband's death had sent her over the edge. A neighbour verified that she saw Feliks staggering home drunk that night. It wasn't unusual. It was assumed he had stumbled head first into the oven whilst trying to take out the stroganoff. Irina died nine months later. She didn't even recognise Pasha when he visited her in the hospital.

There was little money left after his father's drinking and womanising, but Irina had secretly squirreled away some money and a few pieces of precious jewellery she had inherited from her Russian–English parents. It was enough for Pasha to continue his education. A brilliant student he soon came to the notice of the KGB. Three years later, with a degree in engineering and computer science under his belt, he bought a train ticket to Moscow.

He stared up at The Lubyanka in Red Square. This is where his future would begin.

1973–1976

Pasha was sent to Helsinki, a training ground for spies from the Eastern bloc. At the Soviet Embassy on Tehtaankatu Street he crafted his art. This was where the Soviets concentrated their intelligence. Finland was a neutral country so it paid to foster amicable relations on both sides. It was only a ferry voyage on the Viking Line from Tallinn to Helsinki. The KGB used the city as a portal for Soviet spies infiltrating the West. He excelled: no assignment was too onerous for him. He was a natural linguist, like his English grandmother, and mastered several languages.

At first he slipped into Scandinavian countries. Sweden, Denmark and Norway, followed by brief spells in Dublin and Chicago. In London he worked hard perfecting his received pronunciation. By the time he returned to Finland, his English was perfect.

On a chilly day in April he was summoned into the ambassador's office. A man he had never seen before stood near the window.

"This is Colonel Petrov from Moscow."

Pasha's stomach churned, but he managed to maintain his equilibrium. Why had a high-ranking officer turned up from Moscow? Petrov motioned for him to sit down. He leaned against the ambassador's desk and lit a cigarette before continuing.

"We've been watching you for some time. We think you're ready to integrate into American society. An interview, under the name Ralph Wilson, has been arranged for you in the computer science department at New York University."

"But sir, there are others more experienced."

"Yes, but they don't have your specific qualifications for the post."

"What if I don't get the job?"

"You will be highly recommended from within the department. Besides, your research activities and references from Oxford and McGill in Montreal will be impeccable."

Pasha felt a flicker of uncertainty. He had not expected to be sent into the field on such an important assignment this early in his career. They could be testing his commitment and resilience.

"I'm flattered that you consider me capable and honoured to serve my country."

Petrov nodded his head. It was the response he wanted.

"You must ensure that you do nothing that will arouse suspicion. There are hundreds like you in the United States. They live completely normal lives under the noses of the FBI and the CIA. Some of our agents have been over there for over twenty years." Petrov studied him closely for any sign of tension. All that registered on his handsome face was satisfaction and confidence. He was ready. "Success or failure depends on you, Pasha."

PART ONE

1976–1989

—

CHAPTER ONE

California, 1976–1984

Ralph Wilson started his new job the following September. His brief was to build up a reputation for excellence before he was moved on. Two months into the job, he was joined by his 'wife', Andrea. After four years building up his reputation, he secured a post in computer science and engineering at Stanford University in California.

The Wilsons set up home in rented accommodation in Santa Cruz. The commute to San José every day was hellish, but it deterred colleagues from dropping in unannounced. He soon became involved with research projects in Silicon Valley. He befriended anyone where he could glean intelligence for the Soviets.

Sex wasn't a part of the relationship with his 'wife'. The thought disgusted him. The KGB knew about Andrea's secret transgressions, but sexual preference could be very useful to them in gathering intelligence. Her interests leaned towards the pretty girls in the banking complex where she worked as a senior auditor. Pasha took his pleasure with cheap girls in downtown motel rooms, but Andrea baulked at casual relationships.

Two years into the 'job' she fell for Jodie, a blonde cashier of the same persuasion. It was the start of a turbulent affair that frequently flared into bouts of insane jealousy. Pasha only found out about the affair after the blonde discovered where they lived and turned up on the doorstep. She was a threat that had to be eliminated immediately.

Late one night, he tailed Jodie to her home in a small housing community in Palo Alto. He shimmied the window at the rear of the single-storey house and crept into the darkened bedroom. He crept along the narrow hallway looking into every room. As he passed the kitchen, the outer door swung open. A woman stood silhouetted in the light from the veranda that circled the house. The damn door was open all the time! Pressing himself into the shadow of a large bookcase he froze, knife in hand.

"Come on in, honey," Jodie called, "the late show's just finished."

"Darn it, I forgot the wine. I'll go get it; won't be a jiffy."

"Don't be long, the movie's gonna start any minute now."

The kitchen door slammed shut. He heard the woman crunch along the path to the house next door. He only had a few minutes to get the job done before she came back.

Jodie was lounging on the sofa with her back to the door. She was laughing at some animated advertisement for breakfast cereal. Leaning over, he grabbed her head and pulled it back. She kicked out and flailed her arms, but Ralph was too strong for her. Clamping his hand over her mouth he drew the blade across her throat and waited until her body slumped down into the chair. With the tip of the knife he carved a single word on her arm: 'dyke'. He wiped off some of the blood with one of Andrea's sweatshirts and stuffed it into a plastic bag. Now he had to get rid of the other problem, his 'wife'.

Supper was a sombre affair. Andrea was in a bad mood, because her girlfriend had failed to show up at their usual haunt.

"Is something wrong, Andrea?" he asked. "You seem a bit down."

"It's nothing." She didn't know that Jodie had turned up out of the blue a few days previously. "I'm just tired. It's been a hard day."

"Let's have a drink. It will relax you," he said sympathetically. "Help you to sleep."

She loosened up when he offered her a glass of vodka. Knocking it back in one gulp, she poured another. She could match him drink for drink. A fellow graduate of the Tehtaankatu spy school she was no pushover. He had to be very careful not to arouse her suspicions.

After her sixth vodka, her speech started to slur. She staggered into her bedroom and dropped onto the bed. Within seconds she was snoring like a pig. He had spiked her last drink with diazepam. She wouldn't wake up for hours, not that she *would* ever wake up again.

At two-thirty in the morning, he hauled her through the interconnecting garage door and pushed her into her Chevette, dressed in the blood-soaked sweatshirt. He hated the drive through the hazardous Santa Cruz Mountains, but there would be little traffic at this early hour. Fog descended as he drove along Highway 17. Ascending the tortuous highway, he crossed the Santa Clara–Santa Cruz county line through the summit at Patchen Pass. In the distance brake lights winked on and off as a vehicle negotiated Valley Surprise curve.

Driving close to the middle of the road, he let a Ford overtake. There was nothing behind him as he slowed down to a crawl halfway into the curve. Without taking his eyes off the road he leaned over, opened the passenger door, and pushed Andrea out.

5

"Goodbye, bitch!" he said vehemently.

He slammed the door shut and drove off just as a set of headlights rounded the corner. Moments later, he heard the screech of tyres followed by a muffled thud as the vehicle ran into Andrea's body. He drove on another hundred yards, slewed to a halt, and picked up the Harley he had stowed out of sight. Within five minutes he was roaring down the highway towards Santa Cruz.

Two days later he reported his 'wife's' disappearance to the police after seeing a report on the accident at Valley Surprise Curve. Santa Clara County Police found traces of Andrea's blood in her car. The medical examiner's report confirmed that blood found on her sweatshirt matched that found in her car and the body found in Palo Alto. They brought Ralph Wilson in for questioning.

"Can you tell us why your wife would have been in the Santa Cruz Mountains in the early hours of the morning?" Detective Bacanora asked.

"I don't know. She went out about ten o'clock and didn't come back. She was a bit quieter than usual during dinner, but otherwise she seemed all right. We'd had a silly argument about a trip to Miami. It was all planned then suddenly she decided she didn't want to go."

"Did you know about her relationship with Jodie Reynolds, a colleague in the bank?"

Wilson looked stunned by the news of his wife's death. He looked uncomprehendingly at the detective.

"She mentioned her once or twice, but I never met her."

"So, you weren't aware that they were having a relationship."

"A relationship? I don't know what you mean."

"That they were having an affair. A bit of the old rumpy pumpy. Do I have to spell it out?"

"Why are you saying such terrible things? We loved each other! She wouldn't; not with a woman!"

Poor sucker, Bacanora thought. Wilson looked confused, completely out of it.

"A clerk from the bank told us he had witnessed several arguments between Andrea and Jodie, but they weren't about work. Their body language suggested something more than mere friendship. He guessed there was something going on between them, but kept his mouth shut. He didn't want to get involved."

"I don't believe it!" Wilson shouted, covering his ears.

"They had a massive row in the car park," Baconara continued. "Jodie got into her car and roared off. It was the last time he saw either of them."

They didn't have a trace of evidence, either physical or circumstantial, to charge him.

"Okay, you're free to go, Wilson, but we may want to speak to you again." Ralph felt a rush of satisfaction. It couldn't have worked out better.

"Everything points to the wife, Lieutenant," Baconara said. "I think she killed her girlfriend in a fit of jealous rage after they had a row. Jodie's blood was all over the sweatshirt Andrea was wearing. She probably couldn't cope with what she'd done, drove to Patchen Pass and deliberately walked into oncoming traffic. That's it; it's all we've got."

"It fits with the medical examiner's report. Suicide while the balance of her mind was disturbed. Wrap it up Baconara," Lieutenant Kowalski said. "I need more men out on that missing kid case."

CHAPTER TWO

Santa Cruz, California

Ralph reported the deaths to Moscow. They had no truck with her lifestyle, but it was tolerated, even encouraged while she was actively spying in the United States. The KGB conducted its own investigation. Grigory, an undercover agent living in San Fransisco, arrived one night without warning. Ralph admitted killing Andrea and her girlfriend.

"She got involved with a woman in the bank where she worked," he explained. "I had no choice. My cover was being compromised."

"She would have answered for her behaviour when she returned to Moscow, but her decadent lifestyle was useful to us here," the agent said.

"I couldn't risk being exposed now when I was on the brink of intelligence that could prove very useful to us. The research project I'm involved with allows me to collect extensive data on computing, telecommunication and instrumentation."

Playing on the importance of his new research into computer architecture and networking, which could be used by the military, he convinced the agent to recommend he be allowed to remain in California.

"Very well." The agent nodded in agreement. "I'll send my report to Moscow. They will make a decision."

"Moscow was delighted with the official police verdict," Grigory told him a week later. "You are still very useful to them. You must make friends. Scientists talk together; argue the finer points of their research. Let them talk, Ralph."

His job was to listen, to gather intelligence; but scientists were reticent with newcomers. He had to find a way to get close to them.

A few weeks after Andrea's funeral one of his colleagues stopped at his desk. "How ya doing?" Ralph looked up, his face etched with misery. "How about joining the guys for a drink after work?" The poor guy needed to get out. "A couple of beers will do you good."

Ralph feigned reluctance, but his heart thudded with anticipation. Until now he had been outside the group. "I haven't been out much since, you know."

"Come on, no sense in stewing on your own." This was the opening he desperately needed.

After a hard week, copious amounts of bourbon loosened their tongues. They were the crème de la crème in their fields; their own exclusive clique. Ralph was delighted to be part of it. He played the grieving widower, exploiting it to be invited to the homes of scientists, physicists and engineers for parties and barbecues. He had been accepted. Looking lonely and depressed he sat quietly in a corner; all the while listening, gleaning as much information as possible.

Wives neglected by men wrapped up in their work offered him sympathy and friendship. They went round to his home with apple pie and a shoulder to cry on. His first encounter was with Darlene after a Christmas Eve party at her home.

"Hi, Ralph, having a good time?"

"I guess so."

She leaned over with the tray of canapés, almost brushing his face with her breasts. Neglected by her workaholic physicist husband, Arthur, she was an easy conquest. Poor Darlene; a science graduate herself, she was bored and housebound with three young children. It was surprising how much he learned from her about Arthur's projects.

Soon he instigated a number of illicit relationships, playing off one woman against the other. Starved of attention, they responded to flattery, soft music and the promise of illicit sex. Ralph was very careful to treat them with the utmost tenderness and consideration, unlike the prostitutes he picked up on his trips to Los Angeles. They were left battered and bruised, if they were lucky to be still alive when he had finished with them.

Darlene became increasingly possessive, demanding more and more of his time. When she started talking about leaving her husband, he knew he would have to get rid of her. He had his chance when Arthur flew to Philadelphia to attend a conference in late March. After dinner at his house in Santa Cruz they headed to the beach near 26th Avenue. Hand in hand, they walked along the shoreline in the dark, away from prying eyes. Suddenly, Ralph took off his shoes and ran into the sea.

"The water must be freezing!" Darlene yelled.

"Come on in, it's invigorating!"

"You crazy fool!"

Laughing, she kicked off her shoes and ran after him. He was smiling when he caught her in his arms and pushed her head under the water. It was all over in a few minutes. He dragged her body as far out into the surf as he dared and waded back to shore. Next morning a man walking his dog spotted her sodden body washed up on the beach.

Arthur blamed himself for Darlene's 'suicide'. "She had been depressed for a long time. I shouldn't have left her alone so much," he said at her funeral. "I should have taken her to Philadelphia with me instead of leaving her here to brood." If only he knew.

Ralph spent another three productive years in California until he was ordered to resign his position at the university and return to Moscow.

*

Colonel Petrov studied his protégé. He was an exceptional agent. Taking a long drag of his cigarette, he sat down behind his desk. For a full three minutes he said nothing, watching for any signs of anxiety or discomfort. It was a senior position in the KGB, but he was certain he was up to the job.

Finally he said, "Congratulations, your work in America has been noted by the Politburo."

"I'm flattered they have so much faith in me, Colonel."

"Make sure their faith is justified," Petrov said. "From now on you will be known by your new codename, 'Nobeca'. We expect absolute loyalty from you. You are being rewarded for your excellence. Remember, there is no margin for failure."

Within weeks he was in Berlin taking charge of KGB activities in the Eastern Sector. His star was in the ascendancy. His future was secure. Nothing could touch him now.

Devastatingly handsome, impeccable manners; he was a magnet for women. He played his image up to the hilt, but his vanity made him careless. Nobeca thought he was untouchable; too clever to be caught at his favourite pastime, seducing the wives of his colleagues. He never risked harming them physically: that part of his life was reserved for whores he picked up on assignments in the West.

His star exploded on a visit to Moscow. He was caught in bed with the daughter of a government minister. Only her pleading and threat of humiliation stopped the minister from having him arrested on trumped-up charges. He went back to East Berlin satisfied that he had wheedled his way out of it. After that his sexual exploits were confined to pickups in West Berlin. Whenever he was summoned to Moscow his behaviour was beyond reproach. Nobeca promised himself he would not be so stupid a second time. His downfall came when he tangled with Valentina.

CHAPTER THREE

West Berlin, July 1989

Nobeca and the woman wandered off the path crowded with walkers and cyclists deep into the darkness of the Grünewald. Holding hands, like a pair of teenagers on a first date, they settled down under a large tree. As soon as Linda lay down Nobeca fell on top of her. Giggling girlishly at his impatience she tried to push him off. She wanted to be in control, to watch him so filled with desire for her that he would beg.

He pinned her arms up behind her head while she pretended to struggle. She quite liked playing games with him. Her struggling seemed to excite him even more, but when she looked into his eyes her smile froze. They were full of hate.

"Stop it! You're hurting me!" she cried, trying to push him away. Suddenly, he released one hand and punched her in the face. Blood poured from her broken nose onto her lips and down the back of her throat. She tried to scream, but he clamped his hand over her mouth until she could hardly breathe.

"Bitch! You're like all the others."

Eyes full of hate, he drew his fingernails down her cheek until he drew blood then straddled her until he satisfied his lust.

When Linda stirred and tried to sit up he landed another vicious blow to the side of her head. Hauling her up into a sitting position, he shook her violently until she opened her eyes.

"Please, don't hurt me anymore," she moaned. "Please, you can do whatever you want, but don't hurt me."

He would have to kill her, but he wanted her to know she was about to die. Putting his hands around her slender neck he squeezed hard, relishing the abject terror in her eyes.

It was pitch-dark when he carried her body to an isolated part of the lake and pushed it into the black waters. If and when the body was discovered by the West Berlin Polizei, he would be back in East Berlin. Nobody would question him if he was discovered near the Wall on 'official' business. It was part of his job to infiltrate the West.

"Collaboration with the Stasi is important," Colonel Sidirov had insisted when he had taken up the post. "Erich Meikle, the Minister of State security, has granted KGB officers in East Germany the same rights and powers they have in the Soviet Union. This is to our advantage. Don't compromise your position. Is that understood?"

"Absolutely, sir," Nobeca replied.

He wasn't compromising his position. This one didn't count. He was just ridding the world of another slut. He had the perfect cover, always restricting his exploits to the West. No sense in taking unnecessary risks.

*

From his vantage point in a goon tower overlooking the Wall in Glienicke, Nobeca surveyed the main road. It was usually deserted in the dead of night. He nodded at the Grepos as he descended the wooden ladder. His route under the Wall

14

led through a narrow tunnel with just enough space to crawl on hands and knees into the woods opposite. After hauling himself out at the other end, he carefully replaced the camouflage around the exit. Making his way through the damp undergrowth, he listened for the sound of an engine. Once he reached the drop-off point, his false identity papers would enable him to move freely around the city.

The tip of a cigarette glowed near the goon tower. Captain Yuri Morozov of the KGB watched Nobeca creep to the edge of the trees as a motorcycle approached. His orders were to keep him under surveillance.

"He has disregarded authority on more than one occasion, but managed to talk his way out of it," he said to the junior officer at his side. "Sooner or later he'll slip up. His code name has turned out to be prophetic." The young officer looked at him quizzically. "It means 'Lothario'. He's a serial seducer, particularly with wives of senior officers." Fury consumed Morozov like a raging fire. This time he had gone too far. He had put his filthy hands on his beloved Valentina.

Morozov wasn't the only one watching Nobeca. His every move was being monitored by the Stasi, as well as the KGB. Questions were being asked about his lifestyle. How could he entertain so extravagantly on a captain's salary? There were rumours that he was spying for the West and that he planned to defect for the right price. He had wriggled out of the accusations, claiming that he was being targeted, because of his affairs.

His conquests remained loyally silent, for their own sakes as much as his. He had made a big mistake with Valentina. She was young and naive: an easy target. When Nobeca had finished with her, he cast her off like an old coat. She was killed instantly after jumping in front of a train in the Ubahn. Morozov wanted revenge.

*

The Mitte, East Berlin, August 1989

The headline jumped out at him as he passed a group of men idling near a newspaper stand. Nobeca pushed through the crowd, bought copies of *Berliner Zeitung* and *Neues Deutschland*, folded them under his arm and headed down the road to Augustiner's in the Gendarmenmarkt.

"*Bitte*," the waiter asked.

"Pigs' knuckles, potatoes, cabbage and a stein of beer." He could afford caviar and champagne, but he had never lost his taste for the simple food of his childhood. It reminded him of his beloved mother.

Most of the newspapers were running with the same banner headline.

'Body Found in Schlachtensee'.

Casually, he read through the article. The partially decomposed body of a woman had been discovered by a couple of students in a lake in the Grünewald. She had been identified as Linda Jaeger, wife of Hans Jaeger, a senior member of the Federal German Government.

A rage coursed through him. The bitch hadn't told him she was married to a high-profile politician when he offered to take her to dinner. His fists clenched until his knuckles turned white. Linda was like all the others, a whore. He had to get back into East Berlin before the Polizei started asking questions about her movements on the night of the murder. He wasn't due to be picked up for another fourteen hours. He couldn't risk staying on the streets. He would have to hole up in a hotel room for the rest of the day.

Fortunately, he was close to the Hilton built on the site of the old Soviet Domhotel in the Gendarmenmarkt.

"Would you like to book dinner this evening?" the receptionist asked.

"No thanks. I'll have something light in my room. I have a very early meeting tomorrow morning."

Shortly after midnight, he left the hotel and took a taxi to a bar in the Heerstrasse where he had arranged to be picked up. A real dive. Even at this late hour it was crowded, which suited his purpose. He ordered a schnapps and carried it to a dimly lit corner near a window where he could observe the road. His contact should have been here by now. About twenty minutes later he spotted a motorcycle sliding between the cars. He gulped down the dregs of his drink, casually walked out into the car park and mounted the pillion.

"Where the hell have you been? You'll answer for this. Come on, let's get out of here."

Once out of the city the motorcycle gathered speed. Nobeca breathed a sigh of satisfaction when they hit the Kladow-to-Glienicke road. The sooner he crossed over into the Soviet Sector, the better.

The area near the woods in Glienicke was very quiet at night. It consisted mainly of expensive homes where wealthy Berliners escaped for peace and quiet. A few residents used the narrow path through the woods as a shortcut to the bus stop, but never at night, especially since a woman had been attacked.

The motorcycle eased to a stop and dropped him off just inside the trees. Stealthily, he made his way to a large rock hidden deep in the undergrowth. He rolled it aside and lowered himself into the tunnel. With the flat of his hands he eased it back into place. It was just after 3:00 a.m. by the time he struggled out of the tunnel near the goon tower.

Nobeca knew he was being watched by the KGB when he was in Moscow and by the Stasi in East Germany. Did they think he was stupid? From now on he would have to be much more careful. For the next three weeks he threw himself into his work, more to satisfy his growing impatience than diligence. He knew they would act soon, but he would be waiting for them.

CHAPTER FOUR

September, 1989

It was damp and miserable on the Havel, but Nobeca was snug inside the cabin of his motorboat. Few people had ventured out, except for enthusiasts who navigated the waterway in all winds and weather. He had been chugging within the confines of the Soviet Sector all day waiting for it to happen. Only one thought on his mind: permanent escape into West Berlin. He had to stay well clear of Glienicke Bridge, but get as close to the British Sector as possible.

He had discovered the plot by accident after overhearing Morozov talking on the telephone to a senior Stasi Officer.

"We must wait for the right opportunity. We can't act until we are sure it will succeed. His every movement must be monitored."

Positive that they were discussing him, he broke into Morozov's desk and found the manila folder stamped 'SECRET' in bold red letters. It contained a veiled order to eliminate him as soon as possible. He had no idea when or where it would happen, but he would have to be on his guard twenty-four hours a day.

Systematically, he searched his quarters and his vehicle on a daily basis. It wouldn't matter to the KGB if an innocent driver was killed with him. Life was cheap. Every search proved fruitless, but he knew without a shadow of doubt that his assassination was imminent. He would give them an opportunity they couldn't resist. They were clever, but they would never outwit him.

"I haven't been sailing for ages," he told Morozov. He didn't miss the barely perceptible flicker of interest. "Perhaps I'll take my boat out on the weekend. Do you fancy joining me?"

"Sorry, I have a long-standing commitment." Morozov choked back the anger tightening his chest. This could be his opportunity for revenge. "My niece's wedding," he lied.

Nobeca smiled inwardly, imagining the KGB officer's excitement at the thought of finally destroying the man who had ruined his life.

He searched every inch of the boat before he took it out, confident that he would find an explosive device. After prising off a panel under one of the bunks, he discovered it buried at the bottom of a box filled with life jackets and an assortment of tools. The device was set for 4:15 p.m. when he would be on his way back to dock the boat. With a satisfied grunt he settled down to wait.

At precisely 3:30 p.m. he struggled into the wetsuit he had brought with him and checked the equipment in his waterproof rucksack. Wire cutters, clothes, shoes, false passport and identity papers, plus enough Deutschmarks to tide him over for a few days: all sealed in a plastic bag covered with oilskin.

By four o'clock the light was fading. It would be dark soon. A misty rain added to the gloom. Anybody observing him through binoculars would have difficulty monitoring his movements. He locked the steering wheel, adjusted his snorkel, pulled down his goggles and slid into the river. With only the snorkel pipe visible above the water, he swam away from the boat towards the barbed wire separating East and West Berlin.

Suddenly, a loud explosion shattered the stillness. Orange flames lit up the gloom, illuminating debris showering down onto the surface of the water. A searchlight lit up the river on the West side, another on the Soviet side. The boat had all but disappeared. All that remained was a mess of wood floating on the surface. Taking advantage of the commotion, he swam towards the barbed wire. Within seconds he had cut a gap big enough for him to squeeze through. Keeping his head as far under the water as possible, he swam towards the British Sector.

Exhausted, he climbed out onto the muddy bank and crawled into the bushes. Quickly, he peeled off the wetsuit and concealed it in the undergrowth, along with the rest of the equipment. He stared back up the river.

"You'll never defeat me, Morozov," he snarled. "I'll always be one step ahead of you."

Five minutes later, dressed in a warm sweater and corduroys, he walked through the gloom towards a clutch of restaurants.

The smell of roasted meat hit his nostrils as soon as he opened the door. He ordered a large schnapps and downed it in one gulp. After the second one he felt a lot better. He motioned to the waiter.

"*Weinerschnitzel, pomme frites, apfelstrudel und einem bier;* a large one."

A good stodgy meal was what he needed now to warm him up. He smiled inwardly, visualising the chaos after the boat went up. The KGB and the Stasi would be looking for his body, but they wouldn't find anything except bits and pieces of the man who had cleaned up his boat. Nobeca had crushed his skull with a hammer before stowing him below. He had added enough explosives to completely obliterate any remains found, except for some personal effects he deliberately dropped overboard. Enough to convince them he had been blown up with the boat.

On the Soviet bank Morozov and a Stasi officer watched an inflatable dinghy head out towards the wreckage.

"That was quite spectacular, a much bigger explosion than I expected," he said, turning to the Stasi Officer standing beside him.

"*Ja*, they have done a good job. Nobody could survive that blast."

Searchlights from the British Sector swept over the wreckage and the boat moving towards it. There was no sign of life in the water.

"Probably another escape attempt," the British officer surmised. "Poor sod whoever it was."

Glimpsing something floating in the water a Grepo leaned out of the dinghy, fished something out and headed back to shore. Morozov examined part of the sodden jacket. There was something solid in the inside pocket. He pulled it out. There was no doubt about what the Grepo had salvaged. It belonged to Nobeca. He never went anywhere without it. A feeling of intense satisfaction coursed through him. At last the bastard had got what he deserved.

*

With a full stomach and another schnapps on the table Nobeca looked at his options. If he was picked up he could claim he was trying to escape from East Berlin, but too many questions would be asked. British military intelligence would interrogate him and keep him under surveillance. They were far more adept at keeping track on spies infiltrating West Berlin than the KGB assumed. It often served their purpose just to track their movements and let them sneak back out.

His best option was to lie low in an expensive hotel and enjoy the rest. That would give him time to prepare for his new life as a wealthy businessman searching for opportunities in West Berlin. His little liaisons had paid off. Poor deluded women: they had given him expensive presents. Rings, gold watches and artworks that he smuggled into West Berlin and kept in a safe deposit box in his bank.

The coup de grâce was Anna Mettler, a childless widow he met in a hotel bar on one of his forays into the West. He couldn't believe his luck when she told him she was visiting from Zurich. Ten years his senior, he wooed her with an intensity she couldn't resist. He had finally seduced her after dinner and dancing in Haus Carow.

"Anna, my darling, I want to spend the rest of my life with you. Will you marry me?"

"But we know so little about each other," she said cautiously.

"I know all I need to know," he replied, visualising her bank account. "I have waited for you all my life."

Anna's heart fluttered like a schoolgirl. He was such a handsome man. How could she resist?

After that it was relatively easy to gain her trust. They were married in a civil ceremony and set up home. His prolonged absences were explained as essential business trips to West

Germany. Three months later she committed suicide from an 'overdose' of antidepressants.

"She was on antidepressants for months," he told the coroner. "She didn't really settle in Berlin. She wanted to go back to Switzerland."

Before her death he had persuaded her to transfer her entire fortune of fifty million Swiss francs into his name in her Zurich bank. Now all he had to do was wait until things quietened down.

As far as the KGB was concerned, Nobeca was dead. He had been planning his escape for months, long before he discovered the plot to kill him. Every time he slipped into West Berlin, he took something with him. He had already transferred substantial funds from West Berlin into accounts in the Paris and Madrid branches of Deutsche Bank; enough to comfortably start his new life. He was a patient man. It was important to keep a level head and not allow his greed to overcome his ambitions. Now all he had to do was get out of Berlin for good and implement his plans for the future.

CHAPTER FIVE

West Berlin, November 9th, 1989

Nobeca couldn't believe his eyes. He turned up the volume on the television and stared incredulously at an excited newscaster standing amongst a throng of revellers. The Wall had been breached! The East German guards stood helplessly in the background, unsure of how to tackle the milling crowds. Since he had been in the hotel he had eaten in his room, so engrossed in his plans that he hadn't even switched on the television.

There were always the usual idiots shouting obscenities at the Grepos on the other side, but this? How had it happened so suddenly? The footage flashed to a man squeezing through a narrow gap into East Berlin and emerging a few seconds later. Nobeca couldn't resist the temptation to see it for himself. Hurriedly, he went down to the taxi rank outside the main entrance.

"Bornholmer Strasse," he instructed the driver.

At the border crossing people were shouting and singing. Some were dancing a jig as though it were a big outdoor party.

"What the hell's going on? I can't get through the crowd," the taxi-driver yelled over his shoulder.

Sparklers swirled in the misty air lighting up the gloomy night. People were downing champagne and passing the bottle from one to the other. The aura of euphoria sweeping through the crowd was palpable. A gang of teenagers clambered up and perched on top of the Wall. Others pounded at it with hammers and chisels, breaking off chunks of graffiti-covered concrete. This is where it had all started. He got out of the taxi and worked his way through the excited crowds. The atmosphere was intoxicating; almost like being slightly tipsy. He still couldn't believe it was happening. Gates and security barriers were demolished. Buses poured through the border point crowded with East Berliners anxious to meet relatives in the West. They streamed past the suddenly defunct Bornholmer Strasse checkpoint into West Berlin.

He hurried back to the taxi and instructed the driver to take him to Brandenberg Gate. He couldn't believe his eyes. Berliners from each side were walking through the checkpoint watched by bewildered East German guards on one side and British troops on the other. A sense of exhilaration surged through him. He was free!

He went back to his hotel and sent down for a bottle of whisky. Tonight he could afford to celebrate, secure in the knowledge that his passage from the city would be easier than he had planned. When he awoke next morning it was to discover that Brandenberg Gate had been closed until new orders were received, but that would not affect him. To cover his tracks he decided to take a flight to West Germany before moving on. It would be foolish to take risks when his goal was within reach. The grieving widower would access his Swiss account after a suitable period of mourning. By the time Brandenberg Gate opened for good on November 22nd, Nobeca was in Munich boarding a flight for Madrid.

PART TWO

2016–2017

CHAPTER SIX

Gloucestershire, England, March 2016

Colin Lynes had the pasty skin of someone who spent too much time indoors. His nondescript face, ill-fitting clothes and beer belly could be seen on any high street across the country. Carefully, he folded his copy of *The Telegraph* and slid it into a leather briefcase. Taking one last look at the computer screen, he switched it to standby and headed for the exit.

Nodding briefly to a colleague, he eased into the driver's seat of an ancient Ford and drove away. Thirty minutes later he pulled into a side street. As usual it was jam-packed with cars. He managed to negotiate into a space in front of the small, terraced house he had occupied for over twelve years.

The middle-aged woman living in number fifteen tweaked her net curtains and waved at him. He smiled and waved back. "The interfering old bat," he muttered, quickly closing the door behind him.

At least once a month he suffered the tedious Mrs Jepps, her odious husband and their tiresome friends. They would probably try their matchmaking tactics again. He smirked thinking of the plump, granite-breasted divorcee they had tried to palm him off with last time. Dutifully, he had taken her out for a drink to the local pub just to keep them quiet.

He had kept a low profile for years, living a normal life with normal, nondescript people. If only they knew. He hadn't seen his children for over a decade. His son was a grown man now and his daughter was married with a child. A hard knot clenched in his stomach. He had sacrificed so much, missed so much.

At dead on seven thirty he rang the doorbell at number fifteen. Across the street a curtain moved barely perceptibly in the vacant house sporting a 'To Let' notice. Standing well back from the window, a sandy-haired man focussed his binoculars on the pale light shining from the Jepps's bay window, waiting until an invisible hand drew the drapes.

Nodding at his smartly-dressed colleague they slipped out of the front door. For a few minutes they stood talking, gesturing towards parts of the house as though evaluating various aspects: an estate agent showing a house to a potential client.

They had been monitoring the street for weeks, waiting for the right opportunity. Most of the residents left for work early in the morning, but the Jepps's were at home all day. Either her old man was messing about in the back yard or she was sitting vigilantly behind her nets, her opera glasses sweeping the street from dawn to dusk. Unknown to her she was being watched as she watched.

The two men strolled a few yards towards a black BMW and shook hands. The older man eased himself into the car, gave a perfunctory wave, and drove down the street around the corner. Quickly, the sandy-haired man walked along the street, looked around then slipped into an alley that led to a rear lane. He counted the doors until he came to the right garden.

With one agile movement he was over the low, breeze-block wall. Suddenly, a loud bark, accompanied by a metallic scuffling, penetrated the darkness. A security light flashed on.

"It's that stray dog again," a voice shouted. "I'll wring its bloody neck!"

"Oh, leave it, Derek. I'm trying to watch my show!"

Pressing himself into the shadows, he waited until the light went off and moved along the wall until he reached the back door. Taking out a small bunch of miniature tools, he inserted one into the lock. It didn't budge. Cursing under his breath he selected another. This time the lock turned immediately. He slipped into the kitchen and closed the door, freezing as something brushed against his legs.

"Bloody cat!" he muttered.

Cautiously, he made his way to the living room. Light from the solenoid street lamp outside the house lit up the room with an orange glow. An enormous flat-screen television and a shabby sofa, littered with magazines, filled most of the space.

Tapping the telephone was out of the question. It had to be something less sophisticated, something ridiculously obvious. Lynes would check for bugging devices. His eyes rested on the curtain rail above the grubby nets in the bay window. Moving aside the heavy drapes, he unscrewed the filigreed pole end and inserted a tiny bugging device. After placing one in the hallway and another in the kitchen, he slid out of the back door and raced down the alley. The black BMW was waiting for him.

"Come on, let's get out of here!"

The car shot off and disappeared into the stream of traffic on the main road.

31

The postman gave a cheery grin as he handed over the morning mail. Lynes stepped back into the hallway, put his briefcase on the floor and examined the pile of letters. He opened a large buff envelope bearing the words 'Waldean Travel' stamped in red. Quickly, he read the single sheet of paper, stuffed it in his pocket, and walked to his car.

Near the far corner of the street, a road sweeper idled along the pavement brushing up litter. Lynes gave him a cursory glance as he pulled away from the curb and drove off. The road sweeper took a long drag on his cigarette. He threw the butt into the gutter with the rest of the rubbish. His eyes followed the dark-blue Volvo that swept around the corner. It eased into the traffic, keeping three cars behind Lynes's battered Mondeo.

Two miles further on, the Volvo took a sharp right turn onto a parking space outside a pub. Simultaneously, a grey van lurched into the road taking its place. A red Astra parked further along the road pulled out behind it. The van driver peered into his driving mirror and flipped open his mobile.

"Lynes is being tailed," he said. "It's the same driver, but a different vehicle three days running."

He slowed down at the entrance to GCHQ while Lynes waited to turn in. The Astra was right behind him.

"Somebody else is watching him. Be extra vigilant."

CHAPTER SEVEN

Gloucestershire, England, March 2016

Foley walked slowly past the computer station. He bent down to retrieve the ballpoint pen he had dropped.

"See you tonight," he whispered.

Lynes stared intently into the screen, seemingly oblivious to the other man's presence. He peered at the flickering computer screen decoding Russian traffic. He was an expert cryptographer, one of the best. He had spent ten years in GCHQ gaining the respect of his peers. Heart beating wildly, he tried to concentrate on his work. Everything he had worked for was coming together.

He had deliberately set out to recruit Foley. Initially, they chatted during coffee breaks or shared a table for lunch. After a few weeks he invited him round for a game of chess. Lynes noticed the pallor on his skin. Foley was a sick man.

"You don't look well, Bruce. Have you seen a doctor yet?" Lynes queried solicitously.

"It's nothing," Foley replied, "just a bit under the weather, that's all."

Foley stared at the vacant monitor screen as though weighing up his options. Just a small slip-up would make Lynes suspicious. Something indeterminate had been found on his left kidney while having a full body-imaging scan offered by a private company. Worried it could affect his army career, he had taken some overdue leave and booked into a Harley Street clinic for some tests. The bile of anxiety and fear melted away when the consultant telephoned him with the results.

"There's absolutely nothing to worry about," he assured him. "The biopsy shows it's benign familial hematuria. A small minority sometimes develop hypertension, but it's highly unlikely. Rest assured that your army career is safe."

A week later, Foley was summoned to his squadron headquarters in Wales, without explanation. Filled with apprehension, he marched towards the building, his guts churning like a cement mixer.

"Captain Foley," the young soldier announced.

Colonel Bradstock gestured towards the chair in front of his desk. Foley sat down warily, eyeing the muscular man in the dark business suit leaning against the wall. Bradstock sat on a swivel chair behind his desk, swinging slowly from side to side.

"It seems, Captain Foley, that you're friendly with a certain Colin Lynes who works with you in GCHQ." Bradstock leaned back and stared hard at him. "How did you become friendly?"

"We play chess together at his house." Foley felt a momentary flutter of anxiety. Why had they been watching him? Bradstock glanced at the dark-suited man. Finally, he said,

"Gilbert works with MI6. It's not his real name of course. We've had Lynes under surveillance for quite some time. He's good at his job, both of them."

"I don't understand."

"As a cryptographer and as a 'sleeper'. Initially, he was planted by the Russian Security Services. However, his allegiance is somewhat questionable. He was also recruited by a man known only as the Generalissimo. We don't know his real identity yet, but there are a number of possibilities."

Gilbert moved from his position near the wall and perched on the edge of Bradstock's desk.

"We know all about your visits to Harley Street," he said.

Foley sagged in his chair. "So much for confidential medical records."

"We're dealing with national security, Foley," Bradstock interjected.

"You seem to have gained a modicum of trust with Lynes," Gilbert continued. "We have our own game in mind. We'd like you to go on playing chess with him. His job is intercepting Russian traffic, but he hasn't got access to top-secret documents. That's where you come in. You're in a position where you're handling very sensitive information. Sooner or later, Lynes will take the bait."

"And if he doesn't?"

"He will."

CHAPTER EIGHT

Gloucestershire, England, April 2016

Foley glanced around the sitting room, wondering if it had been bugged. It had been six weeks since he had set the trap for Lynes. From then on, it had been relatively easy. Heart thudding in his chest, he dropped his head into his hands, almost knocking over the chess pieces.

"You okay, Bruce? What did the consultant say?"

"It's my left kidney. It's completely shot. The right one isn't functioning properly either. The prognosis isn't good." Foley shuffled uncomfortably. "I'll eventually need dialysis until a donor kidney becomes available. Donors are scarce. What am I to do, Colin?" Voice cracking with emotion, he stared down at his trembling hands. "My army career is finished."

Lynes patted his knee sympathetically. Foley was getting worse. It was time to show his hand.

"It could be years before they find a suitable donor for you, Bruce." He hedged slightly before continuing. "I've heard that you can buy organs on the Internet. Of course there are other ways besides money. There are people who would acquire what you need for... information." He hesitated, studying Foley's face.

"What kind of information?" Foley asked cautiously.

"You work in GCHQ... " Lynes's voice tailed off.

"What are you suggesting? I give you top-secret

information in exchange for a kidney? Damn you, Colin. I'm no traitor! "

Furiously, he marched to the door and slammed out. Lynes sat back in his chair and leisurely lit one of the strong Camel cigarettes he favoured. A habit he had acquired in America in the eighties. *He'll be back*, he thought. *Sooner or later he'll be back.*

*

Lynes drew back the net curtains and peered out. He usually enjoyed his Saturday afternoons watching sport on satellite television. It was the one thing he liked about this decadent country. Much as he hated to admit it, he had missed his weekends with Foley, but there was no room for sentiment. Today, he would come ready to negotiate. He stared through the window at the unrelenting weather.

A watery sun hovered briefly between dark clouds illuminating glistening needles of rain. Wind moaned through the rooftops rustling the leaves on the scrappy street trees. The pavements were dark and slick. Fast-flowing water flooded the gutters sending cigarette packets, lollipop sticks and other detritus swirling towards the drain at the end of the street.

He squinted down the road at Foley's hunched figure bent under a large, black umbrella. He had to tread carefully. He didn't want to scare him off before he gained valuable intelligence.

"I've been in touch with my contacts," Lynes said, taking Foley's wet coat. "The information you've provided is not enough. They want specifics. Blueprints of the technology you've been working on for cyber security."

"But it's highly classified. I don't have access to that kind of information," Foley blurted angrily.

"Do you want to die?" Lynes asked harshly. Foley's shoulders sagged. He seemed too weak and depressed to argue with him. "As soon as you hand over the information you'll be flown to Switzerland. You'll be contacted at your hotel and taken to a clinic in the Alps."

"I'm not handing over the final papers until I reach the clinic. That's not negotiable!"

Lynes was ecstatic. A flutter of excitement surged in his chest. Foley smiled inwardly; the 'sleeper' had taken the bait.

CHAPTER NINE

Bernese Oberland, Switzerland, July 2016

Foley had been in Interlaken for two days waiting for his contact, a man called Joseph. Half-heartedly he prodded the grilled fish on his plate. He would have preferred a juicy steak and a pile of French fries, but he was supposed to be a sick man. Glancing into the mirror on the opposite wall, he stared at his reflection. They had done a good job with the make-up. His face looked gaunt and sallow. Dark shadows under his eyes clouded the usual bright blue. An attractive woman dining alone smiled at him from across the room. Briefly, he returned the gesture then stared into his plate. A woman was the last thing on his mind.

After he had finished his lunch he went into the bar. He ordered a bottle of Evian water and sat in a corner at the back of the room where he could view the entrance. On the table next to him, a florid-faced man conversed loudly with a delicate-looking woman. He grinned at Foley and thrust out a huge paw.

"Ethan Bateman," he introduced himself, "and this is my wife, Ellie. You're English?" Foley nodded. "London is our next port of call then home to the good old US of A."

Bateman wasn't his contact. What if something had gone wrong? Cold sweat beaded his forehead. Suddenly he was overcome by nausea.

"What's the problem, son? You look mighty jittery," the big Texan boomed. "Let me get you a drink." He motioned to the waiter.

"Not for me. I don't drink alcohol. I'll just have some water."

"Well, we're set for a nap," he said yawning expansively. "Enjoy your afternoon."

Turning at the bar entrance, he waved at Foley then disappeared in the direction of the lifts.

Foley shifted in his seat, his long fingers devil-drumming on the table. Nervously, he glanced up every time someone pushed through the doors. Lynes had told him he would be contacted within forty-eight hours. It must be today.

He was about to return to his room when a bearded man sauntered over from the bar counter and sat down at a table next to him. As he did so, he accidentally bumped into Foley's table, spilling his drink.

"I'm so sorry," he apologised. "I'll get a waiter to clear up the mess and order you another drink." As he leaned over to pick up a sodden beer mat, he whispered, "Meet me outside in ten minutes"

Foley's mouth went dry. He had to play along until they got to the clinic. He returned to his room, grabbed his overnight bag, and hurried outside. Joseph was waiting beside a black off-road vehicle.

"Get in!"

After leaving the main highway they headed up a rough road until it narrowed into a trail. The 4 x 4 suddenly slewed to a halt. Joseph ordered Foley out and disappeared behind a cluster of boulders, re-emerging with a motorcycle.

"Ride pillion," he ordered.

There were still quite a lot of walkers about negotiating the trail. They turned to watch the motorcycle labouring up the steep incline.

"This can't be the way to the clinic!" Foley shouted over the roar of the engine.

Joseph didn't respond. Bumping over stones, they climbed higher until they were out of sight of the walkers. Twice they were almost thrown off after sliding on loose shale. Suddenly, they careered to a stop. Before Foley knew what was happening, Joseph yanked him off the bike. Roughly, he pushed him towards the edge of the path that fell away to the valley floor. Foley struggled, flailing vacant air, trying to find purchase on the crumbling edge. Joseph pinned him in a vice-like grip, arching his body backwards over the chasm.

"Give me the microchip!"

Suddenly, voices drifted down from the path directly above them. Without warning Joseph released him, jumped on the motorcycle and roared away. Foley fell forward onto his hands and knees. A man's voice shouted,

"Are you insane? Get away from the edge, you fool!"

Two walkers came hurrying down the path. They grabbed him and pulled him to safety. Trembling from the exertion of his struggle, Foley sank to the ground.

"What happened here?" one of the men asked, watching the motorcycle zigzagging up the trail.

"That maniac almost knocked me down," Foley lied. Together the two men helped him to his feet. "Thanks, but I'm okay now."

"If you're sure, but don't venture any higher. The trail fans out up there. It's easy to get lost in the mountains." He pointed towards the route Joseph had taken. "He'll have to come back down this track. There's nowhere else for him to go. The left fork is impassable except on foot. An avalanche has buried the other trail."

As soon as they disappeared from sight Foley set off. As he climbed higher the path became more and more difficult to negotiate. There was no sound of an engine; nothing except the distant tinkle of a cowbell and the buzzing of insects. There was no sign of Joseph coming back down. Taking a folding walking stick from his rucksack, he unscrewed the metal end to reveal a powerful telescope. Squatting behind a boulder, he scanned the terrain above him.

In the distance he made out the avalanche the walkers had described. It seemed to spill out from below an outcrop of rock. He climbed higher, attuned to every sound and sudden movement until he hit the scattered rocks. The avalanche was more extensive close up. Huge rocks and loose shale spewed over a hundred metres across. Here and there grass and coarse shrubs had pushed their way through the rubble. Screwing up his eyes against the glare, he peered up at the gleaming white peaks of the Alps. Following the direction of the cascade of detritus above the timberline, he saw it had started just below a grass-covered overhang between the rocks. Half walking, half crawling, he climbed up the steep river of boulders until he was almost under the overhang.

Feet slipping treacherously on loose stones, he picked his way up the last few metres until he was directly underneath a sheer expanse of rock. He squatted until he got his breath back and took stock of the situation. Suddenly, he heard a noise behind him: a distinct humming sound. At the same time the butt of a gun crashed down onto his head.

CHAPTER TEN

Generalissimo's HQ, Swiss Alps, July 2016

When he regained consciousness, he found himself lying on a stone floor. Bright light flooded the room, bouncing off his eyeballs. Someone pulled him to his feet and dragged him to a chair. Gingerly, he touched the bump on his head as the room swam into focus. A tall, slim man stood silhouetted against the light flanked by two black-clad figures wearing balaclavas. The uniform didn't disguise the fact that one of them was a woman.

Foley shook his head, trying to clear the fog in his brain. There was something distinctly odd about the man's face; the curious twist of the mouth when he spoke. The man bent over him, his prosthetic mask smiling a hideous smile.

"Now, hand over the microchip. No chip, no surgery."

Foley dragged himself to his feet. He had to play along, buy some time.

"It makes no difference. My doctor says I've been very lucky. I don't need an operation now. My other kidney is functioning perfectly."

The eyes behind the mask bored into Foley. "Then why did you come to Switzerland?"

"Money, the information I have is worth millions, but I'm not a greedy man," Foley smiled slyly. "I'll settle for a million … in sterling."

Suddenly, the man wearing the balaclava grabbed Foley from behind and clamped a pair of handcuffs on his wrists. Systematically, he searched him from head to toe then emptied the contents of his haversack over the floor. The false microchip had been carefully hidden inside Foley's folding telescope. Gilbert didn't want it to look too inexpertly concealed in case it aroused their suspicions.

He closed his eyes, willing them to find it. The woman picked up the instrument and smashed it against the steel frame of the door. With a soft, plopping sound the microchip dropped on the floor. Triumphantly, she picked it up and handed it to the man in the prosthetic mask.

"What about my money?" Foley whined.

"Don't worry, you'll get what you deserve, Mr Foley."

They marched him down the stone-walled corridor and stopped outside a lift. Foley looked at the red numbers on the control panel. They descended two levels in mere seconds. The doors slid back to reveal a harshly lit anteroom.

An antiseptic smell pervaded the air. Fear hit him like a jackhammer when he saw the syringe. He kicked out, struggling to free himself, but they just laughed. Dark eyes gleamed malevolently through the slit-holes in the mask. He felt the sharp prick of a needle on his arm. Suddenly, his legs buckled underneath him. He was being lifted onto a bed. Everything seemed hazy and unreal. The woman pulled off her mask and smiled down at him as he plunged into oblivion.

CHAPTER ELEVEN

Interlaken, Bernese Oberland, July 2016

A woman looked on with disgust as the smartly-dressed man and woman helped Foley through the swing doors of the hotel.

"Please excuse us. A little worse for wear after the party last night," the man apologised.

Holding Foley upright, they dragged him along, leaving damp skid marks on the red carpet.

Ethan Bateman called across the foyer.

"Ya seemed to have had a mighty good time last night, son."

Foley tried to speak, his lips moving soundlessly below his glassy eyes. When they reached his room they manhandled him inside, stripped him and covered him with the duvet.

"Sweet dreams, Mr Foley," the girl said sourly. She bent close to his ear. "We'll be watching you."

Foley woke the next morning with a throbbing headache. A hundred hammers banged simultaneously inside his head. He tried to sit up, but waves of dizziness washed over him forcing him back onto the pillow. He pushed back the duvet, struggled to the bathroom and turned on the shower. For a full five minutes he stood under the hot needles of water, luxuriating in its soothing warmth. Gradually, the pain in his head and body eased to a dull ache.

After towelling himself vigorously, he swallowed a couple of paracetamol and tried to formulate a plan. Why had they brought him back to the hotel? Not to arouse suspicions if he didn't return? They already had the microchip. When they discovered it was dummy information they would come looking for him. He was safe as long as he stayed in the hotel, but he had to get out before they came back. He would act normally, go down to breakfast and stay in the dining room as long as possible.

Except for Joseph, he had no idea what his pursuers looked like, but he would recognise the girl's voice anywhere. He glanced around the room and spotted his overnight bag sitting on top of the suitcase stand. Inside, he found his clothes still neatly packed along with his shaving gear. They had thought of everything. He pulled on a pair of chinos and a Polo shirt, gave the room a quick once over, grabbed his bag, and hurried out.

His gaze swept the occupants of the dining room, coming to rest on the bluff Texan. He signalled to the waiter hovering at the edge of the room and made his way to their table.

"May I join you?"

"Sure, how are ya?" Bateman beamed. "Ya must have had a real humdinger of a party last night. I thought ya said ya don't drink?"

"Well, I don't usually," Foley replied, grateful for the presence of the garrulous American.

Foley lingered over his breakfast until Bateman rose to leave.

"I've got a hire automobile. Ellie and me are taking a trip up to the Piz Gloria if the weather holds. Say, why don't ya tag along, son? The mountain air will clear ya head," he boomed.

I could kiss you, Foley thought, breathing a sigh of relief. If he could stay with them perhaps he could lose himself in the crowd of tourists.

A bearded man, wearing dark glasses, stared after them as they pushed through the revolving doors. The doorman darted smartly down the steps and held open the door of a silver Mercedes. Bateman pushed a ten-Euro note into his hand and squeezed behind the wheel. Slowly, they slid from the curb and nudged into the stream of traffic. The man and woman ran after them, jostling residents aside in their haste to get to a black 4 x 4 parked at the end of the street.

"Follow that Mercedes," the woman ordered, "and don't lose it."

*

Foley and the Americans boarded the front carriage of the funicular in Lauterbrünnen. The doors automatically slid shut seconds after they settled in their seats. Two latecomers raced to the ticket office then ran towards the train.

"The doors are locked. You can't board now!" a uniformed guard shouted.

In the front carriage Foley watched nervously as Joseph yanked on the door. He pushed his face up against the window, a look of pure venom on his face. Mouthing an obscenity he jumped back as the cogs engaged and the train slowly started its ascent.

The funicular seemed to be moving at a snail's pace. Beads of perspiration stood out on his forehead. The very thought of what they had planned sent his mind into a paroxysm of pure terror. He looked at his wristwatch as they left the funicular in Grütschalp and boarded the train for Mürren. His only hope was to try and lose himself in the crowd once they got to the village.

CHAPTER TWELVE

Mürren, Bernese Oberland, July 2016

The effects of the drugs pumped into him hadn't completely worn off. His bowels churned like a mixer. He was feeling nauseous again and scared; very scared. Ellie patted his arm reassuringly. When they pulled into the station he jumped up and headed for the door.

"What's your hurry, Brucey?" Bateman asked.

"Call of nature," he shot back. He ran towards a nearby hotel clutching his stomach. Bateman rolled his eyes.

"The boy can't take his booze."

The Batemans found a table on the terrace of a hotel opposite the station and ordered coffee. Foley rejoined them a few minutes later. He wasn't sure what to do next, but if he stayed close to them at least he'd have some protection. The village was too small to hide in; just a main street flanked by tourist shops. He had to move on before another train arrived.

They ambled down to see the ancient chalet the waiter had mentioned. Ellie nervously eyed the cable car making its way down from Berg.

"You game, Brucey?" Bateman asked.

Foley didn't answer. His eyes were riveted at a spot down the road behind him. Two familiar figures were striding along the street, sidestepping people lingering near the shops. The man pointed in his direction. Panic coursed through him. They had spotted him. Quickly, he pulled out a notebook, scribbled a few words, and pushed it at Ethan.

"Contact Mac."

As soon as the cable car lurched to a halt Foley raced towards to the ticket office.

"Hey buddy, we're all waiting ya know," shouted a young backpacker angrily.

Making his way to the front corner of the car, he scanned the crowd still left on the station. Joseph's scowling face loomed out of the crowd. Keeping his eyes on Foley he pulled out his mobile phone before running back down the main street towards the train station. *It won't take them long to get back down*, Foley thought.

At last he felt the pull of the cable car as it climbed up towards Berg. He had a ticket for the Piz Gloria. They couldn't get to him up there. Breathing a sigh of relief he slumped against the window. Lulled by the smooth movement of the car he relaxed amidst the chatter of voices. The scenery dropping away below him was breathtakingly stunning, almost unreal. Berg station loomed high ahead; beyond it, the Schilthorn and the famous restaurant.

Suddenly, the faint drone of a helicopter caught his attention. In the distance a black dot appeared casting a shadow on the snow-covered peaks. It moved in their direction flying dangerously close to the cable car.

"The fool, he's getting too close! He's trying to take photographs!" a passenger yelled.

Foley squinted against the light. His heart was beating so wildly he thought he would choke. A figure was leaning forwards pointing at something. It wasn't a camera. It was binoculars and they were aimed at him. He shrank back desperately trying to hide behind people. The helicopter circled above the cable car for a few minutes then pointed its nose back the way it had come. It flew up towards the Schilthorn and disappeared over the summit.

Foley's blood turned to ice in his veins. How had they summoned a chopper so quickly? In a blinding flash of certainty he remembered the article he had read about James Bond. The Piz Gloria had a helicopter pad! Panic rose up in his throat. Beads of cold sweat popped on his forehead, dripped onto his collar. He gripped the handrail, his hands slick with perspiration. He had to get out! Suddenly, his legs buckled underneath him. The young back packer grabbed his arm

"I'm just a little dizzy and nauseous. It must be the altitude," Foley lied.

"Well, it ain't gonna get any better up there." He pointed to the Schilthorn towering high above them.

The cable car lurched into the station, swaying slightly before locking into position. Unsteadily, Foley wobbled out and made for the observation terrace. He had no doubt they would be waiting for him at all cable car stations down to Stechelberg. The only alternative was to trek down the steep trail to Berg. If the cable car arrived without him on board they might assume that he was still on the summit. At least it would buy him some time.

Sliding on loose shale Foley staggered down the dangerous path leading from the observation platform on the Piz Gloria. Suddenly, he heard the drone of an engine. Turning towards the Schilthorn he saw a black helicopter flying steeply down the mountain. He tried to duck out of sight between some boulders as it thundered overhead. He was trapped like a moth in a jar. It was losing height, pinning him to the spot. A man leaned out of the open door of the craft wielding a bullhorn.

"It's no use, Foley! You can't escape!"

Mustering all his strength he leapt up and ran like a madman. Another man descended from the helicopter on a wire, unclipping it as soon as he touched ground. Quickly, he caught up with Foley and felled him with a rugby tackle. He clasped a pair of handcuffs on his wrists then shoved him back to the hovering chopper. Bodies locked together, they were winched up inside. Another man was waiting, syringe poised ready to plunge it into Foley's arm. Through the holes in the balaclava a pair of hard eyes bored through him. Foley shrank back against the metal wall, his eyes darting around the cabin. Too late, the injection had taken its effect.

CHAPTER THIRTEEN

Generalissimo's HQ, Swiss Alps, July 2016

A harsh, white light pierced Foley's eyelids. From somewhere far away he could hear voices in muted conversation. His eyelids felt as if they had been glued together. He forced them open, blinking against the glare. Figures materialised in the haze. A blonde woman was bending over him. *She must be a doctor*, he thought. Suddenly, she stopped and pulled a balaclava up over her head.

"You've been too greedy, Foley."

Horror rose up in his throat like a coiling serpent threatening to choke him.

"No! No!" he screamed over and over again.

The girl plunged a needle into his arm and waited for the drug to take effect. She had given him just enough to make him drowsy. Foley's eyes flickered open. She smiled, relishing the terror on his face.

"Goodbye, Foley," she murmured, pressing a pillow onto his face.

Ripping off her balaclava the woman waited for the telltale beam of the retinal scanner. She hated the claustrophobic sensation that left her feeling breathless. The Generalissimo would be pleased. After her handling of Foley he was sure to reward her. The steel door slid open and quickly closed behind her. As soon as she stepped over the threshold a uniformed figure, sporting a gold armband emblazoned with five black motifs, barred her way. A stab of envy knifed through her. Only the highest echelons of the militia wore gold armbands.

Field agents wore silver, red for computer experts, blue for administrators, yellow for security guards. Subconsciously, she touched the three black motifs on her silver armband. Each one represented a step up the ladder. Quietly, the aide tapped on the inner door and stood aside to let the girl through. The masked Generalissimo rose from behind the oak desk. She shifted nervously, waiting for him to speak.

"Why did you show your face, Anya?" he murmured. "You know how dangerous it is to reveal your identity."

Startled, she took a step backwards never taking her eyes from his face. She was perspiring now, terrified of his impending anger. How could she have been so stupid? He smiled beneath the mask, revelling in her raw fear.

"You are a beautiful young woman," he murmured, stroking her face.

Suddenly, he pinched her cheek, squeezing until she cried out with pain. He let go and patted her face. Clasping her hands together she tried to control her trembling. She was brave, he would give her that, but she must be punished. The very existence of the Black Militia was built on secrecy and subterfuge. There was no room for carelessness.

"There will be no more mistakes," she replied, tilting her head with a defiance she didn't feel.

"*Dosvi' daniya*, my little Anya."

"Goodbye, sir."

Trying not to hurry she marched through the door. Silently, it slid shut behind her. A few minutes later the

Generalissimo's aide came into the room and crossed to a stainless steel device set on a table behind the desk. Lifting the lid he extracted a gleaming ladle, poured the contents into a glass and handed it to him.

"Prepare the helicopter immediately."

"*Da*," his aide replied, giving a shallow bow.

CHAPTER FOURTEEN

Interlaken, Bernese Oberland, August 2016

Macaleer had been searching for Bruce Foley for ten days. He had scoured the area around Interlaken, but there was no sign of him. The last time he had been seen was leaving the hotel with an American couple. He decided to retrace Foley's movements, and ride the cable car to the Schilthorn from Mürren. It didn't take long to realise he was being followed when he headed back to the cable car station. It was the same 'tail' every day. Why? The connection had to be Foley. All he knew from Bruce's last garbled telephone call was that he was in trouble. He sounded frightened and disoriented.

"They're on to me, Mac. I'm a dead man!"

"Bruce, where are you? Why are you being followed?"

"I'm on the trail from Schilthorn down to Berg. There's some kind of army... in the mountains... a masked man. Oh God, the chopper's coming back... Gilbert MI6... "

"Bruce! Bruce, stay with me!"

The beating of helicopter blades roared in his ears; a long, drawn-out scream, then complete silence.

*

The lock gave as soon as Macaleer inserted the key to his room. Warily, he pushed open the door. It was a complete shambles. Clothes strewn over the floor, wardrobe doors and drawers wide open. His suitcase had been ransacked. Even his shaving kit had been searched.

He froze as a scraping sound came from the bathroom. Pressing his back against the wall near the door jamb, he peered through the gap. Suddenly, the door slammed back on its hinges. A burly man, his face covered with a balaclava, burst out of the bathroom. He dived on Macaleer throwing him off balance.

Mustering all his strength he lunged at his attacker. The man parried the blow bringing his fists up in front of his face. He jabbed a right hook that connected with Macaleer's jaw sending him staggering onto the bed. As his assailant ran towards the door Macaleer dived for his lower body bringing him down in a tangle of arms and legs. Hauling him face up, he pushed him back onto the floor and sat on his legs.

"Now, you bastard, let's find out who you are."

As he pulled off the balaclava Joseph sat up and violently head-butted him. Temporarily fazed by the bone-cracking blow he rolled to one side, instinctively covering his head with his arms.

"You've just signed your death warrant," Joseph snarled before disappearing into the corridor.

Macaleer pushed himself into a sitting position. He felt as though he had been run over by a twenty-ton truck. Eventually, he managed to half walk, half crawl to the bathroom. Blinking against the light he peered into the mirror. His face was puffed, one eye partially closed. An angry red patch on his jaw was already turning blue. Blood trickled from his nose to his upper lip. Tentatively, he touched his swollen nose. At least it wasn't broken. After a long soak in the bath, fresh clothes and some hot coffee, he lay on the bed. His head teemed with questions. Who was the masked man? Could it really be an army? Why was MI6 involved?

*

Few people would have paid any attention to the man hunched over the table at the back of the dingy restaurant. The wooden plank floors were stained from years of beer spills, stiletto heel pockmarks and ground-in food. Torn leather banquettes, darkened with grime; tattered fringes hanging limply from dirty lampshades. A haze of grey curled above the tables, gathering in clouds that hung close to the ceiling. The whole place stank of stale smoke and boiled cabbage. A faint odour of urine hung in the air near the lavatories.

Near the bar a woman sat on a high stool swinging her legs provocatively, hoping for potential customers.

"*Bitte?*" queried a slovenly waiter who had appeared at his elbow.

"*Kaffee.*"

The waiter noted the way the man's hands trembled. Probably a drunk or a junkie. There could be a bit of business in the offing.

Rob Macaleer glanced surreptitiously round the room. From this vantage point he could watch the entrance. He glanced up as the bar door opened. A thickset man pushed his way in, sauntered to a banquette and ordered a beer. Casually, he strode to the counter, picked up a tabloid newspaper and returned to his seat.

For some inexplicable reason Macaleer suddenly felt uneasy. Throwing some Swiss francs into the saucer on the table he left the bar, glancing behind to see if he had been followed. There was nobody in sight. Quickening his stride, he walked to the end of the street then retraced his steps past the bar. There was still no sign of anyone leaving.

Rounding a corner into a side street, he mingled with a group of tourists before slipping back into the main shopping area. Behind him a black 4 x 4 slid to a stop. The man in the passenger seat smoothed his hand over his chin. Joseph still hadn't got used to being without his beard.

Briskly, Macaleer walked past the gift shops and restaurants heading for the taxi rank. Urgent footsteps clattered close behind. Someone roughly jostled against him. It was the man from the bar! He must have gone out through the back entrance. Suddenly, he turned and faced Macaleer head-on. Every time he stepped sideways Joseph did the same like a pair of comic actors. Patting the bulge in his jacket pocket he glanced towards a group of children, his eyes spewing venom.

"Get in," he hissed, nodding towards the 4 x 4, "unless you want some casualties."

Macaleer's shoulders slumped. He was trapped. Joseph shoved him into the rear of the vehicle and secured his hands with plastic ties. Satisfied he didn't pose a threat, he pushed him down onto the seat. An hour later they slewed to a stop at the end of a disused farm track. Joseph grabbed Macaleer and hauled him out of the vehicle.

As soon as his feet touched the ground he bolted back down the track towards the main road. He could see vehicles passing the turn-in. Close behind him boots thumped on the stone-strewn path. Suddenly, a burst of machine gunfire filled the air. Macaleer dropped to his knees. He was dead before he hit the ground. Two hours later a lone Englishman on the mountain slopes spotted a motorcycle towing a loaded trailer.

October–December 2016

CHAPTER FIFTEEN

Shropshire, England

A faint, low whistle drifted on the autumn air towards the solitary man walking across the field at the edge of the dense wood. Only the soughing moan of the wind through the trees broke the silence. Fine drizzle misted the air, soaking his shoulders. Pulling up his collar he yanked his flat cap down low over his eyes and miserably tramped across the uneven field, mud sucking at his boots.

"I should be like other men out exercising their dogs – real dogs," he muttered. "A Labrador or an Alsatian, not a toy poodle with a bloody stupid bow in its hair." He squinted against the rain, calling softly to the animal snuffling in the damp vegetation.

The dog raced ahead into the gloom, bouncing along as though she were suspended by elastic. With a wild, excited yap she jumped over a grassy hillock and disappeared from sight.

"Come on, girl," he called.

Cursing, he squelched over the wet ground towards the spot. Turning full circle he peered through the gloom, but there was no sign of the animal. It would be dark soon then he would have a hell of a job finding her. Muttering to himself he strode towards the mound and stepped into nothingness.

He felt himself falling; falling like a stone into total blackness. He hit the ground with a squishy, muted thud.

When he tried to sit up waves of nausea surged through him. His whole body shrieked pain. Feebly, he shouted into the suffocating darkness.

"Help! Somebody please help me!"

It was no use. He must try to stay calm and wait until daybreak. The dog walkers would be back out early in the morning and his wife would raise the alarm when he didn't turn up. With a muffled cry he sank into merciful oblivion.

Harsh light seared his eyelids from somewhere above his head when he finally regained consciousness. With a flicker of relief, he realised the shaft of light was coming from a jagged hole high above him. He must have been unconscious all night.

For a few minutes he lay still, trying to gather his thoughts. All he remembered was calling out for the dog, then nothing. Shifting his body slightly to ease the pain, he gingerly prodded his arms and ribs. His right leg stuck out at an unnatural angle, otherwise nothing else appeared to be broken. He felt around the ground until he touched a mess of sticky fluid and fur. With a sharp gasp he drew his hand away. It was the dog. She had cushioned his fall, but there was something else.

Peering into the gloom he made out a bundle of some sort. He pulled at the fabric. In a nanosecond he saw the glassy, dead eyes staring at him, the mouth pulled back across the teeth of the corpse in a hideous death grin. He heard a high-pitched scream; a scream that went on and on. When it finally stopped, he realised that the terrifying scream was his own.

Eyes wild with horror, he pressed himself against the slimy shaft wall. Suddenly, shouting; tramping feet; the frantic barking of a dog; a face hovering high above him. By the time the emergency services arrived he was hysterical; muttering incoherently like a madman.

Dangling precariously, a paramedic lowered himself into the shaft, swaying slightly until his feet touched solid ground.

"It's okay mate, we'll get you out in no time," he said reassuringly.

Expertly, he strapped the man onto a stretcher, secured his head and slowly winched him to the surface. The paramedic hovered over his patient checking his vital signs.

"There's a body down there and it's not very pretty," he said, turning to the policeman at his side.

Inspector Juliff shone his torch into the cavernous hole. A shapeless mound lay sprawled at the bottom. He sighed wearily and ran his hand over his head. He was completely bald except for a tuft of ginger hair that looked as though it had been stuck on near his hairline. Shrewd brown eyes stared from his jowly face like currants embedded in a bun.

About fifty yards away, a group of curious people huddled in whispered conversation.

"What's the story, Inspector?" shouted a man wielding a camera.

Juliff ignored him. "Keep the press away. We don't want the papers getting hold of it until we've established the cause of death. The pathologist and CID are on their way."

Grey-white mist was already wrapping its fingers around shadowy trees silhouetted against a backdrop of murky light; snaking through gnarled trunks, clawing at sodden branches. People walking their dogs stopped to stare at the fluttering blue and white police tape cordoning off the shaft. A black van, doors flung wide, waited a few feet away. White-suited scene-of-crime officers hovered nearby as the body was brought to the surface. Intermittent flashes of light came from somewhere near the line of trees.

"Get over there, Constable. Confiscate those cameras if you have to," growled Juliff. "All right, Pete, you can get your pictures now."

After a couple of preliminary shots Juliff untied the rope securing the blanket. The police photographer moved round the body capturing images of the corpse from various angles.

"That's it, it's all yours Doc," he said. A slim, fair-haired woman stepped forward and squatted beside the corpse.

"Dr Barnett!"

The pathologist's head jerked around at the sound of the familiar voice. Detective Chief Inspector Ben Wallace trudged towards her.

"What have we got?" he asked, in his usual peremptory manner.

"Male, thirty to forty years old. He's been dead for quite some time. No knife or gunshot wounds. Except for the smashed-up face and fingers there are a few bruises. I can't tell you any more at this stage, not until I've carried out a post mortem," she said getting to her feet. "I should have something to tell you by tomorrow afternoon."

"I'll look forward to it," Wallace replied grimly.

CHAPTER SIXTEEN

Shropshire, England

Wallace hated this part of his job. He didn't have a very strong stomach at the best of times. The stink of disinfectant hit his nostrils as he opened the door to the mortuary. Whenever he came down here the smell seemed to cling to his clothing for days afterwards.

He poked his head round the door, his eyes travelling over the tiled walls, stainless steel sinks and the drain in the floor. A still shape lay under a green sheet on a gurney. A technician, writing at a metal worktop, swivelled round in his chair as the door swung open. Dr Barnett pulled down her surgical mask and looked at Wallace, noting his waxen face. Tossing him a pair of rubber gloves she smiled inwardly, relishing his discomfort.

"You're not going to like this one, Ben. It's very strange. There's some evidence of sedative drugs; mainly benzodiazepines. Judging by the shape of these marks I'd say he was also battered with a rounded object, perhaps a large stone. His fingertips have been partially burned away as well. What I can tell you is that he was suffocated before the injuries were inflicted. Also, his right kidney has been removed fairly recently. I'll know more when we get the toxicology reports."

"Whoever killed him had a very strong motive for not

wanting him to be identified. The SOCOs couldn't find anything at all that would identify him," Wallace added.

Dr Barnett handed him a plastic evidence bag containing the filthy sheet in which the body had been wrapped.

"Just there, in the corner. Chemicals from constant cleaning have almost obliterated it, but I'm certain it's a hospital number. It's used to identify bedding for auditing purposes."

"Jo, you're a gem, a real little gem! We should be able to trace this to the hospital it came from fairly quickly."

"I'll let you know if I find anything … "

She didn't have time to finish the sentence. He was already pushing his way through the strip plastic doors.

By the time he arrived at the incident room, set up in the local community hall, it was a hive of activity. At the far end a technician was busy fiddling with a computer set up close to an electronic whiteboard. Cables and boxes of equipment littered the tables.

"Get forensics on to this straight away," he ordered, shoving the evidence bag at his sergeant. "The pathologist found a hospital number on the sheet. It shouldn't be too difficult to trace. Butler, get hold of the police artist. The victim's face was badly smashed up, but he may be able to come up with a rough likeness."

He sighed audibly; there was so little evidence to go on. They were a long way from even establishing a motive for the killing. His eyes felt gritty from lack of sleep. He hadn't had a chance to rest after conducting the arson case before this had dropped in his lap. Wearily, he shuffled into his overcoat and headed for the door.

"There's nothing we can do until tomorrow morning, Butler," he shouted over his shoulder.

"Go home. Get some sleep. You're going to need it."

Butler kicked a box aside as he barged through the throng of bodies in the incident room early the next morning. He pushed a piece of A4 paper at his DCI. Wallace grabbed it and examined it closely.

"Dr Barnett was right. It's a laundry mark."

This was all they had to go on. No wallet, clothes tags, absolutely nothing! Wallace drummed the desk impatiently. He wasn't looking forward to trekking round the hospitals.

CHAPTER SEVENTEEN

Salop Royal Infirmary

The young woman manning reception at Salop Royal Infirmary completely ignored them when they approached the desk. Her eyes flicked from the keyboard to the computer screen and back again.

"I'd like to speak to the hospital manager," Wallace said, producing his ID card.

Perfunctorily, she dialled an extension number. "His secretary says Mr Jessop is about to go into a meeting. You'll have to make an appointment."

Wallace grabbed the telephone. This is Detective Chief Inspector Wallace, Borton CID. Tell him I want to see him *now*."

Mrs Crowley, the secretary, ushered them into the manager's office with a curt nod. Jessop introduced himself in a silky drawl. He motioned them to the comfortable chairs facing his desk.

"We're investigating a murder," Wallace said. "The body was found wrapped in a sheet." He showed him the photocopy of the laundry mark. "We're trying to establish whether it came from a local hospital."

"Mrs Crowley, ask the housekeeping supervisor to come up please, straight away."

A few minutes later she ushered in a grey-haired woman,

an anxious expression clouding her face. She looked from one man to the other as though expecting bad news.

"It's all right, Mrs Glover, nothing to be alarmed about," Jessop assured her.

"This is Detective Chief Inspector Wallace and Detective Sergeant Butler. They are carrying out an investigation." He picked up the photocopy and handed it to her. "Can you identify this laundry mark?"

"All the hospitals in the area use the same one," Mrs Glover replied. "Unfortunately, linen is sent out to private contractors for cleaning." She shot the manager a tart glance. "It could be sent back to any of the hospitals. These days we can only keep track of quantities." She squinted at the faded number then shook her head. "All I can tell you is that it is one used by the trust."

"Are you absolutely sure?"

"I'm positive."

"Thank you, Mr Jessop," Wallace said rising to leave. "We may be in touch again."

Back in the car Butler said, "Not much luck there."

A strand of blond hair fell across his forehead as he engaged the car into drive mode. He was a square-jawed, brawny man. Only his broken nose stopped him from being classically handsome. The result of too many tackles on the rugby field. In a curious way it enhanced his masculine appeal.

"At least we know it's a hospital sheet. That gives us a lead."

It was late afternoon when they pulled up outside a country pub. They found a table in a bay window and settled down with their drinks. Butler tucked into his steak and ale pie while Wallace prodded at his pasta. They had been on the road most of the day. Every hospital, including the private sector, told the same story about their laundry facilities. They had nothing more to go on than they had yesterday.

CHAPTER EIGHTEEN

Police HQ, Shropshire

Wallace barged into the incident room, his face grim. A uniformed constable quickly gathered up some papers and headed for the door, studiously avoiding looking at the DCI. In the middle of the room a knot of detectives huddled together laughing over a lewd joke. Wallace glowered at them malevolently. Everybody scuttled back to their work areas. They knew better than to get in his way.

"Butler!" he snarled at his DS. "I want everybody in the briefing room in five minutes!"

A red flush bloomed around Wallace's collar. Gradually, it crept up his neck mottling his face with raspberry-red blotches. The case was three weeks old. Other than establishing the sheet was hospital property they had made no further progress. He was still smarting from his meeting with his Chief Superintendent that morning. Nick-named 'Crew Cut Charlie', his gelled hair stuck up like a rough brush.

"What have you got so far?" Charles Payne had asked crisply. "I've got the press on my back. I want results, Wallace."

"We're overstretched as it is. I've still got officers on the arson case."

"This must take priority now. Put every man on it until you make some progress. Is that clear?"

Wallace gritted his teeth as he rose to leave. Carefully, he closed the door behind him, resisting the temptation to slam it off its hinges.

Detectives were waiting in the briefing room looking slightly apprehensive.

"I've had the Chief Super on my back this morning. I want the whole crime scene area searched again, another complete fingertip search. There must be something we've missed."

A loose-limbed detective constable, his backside parked on a desk, groaned and rolled his eyes.

"Have you got a problem with that, Baker?" Wallace snarled, his eyes bulging with anger.

DC Baker slid off the desk into a chair behind his colleagues. He was already in the governor's bad books after gaffing in the burglary case.

Wallace stared at the photographs on the evidence board showing various shots of the corpse on its back and front. What was he missing? He looked closer at a blow-up of the battered face. Broken nose, shattered cheekbones and smashed forehead.

Based mainly on guesswork, the police artist had struggled to produce a sketchy likeness for the press. It had been handed over to a forensic sculptor to reconstruct the face, but that would take time. Bending closer he examined the picture of the back of the head. Something flitted into his mind and out again before he could grasp it.

The telephone jangled in the background. Butler snatched it, listened intently and slammed it back into its cradle.

"Sir! They've found another body, on the riverbank near Atcham, half naked."

"The same killer," Baker interjected.

"We don't know that yet!" Wallace snapped. "Haven't you learned anything since you've been in CID. Never assume!"

He stormed out, his face bright red. Pressing his fingers to his temples he took a deep breath. The blood pounding in his temples made him feel slightly nauseous. DS Butler followed him out, fervently hoping the victim was a suicide. Wallace whirled round angrily and glared at him. He looked as though he was about to chew him up and spit him out. Suddenly, his shoulders slumped. Butler was a good detective; intelligent, efficient and a promotion looming. He wondered how much longer he could keep him on the team.

CHAPTER NINETEEN

Bayston Hill, Shropshire

Wallace threw off his jacket, slumped into his favourite chair, and stared out at the rain lashing against the French doors. A low, moaning wind rattled through the trees sending shrivelled leaves sailing across the lawn. Twilight had descended prematurely, closing in: a living, breathing thing threatening to suffocate him. He always hated this time of year; the sense of decay and the wet mush of leaves underfoot. Not even the vibrant autumn colours lifted his spirits.

Maggie, his on-off girlfriend of four years, handed him his usual single malt whisky and water. She was cabin crew on the British Airways transatlantic run. Between his job and her flying they rarely had any quality time together. She stormed into the kitchen to salvage his dried-up dinner, muttering about heart attacks and idiots. By the time she returned he was fast asleep.

From somewhere far away a telephone shrilled. Wallace started out of his chair, momentarily disoriented. Knuckling his eyes he staggered to the coffee table and snapped his mobile open. It was Butler.

"Matt Valens from the *Shropshire Herald* buzzed me a few minutes ago. Apparently, he went to a Fleet Street retirement bash in London over the weekend. According to a pal working on the *Devon Courier*, a naked body was washed up on the beach, not far from Portsmouth, a couple of weeks ago."

"Somebody probably fell overboard off a cross-channel ferry."

"But listen to this. The face and hands had been mutilated."

"Why didn't we see anything in the press?"

"That's the thing, sir. After the police surgeon examined the body it was taken away. The SOCOs just packed up in the middle of their investigations. Not another word was heard about the incident. Matt decided to go down and do some digging. The body never arrived at the mortuary. It smells to high heaven." He chuckled. "Sorry about the pun, sir."

"Get on to Hampshire CID. See what you can find out and tell Valens if he does any more digging around I want to know about it."

It's hundreds of miles away, Wallace mused, tapping his bottom lip. There couldn't be a connection with the body found in Shropshire. Could it be a copycat killing? What if Baker was right about the body on the riverbank? His bowels churned uncomfortably. Slumping into an oversized armchair, he knocked back the remainder of his whisky and closed his eyes. He wasn't looking forward to another post mortem.

CHAPTER TWENTY

Police HQ, Shropshire

Wallace stomped up the stairs to the Chief Superintendent's office and knocked on the partially-open door. In the outer office a grey-haired woman bent over a pile of papers on her desk. Giving him a withering glance over the top of her half-moon glasses, she tapped lightly on the inner door.

"Sir, Detective Chief Inspector Wallace."

Miss Clancy smiled sweetly, closing the door discreetly behind her. Chief Superintendent Payne leaned back into the comfortable leather chair.

"I assume you've made some progress on the Borton Wood murder." Failing to disguise his exasperation he shuffled uneasily. "Our resources are not inexhaustible, Wallace."

Wallace hesitated before speaking, alert to the Superintendent's mood.

"Matt Valens claims a naked body washed up on the beach not far from Portsmouth. The face had been carved up. It's a bit odd."

"That's outside our jurisdiction!" Payne spluttered angrily.

"Apparently, after the pathologist's initial examination, the SOCOs and the fingerprint boys moved in. Less than an hour later, they were called off before they had barely started their investigations. Valens's mate on the *Devon Courier* started digging around. Even more curious, he slipped a backhander to one of the mortuary staff. There was no record of any body being delivered."

Payne chewed on his bottom lip. "Yes, very curious indeed."

"All the local police could tell us was that the body was taken away in an undertaker's van."

"I admit it's strange, but it could be just a coincidence or a copycat. The Borton Wood murder has been prominent in the national press. On the other hand the body may have been dropped overboard from a cross-channel ferry. It's a very crowded sea route. Tankers, container ships, private boats; it could have been dropped from any one of them."

"I'd like to check with Interpol, sir. See if there have been similar cases recently."

"Not Europol?"

"Europol only covers European Member States. Besides, I have personal contacts in Interpol. It could be useful."

"All right, Wallace, but keep me up to speed. I'll discuss it with the Chief Constable at the Police Authority meeting. What about the body on the riverbank?"

"We haven't had the post mortem results yet."

Payne glanced at his watch, waved Wallace out, and bellowed into the outer Office.

"Miss Clancy! Tell my driver to get the car round here as fast as possible. I'd better not be late for this meeting!"

He glared at her, grabbed his hat, and stormed down the stairs towards a waiting police car. Wallace smirked as the car shot off with a squeal of tyres.

"Vain sod!" he muttered as Crew Cut Charlie disappeared from sight, still patting his brush-head into place.

Downstairs the incident room was jam-packed. Extra computers, cables taped to the floor, boxes and files everywhere. A line of grizzly photographs pinned on a board with a map indicating the crime scenes; the usual paraphernalia of a murder investigation. Half-eaten sandwiches lay next to what passed for coffee congealing in a white plastic cup. Three detectives sat with mobile phones glued to their ears.

Valens hadn't turned up anything since his last conversation with Butler. Wallace bit into his dried-up cheese and ham sandwich. Ignoring the shrilling telephone he slurped a mouthful of hot coffee. After the sixth ring he angrily picked up the receiver. It was Chief Superintendent Payne. What did the prat want now?

"I've had a word with the Chief Constable," Payne said. "There's to be no further investigation into the body washed up in Portsmouth – orders from the top. Draw a line under it. It never happened. Is that clear?"

Before Wallace could protest Payne slammed down the receiver. Thoughtfully, he tapped a pencil against his bottom teeth. There was a nasty smell to it all. What was so special about the stiff on the beach? Why was he being warned off? Crew Cut Charlie hadn't said anything about cooling his own investigation. A little call to his old pal in Switzerland wouldn't go amiss.

CHAPTER TWENTY-ONE

Berlin, Germany

Jack Conrad flung his long legs over the side of the bed. Unsteadily he stood up clinging to the bedside table. A wave of dizziness hit him, sending him sprawling backwards. His head was full of cotton wool, his mouth so dry he could hardly swallow. Gingerly, he sat up rubbing the tender spot on his temples, trying to stop the hammering in his head. He took a long swig from a glass of water on the bedside table and slowly eased himself off the solid mattress.

Fluent in German, he had served in Military Intelligence in Berlin in the eighties. Now he worked for the International Military Investigation Corp, a covert branch of military intelligence, answerable only to the head of MI6 and the Prime Minister. His brief was to infiltrate a Neo-Nazi group that had sprung up in the city. Linked with similar groups in Britain it was taking advantage of the unsettled economic climate and mass immigration to recruit jobless ex-servicemen.

Mixing business with pleasure he had met Claus, his old military intelligence contact, the night before. Business finished, they went on a real bender ending up in Tiergarten Quelle, their favourite *bierkeller*. "Never again," he vowed as he stepped into the shower. What he needed now was some food in his stomach.

Jack squinted against the harsh sunlight as he emerged from the Kempinski Adlon on Unter den Linden and walked across Pariser Platz towards Brandenberg Gate. No Grepos or the watchful eyes of the Stasi. Young men, dressed in imitation Soviet and American uniforms, posed for photographs with tourists. The defunct Soviet Sector had changed significantly since the fall of the Berlin Wall, particularly in Mitte. His thoughts were interrupted by the vibration of his mobile phone.

"Get the next flight back to London," a familiar voice said. "Report in immediately you get back."

The line went dead. Conrad groaned and pocketed the phone. He would have to postpone his planned lunch with Claus in the Machiavelli on Albrechtstrasse. He hurried back to the Adlon, ordered a taxi and raced up to his room to fetch his suitcase. Ten minutes later he was hurtling towards Tegel Airport. With any luck he could get the midday flight.

*

London, England

The pilot banked the aircraft gently to starboard before starting his descent. At the front of the cabin the green sign turned warning-red as the steward moved down the aisle checking on safety belts. Conrad picked up his whisky and drained the plastic beaker. It must be something big for Pearce to contact him when he was on official leave. Suddenly, they emerged from grey cloud cover into driving rain onto their final approach. They hit the tarmac and hurtled down the rain-slicked runway towards the terminal buildings. Safety belt already unbuckled, he was the first out of his seat into the tunnel.

When he got to Paddington an intercity train had just arrived. He pushed through the crowd of passengers heading towards the new taxi rank.

"Where to, guv?" asked the burly driver sporting a shaved head.

"Whitehall," Conrad instructed, "and take the quickest route."

Skilfully, the taxi driver negotiated the traffic through the city streets into Trafalgar Square and exited on Northumberland Avenue. A few minutes later he nosed right into Whitehall Place and pulled up outside an imposing Victorian building. A brass plate identified it as 'Trentor Enterprises Global Computer Systems'. The ground and first floor were used for 'legitimate' business. An international computer systems' company set up as a front for their operations. The others housed the nerve centre of IMIC, a highly covert branch of military intelligence.

Conrad paid the driver and mounted the wide steps. He pressed a buzzer on the brass name board. A loud click as the lock disengaged and the heavy door swung open. He ignored the lift in the foyer. Instead he inserted his electronic key card into a door to the left of the reception desk. Silently, the door swung open revealing a narrow corridor. No other entrances or exits except for a steel door sealing the corridor at the far end. He stared at the brass plaque warning 'Executive Staff' and waited for the retinal scan. With a barely audible swish the door slid back and he stepped into the lift. Impatiently, he jabbed the button and quickly ascended to the fourth floor.

In the outer office an attractive woman, in her early forties, sat peering into a computer screen. She looked up expectantly when he entered the room.

"Jack!"

"Isobel, you look ravishing, as usual," Conrad smiled.

She lowered her eyes and stared into her lap. Her heart beat like a sledgehammer whenever he was close to her.

"Flatterer!" she grinned. "Go on in, he's waiting for you."

Clive Pearce, codename 'Breakdancer', moved as though his lanky limbs had been strung with elastic and would collapse into a heap at any given moment. Salt and pepper hair swept straight back: intelligent eyes set in an elongated face dark with five o'clock shadow.

"Glad to see you Jack," he said, offering a bony hand, "take a pew." Jack listened intently as Pearce unfolded the story. "A naked body was found washed up on the beach near Portsmouth. It had a mass of gunshot wounds to the back, probably from a machine gun pistol. By sheer coincidence the pathologist who conducted the post mortem recognized the victim."

Pearce sat back and swung his chair from side to side, his hands steepled under his chin.

"Apparently, six months ago she attended a dinner in Conningwell Barracks to celebrate the Medical Officer's promotion to Colonel. She was dating him at the time. The murder victim was at the dinner. All she could remember was that the MO called him Mac and he had a slight Scottish accent. It turned out to be a Major Robert Macaleer, British Army Intelligence."

"I met him a couple of times. A decent chap. Was he on an assignment?"

"Apparently, he'd gone to the Bernese Oberland on the pretext of a walking holiday in the Swiss Alps. His real aim was to investigate the disappearance of a fellow officer who had overstayed his leave. Alarm bells started ringing when Macaleer failed to make contact at the appointed time."

Conrad's face creased into a frown. He knew Macaleer as a seasoned professional. What could he have discovered that led to his death? It must have been something big.

"I've arranged a meeting with Colonel Bowler, Macaleer's senior officer in military intelligence. Tomorrow morning," Pearce said. "I'll meet you there 08:00 hours sharp."

*

Hampshire, England

Conrad slowed down at the barrier as a guard emerged from a wooden sentry hut.

"State your business, sir."

"Major Conrad. I'm here to see Colonel Bowler."

The soldier consulted a millboard and raised the barrier. He pointed to a stone building on the other side of the parade ground. An NCO was waiting outside. He led him to a small anteroom where a young private was jabbing at a computer keyboard. Immediately, he jumped up and opened the half-glass door behind him. Conrad stepped inside. Pearce was already there, sipping steaming coffee from a large mug.

"Colonel Bowler, I think you already know Major Jack Conrad – military intelligence."

Bowler nodded, handed Conrad a mug of coffee, and settled down behind his desk.

"Rob Macaleer went off to Switzerland to track down Captain Bruce Foley who had been AWOL since late July," he said. He was a decent sort of chap by all accounts. A career officer, fair with the men, enjoyed a joke. For the last two years he was assigned to GCHQ."

"Was there anything strange about Foley's behaviour before he disappeared?"

"He became very short-tempered and withdrawn." Bowler stood up and paced the room, a worried look on his face. "His colleagues said he looked under the weather a lot of the time. The two men were lifelong friends. They went to Sandhurst together straight out of the sixth form. When Foley contacted Macaleer from Switzerland, sounding very agitated, he used some overdue leave to go after him. There's been no word from him since."

"So he wasn't on an official assignment?"

"No, and there's nothing on Foley either. I'm worried. It's not like Macaleer. Damned peculiar if you ask me."

"Thank you Colonel Bowler," Pearce interjected. "I'm sure I don't need to remind you that this must be kept under wraps."

Back at IMIC headquarters Conrad stood up and paced the room, hands thrust deep into his pockets. Pearce sat sprawled in his swivel chair, long legs resting on his desk. He had put out the word to their agents in Europe, but there was no trace of Foley or Macaleer. He would have to send someone into the field. He had only just returned from an assignment in the Middle East before his truncated vacation in Berlin, but Pearce had no choice. It had to be Conrad.

CHAPTER TWENTY-TWO

Wales, United Kingdom

The dark-suited man smiled at the attractive blonde woman sitting in the window seat. Momentarily, she returned his gaze then turned to stare out of the window. Stowing his briefcase and trench coat in the overhead locker, he dropped into the seat beside her.

"Weather's not too bad. With any luck we'll have a good flight," he commented cheerfully.

He was acutely aware of the effect he had on women, but this one was different. This one he would have to court and charm.

There was no indication that she had heard him. Sighing, she extracted a pen from her bag, unfurled a newspaper and started to fill in the crossword. The last thing she wanted was some idiot trying to pick her up. She noticed the chiselled looks, the auburn lights glinting in the rich brown hair. It was difficult to tell his age. He could have been in his late forties or well-preserved fifties.

A stewardess came up the aisle pushing a trolley, reciting her usual spiel. She smiled at the man coquettishly, inviting him to play her game. A real dish she thought, probably with a fat bank balance. Perhaps she could bag him before they touched down.

His eyes above the friendly smile bored into her: hard

balls of ice-blue marble. Involuntarily, she gave a little shudder. There was something vaguely disturbing about him. She felt a sharp stab of fear. Quickly, she started to push the trolley down the aisle.

"Hold on a minute! I'll have a whisky and soda." He raised an enquiring eyebrow at the girl beside him.

She groaned inwardly, knowing she was trapped next to him until they reached Heathrow. Resigned to his company she nodded curtly, "Gin and tonic." Still, he was rather good-looking. Maybe a couple of gins would loosen her up.

"Alex Campbell," he said offering his hand.

"Joanne Howard."

The plane banked, locked onto automatic pilot, and started its approach. Below, the runway lights shone like glow-worms. Suddenly, the plane began to shudder. For a few minutes they rattled around like dried peas in a tin can. Joanne grabbed her drink to prevent it sliding sideways, Alex's hand reaching out at the same time. He let it rest on hers. She didn't stop him.

"Staying in London?" Campbell asked.

"No, I'm flying on to Cardiff International."

"What a coincidence, so am I."

Joanne looked at him suspiciously, one eyebrow arched in disbelief. For some reason she didn't altogether trust him. By the time they landed she reluctantly agreed to meet for lunch at the Hilton Hotel the following day.

*

Joanne glanced at her wristwatch. Twenty-five minutes past one. She idled in the foyer for a while then entered the bar adjacent to the restaurant. Alex was sitting on a low sofa by the window casually reading a newspaper. He was wearing an expensive suit, white shirt and Oxford University tie. Campbell knew he looked good. When he spotted her he rose, flashing a brilliant smile. The man oozed sexuality, she thought. Raising her hand he gently brushed it with his lips. Suddenly, she felt a stirring in the pit of her stomach. She must be careful. It would be dangerous to become too involved with this man.

"I hope you like champagne?"

He smiled, inclining his head towards the bottle of Verve Cliquot resting in a silver ice bucket. A waiter poured two glasses of the pale golden liquid then retreated behind the bar. Slowly, she took a sip and placed it back on the table. Champagne always made her very light-headed. Lulled by the effects of the alcohol, she found herself enjoying his company more than she had expected. Finishing her second glass she sank luxuriously back into the sofa. He grinned disarmingly, reaching for the bottle. She covered her glass with the palm of her hand.

"Not for me. I have to travel to Oswestry later this afternoon."

"Come on," he coaxed. Joanne didn't notice that he had only taken a couple of sips from his glass. "It'll be a waste if it goes flat. You'll be fine once you have something to eat."

During lunch, she found herself warming to Alex. His pharmaceutical company had branches in Bern, Munich and Milan. He appeared to be a very wealthy man. This trip was to finalise details for a new venture near Wrexham.

"I'm driving north later this afternoon," he told her. "Why don't I give you a lift."

They set off around five o' clock catching all the commuter traffic leaving the city on the A470. Driving rain splattered the windscreen of the hired Jaguar obliterating the road ahead. Coupled with high winds, conditions were treacherous and slow. Lulled by the warmth and the rhythmic swish of the windscreen wipers Joanne eventually dropped off to sleep. By the time they reached her modest cottage, north of Oswestry, it was almost midnight.

Set in a sloping cul-de-sac the cottage was surrounded by trees on three sides. Nearby, the shape of another house loomed in the darkness. Rain hammered down as they ran up the path. They huddled under the open porch while Joanne pushed her key into the lock. Alex deposited her suitcase in the hallway. She stood silhouetted against a background of dim light watching him.

"I'd like to see you again," he said, "after I've completed my business."

"It's a filthy night. You heard the flood warnings on the traffic news. I wouldn't want you to be stranded after driving me here. Perhaps you ought to stay here and go on in the morning."

The words were out of Joanne's mouth before she realised it. He probably thought she was coming on to him. Alex hesitated for a few seconds, seeming uncertain, before running to the car to fetch his overnight bag. In another room a telephone shrilled. It was Mrs Blake from the cottage.

"The postman left a parcel for you. It was too wet to leave it outside."

"I'll pop over for it in the morning." The nosey cow must have been watching from her window prying into her affairs, as usual. "Thanks for taking it," she replied, cutting her off in mid-sentence.

"Pour some drinks, Alex. Make yourself at home while I take a shower."

Joanne luxuriated under the hot water, the heat soothing her aching muscles. In the living room Alex, wrapped in her towelling bathrobe, stared into the fire. Carefully, he placed another log in the centre watching the flames lick hungrily at the seasoned wood. It hissed and crackled sending orange flames shooting up the chimney. Satisfied, he relaxed onto the comfortable chesterfield sofa. She had good taste, he reflected, gazing round the room.

"Feeling better now?" he asked when Joanne came into the room vigorously towelling her hair.

He patted the empty space on the sofa. She sat down next to him acutely aware of his proximity. Alex's drink lay untouched on the coffee table. She didn't protest when he topped up her glass. She was beginning to feel deliciously tipsy. Suddenly, he pulled her to him and kissed her tenderly. Smiling, he took her hand and led her upstairs.

At first he was gentle, whispering endearments in her ear as though they had been lovers for years. *I must be insane*, she thought. *I don't know anything about this man.* Something nagged at her, plucking at her memory like a plectrum on guitar strings. Struggling through the fuzz of alcohol, she tried to grasp the thought and hold it before it slipped away back into her subconscious. Without warning Alex's lovemaking became more urgent, almost frenzied. Terrified, she tried to push him off, but he was too strong for her. The more she struggled the more violent he became.

He took something out of the pocket of his open robe. His face was pure evil now. Pinning her to the bed with his legs he brought the syringe in front of her face. A flash of recognition and horror knifed through her. Her heart beat wildly, slamming against her ribcage like a sledgehammer. Suddenly, she knew. It was the eyes; those icy blue eyes. She had seen them before.

Plunging the needle into her soft flesh, he waited until her arms dropped limply onto the bed. Joanne opened her eyes wide, but she couldn't seem to focus. Gradually, she felt herself slipping away; down, down into a dream-filled sleep.

Campbell opened the bedroom door quietly. Joanne lay sprawled out, one arm dangling over the side of the bed as though in a deep sleep. *Such a shame*, he mused. A renewed lust stirred in his loins at the sight of her naked body gleaming white in the dim light.

Hurriedly, he rummaged through her wardrobe picking out a navy trouser suit and matching shoes. He combed her hair, applied a touch of lipstick then forced some brandy down her throat. Roughly, he wiped a trickle of liquor from her mouth. Finally, he put a party popper in her pocket and pulled out the release cord of a second one. With a loud pop, coloured streamers burst into the air settling on her hair and shoulders. Campbell couldn't afford to kill her at the cottage, not with a nosey neighbour about. Besides, she had seen him running inside out of the rain.

It was pitch-black outside. Not a glimmer of light. Jennie Blake's cottage was shrouded in darkness He hoisted Joanne over his shoulder, carried her out to the car and pushed her into the passenger seat. He jumped into the driver's seat, released the handbrake, and let the car slowly slip backwards down the slope. He didn't dare start the engine until the car slid out onto the road.

Dark, rain-sodden trees swayed either side of the road almost touching the roof of the Jaguar. Fog hung low, obscuring the road ahead. Intermittently, the mist lifted for a few yards before enveloping the car in a grey, impenetrable blanket again.

As predicted, it wasn't long before he hit a flood warning sign. Orange warning lights flashed rhythmically from vehicles parked alongside the road. A queue of cars and lorries waited while a young policeman halted the line of vehicles for oncoming traffic to come through. Spotting a break in the flow, he turned to the waiting queue and waved them on. Campbell stopped as he passed and stuck his head through the window.

"What's the trouble, officer?" he queried politely.

"The road's flooded up ahead, sir. We're diverting all traffic."

The policeman leaned into the window. He looked at Joanne who lay sprawled on the seat with her mouth wide open.

"A bit too much to drink," Campbell said, plucking at the streamers, "a girlfriend's hen party."

"Please get out of the car, sir," the policeman ordered. He produced an SL500 Alco meter.

"Blow into this." The constable studied the reading. "Okay, sir. I suggest you get your lady friend home as soon as possible. Have a safe journey." He waved them forward and turned back to the traffic building up behind him.

Campbell drove leisurely. He had no need to hurry now. His ruse had worked beautifully. He gazed at Joanne who was beginning to stir beside him. She groaned and shifted in the seat. Reaching out he ran his hand along the inside of her thigh feeling a hot flush of desire stirring in his loins. She was a beautiful woman. Such a pity they couldn't have longer together.

Near Shrewsbury, Campbell drove up a country lane stopping close to the Severn River. He pulled on a pair of Wellingtons and hauled Joanne over the wet ground to the edge of the riverbank. Slipping on thick mud he pushed her head first into the fast-flowing river. Contact with the icy-cold water seemed to revive her. Suddenly, her eyes opened wide registering disbelief and terror.

Frantically, she rose up and clawed at his face trying to free herself from his vice-like grip. He put his hand over her face and thrust her head back under the water. She was sinking, sinking into an abyss; swallowed up by the black, swirling waters. Campbell waited patiently for a few more seconds until he was satisfied she was dead.

He stripped off her wet clothes then pulled a Stanley knife from his pocket. Holding the body by the head he carved a criss-cross of deep cuts on the face, penetrating the flesh to the bone. Not satisfied, he slashed the skin on her fingertips, picked up a stone and hammered at the face until the skull caved in. He threw the bloodied stone back into the river. The water would soon wash off the blood.

He pushed the body towards the middle of the river waiting for the current to catch it and take it downstream. After washing off the blood he tramped back to the Jaguar, took off his Wellingtons and deposited them into a black bin liner. Back on the main road he called into the car park of a closed store and disposed of them in one of the large recycling bins.

It would be days before they found Joanne, but they

wouldn't be able to identify her easily. He hadn't wanted to cut up her lovely face like that, but it was unavoidable. By the time her body was discovered he would be long gone. It would be quite some time before a link would be made between Joanne Howard, the beautiful young travel agent from Oswestry, and the mutilated corpse.

CHAPTER TWENTY-THREE

Gloucestershire, England

Lynes took a last glance at the flickering computer screen. Yawning loudly, he grabbed his briefcase and jacket.

"I'm whacked," muttered a colleague.

"Me and you both, mate," Colin replied. "Footie on telly and feet up for me tonight."

If the clod only knew what was going to happen. He imagined the faces of his colleagues when GCHQ was thrown into complete panic. A delightful shiver of anticipation coursed through him. Soon he would have everything he had ever dreamed of; everything they had promised. It was all arranged. As soon as he handed over the documents the organisation would fly him to Brazil. His heart fluttered with anticipation and fear. He had to be very careful not to raise suspicions in Moscow. He would give them all the information they wanted except the last batch.

As he drove home a black van pulled out from a side street and squeezed into the line of traffic. The driver picked up a mobile phone from the passenger seat.

"He's on his way. It should take about twenty minutes."

"We are in position."

"The parcel must be wrapped and dispatched immediately. Don't make any mistakes."

The man shuddered at the thought of what would happen to him if he failed.

Negotiating the snarled traffic, not even the grey drizzle dampened Lynes's spirits. He whistled a little Russian folk song, his heart dancing to the rhythm. It would be dark soon. He could draw his living room curtains and shut out the decadent world he lived in. The obnoxious, overpowering Mrs Jepps had gone to visit her sister in Cirencester. At least she wouldn't be waiting ready to pounce, as usual. He drew up to the curb outside his house taking a surreptitious glance at the house next door.

He didn't notice the man sitting huddled in a dark-blue Volvo, baseball cap pulled down over his eyes. Lynes inserted the key into the lock, pushed open the door and stepped inside. It took him a few moments to adjust to the gloomy hallway. He pushed the door shut and stretched out to turn on the light. His hand never found the switch.

Out of the darkness an arm grabbed him around the neck. His assailant's grip was so tight he could barely breathe.

"If it's money you want take it. There's sixty pounds in my inside jacket pocket, more in the drawer under the television. Take it! Take it! Please!"

"I don't want money." Lynes kicked out with his foot, but his attacker just tightened his grip. "We know about your friend, Foley. You have betrayed us."

The headlamps of a passing car shone through the half-glass door glinting on the razor-sharp wire. The garrotte sliced through his throat turning his scream into a muffled gurgle. Blood poured from the wound. He tried to cover it with his hands as he fell onto the tiled floor. From somewhere far away he heard a harsh voice before he drifted into eternal oblivion.

"Your work here is done, Igor. The Motherland thanks you."

CHAPTER TWENTY-FOUR

Geneva, Switzerland

The plane suddenly emerged from a blanket of low cloud and started its descent into Geneva Airport. Lazily, Conrad surveyed the scenery unfolding below him. Snow-capped mountains gleamed in the silvery light. A weak sun glinted on a scattering of clouds hanging beneath the peaks. In the valley below swollen, aqua-coloured rivers snaked through the countryside.

Ten minutes later, the aeroplane kissed the tarmac, hurtled down the runway, and taxied to a stop. He hurried through customs, made for the taxi rank and instructed the driver to take him to the Grand Hotel. A burly man pushed his way into the taxi before he could protest.

"Okay if I share? I'm going to the Grand!"

By the time they reached the hotel Conrad had reluctantly agreed to meet him for a drink that evening.

The middle-aged American was already sitting in a discreet corner of the bar when Conrad walked in.

"Ethan Bateman," he introduced himself.

After they had ordered their drinks Conrad asked, "Are you here on holiday?"

"Business, I'm expanding my empire." Bateman chuckled. "I've got my finger in a lot of pies. Sportswear, roller blades, you name it."

Conrad learned that Bateman was investing large sums of money in Eastern Europe. Manufacturing costs were cheaper and there was a ready workforce. He had already accumulated a substantial fortune. He studied the American. Shrewd eyes, jowls hanging onto his thick neck; thinning, grey hair combed in wispy strands revealing his sunburnt scalp underneath. He had a large gap in the middle of his upper teeth. It gave him an almost comic appearance when he grinned.

He noted the heavy rings on his fingers, the expensive gold watch. Friendly enough, but a man who was used to getting what he wanted.

"Is this your first trip to Europe?" Conrad queried.

"I came here a few of months ago with my wife en route to London. We decided to do some sightseeing before we went back to the States. We met up with one of your lot."

Conrad shuffled uneasily, but he looked Bateman straight in the eyes.

"There are scores of British here all year round. You're bound to bump into one sooner or later."

"Yeah, this guy was staying in the same hotel in Interlaken – pretty place." Bateman ran his tongue over his lips nervously. He was sweating profusely now. His hands trembled slightly when he reached over to pick up his bourbon.

He lunged into a story about a sick Englishman who was going to a clinic in the Alps to recuperate after an operation. He had accompanied Bateman and his wife on a trip as far as Mürren.

"The guy looked very scared," Bateman continued. "His hands were shaking and he was sweating like a pig. He pushed a note into my hand and ran off. It was a telephone number. That's the last I saw of him."

Could it have been Foley? Why was Bateman telling him all this? He was all attention now, tuned in at high frequency.

"Do you know who he was?"

"Only his name – Bruce Foley."

A rush of adrenaline surged through Conrad's chest. His meeting the American was no coincidence.

"Why are you telling me this?"

Bateman related how he rang the number and discovered it was Conningwell Barracks. He contacted the commanding officer on the pretext of making a film about American GIs stationed there during the war. He was at the barracks when Conrad arrived.

"I was in the 'john'. When I came out I noticed the squaddie had accidentally left the door open. I only heard the beginning of the discussion before he closed it, but it was enough. It didn't take me long to put two and two together. From then on it was easy to keep tabs on you."

Abruptly, he stopped talking. His eyes followed a well-built man casually ambling into the bar. Nervously, he took out a large handkerchief and wiped his face.

"When we got back to our hotel the room had been ransacked and my laptop had disappeared. I'm being followed, I'm sure of it. Foley must have had something they wanted and they thought he passed it to me."

Bateman struggled out of the chair and looked at his wristwatch. He glanced nervously towards the bar and then leaned over to shake hands. Clasping Conrad's shoulder he whispered,

"The note also said 'Contact Mac.'"

Conrad watched him barge like a hippopotamus into the foyer. The bearded man sitting at the bar appeared engrossed in the light-snacks menu and paid no attention to the overweight Texan. But Conrad had been observing him closely since he arrived. He had been watching Bateman's every movement in the large mirror over the bar.

Sipping the last dregs of his whisky he ambled into the reception area, pausing at a stand of tourist information and maps near the entrance of the hotel. Through the glass revolving doors he saw Bateman get into a taxi. Seconds later, the bearded man appeared and swiftly walked through the foyer into the street. As the taxi pulled away, he yanked at the locked rear door then ran towards a 4 x 4 parked in one of the bays. Conrad approached the doorman and discreetly slipped him a ten-franc note.

"My friend dropped his wallet in the bar. He's just gone off in a taxi… an American"

"Ah, yes, Mr Bateman. He was going to the airport."

Conrad mulled this over. Bateman had mentioned he was going to a business meeting in Bern the next morning, but there was something distinctly suspicious about the way he had rushed out of the hotel. Why had he been so agitated by the appearance of the man at the bar?

He hurried back inside the foyer and made for the bank of telephone booths on the left. They were all occupied. His eyes raked the area looking for a secluded spot where he wouldn't be overheard. Suddenly, the door of the nearest booth opened. An elegantly dressed woman stepped out. She gave a faint smile as he darted inside and closed the door behind him. He delved into his pocket for his mobile phone and quickly dialled a number.

"Breakdancer."

"This is Regis." He outlined his meeting with Ethan Bateman. "I need a full security check on him as soon as possible."

He was about to go into dinner when his phone rang. It was Pearce.

"Bateman's squeaky clean. Wife and three kids, a wealthy entrepreneur, country club set, regular churchgoer. Well educated – MIT, Harvard, doctorate in physics." Conrad raised his eyebrows in surprise. "He owns two factories in Texas manufacturing surgical and optical instruments and a small design facility in Nevada. Right out in the desert, very hush-hush. He's also a state senator."

"Why would a US senator take it upon himself to investigate Foley's disappearance? It doesn't add up."

"Here's the interesting bit. It seems our entrepreneur has connections in the Pentagon. My CIA source tells me he's been working on some classified stuff for the military. Keep in touch, Jack."

Conrad snapped his phone shut as the line went dead. What was Bateman involved in? Why was he so interested in Foley?

CHAPTER TWENTY-FIVE

Geneva, Switzerland

Conrad pushed his way through the lunchtime throng. Le Cygne Noir was always jam packed at this time of day. Most of the tables were occupied with dark-suited businessmen talking in low voices. A few tourists slumped wearily, cameras hanging round their necks, shopping bags crammed full of souvenirs and chocolate. He looked into a smaller side room. Less formal, it was packed with youngsters in fashionable jeans and designer sweaters animatedly talking by the bar. Casually, he took in the whole room looking for his Swiss contact.

A fair-haired man sauntered in and walked to the booth at the rear. Conrad smiled to himself as women's heads turned to follow him. Alexander Mikhail Leveque, affectionately known as Sasha, was the product of a Russian-American mother and French father. A popular television star, his face adorned magazines all over Europe and the United States.

He had been recruited by Conrad after his sister, Yvette, was caught up in a terrorist bomb attack on the French President. She was an innocent spectator amongst the crowd outside the Élysée Palace. Now, Sasha used his glamorous lifestyle to gain entry to the homes and secrets of the well-heeled and famous. It was part of his cover.

Conrad related the story of Ethan Bateman's encounter with Foley and the note asking him to contact Mac.

"Any sign of Macaleer?" Conrad asked.

"We've checked right across the cantons," Sasha replied. "We know he went to Interlaken looking for Foley after checking out of the Grand. Since then there's been no sight of him. We checked the airports, trains, all the car hire companies. If he'd gone over the border by road he would have been spotted by one of our agents."

"Foley said he was going to a clinic in the Alps, but according to Bateman it doesn't exist. I think I'll take a little excursion into the mountains myself. I'll fly down to Bern tomorrow morning."

"I'll come with you," Sasha offered. "The mountains can be treacherous this time of year."

"No, you're more useful here at the moment. Get on the web and look up all the aerial photographers for the Bernese Oberland. Get hold of any pictures they've taken over the last few years. If there are any new buildings they'll show up. Meet me here in two days."

CHAPTER TWENTY-SIX

Bernese Oberland, November 2016

A glittering white sun hovered in the November sky, partially obscured by heavy clouds that raced above the valley. Clumps of vegetation huddled amongst an avalanche of shale. Higher up clusters of pines stood stark and black against the snow that iced the mountain peaks. No sound except for the whining engine of a motorcycle snaking up the narrow road. Conrad watched it weaving in and out behind enormous outcrops of rock until it vanished from sight.

He peered through his high-powered binoculars raking the landscape ahead of where the vehicle had disappeared. Two gigantic pillars of rock hung over the rough path forming a natural canopy. He waited, expecting it to reappear, but there was no sign of the bike. It seemed to have evaporated into thin air.

The path was an extension of a narrow road through a village about a kilometre away. Nestled against the mountain it was almost invisible to climbers higher up. Just a couple of rustic chalets and a goat pen. The tarmac road ended just beyond this point and narrowed into little more than a dirt track. Without a trail bike it would be impossible to get higher up the tortuous path. The only other way up was on foot. It was the first week of November. Already, a layer of icy snow crackled underfoot. A heavy snowfall would make it even more difficult.

He followed the stone-strewn path keeping up a steady pace on the uneven surface. Suddenly, a shot echoed across the slopes. Instinctively, he ducked and dived for cover behind a large boulder. It wasn't meant to kill him. He knew a skilled marksman could have easily picked him off in the open. No, this was a warning. Two more shots rang out, pinging off the rock, sending slivers of stone flying into the air.

He swept the area with his binoculars. A sudden movement caught his eye about three hundred metres above him. A figure clothed in black wearing ski glasses. There was something familiar about the way he moved as he scrambled up the slope: a certain sinewy litheness. Suddenly, he stopped and looked down, hands planted on his hips. Conrad was almost certain it was the man he had seen in the hotel. With a final glance over his shoulder he was gone.

Warily, Conrad cut across to an isolated chalet on the outskirts of the village.

"*Guten tag!*" he called to a man busily stacking logs against the side of his chalet. "Stocking up for the winter?"

"*Ja*, before the big snows come."

"I expect a lot of visitors stay up here in the clinic in the summer months."

Bemused, the villager grinned and scratched his head. *Tourists*, he thought contemptuously.

"No, there's nothing here. Some years ago there was a hotel and restaurant up there." He pointed in the direction of the rock formation Conrad had spotted. "It changed hands many times, but it wasn't very successful. The last owners started to build an ice hotel for tourists. They burrowed deep into the mountain, but the project soon shut down after two young skiers were killed. There's nothing left of it except a shell of broken timber. Since the avalanche walkers never go up there. It's too dangerous."

Conrad rejoined the main signposted path and climbed steadily for another hour until he reached the Schilthornbahn at Berg. The cable car was locking into position to disgorge its passengers when he approached the station. Following the crowd on board he pushed his way into a corner, pressed in by a group of excited Japanese girls. The gondola rattled over the cable as it left the station. The girls screamed hysterically and covered their eyes, not daring to look at the precipitous drop to the valley floor.

He scanned the surrounding mountains as the cable car slowly descended, straining his eyes for any sign of a building that might house a clinic. Nothing except snow and rocks. A slight bump heralded their arrival at Mürren. He caught the train to Grütschalp down to Lauterbrünnen where he had left his car. Tomorrow he would hire a trail bike.

CHAPTER TWENTY-SEVEN

Shropshire, England

Dr Barnett lifted the sheet covering the body. Wallace sucked in his breath when he saw the mutilated face. Someone had taken a knife to her. Whoever did it was a sadistic bastard, or didn't want her to be recognised for some reason. He stared at the partially-clothed, bloated corpse. Sightless eyes wide open, stripped of dignity. An image of his daughter studying for a degree in London floated in front of his eyes. A thrill of fear swamped his chest. Quickly, he pushed the thought out of his mind.

"Huge bristols," DC Baker smirked near his shoulder.

Fists clenched, Wallace whirled round, his face red with fury. For a split second the pathologist thought he was going to punch the DC. Startled, Baker took a step backwards almost losing his balance.

"In future you'll treat victims with respect. Is that clear?" Wallace hissed through clenched teeth. "Now, get out of my sight before I forget I'm your superior officer! I'll deal with you later!"

He bent over the corpse, quickly zipped up the body bag and signalled to the SOCOs. For a few minutes he gazed out over the fast-flowing water watching it slap against the bank. Heavy rains had swollen the river, flooding the area on both sides. The ground was soft and squelchy underfoot. A furrow of deep mud indicated where the body had been dragged up the bank.

"Who found the body?"

"Some kids out riding their bikes," Dr Barnett replied. "They spotted it from the path, lodged in that partially sunken tree... frightened hell out of them." She pointed to a detached cottage, about two hundred yards away, with lawns sloping down to the river edge. "Apparently, they were heard screaming from that house back there."

Wallace gingerly squelched through the mud to examine the spot. It was a fresh break. The tree had obviously come down the night before during high winds. The body had snagged in the branches preventing it from floating downstream.

"I'll call you in the morning about the post mortem," Dr Barnett said.

"How about dinner tonight, Jo?" Wallace murmured, struggling back to her side.

"I thought you had a girlfriend? Maggie, isn't it?"

"Ex-girlfriend. She left a note before she jetted off to New York; says she sees more of the pilot than she does of me. No strings, scout's honour," he pleaded. "Come on, what do you say?"

"All right, pick me up at eight, as long as it's somewhere outside town."

Wallace had been plucking up the courage to ask Jo out ever since Maggie had dumped him. Their relationship was never going anywhere. He supposed he should feel guilty about it, but all he felt was relief. He realised with a start that he had never really loved Maggie. She was just a comfortable habit he had acquired after his wife had run off with her boss.

A slight thrill of anticipation coursed through him. He was looking forward to his dinner date.

On the way back to Shrewsbury, he reflected on the information forwarded from Interpol. A body had been found floating in the Seine near the Isle de Citè in Paris, completely naked. It had turned out to be a drunken student bent on a late-night swim. Another had been dragged out of Lake Geneva. Now he was waiting for an up-to-date report from his old friend, Ernst Dreher, his counterpart in Geneva, but it was unlikely there was a connection with the murders on his patch.

*

Settled in a bay window overlooking the river, Wallace tucked ravenously into his steak.

"This is lovely, Ben," Jo said looking around the room.

She hesitated to say romantic, but it was. Subdued lighting, pristine white tablecloths; deep-pile carpets muffling the steps of waiters. A log fire crackling in the grate, bathing diners in a rosy glow. It was perfect.

"I always come here when I want to chill out over a quiet meal," Wallace mumbled through a mouthful of meat. "Hardly anybody at the station comes here. Most of them prefer the pubs or a curry house."

They continued their meal in companionable silence. Jo looked at him as she sipped her glass of Rioja. Brooding dark looks, green eyes; he really was quite attractive. She shook herself mentally. Pity he's a policeman. Her relationship with her ex-husband, a superintendent in the Metropolitan Police, had ended acrimoniously. They had both been wrapped up in their own careers, barely noticing they had drifted apart until it was too late. Tentatively, Wallace reached out and covered her hand with his own then quickly withdrew it. It was too soon to start a new relationship, especially while he was so involved with his investigations. His thoughts were interrupted by the vibration of his mobile phone. "DCI Wallace," he said quietly. He listened intently for a few minutes then snapped his phone shut. Before he had chance to speak, Jo's phone rang. She raised her eyebrows as she stuffed it back into her handbag. Wallace cursed under his breath, a scowl darkening his face. They were going to the same place.

*

Wallace pushed aside the plastic strip doors and edged into the post mortem room. Jo Barnett was huddled over the corpse of the girl they had found the day before.

"You're off the hook with that one over there," she commented, inclining her head towards another body under a sheet on the far side of the room. "Massive heart attack brought on by excessive alcohol intake plus a mixture of Class A drugs."

"This one wasn't strangled as I told you yesterday. There are marks on the throat, but it turns out that wasn't the cause of death. The knife slashes on her face were carried out after she had been drowned. Whoever murdered her will have scratches – deep ones. There's a substantial amount of skin and blood under her fingernails. We also found something else." She held up a tweezers.

"Take a look. You'll need this."

Wallace took the outsized magnifying glass and squinted at the sample. It looked like a strand of something. In fact it was several tiny strands. Two were definitely hair. The others could have been fabric. It was difficult to say until forensics looked at them.

"I'll get it off to the lab," Jo said, shooing him out of the door. "Get some sleep. If you keep on the way you're going you'll be under one of these sheets: you too, Butler."

Wallace's shoulders sagged. They had both been up all night. For a moment he felt slightly detached as though his head was floating somewhere above his body. Butler drove home very sedately, too tired to drive at his normal speed.

He was almost asleep when they crunched up his driveway. They screeched to a halt sending chippings flying from the wheels. He tumbled out on wobbly legs, barely acknowledging Butler's parting wave. Stumbling to the living room, he threw himself on the sofa, fully dressed, and sank into blissful sleep.

CHAPTER TWENTY-EIGHT

Bernese Oberland

Conrad parked the car and trailer he had hired and unloaded the scrambler. Fingers of light pierced the sky in the east. He glanced at his watch – 07:00 hours. It would be light in fifteen minutes. Gunning the engine he lurched up the mountain trail that led high up into the mountains away from Berg.

At intervals he stopped to survey the landscape. There was nothing out of the ordinary. Just a couple of chalet-type inns before the trail veered off. When he reached the highest inn the trail looped back to join another that also led up to Berg. He dismounted, went inside and ordered some hot chocolate. The rosy-cheeked woman scurried off and quickly returned with his drink.

"The air is so clear up here," Conrad said. "No wonder people come here for their health."

"*Ja*, they come in summer, along with walkers and climbers, usually to private chalets on the lower slopes. In winter we are usually snowed in. We close the hotel and move to our chalet near Mürren. There's nothing beyond here."

Conrad nodded. If there was a facility higher up in the Alps, it was unlikely to be anywhere near the cable car route to Schilthorn where it could be seen by hundreds of tourists.

He continued riding the trails, stopping occasionally to survey the landscape or an isolated gummi hut. The terrain was much rougher now with a lot of loose shale. When the engine stalled and died, almost throwing him off, he decided to climb higher on foot.

Concealing the bike behind some rocks, he set off at a steady pace. It was a beautiful morning. Overhead, a white sun glittered in an azure sky illuminating the snow-capped peaks. Far below, little clusters of houses clung to the grass draping to the foot of the mountain. It was so still and quiet.

Suddenly, he heard the faint drone of an engine. The dark shape of a helicopter appeared in the distance flying perilously close to the peaks. Conrad followed its shadow on the snow until it dropped behind an enormous outcrop of rock and disappeared from sight. He waited for it to reappear again, but the sky around him remained empty except for a few scudding clouds that had swept in over the mountains.

It has to come back up, he thought, *there's nowhere for it to go*. If it had crashed he would have seen the smoke. It must have landed somewhere up there high above him. He calculated it was at least another two hours arduous trek to get to the point where it had disappeared. He glanced at his watch. Plenty of time to complete his investigations and get back down to the foot of the mountain before dusk.

His breathing became more laboured as he climbed higher into thinner air. His main objective was to reach that part of the trail that ran parallel with the Berg cable car station. He was sweating profusely even though it was a cold, crisp day.

Shortly after midday, he decided he was close enough to the spot. Concealed behind rocks he swept the area with his binoculars, swinging up and across at an angle. Nothing but boulders, sparse grass and a few spindly pines clinging to the steep slopes. He scanned the mountain again, panning over what appeared to be whitish-grey stones on a patch of grass.

"What the hell… ?" he said aloud. He blinked and refocused the lenses. "My eyes are playing tricks on me. Goats! It can't be!"

Except for that one patch of snow-pocked, level grass, it was all stone with sheer outcrops of rock falling away from it. Surely, goatherds wouldn't climb this far up to tend them, especially in November, when there was more plentiful grazing lower down. Besides, it was the only patch of grass to be seen amongst a blanket of white.

He tried to fit the pieces together. Goats on a patch of grass; odd, very odd indeed. Studying a map outlining all the mountain paths, he circled the area where he had seen the animals. It was directly under where the helicopter had gone down. Beneath the goats, a barely visible trail dropped down about two hundred metres. It came to an abrupt end above an outcrop of rock and shale that had collapsed, spreading into a landslide of rubble that tumbled down the slopes.

Suddenly, a cutting wind swept across the slopes. He shivered. The temperature was dropping. Dark, ominous clouds floated across the sun creating a temporary twilight. He had to start his descent if he was to get back to the motorcycle and off the mountain before sunset. With any luck Sasha would have come up with the aerial photographs he asked him to get. That would give him a better idea of how the helicopter managed to disappear into thin air.

CHAPTER TWENTY-NINE

Bernese Oberland

Guests crowded at the lift doors muttered impatiently when the green indicator light paused. It was on its way down, stopping at every floor. Conrad glanced at his watch… seven thirty. Half an hour before his meeting with Sasha. It was quicker to take the stairs. Reaching his room he checked the fine, cotton thread he had placed between the door and the frame. It was still there. A precaution he had taken after being spotted on the mountain by the man who had jumped into the taxi with Ethan Bateman. Conrad had been wearing wrap-around snow glasses and a neck warmer pulled up over his face. He didn't think he had been recognised, but he wasn't taking any chances.

He quickly showered, rubbing vigorously at his arms and legs. His muscles were aching after riding the trail bike and the strenuous uphill walking. So far he had learned nothing concrete, but his gut feeling told him there something significant on the mountain. All he had to do now was get back up there and find out exactly what was going on.

Dressed casually in black trousers and a dark-red cashmere sweater, he strolled into the bar. He found a secluded corner where he could sit with his back to the wall and watch the entrance. Five minutes later Sasha sauntered in, his eyes scanning the dimly lit room. He smiled when he spotted Conrad waving at him. Women stared and whispered, returning his sensual smile, their thoughts written on their faces.

"Sasha old chap, glad you could make it," Conrad said, loudly enough for other guests to hear him. "I couldn't believe it when I bumped into you yesterday. It's been a long time. Are you here on holiday?"

"Unfortunately, it's work. We're filming a new series. I think it's what you British call a 'soap.'" He laughed, exposing even white teeth.

Conrad felt as though they were under a microscope. Every movement was being monitored by surrounding guests. Ironically, the exposure helped. They were just two old friends enjoying some time together. When they had settled with their drinks Conrad related the sighting of the helicopter.

"It was very strange. It just dropped into the mountains and didn't reappear. For a split second I thought it had crashed, but I would have seen the smoke. It must have landed."

"How could it land in the Alps, especially between the summits of the peaks?"

"That's what I'm trying to figure out. Would you say it was normal for goats to be grazing that high up?"

"It's not unusual to see goats in Switzerland," Sasha chuckled.

"About a dozen of them were grazing on a large patch of grass. The peculiar thing is there wasn't a building in sight, not even a gummi hut. Doesn't it seem a bit strange that animals were simply left there to fend for themselves? There's more to this than meets the eye. I'm going back up there."

"I'll come with you. I know these mountains like the back of my hand. At this time of year the Alps can be unpredictable and treacherous."

Conrad was about to protest then remembered that Sasha had been a serious mountain climber since his teens. Dressed in full mountain gear and snow glasses his face had smiled out of all the glamour magazines.

"Okay, you win," he replied, swallowing the last of his drink. "Let's get some dinner then we can take a look at the aerial pictures."

*

Back in Conrad's room they spread the photographs over the bed. Delving into his laptop case he pulled out a magnifying glass. Carefully, they studied the trails and slopes looking for clues.

"According to the map there should be a trail circumventing the area where I spotted the goats." He stabbed at the aerial photograph. "There's nothing but shale and rocks." He handed the magnifier to Sasha.

Sasha scratched his chin thoughtfully. "There should be a path right here." He jabbed at the map. "It's hardly ever used… shoots off diagonally from the main drag then links with another trail higher up, just here. This path doesn't appear on the photographs either. Hold on!" He pulled out another batch of photographs from his valise and studied them intently. "Well, I'll be damned! Take a look. These photographs were taken about fifteen years ago. As you can see the two paths are quite clearly visible."

Conrad compared the two sets of prints. Either somebody

119

had done a very good job of touching up the pictures or the paths had been deliberately obliterated. Whoever was behind it didn't want anyone snooping around. Whatever was up there, he intended to find out.

CHAPTER THIRTY

Shropshire, England

Wallace strode through the incident room signalling for Butler to follow. His early morning walk in the Quarry Park had cleared the fuzziness from his head. Feeling refreshed and energised he squeezed behind his desk. Before he had a chance to settle down his phone shrilled. It was Dr Barnett with the results of the lab tests.

"The sample taken from under the victim's fingernails was a mix of hair, skin and minute traces of fabric. Coupled with Barr tests on the hair, forensics established that her killer was probably a white male, but the tests were inconclusive. What they could say was that the hair was dyed auburn."

"It could have been a disguise or pure vanity." Wallace said, "A lot of men dye their hair these days."

"The strand of fabric was fine mohair; very expensive," she continued. "Only specialist bespoke tailors would use it so it shouldn't be too hard to trace. It's more widely used in Europe, particularly France."

"Could be a foreign businessman, I suppose," Wallace suggested. "That would make it slightly easier to track down."

"More importantly, the girl had a very rare blood group – AB rhesus negative. Only about 1% of the population have that blood group. Oh, and she's had an abortion."

"Thanks Jo, we can do a lot with that information. I'm

off duty tonight. What about dinner over at my place... say about eight o'clock? Spaghetti alla carbonara and a good bottle of Rioja," he coaxed.

"Okay, you've twisted my arm. I'll be over by seven-thirty."

This could be the breakthrough we've had been waiting for, Wallace thought. He strode back into the incident room and instructed Butler to contact the National Blood Transfusion Service. Their records would show if anyone from that particular group had donated blood. There was also a slim chance that hospitals in the area had provided blood for an AB rhesus negative patient recently.

"DS Blakeman, take Baker with you and contact any bespoke tailors in town. See if any of them make quality mohair suits."

Wallace had been observing Baker carefully after discovering the girl's body. He didn't want him going anywhere without a DS with him. He was becoming a liability.

"Going up to the Palace for your knighthood, are you, guv?" Baker chortled.

Butler shot him a warning glance. Wallace's neck flushed blood-red, but he swallowed his anger. He nodded at two young detectives.

"Get round to the hotels. Find out if anyone wearing a very expensive suit checked in over the past few weeks. I doubt anyone would recognise it as mohair. Richards and Connolly, cover the hospitals." He marched into his office, Butler close on his heels.

Yawning expansively, Wallace lowered his lanky frame into an armchair across from his DS. The good news was that Howard's AB negative blood group narrowed it down dramatically. The bad news was that only two men in that group had donated blood in the past six months. No women in the victim's age group. If the victim hadn't had surgery, or donated blood, it would be a hell of a job to identify her.

Wallace slammed down his cup spilling coffee over the desk. They were back where they had started. All the GP surgeries in Shrewsbury and surrounding areas would have to be checked out.

"I'll make a start straight away," Butler said, heading for the door, "but the victim may not have been local."

"The thought had occurred to me," Wallace replied sarcastically.

*

Jo settled herself in Wallace's overstuffed armchair. Mellowed by a large glass of Rioja she smiled at him provocatively over the rim of her glass. She hadn't felt this relaxed for a long time. Wallace smiled back, but said nothing. The long silences between them were soothing rather than discomforting. They were unusually relaxed together, but he didn't want to ruin everything.

"I'm owed some leave so I thought I might take a trip to Switzerland," he said breezily. "Maybe get in a bit of skiing. How would you like to come along?"

"During the middle of a serious murder investigation?" Jo raised her eyebrows in mock horror. "What's the catch?"

Wallace grinned, remembering their passionate kiss after the meal at the riverside inn. Their relationship was moving more quickly than either of them had anticipated.

"Perhaps we could combine business with pleasure."

"I knew it!" Jo exclaimed.

Wallace explained that he had been speaking to Ernst Dreher, his counterpart in Geneva. They had been collaborating on and off for years after investigating an international fraud case while he was in the Metropolitan Police back in the nineties. Since then he had spent most of his winter leave with Ernst and his wife skiing in the Bernese Oberland.

"Ernst inherited his parents' skiing chalet. Sophia, his wife, is Italian… fabulous cook. You'll love her."

He's manipulating me again, Jo thought, *but what the hell.* She was rather enjoying it. Besides she had never been to Switzerland. She held out her glass.

"Pour me another glass of wine and I may take you up on your offer. With one condition; you teach me to ski… deal?"

"Deal," Wallace grinned.

CHAPTER THIRTY-ONE

Geneva, Switzerland

A flurry of snow hit the window as the plane made its final descent towards Geneva's Cointrin International Airport. By the time they collected their luggage and left the terminal it was coming down thick and fast. Passengers huddled in warm coats waited in line for taxis. On cue, a black Mercedes swung in front of the taxi rank slithering to a halt on the slippery surface. A man in an expensive overcoat and Astrakhan Russian-style hat jumped out of the rear.

"Ben, I'm so glad to see you," he said warmly.

The two men shook hands, vigorously clapping each other on the shoulder. Wallace turned around and took Jo's arm.

"This is Johanna Barnett, a very good friend of mine."

"Ah, you are very beautiful," Ernst remarked knowingly. "Come, let's get out of the cold. We have a chalet near Thun, but we stay in our house in Cologny during the week. It's more convenient for my work. We'll drive down tomorrow morning. Sophia is already there making preparations for your visit. She has a feast planned for tomorrow night. I hope you like Italian food?"

"I love it!" Jo replied enthusiastically.

Dreher leaned forward to give his driver instructions then spoke into his mobile phone.

Traffic was heavy as they left the airport. It was ten minutes before they reached La Voire des Traz and finally made some headway. Eventually, they turned into the driveway of a very large house surrounded by lawns and trees heavy with snow. Dreher pressed the intercom. A metallic voice greeted him followed by a click as the lock disengaged.

As they mounted the steps the door opened. A short, rotund man with rosy cheeks beamed at them.

"*Bon soir*. It is a pleasure to see you again, Monsieur Wallace. Please let me take your coats. Coffee is ready for you."

"Thank you, Henri."

Dreher led them across the hall into a room lined with books. Jo looked around appreciatively at the chesterfield, oversized armchairs and expensive rugs. A log fire crackled in the grate suffusing the room with a warm glow. It radiated taste. *Neither his clothes nor this property were bought on a policeman's salary*, Jo reflected.

Tall, dark hair flecked with silver swept back from his forehead, straight nose, finely-chiselled features and penetrating blue eyes. He looked every inch the wealthy aristocrat.

"What a beautiful room and an open fire!" Jo exclaimed.

"My little weakness, I'm afraid. It reminds me of my childhood."

After dinner that evening they took their brandies into the library. Wallace and Dreher reminisced about their skiing holidays in the Alps while Jo admired the books and paintings. Inevitably, the conversation turned to the real reason for Wallace's visit.

"I forgot to mention that Jo is a pathologist. She performed the post mortems on the victims on my patch."

"Sophia is a criminal psychologist," Dreher chuckled. "I'm sure you'll have some very interesting conversations."

"Actually, she could be very helpful to us," Wallace commented.

"Enough! Let's enjoy the rest of the evening. It will keep until we get to Thun tomorrow."

Dreher drew back the heavy drapes and peered out at the curtain of falling snow. Flying into Bern-Belp airport was out of the question. More heavy snow was forecast for the area. It would take a few hours by road to Thun so they needed to make an early start the next morning.

"I'm so tired," Jo said, stifling a yawn. "It must be the Swiss air. I can hardly keep my eyes open."

"Where are my manners?" Dreher said. "Of course you must have your beauty sleep."

She dragged upstairs to her room to the sound of the men laughing uproariously. Seconds after her head touched the pillow she fell into a deep sleep.

CHAPTER THIRTY-TWO

Thunersee, Bernese Oberland

Jo peered through the window at the bleak landscape. Anticipating a tiring drive they had started out early. She glanced at her watch – nine o'clock. They had been on the road for over an hour. Driving conditions were hazardous even with the efficiency of the Swiss in keeping the roads drivable. Cocooned in the warmth of the car the rhythmic swish of the windscreen wipers lulled her into a delicious torpor.

A white mist hung over the Alps obliterating the peaks. It was like a monochrome painting. Dark-trunked trees silhouetted against a background of pure white. Aquamarine rivers washed of colour, like over-diluted cordial. A frozen waterfall, transformed into a giant icicle, hung suspended over the sheer mountainside.

Jo caught her breath. Everything seemed completely still as though life had frozen in a moment of time. She shivered; there was something vaguely malevolent about the towering mountains as though they were trying to draw her in. Suddenly, she felt claustrophobic. She inhaled deeply trying to shake off the feeling.

The lake, set like a piece of jet in a sea of ice-white, disappeared from view as they approached the entry road. A large chalet, perched on a spit of land overlooking the lake, loomed ahead. Logs were stacked along one wall in neat rows. Icicles hung low from the eaves, partially obscuring the colourful murals painted on the walls. The car crunched up the drive between pine trees and stopped in front of carved double doors.

"Sophia!" Dreher called as they entered the hallway. "Sophia!"

A slim, elegant woman rushed into the hall. Olive skin, high cheekbones, liquid brown eyes flecked with green. She was stunning. Behind her stood a dark-haired boy, around fourteen, with the same bone structure and graceful movements as his mother. A little girl pushed between them.

"Papa!" she cried, running to her father.

He swung her round and round until she begged him to stop.

"Christian, my son, and this is my baby Bianca."

"I'm not a baby! I'm seven!" she exclaimed irritably.

Dreher grinned and patted her head. "Off you go now and wash ready for lunch."

After lunch they settled down in front of a roaring log fire. Pleasantly full, a relaxed Wallace broached the subject of the murders.

"Two murders on my patch. The man had been drugged and suffocated. The woman had also been drugged and drowned. Both of their faces had been mutilated after death, especially the girl. She had been carved up pretty badly. Both bodies were completely naked and wrapped in sheets. Another body was washed up on a beach in Hampshire. That one was also stripped naked and wrapped in a sheet. There are too many coincidences."

Wallace's instincts told him there was something more than fishy about the case. It had to be big, so big Payne had stopped the investigations on the Chief Constable's orders. He related how the body in Hampshire had been whisked away and everything hushed up. Dreher rubbed his chin thoughtfully. He was not a man to make rash judgements or decisions.

"What I am about to tell you is highly confidential," he said. He glanced at Jo. "Would you mind if I talk to Ben alone?"

"I think I'll see if Sophia needs any help," she murmured.

Dreher waited until he heard the women laughing in the kitchen before speaking.

"A man named Ethan Bateman, an American Senator, disappeared from his hotel in Geneva recently. The alarm was raised when he failed to return to his hotel."

Wallace shrugged his shoulders. "I don't see the connection."

Dreher devil-drummed on the arm of his chair then got up and paced the room.

"When you contacted Interpol we decided to dig a bit deeper. You're right, Ben. This is big. The man my detectives questioned turned out to be British Military Intelligence. Our local police have been warned off by security services. There's to be no further police investigation."

"Military Intelligence!" Wallace exclaimed, letting out a low whistle.

"However, this situation could have international repercussions which is why I will be working in close liaison with Interpol. We've both been members of Interpol Incident Response Teams. Five years ago on the human trafficking case in Eastern Europe, the international drug smuggling and those stolen art works from Paris."

"What are you getting at?"

"The United States is champing at the bit to find out what happened to one of their prominent citizens, especially a Senator. It won't be long before the CIA start sniffing around."

"Will Lyon send out an Incident Response Team?"

"They don't think it's warranted at the moment. At the same time we have to placate the Americans. You are experienced in intelligence work. I want you to be part of my team if they decide to go ahead. I'll get in touch with headquarters in Lyon. Your superiors will be hard-pressed to refuse such a request."

Wallace chuckled and blew out his cheeks.

"A meeting has been arranged with the British agent tomorrow morning at his hotel. He insists it must be off the record."

Wallace felt a thrill course through his chest he hadn't felt for years. The old familiar tension tinged with excitement before an assignment. Suddenly, he felt alive, vigorous and impatient for action.

"I'd like to see Crew Cut Charlie's face when he hears this."

CHAPTER THIRTY-THREE

Thunersee, Bernese Oberland

There was something vaguely familiar about the figure sitting in the hotel bar, silhouetted against the wintry sunlight pouring in from the huge windows. Wallace couldn't make out his face. It was just the angle of the head, the slight nod to the waiter that stirred up a fleeting memory. The man stood up as Dreher approached him.

"Good morning, Chief Inspector Dreher."

Wallace moved from behind the heavy curtains that separated a small dining area from the bar lounge. Conrad stopped and stared at the broad-shouldered man walking towards him.

"Well, I'll be damned! If it isn't Biker Wallace!" he exclaimed.

"You know the Chief Inspector?" Dreher asked, looking slightly bewildered.

"Captain Ben Wallace, aka Biker, rode his Harley Davidson down Route 66 from Chicago to Los Angeles, hence the nickname. We worked in military intelligence for quite a while. What the hell are you doing here, Ben?"

Wallace related the circumstances of the murders on his patch. The body on the Hampshire coast and the similarities with a body found in Lake Geneva that eventually turned out to be unconnected.

If Conrad was involved it could only mean covert military operations. Wallace smiled inwardly. So that's why he had been warned off by the big brass. His little trip to Switzerland was paying off. He wanted answers and so did Dreher. Cut from the same cloth they had been trusted friends and colleagues for years. Neither of them would be fobbed off with some concocted story. It was too much of a coincidence that British and Swiss police had been told to halt their investigations.

Conrad frowned in concentration, weighing up the possibilities. This had to be kept under wraps. If he told them everything he could risk the whole situation crumbling before he completed his investigations. If he didn't, he suspected they would keep on digging. He was careful not to tell them about IMIC or about its activities. All they needed to know was that he was investigating the disappearance of two military intelligence officers who had gone AWOL in Switzerland.

"Macaleer went out to find Foley who had checked out of his hotel. He didn't return to his unit," Conrad said. He related Ethan Bateman's encounter with Foley and their trip to the Piz Gloria. "Foley pushed a note into Bateman's hand telling him to 'Contact Mac' before running off into a throng of tourists. The senator started snooping around, tracking down Foley's base and eventually following me here. It was Macaleer's body that washed up in Hampshire. He had been shot in the back. It was sheer coincidence that the pathologist recognised him. We don't know what happened to Foley."

Conrad still hadn't worked out why Bateman got so involved or why he was so agitated. It was obvious he was scared stiff. He would have revealed more if he hadn't been frightened off by the guy in the bar. They had to find Bateman and question him, if he was still in Switzerland.

Wallace was equally puzzled by Macaleer's body washing up on a Hampshire beach, if he was supposed to be in Switzerland. Was it just coincidence that the murder victims on his patch were stripped naked? The only difference was that they had been mutilated while Macaleer had been shot. He grinned as Conrad furrowed his fingers through his hair, a habit that Wallace used to find irritating when they worked together.

"Damn! That's it!" Wallace exclaimed.

"I don't understand."

"Your hair, it was always too long. Your cap left an indentation at the back of your head, because it was too tight. The victim on my patch had the same thing. He could have been a military man. Macaleer was washed up in Hampshire even though he was supposed to be in Switzerland. Is it possible that Foley turned up in Shropshire?"

"Come on, you're clutching at straws," Conrad said sceptically.

"Perhaps, but it's worth checking out. I haven't got any other leads. I'll get the victim's blood checked against Foley's army records. We'll have to contact a relative to get a DNA sample."

"It's highly unlikely," Conrad said, "but if by some fluke it does turn out to be Foley we'll have to keep a lid on it. The Chief Constable will be informed. All your people need to know is that the victim remains unidentified, nothing else." Conrad excused himself and dialled a number on his mobile.

"Breakdancer," a voice rasped.

"Regis reporting. I have a problem. It turns out an old intelligence colleague, Detective Chief Inspector Ben

Wallace, is out here in connection with two murders in Shropshire. He also knows about Macaleer being washed up in Hampshire. His old pal from Interpol is also sniffing around, a guy called Ernst Dreher."

Pearce was silent for a few moments anticipating Conrad's anger when he told him about Dreher. He had been active as a covert field agent for IMIC for a number of years.

"Why the hell didn't he tell me?"

"Why would he? He doesn't know you're involved with IMIC."

Conrad wanted Wallace on board, but he had to convince Pearce of his suitability. Wallace had left the army due to wife trouble over his long absences. That didn't augur well, especially as he was due to be promoted to Major. On the plus side his work with Dreher gave him the edge and he had a good record in military intelligence.

"Jack, you know I trust your judgement, but I'd like to run the usual security checks on Wallace. Ring me this evening."

"Why don't you join us for dinner?" Dreher said, as Conrad prepared to leave.

"My wife always cooks enough for a small army. That way we can talk without being overheard."

Wallace grinned at the thought of another scrumptious meal cooked by the beautiful Sophia.

*

Snow fell gently past French doors that opened out onto a wooden veranda stretching along the front of the chalet overlooking the lake. Dreher drew the heavy drapes then placed a large log in the middle of the glowing fire. Within seconds it licked hungrily at the seasoned wood, engulfing it in tongues of orange flame. Mellow light from antique wall lamps spilled over the polished mahogany desk and gleamed on brass fire irons.

Dreher poured generous amounts of brandy and handed it to his guests. Conrad sat down in an oversized armchair and waited until the other men were settled with their drinks. This was as good a time as any to broach the subject.

"Have you ever heard of IMIC?" he asked.

Wallace shrugged his shoulders. Dreher stared intently into the fire, giving it a sharp jab with a brass-handled poker. Conrad quickly dialled a number on his mobile and handed it to Dreher. Looking perplexed, he listened carefully for a few minutes. Without saying a word he handed the mobile back to Conrad.

"IMIC stands for International Military Investigation Corps," Conrad explained. "It deals with anything that relates to the Armed Forces. Military espionage, terrorism, extortion involving personnel, anything that risks national or international security. It's highly secretive with an exclusive executive. Unknown to me, Dreher has worked undercover for them for some time. He has eyes and ears throughout Europe. Not even the CIA know about it, although Breakdancer has his American sources."

"Why are you telling me all this?" Wallace asked.

"We're dealing with the sale of military secrets. MI6 sussed out a 'sleeper' in GCHQ going under the name of Colin Lynes. They don't know how much information he passed on to the Russians before he was rumbled."

Conrad revealed how Lynes had been spying for the Russians for decades and deliberately set out to recruit Foley who had been working at GCHQ when he disappeared.

"What Lynes didn't know was that Foley was playing the same game. MI6 had recruited him to set up the 'sleeper'. He cultivated a friendship with him through their mutual love of chess. Somehow the plan backfired. We don't know what happened after Foley came to Switzerland for his planned kidney transplant."

"What do you mean?"

"That was how Lynes was set up. Foley had been given the all-clear after a blip on his kidney had been found on a private body-imaging scan. MI6 decided to use it to trap Lynes. He offered to obtain a kidney in exchange for military intelligence."

Wallace stood up and blew out his cheeks. "The murder victim on my patch had surgery to remove his right kidney, fairly recently." He shook his head in disbelief. "It *must* be Foley. Don't tell me Macaleer was involved as well."

"Unlikely, but we believe he found Foley. What happened after that is anybody's guess. We have to fit the pieces together."

CHAPTER THIRTY-FOUR

Shropshire, England

Wallace's flight from Geneva had been delayed for three hours. That, coupled with irritating road works, had plunged him into a foul mood. The last thing he needed was this little creep. Baker had put his foot in it again. Butler had only just managed to smooth things over at the Blood Transfusion Unit after a female member of staff threatened to report him for a lascivious remark. His face bright raspberry, he jabbed a finger at DC Baker.

"I'm recommending you go back into uniform. Now get out and close the door!"

Taking a deep breath he willed himself to calm down and think clearly about the flimsy leads they had so far. Richards and Connelly had come up with zilch at the hospitals. The only other lead on Joanne Howard was the fabric sample found under her nails. A young man had ordered a suit in that material from a tailor in Shrewsbury who had a website dealing with quality off-the-peg clothes. He had paid online, but the credit card turned out to be stolen.

Apparently, the owner didn't report it straight away. A number of purchases were made over the space of a few days. The fraud squad was alerted by the credit card company following a query about a statement. However, the fraudster could be ruled out of the murder investigation.

They might have more luck with a travel agent from Oswestry who had also ordered a business suit in the same fabric about a month earlier. One of her office staff, living in Shrewsbury, picked it up from the shop and paid cash. He was furious that nobody had followed it up while he was in Switzerland. His face was purple with rage as he strode into the outer office.

"Butler!" he barked. "Follow up that lead on the travel agent and do it now!"

Butler shot out of his chair and scurried out before Wallace could say any more.

"Touchy sod! He'll have a heart attack one of these days," he muttered.

*

Wallace and Dr Barnett sipped coffee in her office away from the unpleasant smells of the post mortem room. The corpse found in Borton Wood was definitely Bruce Foley. Toxicology tests had already shown evidence of anaesthetic drugs, but he had died from suffocation as Jo Barnett had confirmed. What neither of them could understand was why he had been pumped full of drugs and then smothered. It didn't make any sense. Why was he murdered in Switzerland and dumped over here? Wallace shook his head in perplexity. It had been difficult to make a formal identification, because of the state of the victim's face, or lack of it. His brother had identified a birthmark on the victim's scalp. That and the DNA sample had clinched it.

Foley's brother was also an army man. He knew Foley was working on something top secret so he understood the need for secrecy, but his mother needed closure.

"Once I've had a word with the Chief Constable they can go ahead with the funeral," Wallace said. He gulped down the remainder of his coffee and rose to leave. "I'll ring you later this evening."

Outside, he breathed in the chilly air trying to rid his nostrils of the cloying odour of the mortuary. Humming to himself he strode to the waiting car and ordered the driver to take him back to the police station. Back in his office he closed the door and dialled a number.

"Jack, I've had the results of the DNA tests on the victim. I was right, it's Foley," he said triumphantly.

"Well, that's one mystery partially solved, but we still don't know what happened to Rob Macaleer. The same goes for Ethan Bateman. I may need you to come back out here, Ben, but hold fire on that for the time being. Carry on with the investigation at your end. Dreher wants a chance to do a bit more digging over here."

Wallace replaced the receiver in its cradle. They knew the identity of the murder victim and his connection with Macaleer, but where was he murdered and why would he have been in Shropshire? Why had Macaleer turned up in Hampshire?

CHAPTER THIRTY-FIVE

Church Stretton, Shropshire

Wallace felt ridiculously nervous as he drove through the wrought-iron gates. He pulled up outside a period building with impressive bay windows either side of the front door. This was the first time he had been invited to Jo's home. When she greeted him with a disarming smile his nervousness melted away.

She ushered him through into a large living room with shuttered windows and high ceilings. Cream walls, conker-coloured chesterfield and real oak floors highlighted with antique rugs. A real log fire glowed in the marble grate. Crystal wine glasses and a sherry decanter sat on a coffee table alongside a copy of *The Lancet*. Watercolours of seascapes, enhanced by clever lighting, adorned one wall.

In the dining room an antique table was set ready for dinner. An ornate sideboard took up much of one wall with vintage Queen Anne armchairs in two corners. Overhead, tiny ceiling lights twinkled like stars in the dim light.

"I love antique furniture," Jo said, noting his amused look, "but I just couldn't resist the modern lights. They are *so* pretty."

Taking her in his arms he pressed his mouth down on hers savouring the sweetness of her lips, the scent of her hair.

"Hmm," he murmured. "I love the perfume."

"I should think so," she laughed, pushing him away, "after all you bought it. How did you know Chanel No. 5 is my favourite?"

"Sophia Dreher. I overheard you talking when you were helping in the kitchen. Sherry please, if it's dry," he said.

"Big bad Ben, a sherry man?"

He really rather enjoyed it, but if anyone down at the station found out he would never live it down.

"My parents always had a glass before dinner. It's a little ritual I've become part of whenever I go home. I'm sure they would be delighted to share some with you."

Jo coloured at the implication. Embarrassed, he pretended to examine a painting, acutely aware he had pushed the relationship a step further before she was ready.

After dinner Jo replenished their glasses with the last of the wine. Sitting close together, her head on his shoulder, he felt blissfully content. He hadn't felt so much at peace with himself since the first heady days of his failed marriage.

"Incidentally," he said, "the body found in Atcham: we've got a witness."

"As my report states, he didn't drown," Jo interjected. "He suffered a massive heart attack coupled with excessive alcohol in his blood."

Wallace had interviewed Adam Taylor himself; a respectable married man with kids. He was scared to death his wife would find out he leaned both ways. Apparently, the victim had propositioned him in a pub. They were both blind drunk when they went down to the river for a bit of hanky panky. Afterwards the guy decided to have a paddle. He waded in, half naked, and lost his footing.

All Taylor could remember was the bloke shouting, 'It's

bloody freezing in here!' before clambering up the bank and falling face down in the mud, legs still in the water. Taylor thought he was just goofing around. When he realised he was dead he ran off scared to death. They couldn't charge him with lewd behaviour, because they hadn't been caught in the act, but he was charged with failing to report a death. Wallace wondered how he would explain it to his wife and teenage sons.

"That leaves us with Foley, the woman on my patch, plus the body in Portsmouth."

Jo lifted her head and placed a finger on his lips to silence him. She pulled his head down and kissed him with more passion than she intended. Taking his cue Wallace swept her up in his arms. *To hell with murder*, he thought. *It can wait until tomorrow.*

*

On the horizon, fingers of silvery light probed the sky. A watery sun peeped through metallic, grey clouds. Glittering needles of rain sliced the hazy air like tiny swords, disappearing into gutters overflowing with water from an overnight deluge. A light mist hovered between branches of trees almost bare of their leaves.

Incessant rain had fallen for weeks, high winds clutching at umbrellas almost bowling people off their feet. Winter was just around the corner. Still, Wallace preferred this to the cloying decay of autumn. He hated the slush of wet, dead leaves underfoot. The drooping trees, the clammy feel of sodden foliage dropping on his head when he tried to clear them up. Winter was cold and clean and sharp. That's how he felt this morning. Clear-headed, alert, his mind ready for the onslaught of his working day. Whistling loudly, he marched into the station.

"What's with Wally today?" a young DC whispered. "He looks as though he's had his cake and eaten it."

Wallace beckoned to Butler who followed him into his office and closed the door. "What did you find out in Oswestry, Phil?"

DI Butler relaxed. The guv always called him by his first name when he was in a good mood.

"We spoke to the woman, a Mrs Waterman, who picked up the suit. She told us she delivered it to Joanne Howard, the owner of the firm – Waldean Travel. A few days later her boss went off on a working holiday inspecting hotels in Estonia. Apparently, Howard lived in Eastern Europe for a while. She met her husband, an English university professor, when she was studying for a language degree. That's all she knew."

"How long will she be away?"

"Mrs Waterman had no idea. When Howard goes off on her inspection tours she's away for weeks. They never know when she's coming back until they get a telephone call out of the blue."

"How do they contact her in an emergency?"

"They don't. Mrs Waterman is in sole charge of the business while she's away. Sometimes she's away for two weeks, sometimes a month."

Wallace chewed his bottom lip. It was a peculiar way to run a business, especially in these financially stringent times. Something was not quite right about this Joanne Howard. They needed more information.

"We need place of birth, marriage, friends and any information on her husband. If she was travelling abroad perhaps Interpol could find out more about where she had been living and studying before she came to this country."

"I'll get right on it," Butler said heading for the door."

"And Phil, have a good day."

Butler grinned as he closed the door behind him. Wally must have won the lottery.

CHAPTER THIRTY-SIX

Geneva, Switzerland

Ernst Dreher handed Lukas Merien a cup of steaming coffee. The man was clearly badly shaken up. He had reported what he had seen to the local police who had passed it on to the Federal Police. It all seemed very far-fetched, like something in a film.

Merien lived in Faulensee in the Bernese Oberland, but worked in Geneva three days a week. He had been out walking in the mountains near Interlaken when he spotted a man about three hundred metres below him. Even at that distance he could see he was dragging some kind of bundle on a trailer behind a motorbike. It disappeared behind an outcrop of rocks then reappeared at the edge of a steep precipice and stopped. He was so curious he scrambled down and watched from a safe distance. The man was dressed from head to toe in black. He couldn't see his face, because it was covered up with a balaclava.

"I watched him drag the bundle off the trailer and haul it to the edge of the precipice convinced he was going to push it over the side. Just then a helicopter appeared out of nowhere. It circled around then hovered close to the motorcyclist. I could see someone leaning out raking the area with binoculars."

Merien was perspiring heavily. He extracted a large

handkerchief from his pocket and dabbed his face. His hands were shaking now.

"Whoever it was spotted me. The next thing I knew the helicopter was closing in. A second guy had a gun with a telescopic lens. He pointed the gun at me, but he didn't fire any shots. I don't think they wanted to kill me, just scare me off. I'm convinced they were trying to dispose of a body."

"What makes you think it was a body?"

"It looked very heavy... just the shape of it and the way it was tied up."

"Why didn't you report this to the local police at the time? Why has it taken so long for you to come forward?"

"The more I thought about it the more ridiculous it seemed. I didn't think anyone would believe me." Merien hesitated for a few seconds. He stared up at the ceiling. "I couldn't stop thinking about it. I was sure I wasn't wrong about the gun? It just kept nagging at me until I finally went to the police."

"Thank you, Herr Merien. We may need to speak to you again."

He called to Dupont in the outer office. "Please take Herr Merien back to his office."

Dreher rang Conrad and arranged to meet him later that morning. He replaced the receiver and pressed a button on the intercom.

"Inspector Zinzli, please come to my office immediately."

"Sir?" Bastien Zinzli queried, closing the door behind him.

"I've had some interesting information about a possible murder," he said, relating the story. "I want you to look into it. Somewhere on a trail up to Berg, Merien saw a motorcyclist and a helicopter." He jabbed at the wall map. "I want the whole area covered with a toothcomb. Take Acting Inspector Rast with you. She knows the area like the back of her hand." The detective headed for the door. "And Zinzli, this is to be kept between the three of us for now."

*

Deep in thought, both men sipped their coffee. This was the first lead they had uncovered that fell in with what Conrad had himself witnessed. There was definitely something very strange going on in the mountains. Whatever it was, they were prepared to kill to keep it under wraps. Both Foley and Macaleer had been formally identified. Both had been snooping around in Switzerland. Both bodies had turned up in England.

"What we don't know is why they were both murdered," Dreher mused.

"They must have discovered the microchip Foley gave them held false information."

"I accept that, but why take him to a so-called clinic and remove his kidney? What could they possibly gain from it? Murder, yes, but an operation? It doesn't make sense."

"I must admit I'm as puzzled as you are," Conrad replied. "Wallace is also investigating another weird murder victim, a young woman. He still hasn't been able to establish her identity, but he's hoping to have something for me by tomorrow."

"Come to dinner tonight. If it's all right with you I'd like to run this by Sophia. Perhaps she can compile some kind of basic psychological profile of the killer."

"Good idea. In the meantime," he continued, "I'm going to see Sasha. He may have found out more about Bateman."

*

The man attacking a large steak glanced up casually when Conrad walked into the restaurant.

"Over here!" he called, wiping grease from his mouth.

Two giggling women at the next table leaned in and whispered together. Sasha raised his eyes and beckoned to the waiter serving at an adjacent table. Conrad waited until his lager arrived and looked around before speaking.

"Well, what have you found out? Anything on the clinic or helipads in the vicinity?"

"Nothing. There's no trace of Ethan Bateman either," Sasha replied. "Apparently, he turned up at his hotel looking very dishevelled, sporting a large bruise on his right cheek. After enquiring from the concierge about connecting flights to the States, he booked a flight from Geneva to Paris. Unfortunately, all flights in Paris were grounded," Sasha continued. "Thick fog, so he checked into the airport hotel. He left the following morning and hasn't been seen since."

Bateman hadn't caught a connecting flight from either Charles de Gaulle Airport or Orly. There was no record of him chartering a private plane from Paris-Le Bourget airport or anywhere else. Conrad had a nasty feeling in the pit of his stomach. Bateman was no fool. If he was being followed, he would get back to the States where he would be safe. Perhaps he had gone to London, via Eurostar, hoping to get a flight from Heathrow.

"There's nothing more we can do here," he said.

"So, how about a little fun tonight? Do some of the bars, pick up a couple of girls."

"Sounds fantastic, Sasha, but I think I'll take a little trip to Paris."

CHAPTER THIRTY-SEVEN

Paris, France

Conrad emerged from Charles de Gaulle airport into bright sunlight. He squinted against the harsh light, scanning the line of travellers waiting for taxis. A maroon Bentley swept up to the curb. Silently, the rear window slid down. An elegant woman leaned forward and smiled.

"Bonjour, Jack!"

He climbed in beside her. Taking her face between both hands he planted a loud kiss on her forehead.

"That's not how we do it in Paris," she rebuked with a girlish giggle, "but I like it."

Tall, willowy, auburn hair streaked with blonde, at sixty years of age Patricia Bonnet was still a very beautiful woman. Born Patricia Hemmingway, she had fallen in love and married an aristocratic French banker whilst studying at the Sorbonne.

An hour later her chauffeur calmly negotiated the traffic-snarled Arc de Triomphe. Patricia owned an apartment in the 16th Arrondissment, one of the richest areas of Paris. She used it on her frequent trips into the city.

Conrad studied his surroundings while he sipped his whisky and soda. Everything about the apartment oozed good taste and old money. If it weren't for his assignment he would be delighted to stay here for a very long time. Patricia was an old friend and colleague. Her escapades working for British Military Intelligence were legendary. She had already established that Bateman had left the airport hotel, checked into the Hotel Eiffel in the city, and paid his bill in advance. The concierge ordered a taxi to take him to Charles de Gaulle Airport the following morning.

"When he didn't turn up, the concierge rang his room," Patricia said. "The maid on his floor said his bed hadn't been slept in."

"It sounds as if he was on the run, trying to cover his tracks," Conrad mused. "I wouldn't have thought he'd be stupid enough to make a phone call from the hotel. Still, if he was spaced out, it's possible. I'll get London to check it out their end. In the meantime I'll do some snooping around myself."

Patricia's chauffeur dropped him off near the Eiffel Tower. He gazed up its length. Looking at it at night from the Trocadero, bathed in golden light, it was magical. Undoubtedly, it was a feat of engineering genius, but in daylight it failed to impress him as an object of beauty. Suddenly, his mobile vibrated in his pocket shattering his reflections.

"Breakdancer," a familiar voice intoned, "it seems Bateman made three calls from the Eiffel Hilton on his mobile. One was to his wife in Texas and another to the Pentagon. The third call was to a small boutique hotel. Hotel Parisienne on the Left Bank close to the Latin Quarter. He booked in under the name George Hayes. Proceed with caution, Regis."

With a muted click the connection was broken. Conrad searched the oncoming traffic hoping to see a free cab. Trying to get a taxi in Paris was a nightmare. It was impossible to hail one off the street as he did in London. He decided it would be quicker to get the Metro.

A woman, pulling a small trolley suitcase, brushed past him and joined the taxi queue. Quickly, he ran down the steps into the underground and bought a ticket from the machine. He turned at the sound of clattering footsteps behind him. It was the woman with the trolley case. The train had already arrived when he hit the platform. He stood aside for her to board the train. She hauled her case down the aisle and sat down two seats in front of him.

Back above ground, he swiftly walked from St. Michelle Metro station towards the Latin Quarter. *Boutique hotel is stretching it a bit*, he reflected, looking up at the grimy façade. Inside he was surprised to discover an attractive foyer gleaming with glass and highly polished wood. At reception, a dark-haired girl, with the name 'Yvette' emblazoned on a lapel badge, sat staring at a computer screen. He noted the lift and sequence of room numbers on a brass plaque at the foot of the stairs.

"Good morning, Yvette." Conrad smiled flirtatiously. "It's very smart," he commented, observing the modern prints on the walls. Playing for time he remarked, "It's quite a surprise on the inside."

"The new owners have spent a lot of money on improvements," Yvette replied. "The exterior will be given a facelift in the next few weeks."

"A friend of mine is staying here," he continued. "Mr George Hayes. We've arranged to have lunch. Will you ring his room and tell him Mr Bruce Foley has arrived?"

Conrad watched carefully as the girl punched the buttons

on the desk phone. "I'm afraid there's no reply, sir. Monsieur Hayes must have gone out. Shall I take a message?"

"No, it's okay, I'll pop around later."

Room twenty-six. That's all he needed to know, but he would have to wait and see if Bateman turned up. Shortly after midday Conrad returned to Hotel Parisienne. Yvette was still sitting in front of her computer.

"I'm afraid Monsieur Hayes is still out," she said apologetically. "I'm off duty at five. If he hasn't returned by then I'll ask my colleague to inform him of your visit."

Conrad exited the revolving doors and stepped onto the crowded pavement. He spotted the woman immediately; the same woman he had seen twice that morning. She had discarded her trolley and had covered her black trouser suit with a beige trench coat. She was sitting outside the restaurant next door to the hotel deep in conversation with two men.

They paid no attention when he strode briskly past them. He had harboured a vague suspicion when she trailed behind him after leaving the Metro. Now he was certain he was being followed. After walking two blocks there was no sign of her or the two men. No doubt they would be waiting for him to return to Hotel Parisienne.

Back at the apartment he discussed his plans with Patricia.

"I need to get into Bateman's room. It's just a small boutique hotel. One staircase leads to all the floors. All I want you to do is create a little diversionary tactic to give me time to get up to his room."

"That shouldn't be a problem," she replied with a wicked grin.

CHAPTER THIRTY-EIGHT

Paris, France

The chauffeur edged out onto the Champs Élysées and filtered into the flow of traffic. Lights blazed in Restaurant Le Fouquet. It was crowded with people enjoying pre-dinner drinks. The chauffeur turned his head slightly and grimaced.

"Traffic is heavy tonight, Madame. It will probably be quicker if I go back around the Arc de Triomphe and drive down the Rue de Courcelles."

Conrad never ceased to wonder at the driving skills of the French. Bathed in golden light, the Arch de Triomphe looked magnificent. It was lost on Parisians negotiating the various exists. Honking impatiently they weaved and dodged, totally oblivious of other vehicles. A Renault screeched to a halt a fraction of an inch from a large Citroen. Both drivers opened their windows gesticulating and shouting in Gallic fashion.

Eventually, the traffic thinned out, but progress was still relatively slow. Even in November the streets were crowded with tourists. Pierre, the chauffeur, dropped them off close to a smart restaurant in the Latin Quarter.

"It's only seven-thirty; far too early to be going to a party in Paris. Let's have a glass of champagne first," Patricia suggested. "After all we're supposed to be celebrating my birthday."

An hour later they walked into the foyer of the Hotel

Parisienne giggling like a pair of teenagers. A different girl was sitting in front of the computer. She looked up when they stopped at the desk.

"We've arranged to meet one of your guests here at eight-thirty... a Mr Hayes."

Conrad leaned over the counter letting the whisky on his breath waft over the girl. "Will you ring his room and tell him that we're waiting to take him to the party."

"Of course, he arrived back about five o'clock, just after I came on duty."

She picked up the telephone and punched in a number. Conrad flashed his most disarming smile causing a deep red flush to creep up her neck.

"Strange, there's no reply. He definitely went up to his room and I haven't seen him go back out. He's probably on his way down. Perhaps you would like to wait in the bar?"

Conrad and Patricia strolled into the smart bar that led off from the foyer. They took a seat to the side of the entrance and observed the receptionist still absorbed with the computer.

"She's chatting online," Conrad commented, "to someone called Michel. We'll wait until she's completely absorbed."

Five minutes later Patricia stood up and walked towards the door. Suddenly, she turned on her ankle and lurched forward. Conrad rushed to her aid and caught her under her arm.

"Are you all right?" he asked solicitously.

"It's my damn shoe!" she replied. "The heel's come off."

The girl at reception looked up and stared at Patricia, obviously annoyed at having her online conversation interrupted. Patricia hobbled over to her, brandishing the shoe in one hand and the heel in the other.

"What am I going to do? It's supposed to be my birthday party. Now it will be ruined," she complained. "I don't suppose you have anything, some glue, anything I could use to repair it?"

Sighing, the receptionist examined the shoe. Finally, she picked up the telephone and dialled a number.

"I'll see what the porter can do," she said irritably. "If you'll stay in the bar, Madame, I'll take it over to him."

With that she produced a laminated card stating, 'Back in five minutes', before vanishing through a door at the side of the stairs.

Immediately she disappeared, Conrad launched up the stairs towards Bateman's room on the second floor. He hesitated outside room twenty-six before knocking gently on the door. There was no sound of movement from inside. Extracting a key ring from his pocket, he selected a small tool with a grooved edge. He inserted it into the lock and turned it. It wouldn't budge. He selected another and tried again. This time it clicked open.

Cautiously, he pushed the door ajar. The suite was in complete darkness except for the glow of a flashing neon sign outside. Everything looked perfectly normal. The dregs of a drink sat on an ornate coffee table next to a laptop. He sniffed the glass. Bourbon and a strong smell of almonds. Slowly, he crept towards the bedroom and eased open the door. The bed hadn't been slept in; not even a crease in the covers. Nothing except a single shirt hanging in the wardrobe.

Making his way back into the sitting area he paused studying the laptop. It was still hibernating. Suddenly, the neon sign flashed lighting up the room in a surreal, greenish glow. Beside the sofa terrified eyes stared sightlessly, partially opened mouth frozen into a scream. There was no mistaking the big gap in the front teeth of the jowly face that stared back at him, hideous now instead of comic. Ethan Bateman!

There was obviously nothing he could do for the Texan. Searching around for clues the laptop caught his attention again. He tapped a key and the e-mail page appeared. Bateman had been trying to send an e-mail with an attachment, but to whom? Conrad felt his heart quicken as he read the page. It was very disjointed as though Bateman couldn't coordinate his thoughts. The names Foley, Macaleer and bogus clinic jumped from the page. The writing stopped abruptly after his own name… 'Jack… help!'

He pressed the attachment icon and waited. On the screen a coloured picture appeared.

"What the hell!"

Swiftly, he enlarged the image. Three men, all of them clothed in black, their faces concealed by balaclavas. Arms outstretched, fists clenched in a salute, staring at something outside the frame.

A muffled noise from the corridor brought him up short. Looking at his watch he realised he had been in the room for almost six minutes. He had to get back downstairs before the receptionist came back to her station. He tapped print and waited impatiently for the portable printer to spew out the page. Grabbing the sheet of paper, he sloped into the corridor and raced downstairs into the bar. Patricia was still sitting there nursing a drink when he dropped down beside her.

"Well?" she queried.

"Bateman's dead. Cyanide poisoning. There was a distinct smell of almonds. We've got to get out of here… fast!"

"Madame," said the receptionist. She approached their table, shoe in hand. "This is the best the porter could do, but it probably won't last long. You'll need to get it properly repaired."

"It looks as if Mr Hayes may have gone out after all," Conrad said, nonchalantly leaning against the reception desk. "I'd be grateful if you tell him we called."

Taking care not to rush, they sauntered out onto the pavement. They hurried into the side street where the chauffeur was waiting for them. They spoke very little during the drive back to Patricia's apartment.

"Tell me everything," she demanded.

Conrad sat back in the chair and blew out his cheeks. Taking a large gulp of whisky, he launched into the details of his first encounter with Ethan Bateman and what he had already found out about the connection between Foley and Macaleer.

"Wallace is working with Ernst Dreher, his counterpart in Switzerland. There's something more here than meets the eye, Patricia. Now we've got two army intelligence men and a US senator dead. The Russian 'sleeper' who recruited Foley has also been knocked off. We've got a good idea who recruited Foley. We've got a good idea why they were eliminated, but Bateman. Why? That lead has reached a dead end – literally."

"What are you going to do now?"

"I'll get a flight back to Switzerland in the morning."

Bateman was trying to tell him something before he was murdered. It was obvious the man had been terrified of something, but what? Why was he sending him a photograph of men in what appeared to be fascist uniforms?

CHAPTER THIRTY-NINE

Oswestry, England

A SOCO bagged a hairbrush, items of clothing, a used lipstick, a dirty mug from the sink and a few stray hairs from the back of the sofa. DNA tests would establish if the murder victim and Joanne Howard were one and the same person. Wallace rummaged in a drawer. Just underwear, rolled-up tights and other bits and pieces. Smart clothes sporting designer labels hung in the wardrobe, along with some sweaters neatly folded on a shelf. Wallace fingered a black evening dress. "Very expensive tastes, Butler. This must have cost a pretty penny." On the bedside table were a folded newspaper and a few travel magazines. Nothing to indicate that the victim was anything other than what she claimed to be.

In a small trolley case, propped at the foot of the bed, they found some soiled clothes, a partially eaten sandwich still in its plastic container, two pairs of shoes and some solid walking boots. Wallace turned his attention to the bedside cabinet drawers. Nothing unusual for a travel agent. A passport in the name of Joanne Howard, two hundred Swiss francs, three hundred pounds in travellers' cheques and a return plane ticket from Heathrow to Geneva. Why the Swiss francs and ticket to Geneva if she was supposed to have gone to Eastern Europe? Wallace shrugged. Maybe she changed her mind and went off to Switzerland instead.

Her neighbour had seen Howard running up the path to the cottage with someone. They were bent over against the wind and rain. She couldn't be certain if the other person was a man or a woman. It was too dark. There was no evidence of a struggle or of anyone else who may have been in the cottage. Everything was neat and tidy; too tidy. He pulled an expensive trouser suit from the wardrobe and handed it to the SOCO.

"Bag this with the rest," he instructed. "Hang on!" He patted the jacket then turned it inside out and ran his hand over the glossy lining. "What's this?" His hand rested on a concealed zipper. "There's something inside." He pulled out a silver band. "It looks like an embroidered garter."

"Perhaps she was into some kinky sex, sir," his DI said.

"It's too big for a wristband. Maybe it's an armband." Wallace dangled it in front of Butler. "Why hide it away in a hidden pocket?"

"Do you know, sir, those bits of embroidery look exactly like snow crystals. No two are identical. They're so intricate. That's why a lot of people are sceptical about some of those crop circles. It's hard to believe that anyone could fake something like that overnight," he continued, warming to the subject.

"Very interesting," Wallace replied sarcastically. "Come on, let's get going. I intend to get to the bottom of this, but first we'll call into that little pub near Shrewsbury on the way back. You can wax lyrical about snow crystals over a meat pie."

CHAPTER FORTY

Bayston Hill, Shropshire, England

Wallace swung his Audi through the gates and scrunched to a halt in front of the garage. Head down, collar turned up against the driving rain, he ran towards the front door. A sudden gust of wind sent a pile of shrivelled leaves scurrying across his path. Overhead, lightning streaked across the sky, illuminating everything in white light. It was soon followed by a low rumble of thunder.

He stripped off his wet coat in the kitchen, towelled his hair, and brewed some coffee. He needed caffeine to stay as alert as possible. After pouring a mug of steaming coffee, he went into his study where IMIC had installed a secure line.

He paced to and fro watching the rain lashing against the patio doors. Suddenly, a bright flash of lightning cracked overhead followed by a loud clap of thunder. It almost deafened him, exploding above the house like a bomb. A woman gazing through the window of the house opposite hurriedly drew the curtains. When the telephone shrilled he picked up the receiver and dropped onto the sofa. Conrad's voice came on the line loud and clear.

"Where are you?" Wallace asked.

"Still in Geneva, but I'm off to Dreher's place in Thun tomorrow. I have to get up into the Alps before the weather deteriorates. I found Bateman in Paris. He's been murdered

– potassium cyanide in his favourite tipple. Our GCHQ 'sleeper' has also been knocked off. He had his throat cut from ear to ear by his own people. MI6 had his house bugged for quite some time. It picked up a voice with a Russian accent."

"But why would they exterminate one of their own?"

"As I told you before, he was suspected of taking money from another organisation. The security services ransacked the house. Nothing; not a scrap of anything that could link him with the Russians or anyone else. Whoever killed him swept the place clean. His clothes had been torn apart as if they were looking for something specific."

"Strange, especially as Foley had already taken the microchip to hand over in Switzerland."

"Even a fluffy toy dog, wearing a baseball cap and a silver collar, had been ripped open."

"They were probably looking for the microchip to… " Wallace stopped mid-sentence. No, it wasn't possible. His heart thumped painfully in his chest. "Did you say a silver collar?"

"It was more like one of those stretchy armbands that kids wear – silver and red with four black motifs embroidered on it."

"Wallace's breath caught in his throat. "Think hard, Jack. How would you describe them? Geometric? Senseless doodles?"

"Actually, they looked rather like snow crystals. Reminded me of our Christmas tree when I was a kid."

"You're not going to believe this, Jack. I found something similar in Joanne Howard's cottage in Oswestry. A silver armband emblazoned with three black snow crystals."

Conrad fell silent on the other end of the line. Wallace could almost hear his brain clicking into gear.

"It may be just a coincidence, but what if Lynes and Howard were working for the same organisation? They were both Russians. She could have been another 'sleeper'. That would extend the link to include all the murder victims, the Russian Security Services, GCHQ and the Generalissimo."

"I'm going back to the cottage tomorrow to take another look," Wallace said. "In the meantime I'll put out a bulletin for any sightings of Howard in the days leading up to her murder."

"See what you can find out about the armbands, Ben; what company produces them. It could turn out to be just another kids' accessory like the wristbands they collect."

"I'll get someone on it straight away."

Wallace replaced the receiver and chewed over what he had heard. He picked up his mobile phone and quickly dialled a number. He wanted every last bit of information concerning Joanne Howard on his desk first thing in the morning. A press conference would ensure the media exploited it as much as possible. He wanted her photograph on the front pages and television news channels. His gut instinct told him that Colin Lynes and Joanne Howard were both members of the same organisation. A chill ran through him when he thought about what could happen if genuine top-secret papers got into the wrong hands. Lynes had passed on volatile information before he was rumbled.

CHAPTER FORTY-ONE

Police HQ, Shropshire

Wallace studied his notes for the second time. Joanne Howard had been briefly married to a university professor. Originally from Moscow, she and her family moved to St. Petersburg when her father took up a post at the university. She studied Russian literature and several languages including French and German. Two years after gaining her degree she obtained a visa to study English at Oxford. That's where she met Peter Howard, a computer scientist, with an interest in cryptography.

Occasionally, she travelled abroad to check out holiday resorts. Her husband thought it strange that she never discussed her trips. She seemed bored with their lifestyle and claimed she needed a break now and then. It all came to a head when she tried to persuade him to work in Switzerland. When he asked her what kind of work she was very evasive… mentioned something vague about an organisation. If he pressed the question she clammed up. It seemed the victim wasn't all she pretended to be.

Brandishing a fax, Butler walked into the office, a broad smile on his face.

"Well, out with it. You look like you've won the bloody lottery!" Wallace barked impatiently.

"When I was talking to Howard's 'ex', he mentioned

that he had hoped a child would bring them closer. Apparently, she went for an abortion without him knowing she was pregnant. They had a terrible row. He only found out after complications set in. She haemorrhaged after the operation. They had to rush her into hospital for a blood transfusion."

"Where is all this leading, Butler?"

"Joanne Howard has a very rare blood group… the same blood group as our murder victim."

"Bingo! I could kiss you, Butler, if I wasn't so fussy. That's a real breakthrough."

They would have to bring in the ex-husband to identify her. Wallace yawned loudly and rubbed his hand over his face. He couldn't remember when he had last enjoyed a good night's sleep.

"Good work, Butler. Haul him in tomorrow morning, but warn him it won't be pretty."

The 'ex' had a strong motive for the murder, but they didn't have sufficient evidence to support it. Questioning him would have to wait. Wallace clicked on the e-mail attachment from Dreher.

Joanne Howard, real name Anya Sharapova, born in Moscow in 1979. Her father, Piotr, is a physicist. The mother, Martina, was a linguist like her daughter. Both her mother and brother, Anatoly, are dead: killed in a car crash. Anya and the boy were involved in some kind of radical organisation. Their father disapproved of their involvement. He claimed it had something to do with the death of his wife and son. Apparently, Anya cut herself off from her father when she went to

live in the United Kingdom. She changed her name to
Joanne Sharpe. Howard is her married name.

Russian and involved with some sort of subversive organisation. This put a whole new slant on the Howard case. Especially, as her husband was completely in the dark about her activities during her trips abroad. His thoughts were interrupted by his mobile vibrating in his pocket.

"Conrad here. Anything new?"

Wallace related everything he knew about Joanne Howard then he repeated what Dreher had told him.

"My gut feeling tells me there could be a connection between Foley, Macaleer and Joanne Howard, alias Anya Sharapova," Wallace said.

"That's feasible. I'm flying to Geneva this afternoon. Keep me posted with developments your end."

CHAPTER FORTY-TWO

Geneva, Switzerland

Light snowflakes hit the window as the plane descended towards the runway in Geneva. Below, a channel of lights twinkled into view, appearing and disappearing as they descended through patchy cloud cover. A slight bump and they were on the tarmac hurtling down the runway. Buffeted by high winds the plane lurched from side to side causing a corporate gasp of fear to ripple through the cabin. Eyes tightly closed, a brassy-looking blonde across the aisle gripped the arms of her seat until the plane gradually slowed down and taxied towards the buildings.

Taking advantage of the lull while passengers composed themselves, Conrad unfastened his seat belt as soon as the warning signs turned green. He retrieved his holdall from the overhead locker and made for the exit. Giving a quick smile of acknowledgement to the stewardess he walked down the tunnel, through customs, into the arrivals hall. People scurried out towards the taxi rank dragging suitcases behind them. A bitterly cold wind cut through his thick overcoat when he stepped out onto the pavement.

Dreher's car was waiting outside. The usual plain-clothes officer jumped out and opened the door when he spotted Conrad.

"Good evening, sir. Chief Inspector Dreher has instructed

me to take you to his apartment in Cologny. He will join you later this evening."

"Thanks," Conrad replied, sliding into the roomy Mercedes.

A couple of minutes later they exited the Rue de Chantepoulet and turned right onto Rue de Mont Blanc towards the Quai Gustave Ador and the Rampe de Cologny. Evidence of Cologny's exclusivity was all round in the expensive detached houses and apartments. *Only fifteen minutes from the city*, Conrad thought, *but such a striking contrast*. Narrow country lanes, open fields, vineyards, a proliferation of trees and stunning views of white-capped Mont Blanc.

It was here that Byron had been inspired to write *Childe Harold*. It was also the headquarters of the World Economic Forum. He could almost smell wealth and prestige.

He glanced up at the sky as the car swung into the drive. Ominous clouds, hurried along by an icy wind, swept in overhead. The last thing he wanted was more snow. *I'll have to get up into the mountains before the really bad weather kicks in,* he thought, *otherwise it will be impossible.*

Nursing a large whisky, Conrad settled in a comfortable armchair in the library, pondering on recent events. His thoughts were interrupted by Henri greeting Dreher at the door.

"Jack, so good to see you," Dreher said. While Henri poured him a generous brandy he settled into his favourite armchair. "Have you got anything new?"

"I've been digging deeper into Joanne Howard's life. She was well known in Kiev for being a radical. Rumour suggested the Russian Secret Service, formed after the dissolution of the KGB, tried to ferret out her involvement, but they failed to penetrate the organisation."

"We know that Joanne Howard is Anya Sharapova," Dreher observed, "but the rest is speculation. Who would be powerful enough to fool the Russian Secret Service?"

"Only four people would fit the profile and one of them, a guy named Plushenko, is dead. He was killed in East Berlin in a boating accident a few days before the fall of the Berlin Wall."

"Do you know the names of the others?" Dreher asked.

"Boris Oblensky, Vasily Zhukov and Leonid Morozov, all senior KGB officers during the cold war. Oblensky would have been a strong candidate, but he's out of the frame. He's in a nursing home in Omsk after suffering a series of strokes two years ago. That leaves Zhukov and Morozov."

"Where are they now?"

"Zukhov is living with his daughter in Novosibirk. He's in his late seventies now. Morozov, the youngest, is in his late fifties, still in the Russian Security Services. I don't think it's him. He's right at the top of the tree... secret service through and through. Our contact in Moscow heard he's in line for a big promotion. Still, he remains a possibility. Pearce is also liaising with Langley with regard to Bateman."

"Does Langley know about IMIC?"

"No, the CIA don't know that IMIC exists. As far as they are concerned he's just fulfilling his normal role as General Pearce of military intelligence, heading up the investigation into Macaleer and Foley. It appears Bateman was working for the Pentagon. All they told Pearce was that he was involved with computer security systems. Apparently, the area around Bateman's facility in Nevada is heavily guarded twenty-four seven. Whatever is going on there is highly secretive."

"Don't you think it's rather odd they didn't have him under surveillance out here?" Dreher asked.

"Not really. He's a prominent businessman – travels all the time. Most of his designs have been under wraps, because of industrial espionage, hence the high security. Often a company designs a prototype. A rival firm gets wind of it, covertly procures copies of the blueprints and gets it on the market first. There was no reason to believe that this was anything different. Besides, he had direct access to the Pentagon."

"Have you briefed Wallace about this?"

"I couldn't be sure his line was secure. That's something we need to get sorted. I'll speak to Pearce about it. Ben's CC and ACC know very little about the body on the beach except that it's highly sensitive. We don't want them gumming up the works."

Dreher leaned over and threw another log onto the crackling fire. He waited until the flames took hold then prodded the middle of the orange glow. Conrad sat back luxuriating in the warmth. Suddenly, his eyelids felt heavy; too heavy to stay open. There was something about the air in Switzerland that lulled him into deep relaxation. Sleep came easily to him here. Dreher rose and prodded Conrad awake.

"Go to bed, Jack. You look exhausted."

Conrad stretched, turning his neck from side to side. His whole body suddenly felt limp as though his life force was being sucked out through a straw. Rising to his feet, he tried to stifle a yawn.

"Ernst, will you contact Wallace first thing tomorrow morning and bring him up to date. I'm going up into the mountains again."

In his room he plumped up the outsize pillows and lay, hands under his head, trying to fathom out everything he had seen. Grazing goats, a lush patch of grass, a path obliterated by a mini avalanche. Something wasn't right about it. There was an obvious link between Bateman, Macaleer, Foley and Lynes, but where did Anya Sharapova, aka Joanne Howard, fit in with all this? Why had she been murdered and why had her face been mutilated? Like Wallace, he was convinced the victim was connected to the other murders, but they had no proof. His gut instinct told him that he could find that proof up in the Alps.

CHAPTER FORTY-THREE

Swiss Alps, Bernese Oberland

Heavy rain had washed away most of the early snows in the valleys below, but at this altitude it was deep, hampering progress. Conrad laboured up the steep slope using his ice pick to secure a hold on the frozen snow. The sky was an unbroken blanket of white cloud tinged with silver. The glare hurt his eyes even through the snow glasses he was wearing. Overhead, a dazzling white sun threw its rays onto the snow, temporarily blinding him in its intensity. An icy cold wind knifed through his salopettes and padded jacket.

He climbed at a steady pace, stopping at intervals to rest. The air was thinner up here. The last thing he wanted was a dizzy spell. It was vital to keep a clear head. He took out his binoculars and scanned the area above him. Piles of rubble littered the obliterated path. He could just make out the skeleton of a chalet-style hotel above the trail. The closer he got to it, the more evident it became that the landslide had been deliberately created, but for what purpose?

Reaching the foot of the avalanche, he stopped to assess the situation. There were no signs of life, just the moan of the wind and an occasional alpine chuff wheeling overhead. Slipping and sliding, he scrambled over the rocks until he reached the top and came up against a sheer wall of stone. He couldn't climb any higher. Nothing but a bloody wild goose chase!

Taking a last look, he started his descent. Suddenly, a faint sound caught his attention. It seemed to be coming from the right of the rock face. There it was again, a strange scuffling noise. He felt along the surface of the gigantic rock that had fallen next to the smooth cliff wall. There was a narrow fissure in the stone. It was barely wide enough to squeeze a hand through it. He pressed his face against it and peered through the slit. There was nothing to be seen except another layer of stone wall beyond a grassy area. It looked like some sort of cave.

Suddenly, something moved in front of his vision. It disappeared before he had a chance to form an impression. With bated breath, he waited. Just when he thought he had imagined the whole thing, he saw it again. This time he knew what he was looking at; the top of an animal's head. A goat's head! How the hell did they get in there? They must have climbed over the rocks. He watched as the animals filed from the right towards something over to his left.

What the devil? There was some kind of indentation on the ground. It was the imprint of a heavily-soled boot. So, someone had been up here and fairly recently. Approaching the stone wall under the overhang, he searched for a way to climb up beyond it. An experienced climber could get up there, but this was as far as he could go. He cursed the producers for recalling Sasha to rehearse a scene from his 'soap'. Next time, he would have him in tow.

He turned and started back down the slope again. Behind him a faint humming sound drifted on the wind. Startled, he turned, almost losing his balance on the steep incline. His mouth fell open with disbelief. The wall of rock was moving, opening out towards him, exposing a steel panel. With a swish the panel slid back revealing a brightly lit corridor. Two dark figures, silhouetted against the harsh lights, marched purposefully towards him. As they got closer he could see they were carrying Kalashnikovs. Only their eyes could be seen behind the black balaclavas.

"Put your hands above your head," one of them growled, "and don't try anything or you're a dead man."

Nodding to his companion he waited while he patted Conrad down for firearms. With a grunt of satisfaction he pulled out the Glock pistol and shoved it into his belt. Silently, the other man gestured to Conrad. He prodded him painfully with the muzzle of his gun until he moved into the tunnel. Without a word they marched him down a corridor hewn from the rock face. A few minutes later they emerged into a natural cavern lit with bright, blue-white lights.

Men in black uniforms sat at a bank of computers scrolling down row after row of statistics. A digital map of the world, pinpointing various cities with different coloured lights, took up the whole of the far wall. On both sides men and women studied a changing kaleidoscope of images transmitted from around the globe. It was like walking into a science fiction film set.

A sharp prod in the back sent him reeling forwards towards another steel door at the side of the computer stations where another masked man waited. He faced the retinal scanner and the door slid open to reveal another smaller chamber. It was a miniature of the outer room. Flickering computer screens, digital wall maps and a curious device in one corner. Behind a large desk a man sat with his back to them. As the door clicked shut behind them he turned around, his face partially in shadow.

Long hair swept back, a prominent widow's peak above a wrinkled face. Deep lines ran from the side of his nose to the outer corners of his thin lips. His head looked too big for his slim frame, draped in a black military-style uniform. An old man trying to look youthful.

"Sit down, Mr Conrad," he said, gesturing towards a chair placed directly in front of the desk.

Conrad strained his eyes, registering the facial features of the man. There was something distinctly odd about his face. His eyes weren't the eyes of an old man. Piercing, almost luminous eyes, olive skin and an aquiline nose. The skin colour didn't seem to work with the eyes.

"What the hell's going on here?" Conrad demanded. "How do you know my name?"

"You will find out in due course. May I offer you some coffee?"

The man who had brought him in moved to a table and poured some coffee into a mug. He picked up a ladle, scooped some milk from a container into a jug, and added it to the coffee.

"Who the hell are you? What are you doing here?"

The guard moved towards him in a threatening manner, but the other man waved him away.

"I am the Generalissimo. The supreme head of the Black Militia. This is my headquarters."

Conrad's brain went into overdrive. Foley's organisation! That's why he and Macaleer were murdered. Could this guy be one of the three KGB men on the list he had compiled? It wasn't possible, unless their profiles were bogus.

"Nobody still alive will ever discover my real identity. Those who tried died a swift death."

The guard pulled Conrad to his feet and pushed him towards the door. Moving from his desk the Generalissimo sat down in front of one of the computers. His face lit up with a greenish glow. It was then Conrad realised he was wearing a prosthetic mask.

On the wall above the computer console a replica of the large screen he had seen in the outer chamber glowed green. Pinpoint lights flickered over Washington, London, Berlin, Ottawa, Beijing, Paris, Tokyo: every major capital city in the world. Suddenly, the tiny light on Beijing stopped flickering and remained steady.

"Beijing is ready!" the Generalissimo exclaimed. Turning to Conrad he gave a hideous smile.

"Soon we will be in control."

Conrad lunged at him, hands outstretched to grab at the mask. The butt of the Kalashnikov in his stomach brought him to his knees. Writhing in agony, he lay on the carpeted floor clutching his stomach.

"That was very foolish, Mr Conrad. You will be dead before you can find out who I am. Besides, who would believe you? Nothing can stop us now. Get him out of here!"

Nosing him with the gun, the militiaman pushed him through the door and back down the corridor into the main operations' chamber. Through a haze of pain he peered at the flickering lights. Whatever they were up to straddled every continent, he realised, but what were they up to?

The guard shoved him through the main chamber towards a lift. In seconds they descended two levels. Another guard, waiting outside the lift, prodded him through a wooden door. A dim glow lit up what appeared to be a small cave accentuating shadows and rough surfaces. He whirled around at the loud thud of the door slamming shut. At eye level a pinpoint of light shone through a tiny spyhole. In the corner of the cave, a chair, half a dozen books thrown carelessly on a table, a narrow bed set against one wall and a chemical toilet.

This didn't make any sense at all. Why would they provide him with books? He leafed through an English translation of Russian folklore, a history of famous battles, and biographies of heads of state from various countries. Suddenly, he heard the sound of heavy footsteps approaching. The door creaked open. An armed guard placed a tray on the floor.

"What is this place?" Conrad shouted. "What are you doing here? Let me talk to the Generalissimo!"

The guard didn't respond. Without a word he slammed the door shut and clunked down the corridor.

There was nothing to be seen through the spyhole except stone walls and the same eerie glow. Conrad picked up the tray of food. He prodded it with a fork. Spicy sausages, potato salad and French fries. On the side, a large portion of gateau and a steaming pot of coffee.

Glancing at his wristwatch, he realised he had been on the mountain for over four hours. If he didn't return by nightfall alarm bells would start ringing. Dreher wouldn't be able to send a team out to investigate once darkness fell. They would have to wait until daybreak. *I've got to get out of this infernal place, but first I want to find out exactly what they're up to*, he decided.

The other aspect that puzzled him was why they hadn't killed him like Foley, Macaleer and Bateman. What did they want with him? The Generalissimo said he could be useful to him, but how? Frustrated, he kicked at the chair toppling it over then kicked the solid door. Suddenly, a muted voice filled the cave. It was the Generalissimo.

"Mr Conrad. Please eat your meal and relax. Pick up the chair."

Conrad looked all round the cave, smoothing his hands over the wall to find hidden bugs. He stared at the panel of LCD lights hanging from the stone ceiling and focussed on the centre light. That's where the CCTV camera was located. He would have to disable it, but first he had to warn Dreher.

He cursed; nothing, not even a glimmer of a signal on his mobile. They hadn't even bothered to search him for it. At this level the whole facility was surrounded by solid rock. That's why their computer systems were on the highest level. Shoulders slumped in assumed defeat, he grabbed the plate of food. No sense in letting his energy levels drop. He picked up a book and settled down on the bed.

"That's better, Mr Conrad," a disembodied voice purred. "Enjoy your book. You are to be our conduit to the G8 countries. We will talk again tomorrow."

Conduit? What the hell did he mean? Puzzled, he lay back studying the room over the top of the book. There was no way out except through the door. Resting the book against his chest he pretended to massage his leg, but he was feeling for the mini smoke capsules in a concealed pocket. He only had two so each of them would have to be effective first time round. Throwing the book onto the table, he settled back and closed his eyes. When the guard came again he would make his move. He would only have one chance at it.

Time dragged, but he was used to waiting. His hours on surveillance missions had disciplined his mind to be watchful while he rested. Feigning sleep, he planned his escape down to the last detail. He had to get back down to Berg before the last cable car left otherwise he would have to negotiate perilously steep trails in the dark. Unlike Sasha, his experience of the Alps was limited to skiing on the black runs.

The scraping of the bolt sounded loud and metallic in his ears. Fully alert, he remained on the bed, eyes closed. A key turned in the lock. The guard opened the door and picked up the tray. As he turned to go Conrad reared up and snapped open the miniature smoke bomb. Veering behind the man, he delivered a vicious chop to his neck. He dropped to the ground, unconscious. Conrad didn't waste time tying him up. In a nanosecond he grabbed the Glock the guard had taken from him earlier. Swiftly, he placed a chair under the ceiling light and disabled the CCTV camera. Through the grey haze a disembodied voice demanded.

"Stop him! Stop him you fools!"

He was already out of the door. Cautiously, he moved down the dimly lit corridor towards the lift.

"Come on! Come on!" he urged, punching the up button.

As the doors opened, two guards rushed at him. Before they could grab him he snapped another smoke bomb. Blindly, they stumbled forward into the lift. Taking advantage of their disorientation he sidestepped them, bringing the butt of his Glock down on the shorter of the men. In the confusion the second guard whirled round just as the gun made contact with his skull. Heart thumping, he punched the up button again and waited for the lift to stop on the main level.

Swiftly, he assessed the situation, scanning the walls for CCTV cameras. Nothing but stone walls mottled with damp and a door further along the corridor. *That must be leading into the main chamber*, he thought. *Damn it, another retinal scanner! There was no way he could get out unless... ?* One of the men was still unconscious. He stripped him of his uniform and put them on over his own clothes. Quickly, he yanked on the yellow armband, emblazoned with three black snow crystals, and covered his face with the balaclava.

"They must be security," he muttered, noticing they all wore the same colour.

The other man had come round and was struggling to sit up. Grabbing him under his arms, he dragged him towards the door and pulled him up in front of the retinal scanner.

"Look into the scanner! Keep your eyes open!" he ordered, holding the Glock to the guard's head.

Conrad pushed the guard's face forward until the door swished open. He delivered a rabbit punch to his neck and lowered him to the ground.

Suddenly, the piercing whine of an alarm reverberated around the cavern. Armed security guards marched across the chamber coming and going through various entrances. Conrad squinted against the harsh light. Black-clad figures were still seated at state-of-the-art computers studying the rapidly changing rows of statistics. The enormous wall map gleamed with flickering pinpoint lights. The whole chamber was a buzz of controlled activity. He took a deep breath and stepped into the cavern. Could he bluff his way out?

Drawing himself to his full height, he marched close to the computers trying to read the screens. Each one seemed to be focussed on a different area of the map on the wall. Suddenly, the Generalissimo's voice reverberated around the chamber.

"Beijing is in control, I repeat, Beijing is in control."

"We've registered Beijing," the computer operator replied, punching in a code.

"Now find Conrad! He must not be allowed to escape! Find him!"

Taking a huge breath Conrad moved along the line of computers. Set slightly apart from the others, a man was furiously jabbing at the keyboard. He seemed to be coordinating all the information. All the major cities appeared on a world map on his screen with codes alongside. What the hell was going on? Suddenly, a light flickered on the map.

"Beijing is on board!" he exclaimed.

"Beijing's on board?" Conrad queried, sidling up behind him.

Completely absorbed in his work the man nodded briefly.

"We're on schedule. Another four weeks and our mission will be accomplished."

"Four weeks?" The man looked up at Conrad, a sneer on his face. "What do you expect, you idiot? That we control that many countries in a few hours? Not even the Generalissimo can do that. This is just the beginning."

Conrad froze. He couldn't believe what he was hearing. In four weeks all the cities on the map would be 'on board', but why? Cautiously, he prodded the computer operator for more information.

"What if the mission should fail?"

"Fail?" the man replied scornfully. "The Generalissimo has been planning this for decades. Why are you asking so many questions?"

"I'm interested in computers, but I've never learned to use one," he responded. "It all seems very complicated to me."

The man sniggered. Security guards, no brains, little short of thugs. He grunted and turned back to his screen.

Surreptitiously, Conrad surveyed the chamber registering every possible exit. He had to make a move soon and glean more information before it was too late. Out of the corner of his eye, he spotted an opening leading off to the right of the bank of consoles. Glancing quickly behind him, he marched purposefully towards it. A narrow corridor disappeared round a series of bends that led to a door with a drop-down latch. He lifted the latch and yanked open the door. The handle on the inside hung from a loose screw. Taking a strip of flexible plastic out of his jacket, he propped up the latch and left the door open a crack. He didn't want to get trapped inside.

Both walls of the rough-hewn cave were lined with wooden stalls. So that's where the goats are kept! He peered inside the nearest stall. Fresh straw and a plentiful supply of food had been provided for the animals. The walls were perfectly dry. On the far outer wall a retinal scanner sat like a watchful eye beside a gleaming steel door. That must be a way out where they can graze on the patch of grass outside.

Squatting just inside the nearest stall he waited, deciding on his next move. He couldn't go back, slug another guard and drag him down here to open the door. There was only one way he could get out. His chance would come when someone came to let out the goats. Moving deeper into the stall, he patted a startled animal as it pawed the ground. Keeping very still he settled down to wait. He didn't have to wait long.

Ten minutes later the distant sound of muffled footsteps tramping down the stone-flagged corridor caught his attention. He darted to the door, removed the plastic strip and pulled the door shut. With a muted clunk the latch fell into position. He raced back to the stall, at the same time pulling out his gun.

"Damn this latch. I'd better get it fixed," a voice muttered. When the door scraped open the guard dragged a bale of straw to prop against the door. "Where are you, my beauties?" At the sound of the voice, the goats scrambled out of the stalls. Heavy footsteps clumped across the floor and stopped in front of the steel door. For a few minutes, he petted and talked to the goats milling around him. "Not so fast little ones." He laughed as the goats nudged his legs. "You must be patient."

With bated breath, Conrad waited until the man faced the scanner. As the door slid open the guard turned to the goats. Suddenly, he spotted Conrad crouched just inside the stall. Before he had a chance to react Conrad was on his feet brandishing his Glock.

"One sound and you're dead."

In a knee-jerk reaction, the guard's hand moved to the Kalashnikov slung over his shoulder.

"Don't even think about it! Drop the gun and put your hands on your head!" It fell to the ground with a loud clatter. "Turn around!" The man dropped to his knees as the gun came into contact with the back of his skull.

Conrad felt for a pulse. The guard was alive, but he would probably be unconscious for hours. He pulled the straw bale away from the inner door and raced out onto the grass patch. The goats were grazing contentedly, completely oblivious to his presence. He pushed his way through them and came up against an outcrop of solid rock about three metres high.

Except for a small ledge, about halfway up, it was sheer stone. There were a few decent handholds and scrubby bushes sprouting from crevices above the ledge.

Lifting up his trouser leg, he unwound a length of reinforced steel cord from around his ankle and opened the closed hook secured at the end. Fortunately, his padded trousers had concealed the slight bulge. Holding it over his head he twirled it like a lasso and threw it up over the rocks. All he needed was to get his foot onto the shallow ledge on the rock. The hook fell back to earth just missing his face. At the third attempt it caught on the rock. He pulled gently until he felt enough tension to know it was firmly in place.

Pushing one boot against the wall he started to hoist himself up. The cord was too thin to grip properly. He wound it around his hand until his arm was outstretched upwards. Placing his feet against the rock, he tried to haul himself up again. The cord bit into his hand through the protective glove. Sweat poured down his face. His arms felt as though they were being pulled from their sockets by the dead weight of his body. If only he could get another foot higher he could grab a piece of scrub and haul himself onto the ledge.

With almost superhuman effort he managed to pull himself to the top. He scanned the area for any sign of the guards. It was eerily quiet; too quiet. Dropping to the ground on the other side he stopped dead, expecting a volley of shots. He scanned the rock face searching for concealed cameras. A faint beam of an infrared light either side caught his attention. *That's how they keep out intruders,* he thought.

It was then he realised that there was something peculiar about the wall. He gave it a gentle tap. It sounded vaguely hollow. *So that's it. It's not real stone.* It was artificial like the boulders they used on fairground attractions and in films. An outer layer to conceal the steel door behind it.

Keeping low, he moved to the left away from the beam. It was much steeper, strewn with loose shale, sparse shrubs and craggy rocks. When he was certain he was far enough away, he scrambled down the mountain, slipping and sliding on his backside.

Suddenly, a gunshot cracked the air. The bullet pinged off a rock a few feet away, quickly followed by a volley of shots. Ducking down, he kept on running headlong down the steep slope until he knew he was out of range. He slumped to the ground, under cover of an overhanging rock, panting like an overheated dog.

It was another two hours before he reached the aerial cable car at Berg. Passengers watched its slow descent from the Piz Gloria. Most of them were waiting to go back down to Mürren where they could catch a train back to Grütschalp or a cable car to Stechelberg. Excited American students, backpacks crammed full of equipment, middle-aged, immaculately dressed Japanese tourists and serious walkers crowded round the station to board the last car of the day.

When the cable car arrived they surged forward, anxious to secure a place by the windows where they could use their expensive cameras. Conrad pushed his way towards the corner to the right of the doors. From there he could see if he had been followed. Taking out his binoculars, he scanned the mountain for any sign of activity near the installation. From that distance it just looked like a ramshackle structure. The remains of the failed hotel. Nobody would guess what was really up there.

Breathing a sigh of relief, he slumped against the window trying to gather his thoughts. The Alps were stunningly beautiful. Late afternoon shadows moved across the mountain turning the snow-covered peaks bluish purple. Overhead, a white sun dazzled, glancing off rocks and trees glistening with snow. Conrad adjusted his snow glasses against the powerful glare, watching the peaks recede as they dropped lower.

Suddenly, a movement caught his eye. Rising from the mountain, high above them, a black spot grew in his vision. Instead of receding it was getting bigger and bigger. An excited buzz filled the car.

"Hey look, guys, there's a whirlybird!" shouted one of the students. "He's coming right at us!"

A black Mosquito helicopter zoomed in and hovered about a hundred metres away from the wire. The figure in the passenger seat leaned out and pointed.

"Who's he pointing at?" he yelled. "He's coming closer! Is he nuts?"

Passengers looked around the car trying to work out the object of the man's attentions.

"His face is covered up. I wonder who they are?" piped a short woman. She looked like a miniature barrage balloon in her padded jacket. Wobbling slightly, she moved closer to the window and peered across at the man. "My God, I think he's got a gun!"

Conrad leaned nonchalantly against the window pretending to study a safety notice, but he was observing the helicopter. There was no doubt they were looking for him. Why hadn't they polished him off when they had a chance? It didn't make any sense. Suddenly, the helicopter swung away from the wire and headed back towards the mountain, casting a dark shadow on the snow.

CHAPTER FORTY-FOUR

Interlaken, Bernese Oberland

Conrad luxuriated in the warmth of the hot shower. He felt as though he had been kicked by a horse. His arms were covered with bruises, but the thick padding in his jacket had protected most of his upper body. Standing in front of the full-length mirror, he twisted and turned. No wonder his backside felt so tender. Both cheeks had bruises the size of saucers where he had been sliding over the rubble.

Feeling refreshed, he headed for the bar where he had arranged to meet Ernst Dreher. He chose a corner seat against the back wall where he could watch the entrance. Five minutes later Dreher marched into the bar, a grim look on his face. Spotting Conrad, he manoeuvred his way through the tables and sat down.

"You haven't been answering your mobile all day. I thought you were in trouble," he said accusingly.

"I was," Conrad replied. He signalled to the waiter. "Whisky, *bitte*. What about you, Ernst?"

Dreher nodded. "Just a small one. I'm officially off duty, but the way things are going I could be called in. Now, tell me all about your trip."

"You're not going to believe a word of it, but I swear it's the truth."

He related all that had happened: the hidden installation,

the masked Generalissimo, the Black Militia, their incredible plans.

"They're obviously using the internal skeleton of the old hotel for their activities."

Dreher looked sceptical. "It's hard to believe. Perhaps the computer operator was pulling your leg: trying to impress who he thought was a lowly security guard. Some of these computer nerds are like that."

Conrad knew what he had seen. A covert operation hidden away in the Swiss Alps. All the major cities in the world were online preparing for what – an invasion? It was ludicrous! There was no way they could accumulate an army of that size. Besides they would need more than an army. They would need planes, ships, nuclear weapons. Perhaps that's it. They could be working with a foreign power; one that had secretly stockpiled weapons of mass destruction. His imagination was running wild with possibilities. *Think rationally*, he told himself. *Any suspicion of stockpiling and NATO would have inspectors in there straight away. Besides, it would be tit for tat – Armageddon.*

Chemical weapons would be far more feasible; poison in the water system or the air. It has to be something that would give them control without destroying the infrastructure of the cities. He had to find out more before it was too late.

CHAPTER FORTY-FIVE

Shrewsbury, Shropshire

Wallace weaved his way in and out of the lanes of traffic. He gritted his teeth with exasperation. The one-way system was a damned nuisance at times. Pedestrians took their lives in their hands, darting in front of vehicles with inches to spare. When he reached Pride Hill it was already crowded with early shoppers and tourists. Slowly, he trailed the traffic down Wyle Cop towards the abbey and English Bridge.

His trip to the cottage in Oswestry the day before hadn't turned up anything new. Nor had they discovered anything more about the armbands. Extensive enquiries, web searches and local shops had failed to produce anyone who manufactured or sold them. The only other clue was the tiny fabric sample found under Joanne Howard's nails. The shop in Shrewsbury bought in the material from Europe for a few select clients. Dreher had traced the same fabric to a high-class tailor in Paris whose clientele were the rich and famous. Other than that it didn't give them much to go on.

He was about to go into his makeshift office next to the incident room when Butler waylaid him.

"Sir, we've got another lead from traffic. PC Davies was on duty not far from Oswestry when the roads were flooded. Diverting traffic away from the area onto country lanes. He pulled in a Jaguar. There was a young woman in the passenger seat, pretty worse for wear by all accounts. She stank of drink. The driver said he was taking her home after a hen night."

"Where is this leading, Butler?" Wallace asked wearily.

"Davies thought she resembled Joanne Howard. She looked like the photograph we circulated; the one found in her cottage."

"What about the man? Do we have any information about him?"

"He was smartly dressed, polite and very well spoken; well under the drink drive limits."

Wallace sat on the edge of his desk, folded his arms, and blew out his cheeks. The case was becoming more and more complex. Who was the man? What was his relationship to Joanne Howard? A tap on the half-glass door broke into his thoughts. He beckoned to DS Wilkins to come in.

"Sir, a guy just rang in to say he recognised the victim. Apparently, he was in a conference at the Hilton in Cardiff. Joanne Howard was with a man. They were sitting near him in the bar, drinking champagne. The bartender confirmed it."

Could it be the same man she was seen with outside Oswestry? His description matched with that of the barman in the hotel. Reddish-brown hair; impeccable manners; well-cut, expensive suit. The women in the bar had been giving him the glad eye. The police artist should be able to come up with a good likeness to circulate in the morning papers.

"I checked with reception," the DS continued. "He booked in under the name of Alex Campbell. The barman overheard them talking about their flight from Geneva." Wallace's pulse quickened with excitement. At last they were getting somewhere. So they had both come from Switzerland. It was too much of a coincidence.

"And they were definitely together?"

"Apparently, they met on the plane to Heathrow then flew down to Cardiff. The guy was giving her the full chat-up line. Complimenting her about her figure and looks; saying how fortunate he was to have been sitting next to her on the plane. She drank a lot of champagne. By the time they left together she was quite tipsy."

"Get in touch with Cardiff International Airport security and contact Heathrow. He might have booked a return ticket. If he is the murderer, he may also try to get out of the country from another airport so check out Birmingham and Manchester. They are closer to Oswestry than Heathrow."

If he *was* Joanne's killer he would either lie low or try to leave the country at the earliest opportunity. Now there were five murder victims. Foley and Howard on his patch, Macaleer, Lynes and now Bateman. Four of them definitely connected. Three of the victims had been found naked. Other than that there was no evidence to suggest that Joanne Howard was in the frame. Could it be that the armbands were just a coincidence?

Wilkins poked his head round the door interrupting his train of thought. "It turns out Campbell booked a return ticket from Geneva to Heathrow."

"So, I was right," Wallace murmured. He probably flew back the day after the murder, but he hadn't taken a domestic flight from Cardiff, Birmingham or Manchester. Damn it! He could have travelled up by car or train. Either way, it was all academic if he had already left the country. He dialled the number on his secure line.

"Good morning, Ben," Dreher answered. "How's the weather over there?"

"Cold and wet, as usual." Dispensing with the pleasantries he continued. "We know there's a link between Foley, Lynes, Macaleer and Bateman. My gut instinct tells me there's also a link between Lynes and Howard." Wallace told him about the armband he found in Joanne Howard's cottage and the one Conrad had described. There was silence on the other end of the line then Dreher said,

"Jack is on his way back. He has some very interesting information regarding Joanne Howard. We've reached the same conclusion. She must be connected to Lynes and that they were both involved with the same organisation."

"What kind of organisation?"

"He'll fill you in when he gets back to London this afternoon. Have you made any progress on her killer?"

"That's what I'm ringing about. Apparently, she met up with a guy called Alex Campbell. They flew into Heathrow from Geneva and on to Cardiff International Airport. A policeman reported stopping them on their way to Oswestry when he was diverting traffic through floods after heavy rain. He remembered the incident because the girl, who turned out to be Joanne Howard, was plastered. Drunk after a hen party, or so it seemed. We believe that Campbell flew back to Geneva the morning after Howard was murdered. I'll fax you an artist's impression."

"I'll be in touch as soon as I have some information for you," Dreher said.

Campbell may have been travelling under an assumed name, but if he was in Switzerland Dreher would find him. He wouldn't waste any time getting Interpol on to it.

*

Wallace had only just replaced the receiver when it rang again. It was Conrad. "The boss wants to meet you in London tomorrow morning. Expect a phone call from the Chief Constable. This investigation is way over his head now, Ben. It's way over all our heads."

Conrad gave Wallace the address in Whitehall warning him that complete secrecy was essential. Not even the Chief Constable could be told where he was going. Only that he was ordered to give him carte blanche to pursue the investigation.

Stunned, he slumped into his chair, his brain seething with possibilities. What was so secretive that not even his CC knew about it?

"Butler!" he shouted into the incident room. "If you find out anything else on Campbell give me a buzz. I'm going to work from home over the weekend, possibly up to Monday. I'm due a weekend off."

Butler grinned to himself. It wasn't like his DCI to take time off unless he was up to something. It must be getting serious with Dr Barnett. Lucky sod. He quite fancied her himself, but she was definitely out of his league.

CHAPTER FORTY-SIX

London, England

Wallace walked briskly towards the taxi rank in Paddington. He waited in the queue until he was motioned forward by a man in charge of getting passengers into cabs. He instructed the driver to take him to North Pembury Avenue. The driver shot off up the ramp into the traffic and expertly negotiated the busy streets. Wallace looked out through the window not wanting to engage in conversation with the garrulous cabby. He was too tense for small talk. They slowed down as they negotiated Admiralty Arch then nudged towards Trafalgar Square. It was crowded with people chanting and waving placards.

"Bloody demonstrators!" the cabby fumed.

Impatiently, he nudged the taxi forward towards the traffic lights and onto Northumberland Avenue. Wallace had the door open before the cab stopped outside Trentor Enterprises. He shoved some notes at the driver and ran up the steps.

"Ben Wallace," he told the middle-aged receptionist. "I have an appointment with the managing director."

She smiled, motioned him towards a leather sofa and spoke quietly into the telephone. A few minutes later a woman appeared from a corridor at the side of the reception desk.

"Good morning. I hope you had a pleasant journey? This way, please."

Wallace followed her through a security door to the lift. Conrad had warned him not to use his police rank to avoid arousing suspicions. Trentor Enterprises actually dealt with the public, giving advice to companies on installing computer systems.

The secretary knocked a door and gently pushed it open. Conrad rose from his chair when he entered the outer office and ushered him to a chair.

"You'll be meeting Breakdancer in a few minutes. You won't be able to see him until he's satisfied you can be trusted one hundred per cent. He knows we're old friends, but that won't stop him forming his own assessment of your character and reliability."

"Good morning, Mr Wallace." The deep voice echoed around the room. "Please make yourself comfortable while I ask you a few questions."

Wallace waited for Breakdancer to begin, but there was only silence and the faint humming of the air conditioning. The boss was testing his patience to see how he would react. Finally, the voice came back and asked him a series of questions in rapid succession. Wallace's mouth was as dry as cardboard. Suddenly, the tone changed, became soothing and cajoling, but Wallace didn't let down his guard. This approach wasn't new to him. He could handle it. After an hour of intensive interaction the door opened. A tall, rangy man emerged from the inner office.

"General Clive Pearce," Conrad said.

"Breakdancer?" Wallace shook his hand.

"That's my code name. Major Conrad has told me a lot

about your experience. You've worked together before on Interpol teams and in military intelligence. In fact, we know everything about you from your shoe size to your relationship with Dr Jo Barnett."

Wallace didn't show a flicker of emotion. It was what he expected from an offshoot of MI6.

"We've already code-named you 'Rookie'. You're a policeman and you're new to our organisation. It fits," he said with a chuckle. "Jack will fill you in."

Conrad outlined his discovery of the installation in the Alps and the enormous cavern behind the debris of the derelict hotel.

"There are dozens of state-of-the-art computers. It's obviously some kind of paramilitary organisation controlled by a man known as the Generalissimo."

Wallace let out a low whistle when Conrad mentioned the army of men and women sporting armbands like the one he had found in Joanne Howard's cottage. His instinct had proved reliable. There was a connection between all five murders.

"All the computer people were wearing red armbands, security yellow. A handful close to the Generalissimo wore gold. A lot of them had snow crystals embossed on them. They seemed to indicate seniority."

"What about the silver ones?"

"I didn't see any, but l think they must be for those who work covertly in the field. Probably 'sleepers' like Lynes and Howard."

"Colin Lynes was a computer expert and cryptologist," Wallace cut in. "That's why the crystals were outlined in red. Silver for a field worker and red to indicate his computer know- how. That's got to be it."

"Didn't I tell you he'd be an asset?" Conrad grinned at Pearce. "This may sound crazy, but I believe they're planning to cripple major cities around the world."

"Come on, Jack. You've been reading those science fiction books again," Wallace laughed.

"It's not a joke. Ludicrous though it may sound I watched and listened. They have outposts all over the globe ready and waiting for the signal to attack." Wallace raised an eyebrow sceptically. "Not in the conventional sense. I believe their attack will come through cyberspace."

"There are dozens of claims regarding cyber terrorism on a regular basis," Pearce interjected.

"At the moment it's just speculation," Conrad continued, "but if I'm right they could cripple government computers, business conglomerates, research organisations, nuclear power stations, military establishments, observatories: even GCHQ or the Pentagon."

Wallace shook his head in disbelief. "I knew you were a bit of a Trekkie years ago, Jack, but this is a bit far-fetched."

"Pentagon computers have been hacked into more than once," Pearce said.

"The aim is to paralyze the infrastructure of G8 countries," Conrad continued. "They could even bring planes down. You name it."

"It's incredible!"

"Incredible, but possible," Pearce said. "There are thousands of attacks through cyberspace every single day. Most of them are detected by GCHQ or the Pentagon. That's why the Government recently set up the National Cyber Security Centre. It's only a matter of time before there's an extremely malicious attack on government and business computer systems."

"Colin Lynes was working for the Russian Security Services," Conrad said. Somewhere along the line he got involved with the organisation known as the Black Militia. They wanted his computer skills. More importantly, he was working for GCHQ."

"The last thing we want is to alert the Generalissimo by sending in the SAS. He would be waiting for them," Pearce stated. "They've already tried to scare you off. Be careful, Jack. Next time you may not be so lucky."

"If my theory is correct, we'll have to find a way to destroy the installation before the plans are implemented," Conrad replied. "In the meantime perhaps Sophia Dreher could compile a psychological profile of the Generalissimo."

CHAPTER FORTY-SEVEN

Long Island, New York

Sunlight glanced on the undulating sea, lit up the shore with a soft, pink glow. Seagulls wheeled over the surface of the water and dived towards the beach searching for food. Half a dozen overweight joggers plodded along the shoreline trying to work off a few pounds. A runner in a baseball cap, sunglasses and grey sweats ran along the beach at a leisurely pace. His beer belly flopped obscenely out of his tracksuit top. Breathing heavily, he dragged himself laboriously towards a dilapidated hut close to a wooden pier.

As he approached, a burly figure stepped out of the hut and started jogging alongside him. They ran towards a clutch of weatherboard buildings near a deserted seafood restaurant. The little fat man paused for a few moments to catch his breath. Beads of perspiration speckled his forehead. His face was blood-red from the unfamiliar activity. Too many cigarettes and too much booze had taken their toll on his body.

Across the road from the restaurant an old-fashioned drugstore and ice-cream parlour had opened its doors to let in its first customers. The two men pushed inside and sat on the high stools placed around the counter. Three days previously, the man in the sweats had taken the ferry from Hartford, Connecticut across Long Island Sound to Port

200

Jefferson. He had been careful to take a circuitous route from Boston, travelling by train and road. Too many questions were asked at airports. Security was extremely tight since the bombing of the twin towers in New York City.

The burly agent handed over a set of car keys and a piece of paper. "Everything is in place. We have a safe house in Fort Salonga. Stay there until we receive the signal to move. You'll take the Long Island Railroad to Manhattan: from there a train to Chicago."

He smiled, anticipating the chaos to come. Casually, he clapped a hand on his companion's shoulder in a friendly gesture then walked out towards the beach. The man still sitting at the counter stuffed the paper and keys into his pocket. Without a sideways glance he moved towards the door and headed for the car park near the beach.

An hour and a half later, he drove down the main street of Fort Salonga with its fire station and smart shops. Just outside the small town, he drove up a hill until a white weatherboard house came into view. He pulled into the drive, flicked the remote control, and waited for the garage doors to slide open. Inside the garage, a door led conveniently into the house. He had no baggage. Food, clothing, everything he needed had been provided. In the kitchen he opened the fridge. It was well stocked with fresh food, even a few beers.

Well, I might as well make the most of it, he decided. Kicking off his trainers, Baranski grabbed a beer, went out onto the wooden deck and gazed out across Long Island Sound. In the distance the white tower of a church pierced the azure sky. A soft moan murmured through tall trees. Waves, crested with white horses whipped up by a fresh breeze, rolled to the shore. Any other observer would have marvelled at its beauty, but not Baranski. Beauty was lost on him.

*

Amoral, brutal, totally lacking in compassion, he had never loved anyone. If anything or anybody got in his way he eliminated them, just as he had eliminated his parents who wanted him to study medicine. He was just seventeen years old when he deliberately set fire to their apartment. Black smoke streaming from under the door alerted the neighbours. They found Baranski lying in the tiny vestibule attempting to claw his way to the door. His mother, father and sister died in the fire.

After their death, he lived with his maternal grandmother just outside St. Petersburg. A retired schoolteacher, she took huge pride in her clever grandson. She encouraged him to enrol in the university, even though she was disappointed that he had chosen computer science instead of medicine. She had managed to save a few roubles towards her old age and intended giving it to her grandson as a graduation gift.

"But Babushka," Baranski purred, "wouldn't it be better to give me the money now?" She stroked his cheek. "You will have the money soon, but not until you graduate."

For days he watched her every move until he discovered where she had hidden the money. After a pleasant supper one evening the old lady retired for the night. Baranski knocked lightly on her bedroom door calling softly, "Babushka! Babushka!"

Confident she had fallen asleep he crept in and stood over the bed. The kitchen knife in his hand gleamed in the moonlight. At this moment his grandmother opened her eyes. She tried to sit up, but Baranski pushed her roughly back onto the bed. Smiling down at her he sliced the air with the knife. He wasn't going to kill her himself, just give her a bad fright. He wanted her to die a natural death.

With an evil grin, he made chopping motions with his hand. She clutched at her chest. Her face was grey; beads of perspiration stood out on her forehead.

"My pills," she gasped. "Please, get my pills."

She stretched out an arm to him, eyes wide with terror and disbelief. Devoid of compassion, he watched his grandmother gasp her last breath. When he was sure she was dead, he arranged her body in a peaceful sleeping position and returned the knife to the drawer.

He took her paltry savings from the box under her bed and stuffed it in his backpack. Calmly, he walked to the metro station to take a train to the university. They would assume the old hag had died in her sleep, but her neighbours were suspicious.

They had witnessed his vicious ways when he had strangled their little girl's cat. He had denied it vociferously, but they knew he was responsible. They reported his grandmother's death to the police. He was arrested and questioned.

"She had a weak heart," he explained. "Nobody knew about it. Doctor Yagudin can verify it."

"There will be a post mortem," the police officer said. "In the meantime you are free to return to the university while we continue our investigations."

The post mortem confirmed that his grandmother had died from natural causes. A year later Baranski graduated first in his class.

It was Ivan, the Generalissimo's personal aide, who had recruited him for the Black Militia, Ivan who had recognised his extraordinary ability with computers. He was ready to play his part in realising the Generalissimo's brilliant plan.

*

Baranski spent his days on Long Island eating, drinking, sleeping and watching television. On the fourth day he noticed a delivery van parked on the road. The driver carried a package up the drive and rang the bell. Baranski stopped dead, a forkful of food halfway to his mouth. The bell rang again: five short rings followed by three more. That was the signal! Quickly, he rushed to the door and signed for the package. The courier lingered, waiting for a tip. Fuming inwardly, Baranski dug into his pocket and produced a dollar bill. Bloody Americans and their tips!

Grabbing the parcel, he trudged back into the living room and closed the venetian blinds. He tore open the protective double layer of bubble wrap. This was what he had been waiting for: the promised laptop along with an automatic pistol. He picked up the gun and turned it over in his hands, revelling in the feel of cold metal.

With a thrill of excitement, he plugged in the laptop and waited for it to boot up, impatiently devil-drumming on the arm of the chair. He tapped in the password. A black crystal, edged with gold, appeared on the screen. Within seconds a message replaced it.

Have a great time in the 'Big Apple'. I hope to see your holiday snaps soon.

Baranski felt light-headed with exhilaration. He raced

into the bedroom and changed his clothes. Picking up a billfold crammed with notes, he stuffed it into his pocket. After a last look round he opened the front door and stepped out.

Nobody would have recognised him as the same man who had been living in the house in Fort Salonga. Dressed in a dark suit, white button-down shirt, conservative tie and black wingtips, he looked the epitome of the middle-aged, affluent American businessman. Smiling confidently, he strode towards Long Island Railroad station swinging his laptop case.

CHAPTER FORTY-EIGHT

Manhattan, New York City

Baranski pushed through the crowds surging towards the station exit and emerged into the bustle of Manhattan. Skyscrapers loomed like dark sentinels over the streets. The sudden spell of good weather and blues skies had evaporated as swiftly as it had arrived. Now it was wet, cold and gloomy. He should have brought an overcoat. Still, he didn't have far to go. He felt a sudden stab of claustrophobia as he gazed up through the misty drizzle of a dank December day.

A thousand windows stared at him, rain dribbling down the glass like tears. The city depressed him. He longed for the country and wide-open spaces. Shrugging off the feeling, he quickened his pace. Money, influence, prestige and power; everything his heart desired lay within his grasp. He hailed a yellow cab as he walked.

"Barclay Intercontinental on eastside."

The driver negotiated the heavy traffic, eventually accessed Seventh Avenue and nosed his way through the jam. A few minutes later, the cab slewed to a halt outside the main entrance of the Intercontinental.

"Fifteen bucks," the driver said sourly.

Baranski jumped out and headed into reception. He checked in using the name Tarek Dudek, a Polish name.

"Your passport, Mr Dudek," the receptionist said. She

handed it back with the regulation smile. "Would you like help with your luggage?"

"No, thank you. I just have a small case. I can manage," he replied, running a finger over the pencil moustache he had grown.

"I hope you have a very enjoyable stay in New York. Have a nice day."

Inside the elevator he pressed the button for the executive floor. His room was close to the elevator as he had requested. After looking around the room, he gazed out of the window at people scurrying along the pavement seventeen floors down. Leaving his briefcase on the bed he went back into the corridor noting the fire exits. He tried a door; it opened easily. Grunting with satisfaction, he left his valise in his room and took the elevator down to the lobby.

He would have a cup of revolting American coffee, making sure he was seen. Nodding to an elderly couple, he sat down at the table next to them. He ordered a cappuccino and settled back pretending to admire the spacious lobby.

"Very impressive," Baranski said, loudly enough for the couple on the next table to hear.

"It sure is, mister," commented the man.

"We're in New York for our fiftieth wedding anniversary," the woman interjected, "ain't we, Hank?"

Baranski recognised the mid-western drawl. Country hicks! America was full of them! He finished his coffee and politely wished the couple a happy vacation.

After strolling across the spacious foyer, he exited via an entrance situated close to the hotel gift shop. Directly opposite was the side entrance of the Waldorf Astoria where an escalator carried guests from the pavement into the hotel.

Casually, he crossed the road and rode up the escalator with a group of chattering tourists. What a stroke of luck! It would be easy to slip from one hotel to the other; much easier than he had anticipated.

He lingered for a few minutes then went back down the escalator. Dodging round the corner into East 48th Street, he passed the main entrance of the Intercontinental and made for Seventh Avenue and Macy's, where he purchased a small suitcase.

An hour and a half later, he walked through the side entrance of the Waldorf and rode the escalator back up to the lobby. Reception was crowded with guests booking in and out. Casually, he lingered as though waiting to check in. A middle-aged couple jostled past and headed towards the main entrance. The man was carrying an identical suitcase to the one Baranski had purchased. He stared down at his case and pushed it gently with his foot. It had been switched. It was heavy now, packed with everything he needed for his work. Smiling inwardly he picked it up and headed for the exit.

*

Baranski was enjoying steak and eggs for breakfast at Oscar's in the Waldorf when the call came. Looking round the room he pulled out his cell phone, placed the receiver close to his ear, and listened intently. Smiling at the young woman on the next table he left the restaurant. He made for the main lobby exiting the hotel on Park Lane. He walked down Third Avenue on to 46th Street then walked two blocks to the United Nations building where he was to meet his contact.

He had already sussed out the times of the official tours. After buying a ticket he joined the group trailing the guide.

"On vacation?" a tall, angular man queried.

"Business and pleasure," Baranski replied.

Baranski knew nothing about his contact. Could this be him?

"All the world leaders are meeting here early next week. Ban Ki-Moon will be giving a speech on tackling world poverty," the guide informed them, briefly making eye contact.

"Really, that's very interesting," one of the group murmured.

It could be any one of them, even the guide. The Generalissimo's obsession with secrecy meant that field agents worked alone with complete anonymity. Casually, he shuffled along with the others who were pushing and shoving to get closer to the prattling guide. Just as he decided his contact hadn't shown up he felt a nudge from behind.

"Don't turn around. Look in your pocket," a voice whispered. "Watch and destroy."

Baranski delved into his jacket pocket and fingered the plastic box. It felt like a CD. Disguising his growing excitement, he straggled along with the group until the tour ended. He avoided the others who were discussing what they had seen. Slipping away from the group, he walked back to the Intercontinental as fast as his short, fat legs would allow.

Back in his room, he pulled out the object and examined it. It was an unmarked DVD. Heart hammering in his chest, he slid it into the DVD player underneath the flat-screen television. It contained a list of instructions to be carried out at specific times.

At JFK airport the nondescript man in the first-class cabin of a British Airways flight to Geneva unfastened his seatbelt and settled back with his eyes closed. The Generalissimo's personal aide smiled to himself. Tomorrow the next stage of the plan would be put into action.

CHAPTER FORTY-NINE

Wales, United Kingdom

Wallace slammed the door of his office and thumped the desk.

"Are telling me that the SOCOs haven't examined the hotel rooms?" he shouted.

"The police in Cardiff wouldn't sanction it until they speak to you," Butler replied. "You said you would be working from home, but I couldn't get hold of you, sir."

Wallace breathed deeply to keep his blood pressure under control. There was no time to waste. It would be better if he went down there himself. Any clue, however small, was vital to the case.

Three hours later, they were hurtling down the M4 towards Cardiff. Wallace closed his eyes trying to fathom out the connection between the murder victims and Alex Campbell. Was he involved or was he just a killer preying on women? Either way he had to be apprehended.

As they approached Junction 32 the traffic slowed to a halt at the lights.

"Put the siren on, Butler. We haven't got all day!" Wallace barked. "At this rate we'll never solve the bloody case!"

Before he had a chance to slap a blue light on the roof of the unmarked car the traffic eased forward. Wallace's face was stony. Little did his DI know how much was hanging in the balance. Fortunately, all the lights stayed green as they sped towards the city centre.

Butler tried to squeeze past the police car blocking the entrance of the Hilton Hotel. A uniformed doorman came down the steps and held up his hand.

"You can't park here," he mouthed through the windscreen. "There's a multi-storey car park opposite the Park Plaza, just down there." The doorman pointed down the road to the car park on the right of the street.

Wallace wound down the window on the passenger side of the vehicle. He whipped out his ID card and held it up in front of the man's face.

"Some of your colleagues are already inside, sir." The doorman swiftly opened the door for Wallace to get out.

He pushed through the revolving doors into the plush foyer. A uniformed constable, talking animatedly to the receptionist, stood to attention when he brandished his ID.

"The SOCOs are up in the room now, sir. The chief inspector's with them."

Wallace charged towards the lift. He stuck his foot between the doors to stop them closing, waiting for Butler who was dashing across the foyer. Impatiently, he tapped his foot until the lift doors slid open at their floor. Halfway along the corridor another uniformed officer stood guard outside the bedroom door.

"Chief Inspector Wallace," he said, tight-lipped.

"Come in," a deep voice called from inside the room. A thickset man, dark hair receding to the middle of his head, stepped forward.

"Detective Chief Inspector Harris," he said, holding out his hand. "The SOCOs found a few hairs in the bathroom, fingerprints on the window catches and door handle and some tiny strands of fabric in the wardrobe. A number of people have stayed in the room since Alex Campbell's departure.

"Do you mind if I take a look around?" Wallace asked, struggling to sound civil.

He had to tread carefully. He was on somebody else's patch, always a delicate situation at the best of times.

"Be my guest. We're almost done here. I'll let you know the outcome as soon as I get the results back from the lab. It's highly unlikely you'll find anything more. If you do I expect you to send it over to our forensics."

Harris followed the white-suited SOCOs into the corridor while Wallace and Butler lingered in the middle of the room.

"Bag anything you think might be important," Wallace said.

"But sir, we can't do that! It's not our patch."

"Just do it! I'll take responsibility."

Normally, he would have stuck to the rules, but this was too big to take any chances. There was little evidence of anything except a few bits of lint on the carpet. Wallace doubted that the SOCOs would have missed them. Harris was right; they had done a very good job.

He rubbed his chin thoughtfully. According to the barman Alex Campbell was a snazzy dresser; probably the type who would always be well groomed. He picked up the guest information folder and thumbed through it. Facilities for executive room guests included a valet service. He picked up the telephone and dialled reception.

"This is DCI Wallace. Are you able to tell me if an Alex Campbell used the valet service?"

Wallace heard a muffled conversation on the other end of the line before a receptionist answered.

"Hello, sorry to keep you waiting, sir. Yes, he did use the valet service just after he arrived. He wanted his suit pressed."

"I want to talk to the valet and examine the room where the pressing took place. I'm on my way down to reception now," Wallace growled.

When he and Butler reached reception a shaven-haired man, wearing a gold earring, was waiting for him

"I understand that you pressed Mr Campbell's suit."

"Yes, sir," he replied nervously. "It was a very expensive suit – classy. Charcoal-grey pinstripe. He gave me a very generous tip."

"I'd like you to show me the ironing board you used."

The valet shrugged his shoulders and motioned for Wallace to follow him. "This is it," he grinned. "It's all yours."

The scowl on Wallace's face stopped him in his tracks. He was in no mood for inane banter.

"Have you used this particular ironing board for any other guest since you pressed Mr Campbell's suit?"

"Actually I haven't, sir, it's broken. It collapsed in the middle of ironing the trousers. They caught on the metal when it collapsed, just there on the iron rest. It couldn't be helped, sir."

"Don't worry, you won't get into any trouble. Just go back to your work."

The valet scurried away like a frightened rabbit. Butler smothered a grin. He knew what it was like to be the object of his DCI's wrath.

Wallace squatted next to the ironing board and examined it, running his hand over the fabric. He picked up a thread with a tweezers and dropped it into a plastic evidence bag. He collected a few more bits of lint, a couple of hairs and another minute strand of fabric. Carefully, he dropped them into the bag and sealed it. He knew he would have to send the samples to Harris, but not before his own guys had had a chance to examine them.

CHAPTER FIFTY

Shrewsbury, England

Rain slashed against the windscreen. A cold wind howled through the trees in a frenzy of uncontrolled movement. Overhead, the sky was black and heavy with a blanket of unbroken cloud. Torrential rain, day after day, threatened to swell the Severn River and flood the low-lying areas above its banks. Shrewsbury town centre was too elevated to flood, but it would have a disastrous effect on business if the town was cut off again.

Water cascaded down the windscreen as soon as Wallace switched off the engine. Pulling his collar up tightly around his ears he struggled to open the car door against the force of the wind. Dodging puddles, he ran into the police station and bounded up the stairs to his office. He took off his trench coat and smoothed back the hair plastered across his forehead. *It's well overdue for a trim*, he thought.

Settled at his desk, Wallace picked up the telephone. With growing anticipation he punched in a number.

"Jo, have you got anything for me yet?"

He was waiting for the results from the pathologist and forensics.

"The skin samples found under the victim's fingernails were male. Unless you have some suspects lined up to give DNA samples, there's nothing more forensics can do."

Wallace groaned. They were going back to square one again. His only hope was to establish a stronger link between Joanne Howard and Alex Campbell other than that they had met up as mere travellers.

"It was the same for the fabric samples. Hang on, I haven't finished yet," she complained, sensing Wallace's impatience. "Most of it was of no importance, but… "

"What is this, the bloody X Factor? Spit it out!" he said rudely.

"I'm rather busy. I'll send you a report in due course," Jo replied coldly.

"Sorry, I'm sorry. It's just that I'm strung out with this case, more than you could possibly realise."

"One of the threads you found on the ironing board in Cardiff was exactly the same fabric as the suits found in Joanne Howard's cottage. I suppose they could have bought them from the same tailor."

"Perhaps. Don't forget Howard bought hers in Shrewsbury. We don't know where Campbell purchased his suit."

"Didn't you say the tailor shipped in the material from France?"

"Yes, from Paris."

"So, it's more likely Campbell bought his abroad."

"That's a possibility. It's only a hop, skip and jump from Switzerland to France. Thanks Jo, you're a genius."

"Do I get a reward?"

"Dinner at my place, around eight. It's a filthy day. If it's a filthy night you can stay over. I'd hate to see you get stranded in the rain," he said wickedly.

"I'll bring my toothbrush."

Jo grinned as she replaced the receiver. She had promised herself that she wouldn't get involved with a policeman again, but Ben was getting under her skin.

Wallace replaced the receiver and sat staring into space mulling over what Dreher had told him. Forensics had already established that the fabric samples found in the Hilton Hotel and Joanne Howard's cottage were a perfect match. To all appearances, he and Howard had only met for the first time on the plane from Geneva. Was he just a predatory killer picking women up for pleasure before murdering them?

Judging by the information received from her staff and neighbours, Joanne Howard was hardly a shrinking violet. Not the type of woman to be easily duped. It could be a ploy to divert attention away from the fact that they already knew each other. He was convinced they both worked for the same organisation. If that were the case, why was she living in Shropshire?

With Dreher's help it shouldn't be too difficult to track down tailors that specialised in expensive mohair suits. Of course, they couldn't rule out the killer being a woman. He thought about his female, power-dressing colleagues and winced. Why did women want to dress like men?

Mind whirling with possibilities, he picked up the telephone again and punched in a number.

"Conrad," a voice answered.

Wallace described the events in Cardiff and the new evidence they had uncovered. "Dreher is looking into it. I have a notion that there are more than expensive suits linking Howard and Campbell.

"I agree, there are too many coincidences here. Howard belonged to a covert organisation. Macaleer and Foley were murdered by the thugs in the facility I uncovered in the Alps. Colin Lynes was murdered by the Russians, because he had become involved with the same group. If this Alex Campbell murdered Howard then either he's part of the Russian security services or he's one of the Generalissimo's men."

"If that's the case why kill her?"

"She may have been trying to get out of the organisation. They couldn't risk her spilling the beans."

"Maybe, but we won't know until we can track down Campbell and bring him in for questioning."

CHAPTER FIFTY-ONE

Geneva, Switzerland

Zinzli and his men had covered every bespoke tailor's in Geneva, Zurich and Bern. It was highly unlikely that such a business would exist outside the cities. So far their investigations had been fruitless. Holding the receiver in one hand, he sipped a cup of scalding coffee with the other. Bastien Zinzli was a patient man; meticulous, methodical and cautious. A man who could be trusted to get things right. That's what made him a good detective. He was waiting for information from Inspector Pascal Gaudet in Paris. He put down the coffee when the fax machine beeped. Quickly, he scanned the pages.

Gaudet had tracked down the shop using the photofit he had sent him. They only specialised in bespoke suits using the finest cloth; a bit like Saville Row in London.

> *'Campbell went in to order a suit quite recently. One of the staff vaguely remembered taking his measurements, but his recollection was hazy due to a hangover after a party the night before.*
>
> *There was also a seamstress who gave a positive identification. Apparently, she couldn't take her eyes off him, because he was so striking and charming. But there was something about the way he looked at*

her; something about his eyes that frightened her. The customer didn't use the name Alex Campbell. As far as the seamstress was concerned he was a Frenchman. He spoke the language fluently with a very cultured accent. He paid a deposit under the name of Pierre Fournier.'

Zinzli knocked on his Chief Inspector's door and went in without waiting for a response. Dreher looked up enquiringly, twiddling the Mont Blanc fountain pen Sophia had given him for Christmas.

"That's the gist of it, sir." Zinzli handed over the fax. "From the description given by the valet and barman at the Hilton, Gaudet thinks it may be our man."

"Are you sure the seamstress was positive about him being French? It's possible Campbell could be posing under a false name and different nationality.

"Absolutely positive. He ordered two suits in the same fine mohair, one with a waistcoat. He didn't give an address, only his name and mobile phone number to contact him when the garments were ready for collection. Other than that there have been no sightings of him in Paris."

"Have there been any sightings of him in Geneva or the Bernese Oberland?"

"No, sir."

"What reason would he have to use a false name?" Dreher tapped his lips with the pen. "Certainly not to buy a suit."

"Why would he go to the Bernese Oberland?" Zinzli interjected.

"A man of a similar description was reported to the police in the Interlaken area a few weeks ago," he lied. "A young woman claims he tried to assault her. It's worth a try. Do you ski, Bastien?"

"Yes, my grandfather taught me as a child."

"How would you like to do a bit of skiing in the Interlaken area over the weekend? Take Dupont with you; a couple of friends on a weekend away from the wives. Don't attempt to question anybody. Just keep your eyes and ears open. And don't tell anyone where you're going."

"But sir, what will I tell Dupont?"

"Leave that to me. I'll tell him there's been a sighting of Campbell in the area, but that it's surveillance only. No contact with the suspect, under *any* circumstances, is that clear?"

Looking very confused Zinzli headed for the door then stopped, his hand on the door handle.

"You *can* trust me, sir," he said.

"I know, with my life, but for now *you* will have to trust me on this."

Zinzli nodded and quietly closed the door behind him.

All Zinzli needed to know was that they were on the track of a murderer who had flown from Britain to Switzerland. Sighing, Dreher rested his arms on the desk. He would have to confide in him, but he couldn't tell him everything, not yet. Not until they had more information about the organisation in the Alps. First he would speak to Conrad and Wallace. In the meantime he needed Zinzli to keep an eye on the hotel where Foley and Bateman had been staying.

CHAPTER FIFTY-TWO

Bernese Oberland, Switzerland

Feathery flakes of snow floated down like gossamer, settling on pavements and cars as Zinzli negotiated the Hoheweg. In the distance, dark clouds moved ominously across the Jungfrau Joch. A light dusting of snow covered the pavements outside the Victoria Jungfrau Grand Hotel. The hotel where Ethan Bateman and Foley had stayed.

"This will cost a small fortune," Dupont remarked, noting the plush foyer of the five-star hotel.

"Dreher said that Campbell wouldn't stay in a cheap hotel. It's not his style. Don't worry about it. He has to justify the expense, not us."

Even though they were booked into a standard room, it was plush enough to put a smug look on Dupont's face. His sergeant was a decent man, good with the grunt work, but not over-endowed with brains or investigative skills. Zinzli hadn't questioned the reasons Dreher had given him for their trip, but he felt certain that there was more to it than he had been told. Usually, surveillance meant dreary hours sitting cramped up in an unmarked car, not staying in a plush hotel.

He hadn't told his wife he was going skiing, only that they were following a suspect. She wouldn't have prepared the sausage-filled baguettes he scoffed on the journey if she knew he was going off on what she thought was a 'jolly'.

"Let's go down to the bar," Zinzli suggested. "We can have a quiet drink while we look around."

"You don't have to ask me twice," Dupont replied.

"Remember, we're on duty. This weekend isn't for pleasure."

"A couple of drinks won't hurt. Besides it would look odd if we just sat there with lemonade."

"Okay," Zinzli conceded, "but stay sober. We're here to work. Dreher will be on our backs Monday morning looking for results."

In the foyer a waiter stood sentinel over a table filled with glasses of champagne, handing them out as people passed into the lounge bar. He raised an eyebrow at Dupont when he reached out to take a glass. Zinzli nudged him and shook his head.

"It's for the conference members, idiot! They're all wearing lapel badges."

"They wouldn't miss one," Dupont complained.

The lounge area was crowded with men in dark business suits and women in smart cocktail dresses. Talking animatedly, they quaffed champagne as though it had just been invented. Zinzli scanned the group looking for anyone who resembled the photofit picture in his wallet. They threaded their way through the mass to the bar and grabbed two stools.

"*Zwei bier, bitte,*"

The barman poured two beers and placed a dish of roasted peanuts down in front of them. Dupont immediately grabbed a handful and stuffed them into his mouth. Still munching he asked,

"What time is dinner?"

"Let's give it a little while. We'll wait until this lot have left. Just keep your eyes peeled," Zinzli answered impatiently.

Forty-five minutes later, people started drifting out of the lounge into the foyer. A plump, bespectacled man ushered them towards the glittering La Salle de Versailles. Zinzli casually walked along searching the crowd for any sign of Campbell. He caught a glimpse of glittering chandeliers and round tables with pristine white tablecloths set for dinner.

Only five people remained in the bar, mostly casually dressed. Two middle-aged women, heads together in deep conversation, a man sitting alone reading a magazine and a dreamy-eyed young couple holding hands. Zinzli sighed and puffed out his cheeks.

"This is a waste of time. Campbell may not even be in Switzerland. Come on, let's eat."

Dupont was off the stool and heading for the dining room before Zinzli had finished his sentence.

"We could show the photofit at reception. The doorman may recognise him," Dupont suggested.

"Dreher doesn't want us to arouse suspicions at the moment,"

"I don't get it."

"Neither do I," Zinzli muttered.

After dinner they drove up as far as the funicular at the foot of the Harder Kulm and back down the Hoheweg.

"We'll have a better chance of spotting him if we walk," Zinzli said, pulling into a small car park.

Tourists wrapped up against the cold in padded ski jackets and brightly-coloured scarves ambled along the street, occasionally stopping to gaze in a shop window. Expensive watches, clocks, wood carvings and tablecloths vied with cheap souvenirs in neighbouring stores. Models of the Jungfrau, tin cable cars, handkerchiefs embroidered with edelweiss, Swiss Army knives, postcards and various tat. Across the road, at the edge of the green, golden light spilled from the Schuh restaurant. A few stalwarts huddled outside close to the heaters, sipping drinks and eating the restaurant's famous gateaux.

Suddenly, Zinzli nudged Dupont in the ribs and nodded towards a man staring at some lethal-looking hunting knives in a shop window. His face was slightly distorted by the artificial lighting of the window display. Moving closer, he surreptitiously studied him as he pretended to admire a cuckoo clock. Aware of the presence at his shoulder the man looked into the mirror at the back of the window display and stared at Zinzli. For a fleeting moment a pair of hard eyes held his gaze.

"Come on, let's go back to the hotel for a brandy. I'm freezing!" Zinzli complained. "That's him. I'm sure of it," he said as soon as they were out of earshot.

"What makes you so certain?"

"He was very good-looking, reddish-brown hair, right height and build."

"I'm not so sure," Dupont replied doubtfully.

"His eyes, that's what makes me certain. The seamstress described him as handsome, but his eyes terrified her; made her shudder. If it's not him I'll buy you dinner when we get back to Geneva."

They tailed him down the street, past the Hotel Beausite, and over the river bridge. He seemed to be making for the car park behind the supermarket. The exact spot where Zinzli had left his old Volkswagen. Suddenly, the man ducked into a discount alcohol store.

They waited until he re-emerged carrying a bag and followed him over the bridge to the car park. He jumped into a black 4 x 4 and drove out onto the road.

"That was a stroke of luck!" Zinzli exclaimed, engaging the clutch.

They tailed him at a safe distance, relying on the popular make of car to provide them with some cover. There were lots of Volkswagens in the area, but he knew that sooner or later, the driver of the 4 x 4 would spot them.

"He's heading towards Lauterbrünnen," Dupont said.

They were two cars behind the 4 x 4. It was travelling very fast now, over the speed limit. It slowed down as they reached Lauterbrünnen and drove sedately through the town. Once outside, it raced down the road to Stechelberg. Open grassland on either side of the darkened road stretched out towards the foot of the mountains. Lights twinkled high above them from chalets set into the mountainside.

Zinzli peered through the darkness at the speeding vehicle. Suddenly, a flickering light up ahead caught his eye. At the same time the 4 x 4 veered off the road onto a side track. It headed across the fields towards a dark shape silhouetted against the moonlit sky.

"It's a helicopter!" Dupont exclaimed. "He's heading straight for it!"

Zinzli turned off his headlights and rolled slowly forward. He stopped about two hundred metres away. Two men jumped out of the 4 x 4 and ran towards the chopper. In seconds, the helicopter took off and turned its nose towards the Alps. Zinzli and Dupont watched it rise up and disappear over the peaks until the blinking light disappeared.

Suddenly, the 4 x 4 turned full circle and roared across the fields towards them.

Slamming the Volkswagen into gear, he shot off down the road looking in his rear-view mirror for the pursuing vehicle. All he saw were its red tail lights disappearing into the gloom.

"That was a close call. I could have sworn he'd seen us," Dupont said.

"There's something very odd going on here," Zinzli muttered. "This isn't a landing place. Why doesn't he use a legitimate heliport? Besides, it's lunacy to fly over the Alps without contacting air traffic control, especially at night in adverse weather conditions. Something smells very fishy to me, Dupont. We'll get back to Geneva first thing tomorrow morning and report to Dreher."

CHAPTER FIFTY-THREE

Geneva, Switzerland

Zinzli waited for Dreher to finish his telephone call. After replacing the receiver he sat back in his chair. For a few seconds he swung from side to side tapping his lips with his finger. He had just finished speaking with Jack Conrad in London. He was flying back out to talk to Sophia about the masked man he had encountered in the facility in the mountains. She was an expert profiler, skilled at compiling psychological profiles of criminals.

It should have been a police profiler, but it was vital that knowledge of the Generalissimo was kept within a tight circle. If it leaked out and the media got hold of it, it could cause a panic. He swung around and gazed directly at Zinzli.

"I know I can trust you implicitly, Bastien, but I must emphasise that what I am about to tell you is top secret. It is restricted to only a handful of people. I had to get clearance from the most senior level in Interpol and British Intelligence."

"That's understood, sir."

"We believe the man you were following is linked to an organisation known to British Intelligence as the Black Militia."

"Black Militia? I don't understand."

As the story unfolded Zinzli couldn't believe what he

was hearing. British Military Intelligence had been sourcing this organisation for some time, yet the Swiss police knew nothing about it. Dreher had kept quiet about Wallace's involvement other than that he was investigating murders on his patch.

"Not even Wallace knew from the outset that there was a link between the bodies found in Shropshire and Conrad's investigations. Campbell, the man you were looking for in Interlaken, was also linked to the murder of Joanne Howard aka Anya Sharapova. There are a lot of questions hanging in the air, Bastien. Why did he murder her? What was her role in the Black Militia? What had she done to deserve her execution?"

"This Black Militia, sir; are they mercenaries?"

"Some of them are probably just working for the money. Others may be on a power trip like the Generalissimo. It's hardly an army: more like a small force of discontents and potential terrorists attacking infrastructures through cyberspace."

Dreher suspected there was something more sinister involved than merely hacking into computers. It must be something they had been planning for a very long time.

"What do you want me to do, sir?"

"Go back to Interlaken for a few days. Keep your eyes peeled for any further sightings of Alex Campbell. Don't try to apprehend him or challenge him in any way. Just watch, wait; follow him if necessary. Report back to me personally on anything you consider unusual. On no account give any details to anyone else. Is that clear?"

"What about Sergeant Dupont? He's bound to ask questions."

"You need some backup with you just in case. Tell him that Campbell is suspected of drug-dealing, of smuggling the stuff into Britain. On no account let him know the real reason you're staking him out. By the way, Zinzli, I think you can book into a cheaper hotel this time."

CHAPTER FIFTY-FOUR

Shropshire, England

Wallace's mobile jangled in his pocket. He gulped down the dregs of a mug of stone-cold coffee.

"Wallace!" he barked.

"You sound as though you've had a bad night," Conrad laughed at the other end.

"It's just this bloody case. It's so frustrating! What's up?"

"Dreher tells me that his men spotted Campbell in Interlaken. They followed him to a field just outside Lauterbrünnen where he was picked up by a helicopter. It flew off over the mountains and disappeared in the direction of the installation I uncovered. I'll have to go back up there again."

"You can't go back up there! They'll be on the lookout for you!"

Conrad sighed. "There's no other alternative unless *you* are willing to come out and fish around; see what you can find out about this Militia. I know it's asking a great deal."

"It's a far better option. They don't know what I look like or that I'm involved."

Wallace was ex-military intelligence. He knew the drill and had all the right qualifications. An engineering degree, expertise in military weapons, computer-assisted design and rapid prototyping. He was the perfect candidate. IMIC would create a whole new identity for him. Sexed-up army records, false passport and civilian history.

"Take the afternoon flight from Birmingham tomorrow. You'll find a false passport in your pocket before you reach the check-in desk. Come to Dreher's place in Thun. We can work out the finer details there. There'll be a hire car waiting for you at Geneva International Airport under the name Alan Munro. Don't worry, we've squared it with your Chief Constable."

Wallace heard a click before the line went dead. Quickly, he rang Butler to tell him he would be on special leave until further notice.

"Contact me via my mobile if it's urgent. I want your complete cooperation on this, no questions asked. Is that clear? All you need to know is that I'm working on strict orders from the Chief Constable, but keep that under your hat."

Wallace smiled to himself. Crew Cut Charlie would be furious, especially as he was being kept in the dark. He imagined him spluttering with indignation when the CC ordered him to back off. He stuffed the phone back in his pocket. A thrill of excitement coursed through his veins. Grabbing his car keys, he almost bounced over the drive to his car. A wide grin spread over his face. He couldn't wait to get back into harness again.

CHAPTER FIFTY-FIVE

Thunersee, Bernese Oberland

The plane landed in fog, concealing the airport buildings until they were almost upon them. Dim runway lights glowed in the gloom as they taxied to a stop. Impatiently, Wallace waited for the sign to change to green and unfastened his safety belt. He was travelling light, as instructed. His overnight bag contained a change of underwear, socks, a shirt and an extra sweater. Everything else would be supplied when he got to Dreher's house in Thun.

Barely able to contain his impatience, he shuffled down the aisle behind a line of chattering students rigged out in brightly-coloured skiing outfits. He showed his false passport and drifted towards the exit. Once outside, he headed for the Hertz car park and picked up the Volvo estate Conrad had organised for him. It was a hundred and ninety-one kilometres to Thun. At least two hours driving; more if the fog worsened.

Three hours later he pulled into the driveway of Dreher's chalet on the shores of Lake Thun. The house was a blaze of lights. The sound of children's voices and laughter reached his ears. As he walked from his car the door swung open spilling light onto the snow.

"Ben, come in before you freeze to death," Dreher urged, quickly closing the door. "Jack is already here. We're having a drink while Sophia finishes preparing dinner."

Smells of cooking hit Wallace's nostrils as he walked past the kitchen. He couldn't resist poking his head round the door. Sophia looked elegant as usual.

"I hope you're hungry, Ben?"

"Famished. I've been dreaming about your cooking all the way over on the plane."

Sophia fluttered her eyelashes flirtatiously and blew him a kiss. With a wicked grin she turned back to the stove.

In the living room an enormous log fire burned in the grate throwing flickers of orange light round the comfortable room. Wallace turned his back to it and luxuriously warmed his buttocks until Sophia announced their meal was ready.

After dinner Dreher ushered the two men into the sitting room and settled round the fire with large brandies.

"We already know Joanne Howard and Colin Lynes are linked to the Black Militia," Conrad said. "I'm convinced that Alex Campbell is also involved." Dreher and Wallace nodded in agreement. "Gilbert from MI6 confirmed that Colin Lynes was summarily executed by the Russian Secret Service for diverting information passed on by Bruce Foley to this self-styled Generalissimo. Pearce believes there will be an attempt to interfere with business and industrial infrastructures through cyberspace. From what I've seen the facility in the Alps is gearing up to create maximum impact."

"It's not a new concept," Dreher intervened. "A few years ago the Norwegians discovered that their oil, gas and water supplies were being targeted. GCHQ intercept traffic and computer viruses targeting our infrastructure on a regular basis. The US shared our concerns about this for some time, but they tend to shrug it off for the public. We need to find out more about the Generalissimo. He may be Russian, probably with links to the Russian Secret Service, maybe the old KGB."

"Lynes was a 'sleeper' for a long time. He knew what happens to agents who double-cross the Russian Secret Service. There must have been huge rewards for him to take such a chance," Conrad said.

"What puzzles me," Dreher mused, "is where the Generalissimo gets the money to fund the Black Militia. Could it be from a foreign power?"

"Ben is going to attempt to infiltrate the organisation. Tomorrow, he'll travel to Interlaken and hang out in the hotel bar where Campbell was last seen. Perhaps he can find some answers."

Dreher leaned forward, a thoughtful look on his face. He hadn't told Sophia about the Generalissimo or the Black Militia. She had drawn up a psychological profile based on an imaginary scenario. It seemed to fit with Conrad's assessment. The Militia was in awe of him. Even his trusted aides were terrified of any transgression that could put them into his bad books.

"Sophia believes the Generalissimo has all the classic symptoms of megalomania. If her evaluation is correct it could be very dangerous, Ben. Don't take any unnecessary risks."

"The term 'Generalissimo' bothers me," Conrad mused. "I've been doing a bit of research of my own. We've got the obvious ones like Franco in Spain, China's Chang Kai-shek and Stalin. Hitler also displayed the same characteristics."

"Where are you going with this?" Wallace asked.

"They are not the same as the traditional Imperial Russian Generalissimos. There were only four of them. The most well known was Alexander Suvorov. The ideology changed when Joseph Stalin became the fifth Generalissimo. The first and last one of the Soviet Union."

"You think this Generalissimo has modelled himself on Stalin?" Dreher asked incredulously.

"He's just as cold-blooded and murderous, but our Generalissimo is more cerebral... and patient. He's waited a long time to achieve his ambitions. Pearce has harnessed all possible sources of information. It's stalemate unless Ben comes up with something more specific."

"Zinzli is convinced that the man he saw was Campbell," Dreher said. "He's in the picture, but say nothing in front of Dupont. If he turns up in the hotel Zinzli will mark Campbell out. Now, gentlemen, let's enjoy our drinks before we turn in."

CHAPTER FIFTY-SIX

Interlaken, Bernese Oberland

Wallace sat on a bar stool sipping his lager while he watched the entrance. Zinzli walked in with Dupont and sat at a nearby table. Casually, he started a conversation with a young couple sitting next to him, feigning interest in their skiing vacation. To an observer he was just another tourist.

Two hours later they were still in the bar. *Damn it! Nothing is going to happen here tonight. We would be better off patrolling the main street like last time.* They were about to leave when a tall, elegant man entered the bar. Immediately, Zinzli picked up a coaster and started to tap it against his chin, his eyes following the man. Wallace felt a ripple of excitement. It was Campbell. The stranger settled himself onto a stool, ordered a whisky and soda and eyed the room. Wallace smiled inwardly. Perhaps he was looking for talent. He certainly had the looks to attract women. There was an animal magnetism about the man. It was only when their eyes met that the underlying cruelty revealed itself.

"Excuse me," Wallace said. "Would you mind passing the peanuts?"

"Certainly," the man answered in faultless English.

Wallace's mobile shrilled in his pocket. He pulled it out, listened for a few moments, and snapped it shut.

"Damn!" he exclaimed, knocking back his drink. "Have you got any English newspapers?" he asked the barman.

"Yes, but they're two days old." He pointed to a rack near the entrance.

Wallace marched over, pulled out the paper, and returned to his seat. He flicked through the pages. Staring at a page he muttered,

"I'll get the bastards for this!"

Alex Campbell watched Wallace intently, his eyes flicking to the open page. A picture of Wallace stared out at him under the headline, 'Army Officer Compromised in Drugs Scandal.' Swiftly, he read down the column of print.

> Captain Alan Munro brought dishonour to his regiment after being found drunk at a lap-dancing club in London. The club, allegedly frequented by drug dealers, has been under police surveillance for some time. An undercover officer witnessed drugs changing hands.
>
> Before he could make an arrest a fight broke out when one of the male customers tried to pull a dancer off the stage. One man was seriously injured after being hit over the head with a chair. Another man died on the way to hospital.
>
> Munro, along with three others, was arrested for possession of small quantities of Class A drugs. He denied the charges insisting the drugs had been planted on him during the fight.
>
> He had no previous convictions. The magistrate gave him a suspended jail sentence of six months. Subsequently, he was court-martialled and dishonourably discharged.

"Is that you?" Campbell asked enquiringly.

"I was fitted up," Wallace snarled. "Fifteen years in the army… due for promotion. Not a stain on my character. It's not *bloody* fair!"

Campbell raised an eyebrow quizzically, inviting Wallace to tell him his story. It seemed strange to him that an officer with a long-standing career should be thrown out for one isolated offence. Still, using drugs was very stupid unless it was to enhance physical pleasure. Not that he would use drugs of any kind of course, but the girls he used were different. He smiled to himself.

"Have a drink, something a bit stronger – whisky?"

Wallace shrugged his shoulders indifferently and took a long swig of his drink. Campbell ordered fresh drinks and motioned for Wallace to join him at a secluded table set against the back wall.

"You were framed, you say?"

"Like I said, the cocaine was planted on me. In my line of work you can't afford to be on drugs. Look, I've said enough. Just let it go, okay?"

Campbell held up his hands in a gesture of defeat, but his curiosity had been sharpened. He wanted to know more about his new friend. A few more drinks and Munro would spill the beans. Campbell signalled to the waiter to bring a bottle of single malt. He replenished Wallace's glass and sat back waiting. He didn't want to arouse any suspicions by prodding him too much.

"Dishonourably discharged!" Wallace banged his fist down on the bar top. "A security risk, that's what they called me! When I think of all the years of work designing weapons for those ungrateful bastards, I could kill them!"

Campbell's heart skipped a beat. This man could be very useful. He was angry, disgraced, cast aside without a salary or pension. He was ripe for recruitment. He looked at Wallace sympathetically.

"What are you going to do now?"

"Find work somewhere, probably in computers; maybe design work, if I can get it without bloody references."

"I may be able to help there. The company I work for is looking for new blood. People with design and computer skills like yours." A flicker of interest sprang into Wallace's eyes. "The president of the company likes to give people a second chance. I'm the managing director, his right-hand man. If I recommend you, it will be enough. Have another drink."

Campbell pulled out his mobile phone while he walked out into the foyer. He spoke rapidly into it, snapped it shut, and sauntered back to the table.

"It's all set. I have arranged an interview with our head of technology for tomorrow morning at ten o'clock. Look for a black 4 x 4 at the entrance. The driver will take you to a helicopter and fly you to our computer facility."

"Why are you doing all this? I hardly know you," Wallace said suspiciously.

"I think you've been dealt a rotten hand. Besides, the same thing happened to me. I was deprived of a highly paid career for an isolated incident." His hard eyes glittered. "I wanted revenge. Do you want revenge, Alan?"

Wallace's face hardened, his lips set in a grim line. He looked at Campbell searchingly as though trying to fathom his motive in offering a stranger a job. Through gritted teeth he snarled.

"Oh yes, I want revenge."

Wallace looked at the ground receding below him then concentrated on the mountains looming ahead. He had to make a mental note of every little landmark, anything different from what Conrad had told him.

Campbell had said very little about himself the night before. Wallace, pretending to be wallowing in self-pity, had deliberately not asked. He would find out soon enough. Ten minutes later the helicopter banked and started to lose height. He looked down and saw a large patch of grass sprinkled with small stones and shale. Suddenly, the grass started to move upwards and sideways revealing a gaping cavity.

"What the hell is going on?" he shouted over the pilot's shoulder. There was no response. "Those stones haven't moved. They're stuck to the grass." Suddenly, a platform rose up out of the hole and clicked into place. "It's rigged like a bloody aircraft carrier!" he yelled, as the helicopter settled on the metal platform. The pilot switched off the engine, waited for the blades to stop rotating then spoke into his headset.

Wallace felt movement as the platform started to lower into the ground. As they descended, the cavity doors above his head closed and locked into place. Clever, very clever indeed. Nothing could be seen from the valley below or from the air. Anyone flying overhead would see nothing more than an area of grass. This was a big operation; of that he was certain.

A black-clad man, wearing a balaclava and a yellow armband, opened the door of the helicopter and beckoned him out. He pointed him towards a metal door and followed him through it into the same eerily-lit chamber that Conrad had described. *This is it!* Wallace took note of the workers bent over banks of computers, security staff and others sporting various coloured armbands.

Another figure approached him and guided him towards a small area partitioned off at the side of the computers. Inside, a uniformed man, wearing a red armband with five black crystal motifs, waved him to a chair.

"I'm head of computer facilities known as CE1 – Computer Expert 1. We don't use names here." He spoke with an English accent. "I'll be interviewing you and assessing your expertise."

"Why are you wearing those balaclavas and why are you all dressed in black?"

"It's essential to preserve our anonymity. You are not one of us yet."

"What's the big idea? I thought this was a proper interview?"

"It is, I assure you, but our work is highly secret. You can understand that can't you? After all, you were working on projects for the British military."

"They didn't cover their faces. You might as well be wearing a bloody burkha!"

The security guard edged towards him in a threatening manner and stood behind his chair. CEI waved him away.

He was subjected to an intense assessment of his skills, experience and work he had done for the military. When he had finished CEI tapped something into his computer. A precise, digitally-altered voice spoke directly to Wallace.

"We have been observing your interview. There is no doubt you are highly skilled. However, you will not fit into our organisation if you cannot be trusted. We require total commitment to the job and unquestioning loyalty. If you comply your rewards will be great, if you don't… " The statement was left hanging in the air.

"I don't understand."

"It's very simple. You have seen our facility. Helping you get your revenge is important to us. That way we can be sure of your loyalty – correct?" Wallace stared into the webcam and nodded. "We only reveal our faces to those who are members of the Militia. Strength lies in our secrecy."

Wallace's mind was racing. If he blew it now, he was a dead man. He clenched his fists and stared into the screen, his lips set in a grim line.

"I want to give those bastards what they deserve," he hissed through clenched teeth.

"Excellent," the voice purred from the computer. "We will speak again when you have been acclimatised."

CEI nodded to the security guard. He motioned to Wallace to follow him towards a steel door behind the bank of computers. It led to a rectangular room similar to an army ordinance store. The shelves were stacked with black trousers, jackets, balaclavas, boots, blankets and other items. Arms full of clothing, he was taken to his room.

He noted the number of rooms leading off the corridor. This was obviously part of the original hotel. An open door revealed a sparsely furnished dormitory with six beds. Wallace caught a glimpse of a shower cubicle and lavatory.

All the external windows had been bricked up. The only light came from discs set in the ceiling and reading lamps on the bedside cabinets. Another series of single rooms, either side of the corridor, displayed a black crystal on the door outlined in either red or blue. Computers and administrators, he guessed. The security guard motioned Wallace into a similar room. It was just as basic as the dormitories: a chair occupying one corner, a table with a booted-up laptop and a curtained-off wardrobe.

He changed into his uniform and sat down in front of the laptop. Before he touched the keys the Generalissimo's voice pierced the room from somewhere above him.

"The laptop is for you to work when you are off shift. It is on a network. It is not for personal use except for entertainment. Everything you do will be monitored so I wouldn't advise you to try to contact anybody outside the facility. Report to the computer area where you will be allocated your duties."

Wallace marched back to the bank of computers in the main chamber. He listened carefully while CE1 ran through a complex set of instructions.

"Today you'll shadow CE5, but tomorrow you'll start to work alone."

Wallace's eyes took in every screen as he was directed to his place. Periodically, the screen switched from lists of statistics to a map with pinpoint lights. Conrad had mentioned Beijing had been on board. Now Tokyo and Ottawa were also ready, but for what? What was the timescale?

*

Wallace had been working non-stop for three days, decoding information that was coming through at an alarming rate. He needed more precise information of the Generalissimo's intentions. How exactly was he going to make the cyber attack?

It was obvious that the man on the computer next to him was Caucasian. When he tried to have a joke with him he just grunted and turned away. He was luckier with the guy on his other side.

"Where do they all come from?" Wallace asked, indicating the computer workers.

"All over the world. Some don't say much, especially the Chinese and Russians, but there are a few Americans like me and a few Brits."

"What's the Generalissimo planning? When will it happen?"

"Only CE1 knows that; the rest of us will be told when they're ready to move, but it's soon. A few weeks at most, but when it does we'll be in clover, man."

The Generalissimo was clever. According to the Yank, everything was on a need-to-know basis. When the plan came to fruition the Militia would be disbanded. Everybody, except the Generalissimo and his closest aides, would be sent packing with enough money to live the life of Riley.

"Most of the guys here have an axe to grind. See that stocky guy behind you. He was in Chinese intelligence. I was kicked out of the Pentagon – security risk, so they claimed. I was framed," he spat vehemently, "but those bastards will pay!"

Every day Wallace watched computer operators send thousands of hostile e-mails round the world in an attempt to destabilise government departments. But they were only playing, keeping up the pressure until they mounted the ultimate attack through cyberspace. It was on the fifth day that Wallace made a breakthrough.

"I want you to take a look at this," CE1 said, waving him over to his console. "It's a new type of weapon the Americans are developing – high-powered and lethal. Our hackers have infiltrated a facility in the Nevada desert. We managed to access the blueprints. That's where you come in. We want you to assemble it on screen. Show us how it works before we sell it on."

So that's how they fund the Militia, Wallace thought, *by selling blueprints to the highest bidder. That's why they were after Ethan Bateman. It was his top-secret facility in Nevada.*

Wallace had to find out more about the operation. He didn't have long to wait. His opportunity came the following day when he was summoned into the presence of the Generalissimo himself. Conrad had warned him about the weird mask. *Weird is right,* he thought. *He looks like a warmed up corpse.*

"You have done well. I am impressed with your skills," the digitally-altered voice said. "They will make a great contribution to our cause."

Wallace didn't respond. He decided to wait for the Generalissimo to offer more information.

"You are not an inquisitive man?"

Wallace shrugged. "No, as long as they pay for what they've done to me, I couldn't care less."

"CE1 mentioned Operation Black Crystal to you?"

Wallace felt a stab of alarm, but maintained his calm stance. The Generalissimo smiled his hideous smile.

"So, what is Black Crystal?"

"A killer virus. Once it infects a computer it will wreck systems all over the world. We can do whatever we like. All their secrets will be ours. First of all we will cripple their critical infrastructure. Nuclear power stations, oil and gas installations, electricity grids, banks; all will be destabilised. We will be in complete control of the G8 countries, then the

G20. Eventually the entire world." He shrugged. "Not even The Pentagon and GCHQ will be able to stop us. We will have access to highly volatile military secrets. The rest will be simple."

"When will this happen?"

"Soon, very soon."

I'll have to work fast, Wallace thought as he returned to his position. As far-fetched as it sounded it wasn't outside the bounds of possibility. Could Operation Black Crystal be stopped once it was set in motion? Time was running out for him. He had to act swiftly and decisively to get the information back to Breakdancer. If only he knew when the attack would take place. For the moment he was powerless to do anything other than carry out his work tasks. Once he had gained their confidence perhaps they would start talking.

CHAPTER FIFTY-SEVEN

London, England

Clive Pearce, aka Breakdancer, crossed his long legs on the highly polished desktop. He leaned back rubbing his chin thoughtfully. Characteristically, he closed his eyes, appearing to be asleep.

"We've got a madman on our hands, Jack. Not your average off-his-rocker nutcase. Our 'sleeper' in Moscow has been digging around. The only man capable of this plot is Plushenko, but he's dead; or is he?"

Conrad raised his eyebrows sceptically. "There's no way Plushenko is alive. He was killed in East Berlin in 1989."

"The body was unidentifiable."

"But the KGB would have investigated the accident. They wouldn't leave any stone unturned."

"There were no stones to turn, Jack. The boat caught fire, exploded. Only a few charred remains were found. All that was left was some debris floating on the surface. Only bits of the body were recovered."

"I still think the KGB would have sniffed around a bit more."

"It was only days after the Wall came down. It was pretty chaotic in the East. They had more important things to think about than Plushenko."

Pearce pushed a buff file marked 'Highly Confidential

– Eyes Only' across the desk. He settled back in his chair, slowly swinging from side to side. Conrad flipped it open and read the first page. By the time he had finished reading the file, his face was set like granite.

"If this is genuine we're in big trouble, Clive."

"Oh, it's genuine all right. Straight out of the old KGB files. Plushenko had become too much of a risk to them. His 'accidental' death was planned by the Soviets. Our mole thinks that Plushenko got wind of what they were up to, knocked off someone else, and substituted the body along with identity papers and other personal items."

Conrad looked at the file again. Everything pointed to it. Rumours had been rife regarding the 'accident'.

"Plushenko always carried a hip flask of water engraved with his initials: P.L.P. – Pavel Leonid Plushenko. The flask was found washed up on the bank. No further investigations necessary."

Even in the West, Plushenko was known for his cruelty and delusions of grandeur. He had no qualms about torturing suspects. He was completely paranoid, a cold-blooded, vicious killer. He believed he was untouchable. The file showed that the KGB had ordered his elimination.

"Has Wallace been in touch yet?" Pearce asked.

"Not yet. We know he's up in the facility. Zinzli followed him and watched him taking off in a helicopter. It's been five days now. Wallace is very experienced, but I'm getting worried. I'm going back out to Geneva in the morning to meet with Dreher."

"I'm keeping a lid on the police investigations into Foley and Joanne Howard on Wallace's patch. They suspect a link between Macaleer and Foley, but that's as far as it goes. I want to keep it that way."

If the real facts got into the press it would create panic across the globe. They didn't know what kind of attack was planned. Until they did, they were powerless to do anything to stop it. Their only hope was Wallace.

"Like it or not, Clive, if Wallace hasn't been in touch within the next few days I'm going back up into the mountains to find him."

Pearce sighed and knuckled his eyes. Black shadows enhanced his gaunt appearance. His cheekbones stuck out like razor blades. Suddenly, he looked all of his fifty-eight years. He had been in the business too long. He nodded, knowing his assent made little difference to Conrad.

"The CIA have men out there investigating Ethan Bateman. Try not to step on their toes, Jack."

"I'll do whatever has to be done," Conrad replied, heading for the outer office.

Pearce stared after him wondering whether he would ever see him or Wallace alive again.

CHAPTER FIFTY-EIGHT

Manhattan, New York City

Baranski opened the small suitcase. Inside was a uniform, the same kind worn by security at the United Nations. He unrolled a cloth-covered bundle and smiled when he saw the long-barrelled Magnum. He screwed on the silencer, pointed the unloaded gun at the curtained window, and squeezed the trigger. Yes, this would definitely do the job. For the next few minutes he loaded and unloaded the gun, checking how much time it took. Speed would be vital to his mission. After a final check he packed it into an overnight bag and made his way down to the foyer. Rather than take the risk of being recognised by a cab driver, he walked from East 48th Street to the United Nations building.

He pushed his way through the crowd watching the delegates' limousines driving into the United Nations. The conference was in the General Assembly Building. Security was intense around the American President and other major world leaders since 9/11. They were surrounded by bodyguards. It would be difficult to get a good shot. His mission was to assassinate one of the other delegates. It didn't matter which one as long as it created as much chaos and fear as possible.

His contact had supplied him with a rota of guards who worked in or around the General Assembly Building. At the end of every shift he walked along the line of colourful flags sporting various disguises. It didn't take him long to spot the man he wanted. A specific type, a loner, not one who stuck to habits like drinking in the same place every night after work. Someone with few friends who had recently joined the workforce. Baranski followed him to Grand Central Station and on to Brooklyn. Keeping a safe distance he trailed the man until he climbed the steps of an old Brownstone block of apartments. Bishop was living on borrowed time.

*

Larry Bishop pushed open the door of his bedsit in Brooklyn and reached for the light switch. He didn't have time to struggle. Before he closed the door behind him the knife slashed his throat, severing his windpipe. Baranski dragged him into the bathroom and left him pouring out his lifeblood onto the grimy, tiled floor. Blood-speckled foam seeped from his mouth. His dead eyes bulged with terror and shock.

Out of the darkness an old cat meowed, looking for its expected meal. It padded through the blood and climbed onto Bishop's chest leaving bloody paw prints on his jacket. The cat's tongue rasped against the lifeless face, anxious to be fed. When it sidled against his legs Baranski picked it up and snapped its neck like a brittle twig.

"You'll never need to meow for your food again," he laughed.

Baranski felt good, revitalised. The thrill of the hunt, the feeling of absolute power over another human being filled him with exhilaration. Cold, detached; remorse was alien to him. All he felt was an intense satisfaction, almost glee at the prospect of another kill, but the next one wouldn't be so enjoyable for him. He liked to be 'hands on'.

He peered round the door of the bedsit into the corridor. Flaking, sickly green paint, interspersed with patches of black mildew, covered the walls. All the battered doors were closed, but he had to be careful. If anyone was spying through a peephole he was in trouble. The sound of a voice on the metal stairs opposite forced him back inside the bedsit.

He pressed his eye against the peephole and waited. Two middle-aged women, wearing ridiculously short miniskirts and thick make-up, stopped at the top of the stairs. He willed them to move on, but they stood talking and laughing raucously, making obscene comments about some man in the bar where they worked. Eventually, the taller of the two clattered up the stairs to the upper floor calling back,

"See ya later, Nikki."

As soon as they disappeared from view, he lunged out of the bedsit and down the stairs. He emerged onto the pavement letting out a great breath of air. Nobody had seen him go in or out of the building. By the time they discovered Bishop's body, his mission would be completed. With a spring in his step he walked briskly towards the subway.

*

Baranski pulled on the uniform. It was a bit snug, but he could get away with it. He grimaced with discomfort at the tightness of the belt and the weight of the regulation weapon. Some improvements were needed. His hair was too long, but that was easily remedied. Patting a bushy, false moustache into place over his own neat version, he put on a pair of gold-rimmed spectacles. He grinned owlishly into the mirror. *Yes, you'll easily pass for that fool Larry Bishop*, he decided. Now, he would go to work and suss out the area. Bishop had only been employed with security for a few days before he had murdered him, not long enough to form friendships. That's why he had chosen him in the first place. Now he needed time to plan his escape route after the assassination.

Luckily, Bishop's duties were outside, monitoring vehicles and patrolling the area around the General Assembly Building. Baranski wanted a clear shot at the delegates. Once the first one dropped all hell would break loose. That was the specific aim: to create panic and confusion inside and outside the United Nations. Then the brown stuff would hit the fan. Accusations and counter-accusations would be flying thick and fast. Plots by the Russians, cover-ups, CIA investigations. It was enough to keep the Americans busy; so busy they would be unaware of the real attack going on under their very noses until it was too late.

CHAPTER FIFTY-NINE

Bernese Oberland, Switzerland

Wallace wriggled his shoulders to ease his muscles. He had been bending over the computer for hours every day; working on the blueprints stolen from Ethan Bateman's facility in the Nevada Desert. Outwardly, he seemed engrossed in his work, but he was taking note of everything going on around him. The pinpoint light over New York had stopped flickering that morning. One by one, the G8 countries were indicating they were on standby.

There was a sharp tension in the air. Wallace knew that the attack would happen very soon. What were they waiting for? It must be some event on a world level that would act as the catalyst for the attack.

"When will we be ready?" he asked CE1.

He didn't answer as he brushed past Wallace to speak to an operator on the far side of the computer banks.

"I overheard CE1 talking to the Generalissimo's personal aide when I passed by his office," the man next to him whispered. "They're waiting for some meeting in New York. Whatever they've planned will kick off then. It's bound to be big, buddy, very big."

Wallace racked his brains trying to think what could be going on in New York. Suddenly, a news broadcast about world poverty hit him like a lightning bolt. That's it! It must be! Delegates from the G8 nations and a host of other countries would be at the United Nations in three days time. What was the Generalissimo planning? To disrupt the conference, access their computers? A shudder of realisation ran through him. What if they planned an assassination? He had to get out and warn Conrad before it was too late.

*

Conrad glanced at his wristwatch: 07.30 hours. He had started out before daybreak determined to cover as much ground as possible. In the east, pink fingers of light probed the pre-dawn sky. Too early for the cable car, he had travelled to Mürren on a cross-country motorcycle then set out on foot. He was halfway to the facility, ploughing up the mountain through snow that had fallen overnight.

The thin layer of ice underfoot crackled like crisps being crushed in a bag. The air felt rare and pure, so cold it hurt his lungs. No sound except for the occasional plop as snow dropped off one of the straggly pines. An alpine chuff wheeled overhead, dived and disappeared behind an outcrop of rock. Adjusting his snow goggles, he peered up towards the path that led to the old, abandoned hotel. Deep inside the concealed installation Wallace was putting his life on the line. If he had been discovered, he was probably already dead.

Dressed from head to toe in winter camouflage, he knew he was still an easy target for anyone watching from the abandoned hotel. Cautiously, he moved forward using the overhanging rocks and shrubs to conceal his progress. Every few minutes, he stopped and waited for any sign of activity high above him. There was also the Militia helicopter. If that took off they would be likely to spot him and pick him off. He pulled out his satellite phone and punched in Dreher's number.

"I'm almost there." Conscious of the stillness in the air, and the way sound carried in the mountains, he whispered. "Be ready with the chopper when I give you the signal."

"Don't worry, Jack. We're ready."

He retracted the aerial and stuffed the phone back in his pocket. It had a global positioning system that could pinpoint his whereabouts when he was ready for the helicopter. Crouching down behind a fall of rock, he swept the path leading to the facility and the fake stone wall. He waited a few minutes. Still no sign of any movement – so far, so good.

Underneath his winter camouflage, he was wearing black trousers and a black sweater. Around his neck, a black balaclava ready to pull up as soon as he de-suited. He was only a few hundred metres from the facility now. As he scrabbled up the path, he lost his balance on loose shale. The stones trickled noisily in the still air coming to rest up against a large stone, every sound dangerously magnified. He held his breath waiting for a shout from above; nothing, except the faint whine of the wind. Suddenly, he felt slightly giddy and lurched sideways off the path into crisp snow, almost losing his balance. He inhaled deeply in an attempt to steady himself, but it made him even more light-headed. All he needed now was an attack of altitude sickness.

Breathing heavily, he edged upwards until he was close to the fake stone wall. He crouched down low and scurried across to the adjoining rocks. On this side it was easier to climb. He didn't need to use a grapple hook. Using foot and handholds, he hoisted himself up and over the wall.

He landed with a gentle thump amongst the startled goats milling around their winter feed trough.

Keeping low, he edged toward the partially open steel door. It wasn't just luck that he had arrived when the goats were out. He had spent a whole day at a safe vantage point scanning the area, noting their feeding times. Not once had he seen a guard. They were careful to stay out of sight, away from prying eyes. His intention was to get back in the way he had escaped. The door wouldn't be closed until all the goats were back inside. He would only have one shot at disabling the guard before the alarm went off.

He pressed himself against the rock at the side of the door and waited. Standing immobile, the cold cut through his padded jacket. His feet inside the fur-lined boots felt frozen stiff. Suddenly, he heard the familiar call.

"Now then my beauties, let's get you in out of the cold."

On hearing the guard's voice the goats padded towards the warmth of their stalls. Nudging against each other they ambled inside, the guard calling the stragglers by pet names.

As soon as Conrad heard the electronic hum of the door closing he dived in, all his senses alert. The guard didn't have time to turn around before he clubbed him on the back of his skull. He fell to the ground, his head hitting the metal rail of the stalls. The guard's dead eyes were wide open. Blood trickled from his nose and mouth. He dragged the man into the stall nearest the outer door, covered him with straw, and pulled off his black parka.

Stripping off his winter camouflage, he rolled it into a ball and threw it into the nearest stall. Dressed all in black, the balaclava pulled up over his head, he may be able to mingle with the Militia unnoticed. All he needed was enough time to search for Wallace and get them both out of there. He patted the yellow armband, embroidered with three black crystals, he had removed from the security guard. It was just enough seniority to give him a bit of clout. With any luck, he could wander freely around the chamber watching the workers' every move.

Pulling a thin strip of rigid plastic from his pocket Conrad squeezed it through the door under the drop latch. He jerked it upwards expecting the latch to go with it, but it wouldn't budge. *Sod it!* Taking a deep breath he tried again. This time the bar moved an inch or so then stopped. Using all his strength, he jerked the plastic strip up again and held it open with his foot. Muted voices, footsteps and the electronic whirr of machinery came from the main chamber.

Cautiously, he stepped outside, closed the door behind him, and walked down the narrow passage. Hugging the side, he peered round the last bend into the chamber assessing the level of security. Black-garbed men and women roamed around wearing coloured armbands; mostly administrators and security guards. There was no sign of the upper echelons of the hierarchy.

Seven guards at most, stationed at various points. One at each of the three entrances and two wandering amongst the computer banks. Another seemed to be making equipment checks; lighting, digital scanners, computer leads. Occasionally, he bent over switches and points before recording his findings in an electronic notebook. They all seemed completely engrossed in their work. No need to worry about them. The one to watch was the tall, sinewy guard elevated on a small platform. He was obviously surveillance. His eyes darted round the chamber watching everything and everyone. Conrad swore under his breath. It was like the bloody Grepos on the Berlin Wall. They were all watching each other.

Taking a deep breath, he stepped out and marched purposefully across the chamber, lingering a few moments near a group of administrators. He bent forward as though examining their work and moved on: all the time watching the surveillance guard out of the corner of his eye. Two circuits of the chamber later, another man stepped up onto the small platform. The surveillance guard nodded at him, jumped down, and hurried off down the far corridor. The new man folded his arms and looked round the room. For a brief moment his gaze settled on Conrad then turned away. He breathed a sigh of relief. Now all he had to do was find Wallace. If he was still alive he would be working on a computer, but which one? There must be at least a hundred.

Casually, he wandered in and out of the rows of computers, gazing intently at the uniformed workers. He studied their build, discounting women and anybody too thin to be Wallace. That still left around fifty. Occasionally, he bent over a screen and waited for the operative to look up. He wanted to see their eyes. His heart lurched when he caught sight of a thickset man bent over a screen filled with rolling statistics. He hovered close to him until the man looked up – brown eyes.

He moved on to a small section set away from the others. Eight men and two women bent intently over screens, in two rows of five, facing each other. Slowly, he moved around the group studying the operators' faces. The man directly opposite lifted his head enquiringly. Green eyes! He would recognise those gold-flecked eyes anywhere. Conrad sidled over and whispered close to the man's ear.

"What are you working on, Biker?"

Wallace's head jerked up and stared directly into Conrad's eyes.

"How the hell did you get in here?" he whispered through the side of his mouth. "You'll be dead meat if they discover you. You bloody idiot! I know what they're planning, and it scares the shit out of me."

"Just listen and do exactly what I say. Take a break. Go into the restrooms. Give it exactly five minutes. When you come out I'll be standing close to entrance two. There's another unmarked corridor that leads off from the right-hand side of that entrance. When you see me go in follow me as fast as possible."

"Save it for when we get out," Conrad snapped when Wallace started to protest.

Keeping his eyes on the surveillance guard, Conrad continued traversing the chamber. Gradually, he moved towards entrance two and stood with his back to the wall, letting his eyes wander around the chamber like the other security guards.

Heart pounding in his chest, he glanced briefly at his wristwatch: four and a half minutes. His stomach tightened – another thirty seconds. Conrad tensed when a man came out of the restroom and walked across to the administrative section. Another man emerged checking his zipper. Briskly, he strode across the chamber towards entrance two as though heading for the computer section. Conrad shot a swift glance at the surveillance guard then darted inside the passage. Seconds later, he heard Wallace's boots clumping behind him.

"Let's get the hell out of here!" he whispered. "We have to get out and down the mountain before they realise you've gone."

He put a warning finger to his lips and scurried down the winding corridor to the door. Carefully, he lifted the bar and pulled it open slightly. A scraping sound caught his attention. There was someone inside! He peered round the door at the back of a militiaman replacing the straw in the nearest stall.

"That's buggered it!"

"He's wearing earphones," Wallace whispered. "I think he's listening to an iPod."

He peered round the door again. The guard was nodding his head and sweeping in time to the beat of the music. Conrad opened the door wide, lunged at the man, and fell on top of him. Before he had a chance to cry out, they gagged him and stripped off his hood, padded jacket and gloves.

"Put these on," Conrad ordered, handing Wallace the guard's clothes. "It's bloody cold out there."

They hauled the man to the outer door. Conrad put his hand under the man's chin and held his face in front of the scanner. "Keep your eyes open!" He pressed his Glock into the back of the man's head. The outer metal door swished open. "Go! Go! Go!"

Conrad floored the man with a rabbit punch and darted into the grass enclosure. He threw a grappling hook over the rocks and hoisted himself up and over. Seconds later, Wallace dropped to the ground beside him.

"Get down as low as possible. That sheer wall is a fake. There's a scanner and surveillance camera set either side of it. Get to the other side and keep off the rubble path. They're sure as hell to see you there."

Wallace scrabbled across on all fours and lunged ankle-deep into crisp snow. He stumbled over a stone and rolled down thirty metres before he could stop. Groaning, he sat up in the snow rubbing his elbow.

"Are you okay?" Conrad asked, skidding to a halt beside him.

"I haven't forgotten how to roll, mate. It's just been a long time since I did it."

"They haven't spotted us yet, but they will. Come on!"

As they reached the bottom of the covered trail a single shot rang out, echoing on the still air. It pinged off a boulder sending them scurrying for cover below an outcrop of rocks. Tentatively, Conrad raised his head. Another single shot rang out. They were trapped, unable to move out of cover.

"We're stuck here, that's for sure. From up there they can pick us off like sparrows. We have to get back down before dusk or we'll freeze to death," he said. "There's nothing here to provide shelter and the wind is building up."

Wallace didn't respond. He was gazing up at low-hanging mist drifting down from the peaks. Within minutes it had almost obscured the dilapidated wreck of the abandoned hotel and was swirling down the mountain at an alarming rate.

"There is a God," he breathed.

"Once it hits us, move out." Conrad nudged Wallace and pointed up towards the facility. "They're on to us."

A group of black-clad Militia swarmed like ants down the mountain less than three hundred metres above them. It took all their willpower to stay put until the mist enveloped them. Then they were on their feet, one to the left, the other to the right, zigzagging down the mountain at breakneck speed. This time a volley of shots rang out followed by another prolonged blast of firing.

"They won't catch us now," Wallace yelled above the noise.

They ran ahead of the fog until they reached the outskirts of the little village.

"Okay, Biker, I'll ride pillion," Conrad said, dragging a motorcycle out from behind a stockpile of winter logs. "Just remember, this isn't Route 66."

CHAPTER SIXTY

Bernese Oberland, Switzerland

The Mercedes slewed to a halt outside Dreher's chalet on Lake Thun. Before they had a chance to get out of the car the door burst open. Light poured out, puddling the snow-covered drive with pools of liquid gold. The mist had lifted revealing a midnight-blue sky scattered with bright stars. Towering mountain peaks glowed ethereally in the moonlight. Conrad breathed deeply, welcoming the sharp rush of air into his lungs.

The chalet was warm and cosy. From the comfort of the living room, they savoured the tantalising smells emanating from the kitchen. Dreher insisted they eat before discussing what Wallace had discovered in the facility. Later, they sat in front of the blazing log fire sipping brandies.

"The Generalissimo asked me to build a futuristic weapon from blueprints stolen from Ethan Bateman's laboratories in the Nevada desert," Wallace said. "He was obviously onto them so they had to eliminate him. They fund the Militia from selling on government secrets and industrial espionage. Macaleer must have discovered what they were up to in the facility. That's what he meant when he told Colonel Bowler about an 'army'. It was the Black Militia, as the Generalissimo calls them."

"How does Foley fit in with all this?" Dreher asked.

"I think I can explain that," Conrad interjected. "Foley had infiltrated the facility. We know he went up into the Alps pretending to be booking into a clinic. Bateman told me Foley was scared witless. He babbled something about not needing an operation any more so he was going home. We've had the whole story on that from MI6. Colin Lynes had arranged for a kidney transplant in exchange for military secrets. I believe they took out his good kidney to sell to the highest bidder."

"The bastards!" Wallace fumed. "Why would they do that?"

"Payback – they knew Foley would expose them."

"They're not just in the business of selling secrets," Wallace continued. "That's just a sideline. Their main purpose is to bring the G8 countries to their knees, then all the G20."

"It's impossible!" Dreher exclaimed.

"That's where you're wrong, Ernst. I'm convinced their plan will be put into action during the United Nations summit on world poverty in New York. I'm not sure how yet, but I'm certain it's the catalyst that will set it in motion. They'll wage a war from cyberspace. For years, malicious e-mails have been sent round the globe in an attempt to infiltrate government and industrial systems. Some from Chinese and Russian hackers, but a lot were sent out from that facility in the Alps."

"So why didn't they act before?"

"The Generalissimo is a patient man. He's waited a long time for this – years. He doesn't intend to fail. He's spent decades creating a deadly computer virus named Black Crystal. It will bring systems to a standstill, even the Pentagon and GCHQ."

"We'll have to go back up there," Conrad said. "The only way we can stop this is from inside the facility. We have to take out the Generalissimo and destroy all the computers."

"I agree. It's the only way," Dreher added. "Explosives are out of the question. The whole mountain would start moving."

Conrad took out his phone and punched in Breakdancer's number. He related what Wallace had discovered.

"We can't keep this to ourselves any longer, Jack. There's too much at stake. I must inform Gilbert immediately," Pearce said.

"Wallace and I are going back up to the facility in the early hours before dawn. It won't be easy. They'll be on the lookout for us now. Dreher will provide as much backup as possible this end. I'll take Sasha with us. He knows the mountains like the back of his hand."

"I'll see that the SAS are on standby. Good luck."

"Ernst, we'll need trail bikes, the usual clothing, equipment and weapons." Conrad patted his jacket. "I've got my Glock, but we'll also need semi-automatic pistols, light machine guns, grenades and tear gas."

"They'll be ready for you." Dreher snapped open his mobile phone. "Zinzli, listen carefully. There's a lot at stake."

Zinzli was wide awake sitting on the edge of the bed. His wife snored gently at his side. His eyes widened in disbelief as Dreher outlined the situation.

"This must be kept quiet. We don't want to create mass hysteria. Is that clear?"

"Yes, sir, absolutely clear!"

"And if that clown Dupont starts asking questions, send him off on some wild goose chase!"

Sophia came out of the kitchen with a steaming percolator just as the door was slamming shut behind them.

"Ernst, where are you going? Your coffee!"

The Mercedes crunched up the drive, slithered onto the lakeside road and shot off into the frosty night.

CHAPTER SIXTY-ONE

The Alps,Bernese Oberland,

Moonlight shimmered on the snow-covered trail snaking up the mountain. Dark outcrops of rock cast shadows in their path as the three men concealed their bikes behind an overhanging boulder. Conrad cursed the moonlight, praying for cloud cover to conceal their progress.

"Fan out and climb in a zigzag fashion until we reach the foot of the facility," he whispered. "Stay in the shadows as much as possible. Sasha will lead and we'll follow. He knows these mountains better than us. Don't lose sight of him. If we get lost up here we've had our chips."

Silently, Sasha moved out and beckoned to the others to follow. They laboured slowly upwards, nostrils blowing white vapour. Climbing too fast would make them dizzy and disoriented. Difficult enough during the day, but climbing at night was extremely dangerous. Not even the Black Militia would have men out on the mountain in these conditions. It was madness, but they had no choice.

They had been climbing for over three hours, keeping to the barely visible trails as much as possible. Luckily, the moon had disappeared behind thick cloud, but its concealment had brought new hazards. Snow drifted down in fat flakes blown into frenzied swirls by a cutting wind. It was freezing cold. Conrad's feet were already like blocks of ice inside his thick woollen socks and snow boots. Snowflakes settled on his face, danced in front of his eyes, found their way into his mouth. He could hear Wallace gasping for breath over to his right. He tightened the strings of his snood and pulled up his hood. Suddenly, he came up against Sasha's bulky frame crouched low under an overhang.

"We're at the foot of the concealed trail," he whispered.

Conrad peered upwards towards the facility through his night vision goggles. There wasn't a glimmer of light or activity. If they had been spotted the Militia would be waiting for them.

"Check your weapons," he ordered. "We'll rest for five minutes." Wallace slumped down beside him. "Take some nourishment."

He pulled out a chocolate bar, bit off a chunk, and took a swig from a high-energy drink.

"Okay, synchronise your watches. Wallace knows his way around so stick with him," he warned Sasha. "It's easy to get confused with the labyrinth of corridors. I'm going after the Generalissimo."

Thirty minutes later, they crouched under the fake wall. Scrambling to the cover of rocks surrounding the goat enclosure they stopped, expecting at any moment to hear gunshots or feel the prod of a rifle in the back. Nothing, except an eerie silence. One after the other they scaled the rocks and dropped down into the goat compound.

"They're bedded down for the night," Conrad whispered. "We'll have to force open the steel door. Let's hope it doesn't set the goats off. Get your gear out."

He lowered his backpack and took out a reinforced crowbar. He placed the crowbar at the top side of the door

271

and another at the bottom. Sasha covered a large stone with a thick cloth and pounded at it. On the third blow the sharp end nudged inwards, but it hit metal. Conrad angled the crowbar slightly. The next blow sent it into thin air. He wiggled it up and down. It was through! Wallace did the same at the bottom of the door. Both men put their weight to it, but the door wouldn't budge. Exhausted, they slumped to the ground.

"Sasha, we'll hold on to ours while you drive a third one into the centre," Conrad instructed.

Gasping with the effort, they hauled with all their strength. The door slid sideways a fraction.

"Don't let go," Wallace gasped. "Keep up the pressure."

Suddenly, the door slid back. The chisels clattered against rock and fell into soft snow. With bated breath, they pressed themselves against the rocks either side of the door.

"Okay, let's go!"

Conrad lunged inside the goat pen and dropped low beside the first stall, the others hard at his heels. It was empty. He crept to the next one. Empty. They were all empty. Not a goat in sight. He shone his Maglite at the internal door. It was slightly ajar. Raising his hand in warning he gave it a gentle push. The passageway was empty. Weapons at the ready they moved into the corridor, their senses alert to every sound and movement. There wasn't a glimmer of light. Everything was eerily quiet; too quiet. Not even the muted hum of computers. He waved his torch signalling for the others to follow.

"What the hell… !" Wallace exclaimed.

It was bare except for a single chair and some snaking electrical leads. It was stripped of computers, desks, lighting;

completely derelict. Doors leading from the chamber stood wide open. Everything had gone. The Generalissimo and his Black Militia had moved out. It was almost as though the facility had never existed.

"You and Sasha investigate the corridors. There are a few rooms leading off from them."

Conrad headed for the corridor to the left of where the computer bank used to stand. "If you find anything blow your whistle."

Gripping the Glock firmly in both hands, he moved down the corridor keeping close to the wall. Like the main chamber, everything was abnormally quiet. He kicked open every door and peered inside. Suddenly, a faint sound caught his ear. He held his breath. There it was again, coming from lower down the passageway. The Generalissimo's room! The door was partially open. A thin beam of light swept from side to side. Someone was in there searching for something.

Heart thumping, every sense attuned to his surroundings, he edged quietly forward. He listened intently to the scuffling noises. With one swift movement he kicked open the door and lunged in. A black-clad man spun around and went for his gun.

"Drop it! Put your hands over your head. Kick the gun over to me."

Conrad shone his flashlight into the man's masked face. He winced and bent over trying to cover his eyes. Like lightning, he pulled a knife from his right-hand boot.

Conrad brought his Glock down hard on his hand.

"Okay, you bastard, tell me where they've gone!"

The militiaman struggled to free himself. He twisted and smashed his fist into Conrad's face. Suddenly, the shrill of a whistle sounded on the air. Startled, the man's head jerked around. Still dizzy from the blow Conrad lunged at him sending him sprawling to the ground. He was on his feet again in seconds. Before Conrad could stop him he bolted through the door.

The whistle shrilled again. Conrad dragged himself to his feet. He shook his head to clear the fuzziness. Hot pain surged through his skull threatening to bring him down again. He staggered to the door. The militiaman had disappeared. Cursing loudly, he chased after him giving a series of sharp blasts on his whistle. The sound reverberated round the walls, echoing down the corridors. Boots clattered on bare concrete sounding like a squad of soldiers on a march.

He dived round a corner and came up short. Above him, he could just make out the grass-covered canopy slowly closing. A rush of wind and loud roaring filled the air as a helicopter rose overhead, its tail light flashing. The platform started to descend to the floor inside the cavern. The pilot banked to the right, straightened and headed off. Conrad watched the tail light flicker and vanish into a bank of low cloud.

"What the hell was that?" Sasha shouted, running into the cavern.

"Remember the helicopter I mentioned disappearing over the peaks. This is where it was going," Conrad muttered through clenched teeth.

"It's the way they brought me in," Wallace said. "Whoever it was either came back for something or he was completing a final check."

"Come on. I want to search the Generalissimo's room. There may be something there that will give us a clue."

Three flashlights pierced the darkness of the Generalissimo's quarters. There was little to be seen. Whatever the masked man had been searching for, he must have found it. Conrad spotted a stainless steel bucket and ladle protruding from an open cupboard set against the back wall. Yanking it out, he examined it closely. Something flashed into his memory and flashed out again. He couldn't get rid of the nagging feeling that he had missed something.

"We're not going to find anything more here. Let's get going."

Dawn had broken by the time they left the facility. They emerged into blinding white light that seared their eyeballs. Quickly, they donned their snow glasses and secured their parkas. It was snowing much more heavily now. Every blast of icy wind sent thick flurries billowing across the Alps. Conrad pulled out his binoculars and swept the mountains. Through breaks in the flurries, he could just make out the hazy outline of the cable car wires stretching up to the Piz Gloria.

The going was rough, the rubble path obliterated by snow, concealing the hazards underfoot.

"Sod it!" Wallace cursed as his foot sank between two jagged stones.

"Take it easy," Conrad called over his shoulder. "The last thing we want is an injury up here. It could be fatal."

"You think I don't know that!" Wallace answered in a surly tone.

They had reached the bottom of the obscured trail when Sasha stopped dead. He cocked his head to one side.

"Did you hear that?"

They strained their ears then they heard it: the faint

drone of an aircraft. Suddenly, a chopper loomed out of the curtain of snow. A shot rang out, then another.

"He's trying to pick us off," Wallace shouted, pulling at the AK-47 on his back.

"Aim for the fuel tanks," Conrad yelled, letting off a volley of gunfire. An answering volley chattered back, echoing across the mountains. "There's only one guy shooting. The pilot is having enough trouble staying airborne."

The helicopter was veering dangerously left and right as the pilot fought to keep it under control. Another burst of gunfire filled the air. Suddenly, the chopper slewed sideways, completely out of control.

"We've got him!" Sasha bellowed over the roar of the wind. "He's going down!" They followed its progress as it lost height, bouncing crazily in a drunken dance of death before disappearing. Suddenly, a loud bang reached their ears. "They've crashed!" The smell of smoke drifted upwards.

"Rescue teams will be out in minutes," Conrad yelled. "It's unlikely anybody survived. We have to get to the wreckage before they do."

They slid down at breakneck speed. Conrad groaned as he hit a rock full on, knocking the breath out of him. The mangled wreckage of the chopper lay embedded in deep snow.

"He must have been one hell of a pilot," Wallace remarked grudgingly. "The fuselage is still in one piece."

The pilot lay slumped over the controls. His mouth and eyes were wide open in a silent scream. A deep gash ran from his forehead down the side of his face. Wallace stuck his hand through the shattered window and felt for a pulse. Dead as a door nail. Another man lay sprawled face upwards in the snow, arms and legs akimbo like a snow angel. Conrad pulled off the man's balaclava.

"This one's still alive!" he shouted. He bent over the man. "Tell me *where* is the Generalissimo?"

"You… can't… stop… him… now. It's… too… late." Blood poured from the corners of his mouth.

"Tell me!" Conrad shook him roughly. For a brief moment the man opened his eyes and grinned devilishly.

"Where is he, damn you! Tell me!" The man's head slumped backwards, his eyes still wide open.

"Stop it, Jack! Enough, he's gone."

Conrad sat back on his haunches, his breath coming in painful gasps. They would never find the Generalissimo now. What the hell were they to do? What was so important that he came back for it? He stripped off the man's parka, revealing a gold armband emblazoned with a single black crystal. There was nothing else on him except a Swiss army knife, a small compass and some soiled tissues.

"One of the inner circle, but only just," Wallace muttered. "Trusted enough to be sent back to get what the Generalissimo wanted."

"Even soldiers have old ticket stubs, receipts, a wallet. There's nothing on this guy to identify him. Take the balaclava. There's a chance we can get some DNA results from saliva around the mouth opening. If he's got a record, Interpol will have it."

Conrad gazed upwards. Black, ominous clouds were rolling over the peaks. The wind had picked up blowing flurries of snow against rocky outcrops. Whipping out his satellite phone he punched in Dreher's number.

"Ernst, listen carefully. A helicopter has crashed up here.

The emergency services are probably on their way. You must stop them. We need time to search the wreckage. The pilot and another militiaman are dead."

"The rescue team will have started out... "

"Just stop them, Ernst!" Conrad cut in.

He stowed the phone and trudged over to the wreckage, his legs knee-deep in snow. Wallace was already picking through the debris and throwing bits of metal aside. It took all their strength to tear off the door on the passenger side. Conrad squeezed inside and looked around the mangled cabin. He could see that a piece of metal had pierced the pilot's stomach. His dead hands clutched at it in a futile attempt to rid himself of his pain. Something was protruding from under the pilot's seat. The man's weight had it firmly wedged underneath.

"There's something here, but I can't get at it! Help me get him out."

Wallace cut through the safety harness and hauled him out onto the snow. Conrad slid his hand under the seat and tried to drag the object out. It wouldn't budge. He wiggled it from side to side to loosen it and managed to get the tips of his fingers behind it. Slowly, it started to edge towards him until he was able to grasp it and pull it out. It was a black leather case.

"There's a memory stick inside. We have to get back down the mountain as fast as possible. Whatever is on it is important enough for the Generalissimo to send back one of his minions to get it."

Black and baleful, the sky threatened a serious blizzard. The wind had whipped into a frenzy howling across the mountain. They could barely stand up against its force. It seemed to change direction: now lashing at their faces; now pushing them from behind.

"Keep going! Don't stop!" Sasha yelled, as Wallace plunged face forward into the white stuff.

They half walked, half tumbled down the mountain. The trail had been completely obliterated by thick snow. Conrad stopped to take his bearings. For a split second panic rose in his chest then his military training took over. He hadn't experienced conditions like this for years. Most of his fieldwork had involved fighting the heat of the desert in Iraq and Afghanistan.

He whipped out his binoculars and peered through the blinding whiteness. Momentarily, the wind parted the curtain of snow. He could just make out the sharp ridges of the outcrop of rock where they had left the trail bikes before the blizzard had put them off course.

"Over there," he shouted above the cacophony of noise.

The path was covered in snow, but it wasn't as deep and the wind wasn't as fierce as higher up. Still, it was only a matter of time before the mountain was impassable.

They hauled out the bikes and sat astride, ready to kick-start them into life. Luckily, Conrad's started first time. Wallace turned his engine over. Time after time the engine sputtered and died.

"Damn it! If it doesn't start you'll have to go without me! There's no pillion seat on these bloody contraptions."

Suddenly, the engine burst into life. "Thank you, God!"

"I'll go first," Sasha said. "Keep me in sight and stay in the centre of the track. It's barely visible. One false move and we'll be over the edge."

Wind and snow lashing at their faces, they slid their way

down the icy mountain, acutely aware that an uncontrolled skid could send them hurtling into oblivion. Gradually, the path widened and took them away from the edge.

"We're almost there," he shouted.

Just below them the lights of the village burned hazily in the gloom.

*

The tension in the air was palpable as Dreher inserted the memory stick into his laptop. Suddenly, an image of a black snow crystal filled the screen then quickly faded. For a few seconds nothing happened. He tapped the enter key impatiently. Still nothing happened.

"Whatever is on it is locked in," he muttered.

Conrad leaned over and tapped in 'Generalissimo'. Immediately, 'access denied' flashed onto the screen. He continued tapping words and phrases – 'snow crystal', 'black militia'. Still nothing happened. He rubbed his chin thoughtfully.

"Let's try this," Wallace said, tapping in 'Operation Black Crystal.'

Nothing happened. He slumped back into his chair and then bounced up again. He punched in the words again, but this time in capital letters. 'OPERATION BLACK CRYSTAL' zoomed onto the screen along with various icons.

He placed the cursor on an icon of a crystal. The screen filled with the map he and Conrad had seen in the facility in the mountains. Another icon brought up rows and rows of statistics. He scrolled down the columns of figures.

"It's incredible! It's a list of their finances: all the deals they've done to raise money to fund the Black Militia. Look at this: 429,372,900 North Korean Won for military secrets relating to the harvesting of uranium. How much is that?"

"About £2,000,000," Conrad interjected.

"Another 7,000,000 Euros from the sale of weapons to insurgents in third-world countries. The last entry is for 60,000,000 Swiss francs from a Middle Eastern agent for Ethan Bateman's blueprints."

"There are years of payments here," Dreher commented, "all in alphabetical order. See if you can narrow down the payments by date."

"Oh my God!" Wallace inhaled deeply. His eyes were glued to an entry two rows up from the bottom of the screen. "It's a payment for Foley's kidney. The bastard!"

"The Generalissimo is absolutely unscrupulous. If Sophia is right he's completely amoral, but he's also methodical and patient," Dreher interjected. "There are payments here dating back to 1989. It's unbelievable. He's been planning all this for more than twenty-five years."

Pages of details about the organisation filled the screen. No names, just codes to identify nationalities, gender, expertise, and field agents in various countries. It outlined the career structure of the Black Militia with established routes for promotion within all categories. Only five were accorded inner circle status with just two holding six black crystals.

"I can't quite take it in. It's like a plot for a novel," Wallace said.

"It's a plot all right, but a very real one!" Conrad got up and paced the room. "How the hell can we stop him when we don't even know where he is? There has to be something on here that will give us a clue. There has to be! Go back to the icons," he instructed. "Try that one."

Ernst clicked on another icon that resembled a crest. Immediately, another map flashed onto the screen.

"That's odd," Wallace remarked. "There are no place names, just geographical features."

He peered intently at the screen. The thread of blue was obviously a river. There was something very familiar about it. Suddenly, it hit him.

"It's an old map of Shropshire with the place names and points of interest removed. That's the connection! Joanne Howard, Foley's body in that old well outside Shrewsbury. That could be where they've gone!"

"A Lear jet is on standby at Geneva airport," Conrad said. "I'll brief Pearce in London then I'll travel to Shropshire to join you, Ben. We'll fly you down from Heathrow by chopper. Pearce will brief MI6 and the Prime Minister. We may have to call in the military. There's not much you can do this end, Ernst, but be alert."

Wallace was wondering how much he could tell Butler. He would have to play it by ear. His DI wasn't stupid. He already suspected there was something going on other than the murders. The men would have to be given some plausible reason for a search party… an armed gang at large? Anything but the truth.

There were a number of old mines, limekilns and a few dilapidated historic ruins scattered throughout Shropshire. They could be holed up anywhere. It would take a lot of men to cover the area.

"Your Chief Constable will ensure you have the

resources," Conrad said. "Men will be brought in from other forces, if necessary."

Wallace had come full circle back to the scene of the original crime.

CHAPTER SIXTY-TWO

London, England

The man in the black pinstriped suit looked up as Conrad entered Breakdancer's inner sanctum. Tall, heavily built, slightly crooked nose, hair unfashionably long; he looked more like a heavyweight boxer than secret service. He noted Conrad's muscular frame, the confident manner, the precise military tones. This was a man to be reckoned with, a man who trusted his own judgement.

"Come in, Major Conrad," Clive Pearce said, waving him to a leather armchair.

As usual, Pearce was cool, unruffled and self-assured. Nobody would have guessed that he had a catastrophic global crisis looming. But that was why he was head of IMIC. He dealt with crises as though he were organising a monthly board meeting.

"You know Gilbert, MI6." Conrad nodded.

"Major, I want you to tell me all you know about the Generalissimo."

"You know about him!" Conrad exclaimed, looking accusingly at Pearce.

Pearce held up his hands in a warning gesture. This was not going to be an easy meeting.

"Well, not exactly. When we sent Foley out into the field, he encountered the man you call the Generalissimo. As you know, Foley was working on top-secret work before he went to GCHQ. It wasn't coincidence that he had been sent there in the first place. We knew all about Lynes, but we wanted to use him for our own purposes."

"Why the hell wasn't I told?"

Ignoring the question, Gilbert continued. "Foley came face to face with him in some so-called clinic in Switzerland. His final telephone call was garbled and incoherent. He was going on about a man in a mask, an 'army' in black uniforms. He sounded dazed as though he had been drugged up to the eyes. You know the rest, poor sod. We didn't know about Macaleer until Pearce informed us that *two* military men had disappeared. It was a stroke of pure luck that Macaleer's body was identified by the pathologist."

"So MI6 commandeered his body."

"National security is involved so we had to hush it all up. Pearce reports exclusively to me. I report directly to the Prime Minister."

"You knew about this all along?" Conrad asked Pearce accusingly.

"Pearce put two and two together when you informed him about the Generalissimo and the facility in the Alps. How likely is it that there would be two masked men up there?" Gilbert asked with a hollow laugh.

Conrad related the whole sequence of events. His own encounter with the Generalissimo and Wallace's infiltration of the facility.

"We went back up there yesterday before dawn. They've disappeared," he said flatly. "Moved out lock, stock and barrel. There's nothing left to indicate that anyone has been there for years. The 'army' Foley mentioned is a small, well-disciplined force of around three hundred men and women, most of them highly skilled in specific fields. It's run on strict military lines with distinct ranks. Different coloured insignia depicting their speciality and seniority. Each member has a code; no names. Everything is conducted in total secrecy on a need-to-know basis."

"There must be some clue as to where they've gone?"

"We discovered a militiaman in the Generalissimo's quarters. He bolted and escaped in a chopper, but it crashed in the blizzard. The pilot was already dead when we got to him, but the sniper was still alive. We found this." Conrad handed over the memory stick. Pearce inserted it into his computer. In total silence they watched as Conrad called up the map.

"It doesn't look much like Switzerland," Gilbert commented.

"It isn't, it's a map of Shropshire. I'm convinced that's where they've gone and that there's a connection with the bodies found there. That's not all."

Gilbert gasped as columns of statistics filled the screen. "It's unbelievable!"

"Wallace is convinced the Generalissimo's plan will be implemented in New York City. Probably during the conference on world poverty at the United Nations. He thinks they're planning an assassination. Hundreds of delegates from countries all over the world will be in attendance, including our Prime Minister and the President of the United States."

"Washington and Langley have already been informed of a possible assassination attempt," Pearce interjected, "but I don't want them to know about the Generalissimo yet."

Pearce wanted to keep quiet about the cyber attack until

they had scoured Shropshire. They had to find him before he saturated cyberspace with the Black Crystal virus. If they didn't…

Wallace was already in Shropshire with every possible resource available to him. Vehicles, weapons and as much manpower as needed to cover the entire county. The SAS would be standing by, but he didn't want them visible unless it was absolutely necessary.

If the virus couldn't be controlled, the lights could go out sooner than the environmental buffs had forecast. There would be panic in the streets in Europe and across 'the pond'.

CHAPTER SIXTY-THREE

Manhattan, New York City

Baranski watched the limousines roll up to the entrance of the United Nations Assembly Building. Dressed in regulation security uniform; white shirt, black peaked cap, security pass on his right breast, glasses perched halfway down his nose, he stood pretending to study the millboard he was holding. He was in charge of photographing visitors and directing them to the visitors' lobby under Foucault's Pendulum.

There was a hold-up with one of the visitors being refused entry. It was getting pretty ugly. His aides were shouting and gesticulating, but his fellow officer wouldn't budge. Baranski smiled: this little débâcle was helpful to him.

"Hey, Bishop, get on to head of security while I keep these guys occupied."

"Sure thing, Clementi." Baranski pretended to speak into his radio then shouted to Clementi.

"He's sending backup. I'll keep the queues moving."

The queues for entry stretched out beyond the main entrance. This was exactly what he had been hoping. He watched the flags of the United Nations fluttering just inside the perimeter fence. To succeed in his mission he would have to act now. He waited for the snarl-up behind the frustrated delegate to get fidgety. Smiling at the visitor staring into the camera, he waited a few seconds then handed him his pass.

"Thank you, sir. You may proceed to the visitors' lobby."

Stepping back into the booth, he turned his back to check his concealed weapon then stepped out. He passed the furious delegate who was insisting on entry, walked casually through the entrance, and stood alongside the waiting queue as though checking numbers. Abruptly, he pulled out his gun and fired indiscriminately into the crowd.

Pandemonium broke out. Like scurrying ants the crowd dispersed, running blindly in all directions. A woman screamed and dived behind a black limousine. There was no specific target in mind. The whole exercise was to create as much mayhem as possible. Baranski aimed at the limousine. Terrified, the driver dived sideways. Too late, a bullet struck him in the head through the open window of the vehicle.

Passengers and drivers spilled out of automobiles and ran towards the buildings on 43rd Street. A middle-aged man clutched his chest and fell to the ground, his eyes wide with disbelief. Baranski fired again and brought a colourful African delegate to his knees. Ripping off his false moustache he threw it, along with the gun, cap and security pass, into some nearby bushes. He darted across the United Nations Plaza onto 43rd Street, past the Ford Foundation, and crossed Second Avenue onto East 42nd Street.

He had paid his hotel bill the previous night, claiming he would be leaving for Washington on an early flight. Instead, he booked a day room in a cheap hotel nearby and slipped unnoticed out of the back entrance of the Intercontinental.

Face partially covered by a scarf, he hailed a taxi. In the distance the wail of sirens sounded and faded. By now the emergency services would be on their way. Security would be scouring the area looking for the perpetrator.

In the chaos nobody had spotted him running through the United Nations entrance with the rest of the fleeing crowd. Instead of staying within the relative safety of the perimeter fence, terrified delegates surged out to join the overspill milling outside. It couldn't have worked out better.

"Where to, buddy?" the cabby asked.

"Penn Station."

The taxi moved slowly down Madison Avenue and crossed over Fifth Avenue onto East 34th Street. Baranski stiffened when a police officer held up his hand, slowing down traffic ahead of them. He put his hand on his gun, every sense alert. A fire engine, parked against the curb, started up and edged into the flow of traffic. The cop waited a few seconds then waved Baranski's cab forward.

"You on vacation?" the cabby asked. Baranski ignored the question.

The Empire State Building loomed ahead. Not far to go. He breathed a sigh of relief when the railroad station came into view.

"Front entrance," he shouted through the dividing window.

The cab slewed to a halt. He shoved some notes at the driver and darted inside to join milling passengers in the concourse.

Under his Polish alias, Tarek Dudek, he had booked a first-class sleeper on the Amtrak to Chicago. He cursed inwardly. It only ran once a day in the afternoon. Americans! They couldn't even run a decent train service. He froze when he spotted two uniformed cops watching passengers in the main concourse. Another two stood at the top of the staircase surveying the crowds below.

Earlier that morning he had left a second suitcase in the first-class lounge, telling the attendant that he was going to spend a little time sightseeing until his train was due. After showing his ticket to the overweight receptionist in club class, he found a seat where he could observe the entrance.

The lounge was full of passengers: tired looking businessmen, tourists drinking free coffee from polystyrene cups. Two small boys ran riot amongst the feet of disgruntled passengers, their parents happily munching on potato chips.

In thirty minutes he would be on the train. He could barely conceal his impatience. One of the children tripped over his feet. He glared at him over the top of the New York Times. Something about his look sent the child scurrying and blubbering towards his parents. *Little brat*, he fumed inwardly. *No discipline. No wonder Western youths were so decadent.*

"The train for Chicago is now boarding," a metallic voice announced over the loudspeaker.

Baranski looked at the platform number on the overhead monitor. A Red Cap pushed in through the door.

"Passengers for the Chicago train?" he asked enquiringly.

Baranski stood up and followed an elderly couple with two large suitcases. The Red Cap loaded their cases onto a buggy while the couple eased themselves onto the back seat of the cart. The Red Cap motioned to Baranski.

"Jump on, it's a long walk to the platform," he said.

Reluctantly, Baranski hopped on the buggy and smiled at the elderly couple. He didn't want to attract any undue attention When they reached the platform he passed a five-dollar note to the Red Cap and boarded the train. He climbed the spiral stairs to the top deck and edged his way along the corridor to his first-class compartment. After stowing his case, he drew the curtains across to avoid prying eyes from the corridor. Outside, the platform was a hive of activity with last-minute passengers rushing to board. He breathed a sigh of relief as the porter closed the platform gates.

Swaying from side to side the Amtrak groaned away from the platform. Baranski felt as though he was on a roller coaster. Once the train had left the station and gathered speed the sideways rolling stopped and it settled into a straight line.

They passed the same depressing scenery found in all major cities. Rows of warehouses, tenement blocks, breakers' yards. Gradually, concrete buildings petered out into countryside. They lurched over points on poorly maintained tracks, so violently he thought his head would hit the ceiling. Nineteen hours of this hell until he reached Chicago.

The train bounced on the rails, lurching from side to side, up and down, as though driven by a drunken driver. If only he could have flown to Chicago, but it was not an option. Security was very tight since 9/11. They would be scouring the airports first. After Chicago he had to get to Los Angeles. Three nights on the train trundling across the country was tedious, but the safest option. Now he could sleep for a few hours.

The sound of the door sliding back brought Baranski to full wakefulness. A steward poked his head inside.

"Dinner will be served in the dining car between six and eight. Will you be eating sir?"

Baranski nodded perfunctorily. He would prefer to stay in his compartment, but it would draw attention to him. Besides, he was very hungry.

"Yes, thank you," he replied. "I'll eat at seven forty-five."

"It's communal seating sir; four to a table."

Baranski groaned inwardly. The thought of sharing a table, coupled with inane conversation with strangers, was almost more than he could bear. Gritting his teeth, he smiled at the steward.

"Would you like your bed made up while you eat?"

"Yes, I'd like an early night."

At nine o'clock, Baranski gratefully escaped from the elderly couple travelling to Montana for their niece's wedding. They asked far too many questions.

"See ya at breakfast," they said, as he rose to leave.

Not if I can help it, he thought.

Back in his compartment, he drew the curtains across the door and windows and tumbled into bed. The mattress was rather thin, but it was surprisingly comfortable. He lay with his hands behind his head thinking about the days ahead. Soon he would be a very rich man. The steady motion of the train lulled him into an uneasy sleep, broken by the blare of the train's horn every time it trundled through towns on its way to the windy city.

*

Baranski shot upright, temporarily disoriented by his strange surroundings. Doors along the corridor slid open then slammed shut again.

"Breakfast is now being served in the dining car," the steward called down the corridor.

Seven-thirty – passengers were already dragging down the corridors queuing for the toilets. He relieved himself in the toilet cum shower then made his way to the dining car.

He breathed a sigh of relief when he spotted Chuck and Dora sitting with another couple. His relief was short-lived. He had no sooner sat down than a young Japanese girl and her mother sat down opposite him. Thankfully, they were too tired to engage in conversation for very long.

He looked around the carriage at the other diners. There were a few businessmen, one or two families, a couple of lone travellers, but mostly American tourists. What a strange country. Filled with people who never ventured outside the United States and had never held a passport. Some had probably never travelled outside their home state before. He settled back to enjoy his eggs, over easy, as the Americans called it. Another three hours and they would be arriving in Union Station, Chicago.

*

Chicago, Illinois

Baranski lifted his small suitcase off the overhead rack and made his way along the corridor to the head of the stairs leading to the lower deck. He waited for a clutch of passengers to leave the train and tagged on behind. His train to the west coast wasn't leaving until eight that evening; plenty of time to do what he had to do. Leaving through the main entrance he crossed the road onto the old Route 66, surrounded now by stores and offices. Only a plaque attached to a post indicated that this was the famous road to Los Angeles.

After a leisurely coffee in a side street diner, he caught a water taxi to Navy Pier. He made his way to where small boats and pleasure cruisers were moored. Most were now laid up for the winter.

He walked briskly, examining the boats, hardly feeling the cold and the lashing wind whipping across the lake. There it was, the 'Moonfleet', a large motor launch. His gaze swept the pier, noting a few tourists braving the cold and wind. He stepped onto the boat, felt for the keys concealed under the portside window rim and ducked into the cabin. It was almost as cold inside as outside, but that didn't matter. He chuckled: it would soon hot up.

Lifting up one of the seats, he searched underneath. Yes, there it was. He pulled out a waterproof package and opened it. Inside was a quantity of plastic explosives and charges. Carefully, he taped some Semtex onto the wooden side of the lower bunk, set the timer and locked up the boat.

A sudden lashing rain added more misery for the few people braving the elements. They ran for shelter in the terminal building. The pier was deserted now. The only signs of life were a lone sailor, swathed in oilskins, and a bus taking passengers back to the city centre.

Head bent against the wind, he walked along the row of bobbing boats until he came to a pleasure cruiser shut up for the winter. Deftly, he jumped aboard and disappeared round the stern. After setting the explosives, he moved on to two smaller boats at the far end of the pier. All four were detonated to go off at five-minute intervals. More distraction tactics to keep the Americans busy while the Generalissimo went after the real prize. Satisfied with his work, he caught the next water taxi back to Union Station.

In a restaurant opposite the station, he bit into a huge beef burger with a slight feeling of disgust. He hated fast food, but he didn't want to waste time sitting around waiting for a meal. By the time the explosions went off, he would be well on his way on the cross-country trek to Los Angeles.

*

Amtrak – Southwest Chief – Chicago to Los Angeles

Baranski smiled at the gangly man sitting opposite him across the table in the dining car.

"We're from Kansas," he drawled. "First time for me and Betsy to travel across state on a train, ain't that right Betsy?"

"Sure is, Carl, sure is," Betsy replied, chewing noisily. "We're going all the way to Albuquerque."

"Where you headed?" Carl interjected.

"Los Angeles… to visit relatives," Baranski added hastily.

His heart raced. He looked at his wristwatch – eight forty-five. The explosives should definitely have gone off by now unless something had gone wrong. Just as he was about to leave the table, a man sitting behind him stood up.

"Hey! There's been a big explosion on Navy Pier back in Chicago. Half the pier has been blown up."

"Where did ya hear that?" a woman opposite asked sceptically.

"I just opened a text message from my brother. It's on all the radio and TV channels. A pile of boats has gone up in smoke. The whole place is ablaze!"

Baranski sat back in his seat, a warm glow of satisfaction suffusing his body.

"Do they know what caused it?" he asked casually.

"Lost the signal!" He jabbed numbers into his cell phone, pressed the phone to his ear and listened intently for a few seconds. "Got something! Hey Marco, you got any more info on the explosions? You don't say! Thanks bro. Nobody knows what happened," he said, turning to the enquiring faces. "A guy working on his boat was blown right up in the air. He was dead on arrival at hospital."

There was no reason for anyone to suspect that the shooter at the United Nations had planted the explosives in Chicago. Still, it was only a matter of time before the FBI and CIA discovered the connection. Baranski went back to his compartment confident he would sleep like a baby.

When they finally reached Albuquerque he had enough time to hop off the train. Dodging the Navajo Indians selling their wares on the platform, he walked to a nearby news stand. He inserted a coin and pulled out an early edition newspaper. Just as he thought, the explosions were all over the front page. Photographs showed wreckage plastered all over the pier and paramedics carrying a stretcher containing the body of the dead sailor. He felt no remorse, just a feeling of intense pleasure. All over the United States seemingly random explosions were taking place. Black Militia field agents were hard at work in Washington, New Orleans, and Dallas; too far apart for them to be connected to him. Whistling to himself, he walked jauntily down the corridor to his compartment.

CHAPTER SIXTY-FOUR

Shropshire, England

The incident room resembled the aftermath of an all-night party. A detective lay slumped in his chair, mouth wide open, head hanging on his chest. Another sprawled, feet on desk, a sheaf of papers strewn where they had fallen. A woman detective, dark shadows under her eyes, yawned loudly. She delved into her handbag, retrieved a small compact and briefly examined her face. She wasn't giving any of her male colleagues the opportunity to make sly jibes about her appearance.

Polystyrene cups and half-eaten sandwiches littered the desktops. Power cords snaked across the floor. Computer screens glowed in the early morning gloom. The stale smell of body odour clung in the air. They had been working flat out for almost forty-eight hours.

Butler sat waiting for Wallace to speak. His boss looked haggard. Deep lines furrowed his forehead. They had barely left the incident room in almost two days. He knew something big was up, even before Wallace had left him in charge, but he was shocked to the core to learn that he had been in Switzerland.

"My God, sir, are you sure? Perhaps it's some kind of scam circulated on the Internet."

"It's no scam, Butler. I went up into the Alps and saw the facility for myself. Damn near had my head blown off by snipers. This doesn't just concern the United Kingdom; it's global. I've been working with Interpol and British Army Intelligence. I used to be in military intelligence myself before I joined the police."

He didn't mention the highly covert IMIC. "The whole facility has been dismantled. We think it may have been re-situated somewhere in Shropshire, probably in a remote area in the countryside. On the other hand there are a lot of old mine workings, derelict stations and shunting sheds where they could set up. We have to stop them before they put their plans into action. I can't tell you any more than that at the moment. There will be big trouble if this leaks to the public and people start panicking. This must be kept strictly between us. Is that absolutely clear?"

He had already briefed the team. As far as they were concerned they were searching for a dangerous armed gang who had robbed a bank in Birmingham. The fake robbery had been set up that morning. It had already been leaked to the press. Television stations would run the story on the lunchtime and evening news. He had arranged a press interview warning the public not to approach anyone they suspected might be connected to the robbery. The Armed Response Team was on standby. That should be enough to keep them happy for now. He picked up the telephone on the second ring.

It was Superintendent Charles Payne, furious that he had been left out of the loop. In icy tones he informed Wallace that the Chief Constable had ordered him to make every available resource at their disposal.

"Orders directly from me," Wallace said, replacing the receiver, "with no intervention from higher up unless requested."

Butler suppressed a grin. He pictured Crew Cut Charlie when the Chief Constable summoned him to his office. With a smirk on his face, he went into the incident room. The team struggled to look wide awake and interested.

"Shape up! Get some breakfast inside you," he barked. I want you back here in thirty minutes. No stragglers."

The team looked shattered, but they would do the job. The men would ask questions – rightly so. It wouldn't be easy to comply with Wallace's instructions without them getting suspicious. Half an hour later, the team drifted back into the incident room carrying cups of steaming tea and coffee.

DC Williams raked his hands through his luxurious mop of dark hair and patted it into place. They looked a bit more alert now. Still, they were all tired from working through the night.

"Okay, let's start with you," Wallace said.

"We've researched all the old mines," DC Williams said. "There are some derelict coal and copper mines and some lime quarries where they could hide out. The copper mine near Clive is well known so I wouldn't put money on that one. There may be some dilapidated buildings on the surface, but the mines would have been sealed off years ago. There's no way they could get inside."

"I don't understand, sir. Why would an armed gang hide out in an old mine?" Blakeman queried.

Ignoring the DC, Wallace turned to a tall brunette perched on the edge of her desk. DS Hembrow picked up a computer printout from the desk.

"There are a number of abandoned stations. Some still have a bit of rusty track running to them, but they're mostly overgrown after years of neglect. One or two show

300

rundown buildings where they could hide." Butler looked at her enquiringly. "Google Earth – I could actually see the old rails."

Nobody else had come up with anything concrete. No sightings, no strange activity, nothing! They had checked with their counterparts over the border. North Wales Police had drawn a complete blank.

"Okay, I want you out scouring the area. DS Risdale and Blakeman, investigate the old mine workings. Hembrow and Williams, check out those old stations. If any of you spot anything suspicious call for backup immediately. Surveillance only – is that clear to everyone? Baker, I want you to stick with DI Butler."

Wallace had recommended that Baker be moved out of CID. He had excellent investigative skills; skills that could prove useful, but he lacked tact and discretion. This was his last chance to redeem himself. In the meantime, one cack-handed mistake and he was out for good. He was young and full of himself. Butler had given him a good talking-to; warned him he was definitely back into uniform if he didn't change his behaviour. He would have his guts for garters if he messed up again.

CHAPTER SIXTY-FIVE

Shropshire Countryside

The huge, articulated lorry slewed its way along the narrow country road, its sides brushing the hedgerows. Early snowfalls had made the going treacherous. It was bad enough on the main highway, but driving on unsalted, icy side roads was lunacy. All the weather reports had warned drivers not to venture out unless it was absolutely necessary. Bill Fuller was carrying equipment for a dairy farm deep in rural Shropshire. It was all packed into enormous crates. They would need a forklift truck to get it out.

He owned a small fleet of six articulated trucks, a couple of smaller lorries and a dozen self-drive delivery vans. Fuller and Sons had been started by his father back in the 1960s. Now, the old man managed the office while Bill, his two sons and his brother, Derek, did most of the driving. This job couldn't have come at a better time. The business had been struggling during the past two years. It would help keep the books in the black for quite some time.

When he had seen the severe weather forecast he tried to postpone the delivery, but the man at the other end of the telephone was adamant.

"The equipment is needed immediately. That's why we're paying you top rate for delivery – on time!" he emphasised.

"But… "

"No buts!" the voice replied.

Bill glanced up at his mirror. Derek's articulated truck was right behind him, but the van was out of sight round the bend in the narrow road. They had been on the road since the early hours of the morning driving at crawl-speed. Twice they had been pulled aside by the police and advised to park up until conditions improved. Bill cursed the idiot! If it wasn't for the generous payment, he would have turned around and gone back to the depot. The disembodied voice of the satnav interrupted his thoughts.

"Exit ahead – after four hundred yards, turn left."

Bill flicked his left-hand indicator and touched the brake to take the turn. The wheels skidded on the glassy surface, threatening to send the vehicle over the crossroads. He turned into the skid and felt the truck right itself. Blowing out his cheeks in a huge breath of relief he swung the vehicle left.

"After five hundred yards, turn left." This road was even narrower, little more than a wide lane. "After three hundred yards you have reached your destination."

"Thank God for that!" Bill muttered aloud.

The final part of the journey was extremely hazardous. The road was full of potholes, covered with ice and snow, threatening to bring the vehicle to a halt at any moment.

"You have reached your destination."

Cautiously, Bill swung up the slight incline towards iron gates set in a high stone wall. The truck laboured up the slope, its wheels spinning on ice. At last it found purchase and edged forward. Bill had been instructed to stay in his vehicle and wait. Picking up his radio he spoke briefly to the other drivers.

"We have to stay put until someone comes to open the gates."

"Well, I hope they hurry up. I'm dying for a pee," Derek yelled back.

"Use the portaloo in your cab."

"I would if I could stop this bloody thing long enough!"

Suddenly, a mud-splattered 4 x 4 appeared in the distance and careered towards them down the bumpy cart track. It stopped at the side of the gate. A figure, huddled inside a parka, pointed a remote control and the gates swung open. From the build and stance, Bill knew it was a woman.

Staying in the 4 x 4, she waved the trucks inside, one by one, and gestured for them to stop on the track. Bill heard the faint click as the gates locked into place. *Funny kind of farm*, he thought. *I know they have to keep the gates locked to stop animals getting out, but this seems a bit over the top.* Expertly, she made a three-point turn and signalled for them to follow her along the road.

The trucks bumped over a mile down the track until they reached a shallow valley clustered with buildings. An old farmhouse, stables, cowsheds and three huge barns stacked with winter feed. The woman in the 4 x 4 drove towards the barns and slewed to a halt throwing up mud and slushy snow. She held up a hand when she saw Bill's cab door open slightly. Derek poked his head out through the driver's window.

"Hey, miss! Is there a loo round here?"

While they were waiting he had relieved himself in the portable loo, a necessity for long-distance drivers, but he was hoping the farmer's wife would call them in out of the cold for a mug of tea. They might even get some food. He salivated at the thought of a succulent farm fry-up.

The woman didn't answer. She marched into the nearest barn closing the Judas door behind her. Within seconds the large doors swung outwards. A forklift truck nosed out followed by two more. They drove alongside the trucks and motioned Bill out of his cab.

"Open them up," a gruff voice ordered. He had a scarf pulled up covering most of his face. "No, just you," he added when Bill motioned to his brother and sons to get out of their vehicles.

"But it will take twice as long doing it that way," Bill complained. He jumped down from his cab. "Surly sod," he muttered under his breath.

By the time he had unlocked the vehicles his fingers were stiff with cold. The man waved him back into his cab.

"After they've been unloaded reverse over there and drive back out the way you came in. She will open the gates for you," he said, indicating the woman.

"Any chance of a cuppa?" Derek yelled through his window.

The man turned away, but a shout from inside the barn brought him up short. He hurried inside while the drivers started to reverse their trucks. He reappeared just as the first truck straightened up ready for the return journey.

"All right, when you've finished unloading go to the farmhouse. You'll be given tea and some hot food. Go on, it will be waiting for you."

Inside the barn a man watched the men jump out of their trucks and head for the farmhouse. The last thing he wanted was a bunch of lorry drivers moaning when they reached the nearest transport cafe. It would soon circulate amongst the driving fraternity how they had driven hundreds of miles, in terrible conditions, without even being offered a hot drink from the farmer's wife.

The four men trudged towards the stone-built farmhouse and knocked on the door. There was no response. Derek tried the door. It was open. Giving it a gentle push he looked round the door into a flagstone hall. The only decoration was a stag's head on the wall and a threadbare rug in the centre of the floor. Smells of bacon and frying reached their nostrils.

"Just what I need," Derek grinned, rubbing his hands in anticipation.

They followed the smell of cooking into the kitchen. Plates of bacon, eggs and sausages lay on the table. A steaming pot of tea sat on the Aga cooking range. There wasn't a soul in sight.

"Hello, missis!" Bill shouted. Complete silence then a woman's voice called from upstairs.

"I'm busy with my work. Help yourselves!"

"Thanks, missus," Bill replied, sitting down at the table.

The men finished their meal, gratefully sinking two mugs of steaming hot tea.

"I need the loo again before I go back out," Derek stated. "The cold plays hell with my bladder."

There was no lavatory on the ground floor. Cautiously, Derek crept up the stairs. Halfway along the landing a dim light showed through an open door. He cursed as a floorboard creaked underneath him. Fortunately, the howling of the wind outside muffled the sound. He was bursting now. His bladder felt like an inflated beach ball.

Tiptoeing to the door, he pressed himself against the wall and peered inside. A black-clad figure wearing a balaclava, obviously a woman, stood looking through the window.

Startled, he stepped back, his heart in his mouth. She had a gun in her hand. For a fleeting second he thought she must be in fancy dress. Turning slightly away from the window, she emptied a box of bullets onto the bed and reloaded the weapon.

He stood frozen to the spot, his mind a whirl of uncertainty. He didn't dare reveal his presence. His breathing was so shallow he thought he would pass out. He had to get a grip. When she turned her back to look out of the window, he crept back along the landing and down the stairs, expecting at any moment to feel the prod of a gun in his back. The others were waiting in the hallway.

"Come on, let's get out of here!" he urged.

"What's the matter?" Bill asked, staring at his brother's ashen face.

"Don't ask questions. Just get the hell out of here."

"If this is one of your pranks again I'll knock your bloody block off!"

They followed Derek across the frozen farmyard to where their trucks were parked near the barn. Bill tugged at his arm.

"What the hell's wrong with you, man? You look like you've seen a ghost!"

"Keep walking. Just look as natural as possible!"

The gruff-voiced man was watching their progress from just inside the barn door.

"Thanks, mate!" Derek shouted. "That grub's set me up for the day!"

The man huddled inside his parka and pointed to the farm track. The woman with the 4 x 4 was waiting to escort them back to the main gate. From the farmhouse bedroom, the other woman studied their departure as they bumped through the gate and drove away. She smiled to herself. The man with the big mouth would have to be silenced before he could pass information on to others.

Bill peered through the windscreen. It had stopped snowing, although the sky was still heavy with dark clouds. They had almost reached the crossroads when his two-way radio crackled.

"Bill," Derek yelled. "There's something funny going on up there in the farm. I saw a woman dressed from head to toe in black. I couldn't see her face. She was wearing a balaclava and she had a gun!"

"Come off it, Derek. This is you and your practical jokes again."

"I swear on my boy's life, this is no scam."

Bill stared ahead. There was no way his brother would swear on his son's life. She must have scared the hell out of him.

"Do you think it may be that armed gang they mentioned on the news?"

"I admit it does seem a bit odd," Bill replied. "Come to think of it, nobody showed their faces and why have electronic gates?"

Suddenly, Derek's vehicle slewed from side to side. Instinctively, Bill touched the brakes, momentarily losing control of his vehicle. Ahead of him, his brother's truck careered from side to side then ploughed into the hedgerow. The vehicle jack-knifed, turning the cab upside down, its wheels spinning furiously in the air. Bill righted his truck just as it reached the crashed vehicle. Skidding to a halt, he jumped out of the cab and slithered over the ice. Derek was slumped at a crazy angle over the steering wheel, blood oozing from his mouth and nose.

Between them they yanked at the mangled cab door, but it wouldn't budge. Suddenly, it gave way, sending his son sprawling into the icy ditch. Bill felt for a pulse. "Thank God, he's alive! Ring 999!"

They were still waiting for the emergency services when the drone of an aircraft approaching caught their attention. Squinting against the light they watched it battling the wind as it flew towards them.

"It looks like a police chopper," Chris said.

"No. It hasn't got any markings."

The helicopter flew overhead. Inside the cockpit, Ivan stared down at the stricken vehicle through his binoculars. He could see Derek's slumped body, the blood over his face. He couldn't be sure he was dead, but he was obviously unconscious. They had fixed his brakes while he walked back from the farmhouse. It would look like another accident on the icy roads.

Bill waved frantically, trying to catch the attention of the pilot. He must be able to see the crash. Suddenly, it circled overhead and flew away quickly disappearing into the murk. It seemed like an eternity before the wail of a siren filled the air.

"Thank God!" Bill exclaimed. A police 4 x 4 and a paramedic vehicle slewed to a halt.

"What's his name?" the emergency doctor shouted.

"Derek Fuller; he's my brother," Bill answered, his bowels churning with fear.

"Derek, can you hear me? We're going to give you an injection to stop the pain then we'll fit a neck brace." He turned to the policeman. "An air ambulance is on its way. Once Fire and Rescue get him out, he can be winched up from here. Luckily, there are few trees, just open fields."

As soon as the firemen had cut off the truck door, the doctor checked Derek's vital signs then moved aside while they eased him from the cabin. His eyelids flickered and opened for a few seconds. Bill grabbed his hand. "You'll be okay, bro, you'll be okay."

The drone of the air ambulance cut off his words as it flew into sight. Bill breathed a sigh of relief when Derek was winched aboard. He watched the helicopter circle and fly off towards Shrewsbury.

"What happened here?" the young constable asked.

"His truck just slewed over the road. He must have lost control of it," Bill answered. "I'd like to go to the hospital with him. My sons will give you as much information as they can."

"Well, these trucks are stuck until we get a recovery vehicle to lift that one out. There's no point trying to reverse back into the farm entrance. The road comes to a dead end about half a mile beyond it. We'll take you all to the hospital, but we'll need to question you as soon as possible."

"My brother thought there was something odd going on at the farmhouse where we delivered the equipment. He said something about a masked woman with a gun."

"A gun?"

"Yes, he was scared stiff. Could it be that armed gang on the run?"

Looking thoughtful, the policeman returned to his car and reported what he had been told.

"Unlikely, but I'll patch it through to DCI Wallace," the duty sergeant said.

*

Wallace paced to and fro in the incident room, his face haggard from lack of sleep. His frustration was evident for all to see. He perched on the edge of Butler's desk impatiently devil-drumming. It was getting on his nerves, but he dared not complain, not when the Guv was in a mood.

"Damn it, Butler! We have to get a lead on this case! If we don't… "

He was interrupted by the telephone shrilling in his office. Leaving the words hanging in the air, he marched back to his room with Butler at his heels.

"Wallace," he said curtly.

"Sir, duty sergeant. There's been a road traffic accident about twenty miles from Shrewsbury."

"I think you've got the wrong department," Wallace answered sarcastically.

"PC Perkins insists on speaking to you. He says he's got important information regarding the armed gang."

Wallace sighed. "Okay, patch him through." This had better be good. "What have you got, Perkins?"

"Sir, Bill Fuller, the driver of one of the trucks, seemed to think there was something funny going on in the farm where they delivered some equipment. His brother was injured in the accident, but he told him just before that he saw a masked woman with a gun. He thought it may be the armed gang on the loose. He didn't say any more than that."

"Did they question the brother?"

"No, sir. He's still unconscious: probably serious head injuries. He may not come out of it."

"Whatever you do, don't go near that farmhouse and

keep quiet about this. We don't want to stir up the local community. The last thing we want is a bunch of vigilante farmers toting shotguns. Is that clear?"

Butler was all ears now, leaning forward in his seat like a cat waiting to pounce. Wallace replaced the receiver and looked at Butler without saying a word. Could it be where the Generalissimo had set up his new camp?

"Get this Bill Fuller in for questioning. I want undercover officers and an armed response team on standby."

"The Super's not going to like this, sir?"

Wallace didn't care what Payne thought. The Chief Constable would give the go-ahead for whatever he needed. His officers would have to keep a low profile. He didn't want to put the wind up the 'gang' and give them a chance to disappear again.

"Get as many men into the area as possible. I want the farm and its surroundings completely covered. For now, this is a covert operation. No heroics, otherwise it could all blow up in our faces and I don't mean just figuratively. Then I want you back here ready for when Fuller comes in for questioning."

"I'm already on it!" Butler replied, heading for the door.

*

Bill Fuller sat opposite Wallace and Butler, his face drawn and anxious, waiting for one of them to speak.

"I'm sorry about your brother, Mr Fuller. Everything possible will be done for him."

"Thank you," Bill replied nervously.

"Mr Fuller, can you relate to us exactly what your brother

told you when you were at the farmhouse?"

"I've already told the officer when he came to the scene."

"I appreciate that, Mr Fuller, but I'd like you to tell me again. What exactly did he say?"

"We'd had two big mugs of tea. Derek went upstairs to find the loo. When he came back down he seemed scared. He said he saw a woman loading a gun."

"He was sure it was a real gun? Not a replica or a child's toy?"

"Derek was in the army before he joined the business. He'd know if it wasn't a real gun. He said she was dressed in black, from head to toe, and wearing a balaclava."

"Can you describe the person who put in the order for equipment?"

"No, the whole business was a bit strange. I dealt with the orders and delivery schedules. Everything was done by e-mail, but I could only reply to queries. I couldn't contact anyone myself."

"Do you have the e-mail address?"

"No, it changed every time they sent one. It's not how we usually do business, but it was too lucrative a contract to turn down. The business has been struggling a bit lately."

"Did you see anyone else or anything that seemed a bit odd?"

"When we got to the farm a woman met us at the gates. We only saw one other guy. I don't know what they looked like, but they were dressed in black. Both of them had their hoods zipped up over their faces. There was nobody in the kitchen either. The food had been left on the table. It just seemed a bit peculiar, that's all."

"Thank you. You've been very helpful to our enquiries.

DI Butler, get someone to take Mr Fuller back to the hospital."

"Bingo!" Wallace slammed his fist into the palm of his hand. It had to be the Generalissimo's men hiding out in the farmhouse.

CHAPTER SIXTY-SIX

Los Angeles, California

Baranski was tired after the long train journey. He was bored with inane small talk every mealtime, but he had to act as normally as possible. Twice they had collided with cattle walking across the tracks as they trundled across the Mojave Desert. He watched a string of cars snaking around the Cajun Pass in the receding light. The train was already hours late after hitting a cow on the track.

By the time they reached Los Angeles, Baranski was stressed out. Fuming inwardly, he called a cab to take him to the Hertz rental. Using his false name and passport he picked up the keys to a Pontiac.

Following the instructions he had been given, he drove to the end of Canyon Drive and parked up. This wouldn't be easy. His target was under surveillance twenty-four hours a day. It was almost dark when the last few stragglers wandered down to their parked cars and drove away. Baranski trudged up the wide trail, dodging piles of horse dung, until he came to a paved road. Making a left turn, he laboured up the last hundred yards to where his target loomed over the city.

Thanks to local residents threatening lawsuits, it wasn't lit up at night. His first task was to disable the high-tech alarm systems. He fished out a small object, similar to a garage remote control, and pointed it at the security gate until he heard a faint click. Tentatively, he pushed it open. He waited a few seconds expecting the alarms to kick in. Nothing happened. Cautiously, he climbed up the hill until he was right underneath the target. He placed plastic explosives at three points along the base, set the charges and scrambled back down.

He jumped into the car and shot off in a cloud of dust, along Mulholland Drive onto Cahuenga Boulevard. This would give him a clear view of his handiwork. There were only three other empty cars parked up at the viewing point. Baranski mounted the steps and stood at the edge of a group of sightseers admiring the city spread out below them.

"Wow, what a spectacular view!" exclaimed a young woman staring out across the Los Angeles Basin.

Baranski smiled. It would be even more spectacular in a few seconds. Suddenly, a loud explosion filled the air. The famous HOLLYWOOD sign exploded like matchwood sending debris shooting into the night sky. Another blast, then another, quickly followed. The group stared in disbelief as debris fell to the ground. A huge cloud of dust temporarily clouded their view. When it cleared all that was left of the sign was a single spar of the letter 'H'. From a distance sirens wailed; the drone of a helicopter came closer. It flew through the dust circling the empty space where the sign had stood. Baranski exhaled a sigh of satisfaction. Soon his work would be done.

CHAPTER SIXTY-SEVEN

Las Vegas, Nevada

Jake Harrison eased his shoulders and neck muscles. He had been sitting at his computer for hours. Daytime temperatures were unseasonably hot for December; almost fifty-five degrees Fahrenheit. The sun glared through the enormous plate-glass window. It was time for a break. He looked down over the concrete mass of Las Vegas, stark and uninviting in daylight. It looked like an enormous building site. Two hotels had been blasted to the ground a few months before. Now, towering skeletal frames rose out of the ground ready for the rebuild. Lavish amounts of money would be spent creating yet another fabulous hotel.

All sorts of people visited Vegas. Hardened gamblers who played the tables for a living, saddos who lost their shirts on the turn of a card; prostitutes, wannabe celebrities and get-rich-quick merchants, But it was mainly the tourists who kept the place going. Over two and a half million people turned up in December. They spent their time idling along 'the strip', standing on moving pavements that took them from hotel to hotel: shopping in the two-mile arcade or huddled over tables in the casinos.

His stomach growled, reminding him that he hadn't eaten since eight that morning. He grabbed his jacket and headed for the shopping mall. There was a great little restaurant that wouldn't be too crowded this time of the evening.

Jake sat under a reproduction vintage lamp post and stared up at the artificial sky that covered the length of the mall. It had been created to give tourists the feeling of being out of doors. In the summer months they crowded inside to escape the searing heat. He glanced at his watch – almost five o'clock. It would be dark soon, bringing the crowds out to admire the illuminations.

It was close on seven by the time he finished his giant steak and fries. He gulped down the last of his lager, slapped a twenty-dollar bill on the table, and retraced his steps to the main entrance. Outside it was pleasantly cool and quiet. He inhaled deeply, savouring the cool air. The sidewalks had already filled up with ambling tourists.

Outside the Bellagio, a crowd watched the fabulous, illuminated fountain display. Jets of water danced to the strains of Elvis Presley's 'Viva Las Vegas'. Seeing the strip lit up always gave him a kick. He ran across the road towards the Bellagio, dodging taxis taking people to shows or down to Freemont Street, the original Las Vegas of the fifties. He felt like an hour in the casinos and a couple of drinks.

Settling at a vacant machine, he signalled to one of the waitresses carrying trays of free drinks around the casino.

"Bourbon on the rocks."

"Your drink, sir," the attractive brunette said, handing him a drink from her tray.

"Thanks, babe."

He pressed a dollar bill into her hand and turned back to the machine. His finger was poised on the 'hit' button when all the lights went out.

"What the hell?" He whirled around at the sound of breaking glass behind him. The casino was in complete darkness. "Must be a total power cut," he muttered.

Punters were still sitting down waiting for the lights to come back on. Pulling out the penlight he always carried, he threaded his way through lines of disabled machines towards the tables near reception. He shone his flashlight over the long counter. Shadowy figures scurried behind it issuing instructions to guests.

"Please stay where you are until the lights come back on. The emergency generator will kick in shortly. It's just a power cut."

Suddenly, the auxiliary lighting kicked in restoring some normality to the scene. Seconds later, the lights flickered and died again. Jake never did like being caught up in crowds, particularly in the dark. He felt claustrophobic. He couldn't breathe properly. Pushing his way towards the glass entrance he lunged outside into complete blackness.

Not a single light glimmered along the strip. Just the faint image of the imitation Eiffel Tower indicated the existence of the Paris Hotel. The jabber of shuffling, frightened crowds lining the path from the Bellagio to the road filled the air.

"Hey!" a woman shrieked. "Someone's stolen my purse!"

People started shoving and pushing. Others ran aimlessly across the road to the mall. Tyres screeched followed by a dull thud and a loud scream.

"Someone's been hit!"

In the middle of the road a group of tourists stood frozen in automobile headlights like frightened rabbits. Cigarette lighters sparked. Children waved their light sticks, catching faces in an eerie, green glow. Suddenly, pandemonium broke

319

out. People started screaming and running towards the hotels.

Jake ran into the middle of the road waving his arms at the line of stationary cars by the broken down traffic lights.

"The whole place is blacked out!" he yelled. "Turn your vehicles at an angle and fix your headlights on the sidewalk. Let's get some light over there."

Jake ran along the line of cars shouting instructions. Suddenly, a blaze of light lit up the crowds. It had an immediate calming effect. A few tourists giggled nervously; mothers soothed frightened children. In the distance a siren screamed. At *last*, the cavalry had arrived.

Police, ambulances and emergency services positioned themselves all along the strip.

"Please stay where you are until the situation has been assessed!" a police officer shouted through a bullhorn.

"When will the lights come back on?" a woman yelled. "That's what we came here for; to see the lights! I'll be contacting my attorney about this!"

"Shut up, Janie," ordered the burly guy with her.

"What's up?" Jake queried, approaching Lieutenant Benny Squires.

He'd known him since he was a detective sergeant and Benny was a gangly rookie, looking like a schoolboy in an oversized suit. He had been assigned to Jake for his first stint in plain clothes. They were partners for ten years until Benny got married. His wife was ambitious for him. She didn't like him hanging around with 'that loser', as she referred to Jake, when he left the police force and set up his own detective agency.

"Two murders already tonight. Just what I need. The crime rate will shoot up if this isn't sorted out fast." The squad car radio crackled. "Hold on, Jake. Yeah, Squires. Say again. Ya gotta be kidding me? It's the precinct duty officer," he said, turning to Jake. "Los Angeles is completely blacked out. Two trains crashed in the subway." He shook his head in disbelief.

"I don't believe it! Some nut tried to blow up the Hoover Dam! They think it's a terrorist attack. We've gotta get these people off the streets."

"I'll get back over to the Bellagio," Jake said.

"Thanks, Jake; Leiberman can go with you."

Squires sent two uniformed cops to cover Caesar's Palace. There was nothing more he could do until backup arrived.

People were already gravitating towards their hotels as best they could, feeling their way along in the moonless, overcast night. A huge groan, like a disturbed animal woken from sleep, rolled along the strip as people realised they were being corralled indoors.

"Take your hands off of me, bub!"

Jake felt the full force of a fist connect with the side of his head. He lashed out in the gloom and made contact with the flabby guts of the man who had swung the punch at him. He groaned and dropped to the ground, temporarily winded. Jake hauled him to his feet and poked him in the ribs with his penlight.

"Okay! Okay! I'm going inside. Stash the gun."

Slowly, the crowds diminished. There was very little noise now, just the shuffling of feet and the occasional whimper of a small child.

Jake picked his way through the throng in the Bellagio lobby. Dark figures moved between the tables scooping up scattered chips. There were no cameras to monitor their progress. Someone appeared at his side with a storm lantern. It gave out just enough light for him to pick out the nearest bodies sitting on the floor. He clambered up onto the reception counter.

"Okay," he shouted above the noise. "The elevators are down. Anyone with rooms on the first or second floors can walk up. Let Officer Leiberman know. He's standing right next to me. We'll let you up one floor at a time. The rest of you remain here. It's too dangerous to walk up to the other floors without lighting. I want a show of hands. How many of you are staying at other hotels?"

A few dozen hands shot into the air. "Okay, you'll have to bed down here in reception for the night. It's lucky it's been so warm, because there's no heating. Keep yourselves as warm as you can. Those of you who are guests will be more familiar with the outline of the hotel. There are plenty of carpeted public areas where you can make yourselves comfortable, if you can find your way. Those of you with torches or lighters use them sparingly. You may need them during the night. Reception staff will direct you to rest rooms."

*

In out-of-town retail outlets and malls, looters took advantage of the absence of thousands of tacky neon lights. The 'night' girls, entwined with their latest punter when the lights went out, fearfully forced them out onto the street.

In a sleazy room off the strip, a brassy blonde plied her trade without enthusiasm. Holly Jackson, otherwise known as Roxy to the punters, struggled with the flashy tie around her neck. She clawed at the man bending over her. She couldn't see his face now. His charming veneer had swiftly transformed into sadistic brutality. As she drifted into unconsciousness she wondered why the lights had gone out. One last pull on the tie and she was silenced forever. She wouldn't work again, not tonight, not ever.

The man unwound his tie from Roxy's neck and casually put it in his pocket. Carefully, he set her body straight on the bed and pulled the sheet up to her neck, covering the wheals. He flicked on his cigarette lighter. Leaning over, he closed the terror-filled eyes. She looked so peaceful, almost like a little girl, with her lips slightly parted. Only the specks of blood staining the sheet belied her peaceful pose.

For a moment he stood and watched her. So beautiful, but she was expendable. He dabbed the scratch marks on his face with a handkerchief and tucked it away with the tie. He would have to dispose of them. Snapping his lighter shut, Baranski stepped into the corridor, quietly closing the door behind him. He smiled to himself. One more city and his mission was complete.

Somewhere in the Bible Belt of America, Holly's parents gazed lovingly at the photograph she had sent them. A fresh-faced girl, standing outside a realtor's office with a millboard in her hand, smiled at them. On the back of the photograph Holly had written, 'This is where I work.'

"Our Holly's doin' mighty well for herself, Emmy, mighty well."

In Freemont Street, Baranski moved as sure-footed as a cat in the blackness of the night. Frightened revellers had sought safety inside restaurants and bars lit with feeble candlelight. Everywhere, panic and fear roamed the darkened streets.

CHAPTER SIXTY-EIGHT

San Fransico, USA – Canada

It took him over eight hours to reach San Francisco on the freeway, dodging in and out of traffic on the multi-lane road. He stopped in a motel on the outskirts of the city. He didn't sleep, just passed time drinking coffee and occasionally dozing.

Around nine o'clock the next morning he checked out and hit the road. Spotting a roadside diner, he pulled in and ordered an enormous breakfast. His work had made him hungry. Besides, he didn't want to arrive at his hotel too early. He wanted to make sure his room was ready. He checked in just after midday.

"Your room is ready for you, Mr Dudek. Have a nice day."

In his room Baranski opened his suitcase. He could only carry a limited amount of explosives from Chicago, enough for his last job. What he had left was just enough to cause confusion and fear, not enough to blow up the target.

At two o' clock, he left the hotel and headed towards the Golden Gate Bridge. He paid the six dollars toll and drove down the access road at the regulation speed. His hand rested on the holdall he had purchased earlier. Sweating with anxiety, he pulled it onto his lap. The traffic was heavy, threatening to hold him up. He must be in a clear flow of traffic if he was to come out of this alive. He had set the charges to allow him time to get off the bridge.

When he reached the middle point, he threw the holdall out onto the road and drove on. As he exited the famous landmark, a loud explosion rocked the bridge. Cars screeched to a halt, jack-knifing across the lanes. Baranski drove on. He had to get away before the emergency services and police arrived. He headed for Interstate 5. It would take him right up to the Canadian border to British Columbia Highway 99. Tomorrow morning he would be on his pre-booked flight from Vancouver to Geneva.

*

British Columbia, Highway 99

He had been driving for hours through freezing fog and rain. He cursed the weather and the slow progress of traffic. Ahead, the queue of vehicles moved at a snail's pace through border control. Baranski felt the perspiration rolling down his neck, soaking his shirt collar. Quickly, he wiped his face with a handkerchief and took a brief glance at himself in the driver's mirror. The long hours of driving without a break showed in his pasty face.

Slowly, he nudged forward. His heart skipped a beat. Police! Three patrol cars were parked up diagonally across the highway. Something was up! *Don't be a fool*, he chastised himself. They were bound to have alerted border police. Just stay calm. He came to a stop beside the Border Protection booth. He didn't anticipate any problems, but he had to be extra careful not to display any signs of nervousness: anything that would alert the craggy-faced man behind the window.

"Your passport, sir."

"Filthy day," he commented.

The cop ignored the pleasantry. "Polish?" He looked searchingly at Baranski. "What's your business in Canada?"

"I'm a wine dealer. I visit the United States a couple of times a year, usually to the Napa Valley. I decided this trip I'd take some time out and drive up to Canada. I'm meeting up with some old friends. They're on holiday in Vancouver."

"Visa?"

Baranski produced his forged visa. Poles didn't have much chance of getting an official visa, especially for America. It was usually hit and miss.

"Where are your friends staying sir?"

"The Sheraton."

An overweight cop, with his hand on his gun, lowered his head to the window.

"Step out of the car, sir."

"I've done nothing wrong! I'm just a businessman taking some leisure time."

"Just do as I say. Step out of the car. Anything other than personal luggage in the trunk?"

"Just a pile of wine catalogues and a box of souvenir glasses."

The policeman nodded to his partner. He walked around to the trunk and yanked it open. After rummaging around amongst the contents, he leaned into the car and searched the glove compartment, under the seats and the door storage area.

"Will you be travelling back to the US?"

"Yes, in about a week's time," Baranski lied.

"Okay, you can get back in the car, sir."

The policeman waved him on and walked to the next vehicle in the line. Baranski smiled as he drove into Canada. There was no reason for them to suspect Tarek Dudek.

CHAPTER SIXTY-NINE

Washington, DC

The United States National Security Council, along with representatives of G8 countries, sat around the table with grim expressions on their faces. The shooting in New York, and a series of bomb attacks across the United States and Europe had made their impact. Most were minor with very little loss of life, but it was enough to scare them.

The group stirred when the doors behind them opened and two men entered the room. A bleak expression on his elongated face, Clive Pearce loped to a chair at the head of the table.

"Good morning gentlemen and *ladies*," he added, noting the two women sitting at the far end of the table. "This is Major Jack Conrad, British Military Intelligence. What he has to say is of vital importance to all our countries."

Conrad stood up. "The bombings in America and Europe are part of an organised plan to weaken morale," he stated. "Similar incidents have occurred in Russia and the Far East. So far most have been relatively minor in terms of loss of life. I believe that the intention is to divert attention from the real purpose. The bombings and attacks on utilities are just the beginning: the tip of the iceberg. They've been executed by an organisation known as the Black Militia."

A whisper of consternation and expressions of disbeliefs echoed round the room.

"I've actually seen this Militia. It's not an army in the conventional sense. More an organisation composed of a few hundred people, but extremely powerful. It's led by a man known as the Generalissimo."

"Come on, you can't be serious!" a highly decorated military man exclaimed.

"I can assure you I'm deadly serious."

"It's Islamist terrorists. Look what's happened in Germany, France, Belgium. They're all over the place."

"That's true, but these attacks are different. They are not based on religious fundamentalism, although his aim is world domination."

"Go on, Jack," Pearce said.

"After discovering their facility in the Swiss Alps I was taken captive, but I managed to escape. I was investigating the disappearance of two British army officers. It transpired there was a connection between them and murder victims found in Shropshire on Detective Chief Inspector Ben Wallace's patch."

"Do ya think we wouldn't have uncovered this plot?" a heavy-jowled man in his sixties questioned. "The CIA don't need any lessons from British Intelligence. Langley would know."

"Let him finish," Pearce interjected.

"They were also connected to one of your senators; Ethan Bateman," Conrad continued.

A corporate gasp emanated from the Americans when he disclosed the theft of top-secret research papers from Bateman's facility in the Nevada Desert. He described how he had found him murdered in a hotel room in Paris and the plea for help on his laptop. Finally, he told them how they had traced a Russian 'sleeper' in GCHQ and set him up using Foley as bait.

"Colin Lynes had been put in place by the Russian Security Services, but we believe he was also working for the Generalissimo. We had no idea at the time that this Black Militia existed. British Intelligence has been working non-stop to flush them out. Wallace is ex-British Military Intelligence. We planted him in the facility to discover what was going on."

"Major Conrad, are you telling us that this Militia is going to wage war on us?" the Attorney General asked.

Grunts of amusement ran round the room. The German representative stood up, a scowl on his face.

"The Black Militia, the Generalissimo. Do you think we are fools to swallow such nonsense? You say they will wage war against the most powerful countries on the globe?"

"Not a conventional war. What has happened so far is a mere distraction while he puts his plan into motion. I believe the real threat will come through cyberspace."

"These threats have been in existence for years," the Homeland Security Advisor interjected. "Every day hackers try to get into systems. The Pentagon has scores of e-mails containing computer threats. It's a constant. Every major country is aware of this hacking and they deal with it."

"This is different. The Generalissimo has recruited computer experts from all over the world. He's promised them riches beyond their dreams in exchange for their total loyalty and expertise. We believe that the Generalissimo is ex-KGB."

"I protest!" a surly voice shouted. "It is a trick to implicate us!"

"No," Pearce interjected. "We believe it is a man called Pavel Alexei Plushenko."

"Now I know it is a fairy tale. Plushenko died in a boating accident in 1989 in East Berlin. If what you say is true, our security services would have captured him." He shrugged his shoulders. "It is not possible."

Hear me out," Conrad said. "Our intelligence has informed us that he foiled a plan to murder him, because he was a loose cannon. He's been planning this 'war' for over twenty-five years. Plushenko is a psychopathic megalomaniac who thinks he can rule the world. There have been others in history," he added, avoiding the gazes of the German and Russian representatives. "Their intention is to strike when morale is low. The Generalissimo's experts have developed a computer virus known as 'Black Crystal'. It's deadly. Once one computer is infected it will shut down systems all over the world."

"Do you really expect us to believe that this ex-KGB guy is capable of infiltrating the Pentagon and the NSA?" General Logan interrupted.

"Imagine what would happen if all power stations, oil rigs, banks, industries and military systems closed down," Conrad continued. "They would have complete control over everybody, every organisation."

"It wouldn't be the first time someone hacked into the Pentagon," Pearce interjected.

The Americans shuffled uncomfortably. Behind them the door swung open. A young subaltern marched smartly towards the table and handed an envelope to Pearce. Quickly, he read the contents then stuffed it into his pocket.

"We have the full support of the Prime Minister," Pearce said.

The tension in the air was palpable as the group rose to leave.

"I'll inform the President." the Chairman of the Joint Chiefs of Staff said, rising from his chair. "Mr Conrad, how much time do we have?"

"Operation Black Crystal is imminent."

CHAPTER SEVENTY

London, England

Clive Pearce breathed a sigh of relief when the military jet kissed the runway and taxied to a stop in RAF Lakenheath. The whopping of helicopter blades nearby filled the air. He hastened down the steps and ran the hundred yards to the chopper. Within seconds they were airborne and on their way to the London Heliport in Battersea where a car was waiting to take him to IMIC headquarters.

Frustrated by heavy traffic and Christmas shoppers, he cursed under his breath until they arrived at Trentor Enterprises. Isobel was still glued to her computer when he barged into the outer office.

"Contact Lambert and Ryder," he said.

They operated with a small team of highly experienced agents when engaged in covert assignments. Besides Conrad, only two others knew Breakdancer's real identity or the location of IMIC headquarters. Tim Lambert and Steve Ryder would have to be briefed. He wanted them out on the streets of London immediately.

*

A buzz of excitement and conversation circulated throughout the theatre. Ryder glanced sideways at his long-suffering girlfriend. Charlotte was a beautiful woman with shining chestnut hair that she wore just shoulder length. When he knew she was coming up from Oxford for the weekend to do some Christmas shopping, he had bought tickets for *Jersey Boys*. Suddenly, the lights dimmed and the crowd hushed in anticipation. Charlotte tapped her foot in time with the rhythm throughout the show.

"They're fabulous," she enthused as the curtain fell. With a roar of approval the crowd was on its feet clapping and whistling with delight. Fortunately, they had end seats so they started for the exit before the crowd.

"I wonder where Tim is? He promised to meet us for a drink before the show. It's not like him to let us down."

"He's probably tied up in a meeting. I'm sure he'll be waiting for us in the hotel when we get back," Ryder said.

He sighed when his mobile vibrated in his pocket. Charlotte glared at him when he flipped it open. "Business, I won't be long. Wait in the bar." It was always the same whenever they went out for the evening.

"I want you in immediately," Pearce said. "I've just arrived back from Washington DC. All I can tell you over the blower is that the 'deal' I'm working on is highly confidential and very precarious. The 'business' may be going global."

There was an urgency in Pearce's voice, a hint of fear that he had never heard before.

"Understood," he replied, instantly recognising the coded language they used.

"You must be on the alert at all times. Things could happen in the 'business' that are out of our control. It's not just our British-based 'companies'. Our global enterprises are being seriously threatened. Please be extra careful in your 'negotiations'. There's a possibility that the 'market' will drop very soon."

Ryder heard the receiver click at the other end followed by the call-disconnected sound. What the hell was going on and what had Peace been doing in Washington DC? His expression was grim when he entered the bar. Charlotte frowned. She had seen that look before and she didn't like it one bit.

"Weren't they wonderful!" Charlotte exclaimed.

Before he could respond, all the lights went out. People muttered nervously in the darkness.

"Come on somebody. Put the lights back on."

Suddenly, a metallic voice echoed throughout the theatre.

"The lights will be back on as soon as possible. Please remain where you are. I repeat, in the interests of safety, please remain in your seats."

"Come on, let's get out of here!" Ryder urged.

"No, I can't see. It's safer to wait until the lights go on again."

Ryder grabbed Charlotte's arm and pushed her towards the door. His training always kicked in whenever he was inside a building. He knew exactly how to get to the nearest exit. Feeling his way along the wall and down the stairs they reached the foyer. Everything was in darkness. With Charlotte in tow, he pushed through the doors onto the pavement.

There wasn't a glimmer of light anywhere; not from the restaurants, shops or other theatres. The only light was from the headlights of passing vehicles. Was this to do with Pearce's warning? No, it was probably sheer coincidence. He hailed a passing taxi and bundled Charlotte inside.

"Royal Horse Guards Hotel. Any idea what's happened?" he asked the cabby.

"Not a clue, guv. Drivers have been reporting in from all over. There seems to be a power cut all over the city."

He was interrupted by the wail of police sirens behind him. He pulled over to the side to let them pass. Four cars passed, one behind the other.

"Bloody terrorists, that's what it is, bloody terrorists! Well, mate, I aint gonna let 'em affect me business again, that's for sure! I'm staying wiv me cab!"

Hotel reception was in complete darkness, except for a few flickering candles and a couple of storm lanterns. Ryder escorted Charlotte to the bar.

"It's safer to sit in the public areas until the situation has been remedied."

"Actually, it looks quite cosy in here," she remarked, noting candlelight reflecting on mirrors and glasses.

People sat huddled together, giggling and talking in low voices, enjoying the comforts of a four-star hotel even in a crisis. Ryder settled Charlotte with a group of people who had obviously been to see the same show earlier in the day.

"I won't be long," he said. "I'm going to see if I can find out what's happened."

He made his way out onto the street and walked towards the embankment. Not a single street lamp glowed in the darkness. The vague shape of the London Eye towered over the Thames. Faint lights flickered and died in some of the cabins. Stranded passengers were using cigarette lighters to attract attention. Suddenly, an icy wind whipped up, sweeping the clouds away like a harried housewife. Briefly, a pale moon peeped through, illuminating the streets, before disappearing behind a fresh band of cloud.

Turning on his heel, he retraced his steps past the hotel. He made his way into Northumberland Avenue and swiftly walked to Trafalgar Square. Crowds of tourists and Christmas revellers thronged the square, their faces temporarily caught in the glow of a match or cigarette lighter. They had been admiring the enormous Christmas tree when the lights went out. With a screech of tyres a police car pulled up. An officer got out and stood on the pavement at the edge of the crowd, a bullhorn at the ready.

"Please remain where you are until further instructions. Hold on to your valuables and handbags and watch out for pickpockets. Everything possible is being done to remedy the situation."

"Why can't we go back to our hotels?" a voice shouted from the crowd, "We'd be safer there." A chorus of voices agreed, but the officer was adamant.

"I repeat, stay where you are!"

"It's terrorists. They must have planted a bomb!" a woman shrieked.

Suddenly, the mass of bodies started shoving and pushing to get to the edge of the square, knocking people over in the process. Unable to control the crowd, the police officer ran to his patrol car and radioed for backup, but it was too late. Panic rippled through the crowd. An elderly man sank to the ground as a hefty teenager pushed him violently aside. His wife screamed hysterically in the darkness. "Danny! Danny! Where are you?" The milling bodies pushed her forwards to the edge of the square. Nobody paid any attention to Danny, lying bleeding and unconscious under their feet.

A little girl screamed in fear. Her father hoisted her onto his shoulders and tried to barge through the crowd, his wife clinging to his arm. Suddenly, the man stumbled and lost his footing. The child fell backwards from his shoulders landing heavily on the ground. Lost under a hundred pounding feet; kicked like a football under a mass of fleeing bodies.

Ryder lunged across the road battling the surging crowd rushing towards him. He hailed a passing taxi, which was miraculously still running.

"North Pembury Avenue and step on it!" he instructed the driver.

He had to get to IMIC headquarters to find out what was going on. Ryder had the cab door open as it screeched to a halt. He shoved a note into the driver's hand and raced up the steps. Trentor Enterprises was closed for business at this time of night. He pressed the buzzer for Isobel's office and waited for her to answer.

"Sky diver," he said using his code name. "I'm on my way up."

The whole building was shrouded in darkness. The lifts would be out of action. He would have to access the emergency stairs. Fishing out his penlight, he shone it along the counter to the right of the reception area until it hit the fire exit door. He felt his way up the stairs to the second floor and exited into the corridor.

It was pitch-black, devoid of any windows to let in even a glimmer of external light. Cautiously, he moved along the corridor until he came to two doors next to each other marked 'Private – Staff Only'. One was a small store cupboard full of cleaning equipment. The other was lined with heavy filing cabinets from floor to ceiling. Pulling off the front of a dummy electrical point, he pressed a button. A set of cabinets swung out revealing a metal staircase leading up to IMIC's headquarters on the fourth floor.

A faint gleam of light showed under a door in the darkened corridor. He pushed it open. Isobel waved him in. Her office and Pearce's were lit with wind-up storm lanterns. She held up a hand while continuing to listen on her satellite phone. Finally, she turned to him.

"There are electricity cuts in cities all over the country, from London to Edinburgh and Cardiff. A lot of big towns are also without power. It's not just domestic usage; it's shops, factories, hospitals. Fortunately, hospitals have been able to switch to emergency generators."

"I've just come from Trafalgar Square. It's absolute chaos. The police can't keep the crowds under control. Pearce rang me on satellite phone. All the landlines are down, even the high security lines. What the hell's going on, Isobel?"

"I don't know, Steve," she shrugged. "Jack Conrad and Tim Lambert are already here."

Ryder was a big man, six feet three inches tall with shoulders like a rugby fullback. Brown eyes and dark hair cropped close to his head, giving him a bullish appearance. In his tweed suit he looked more like a well-off farmer than the product of one of the top public schools in the country.

"Oxford Street is like a bloody war zone!" he exclaimed, slumping into a chair opposite Clive Pearce. "I've seen films about the blackouts during the war. It's eerie. Not a light anywhere in the city, but it's not like the Blitz. There's no community spirit out there. Thugs are breaking windows and looting stores, grabbing as much as they can. They're making the most of it."

"That's not all," Tim interrupted. "I contacted a doctor pal of mine working in A&E at Charing Cross Hospital. They're snowed under with muggings and accidents caused by the blackout. That's not the worst of it either. They received five people with serious knife wounds and a young girl brutally raped and beaten. She's on a life support machine."

Lambert was the exact opposite of Ryder. Softly spoken, sandy hair flopping over his ice-blue eyes and a pale complexion. There was nothing robust-looking about him, but his body was hard and toned from physical activity. An Oxford Blue, an Olympic-standard swimmer and a computer expert. On top of that, his IQ was off the chart.

"It's chaos across the States," Conrad interjected. "Las Vegas, Los Angeles, San Fransisco, New York, Philadelphia, Chicago and Boston; all blacked out. Apparently, Toronto and Montreal have also been hit by power cuts. The lights went out at night and came back on the following morning. The Generalissimo is playing mind games, but this is just the beginning." He stretched his long legs and eased his shoulders. The flight had been fast, but uncomfortable. He looked as grim and haggard as Pearce. Steve Ryder and Tim Lambert looked incredulously at him.

"What the hell's going on?"

"An organisation run by a man known as the Generalissimo intends to launch a global attack through cyberspace."

"There have been threats from hackers like that for years," Lambert retorted dismissively. "He's probably another nutcase. Remember the fiasco with those Chinese hackers a few years ago?"

"This is different," Pearce interjected. "They've developed a computer virus known as 'Black Crystal'. He's recruited computer experts from all over the world."

"Do you remember Ben Wallace?" Conrad asked. "We worked on assignments together when we were both in military intelligence."

"Yes, a good man."

"He's in the Police Service now, a Detective Chief Inspector in Shropshire, but he's working covertly for us. I discovered the Generalissimo's facility in the Swiss Alps. Wallace managed to infiltrate it. What he discovered is terrifying."

"Whoa! Whoa! Start at the beginning. What were you doing in Switzerland in the first place?"

Pearce rested his long legs on the desktop and settled back in his chair. Lambert's expression turned to disbelief as the story unfolded.

"These power cuts are only the start; just a warning," Conrad said. "He'll target industry, banks, the military. Once the virus infects systems it will be deadly. Everything will shut down. Nothing will stop it. Can you imagine the chaos?"

Their main problem was that they were fighting an unseen assailant. They didn't know in what form the virus would be sent through cyberspace. It was unlikely to be like an ordinary e-mail virus. This had been planned for ultimate destruction of even the most advanced, sophisticated systems. They didn't even know the timescale, only that it would happen very soon.

"This recent spate of power cuts is the most major so far," Pearce said. "The Generalissimo wants to create uncertainty;

to play on people's fears. By tomorrow morning the lights will probably be back on again. People will get on with their daily business. That's when he'll strike; when the country is least expecting it."

"Do you know the identity of this so-called Generalissimo?" Ryder asked.

"We believe it's Pavel Plushenko."

"Plushenko! Impossible, he's been dead for years! I was in West Berlin when it happened. British Intelligence was all over the place."

"It was a set-up. Unbelievably, he foiled the KGB. As you know the 'accident' was conveniently on the Havel where dozens of people in East and West Berlin could witness it. Military Intelligence started investigating, but Major Bryant was warned off."

So that's why Bryant had closed the file after the Soviets announced Plushenko's death. It was a politically crucial time. The Wall was in the process of being torn down. Intelligence had to tread very carefully. What the Soviets did with their own agents didn't really concern them, but it explained why Bryant made a U-turn.

"I had Plushenko and another guy, Mikhail Rykov, under surveillance for weeks," Ryder continued. "The Russians won't like the idea that Plushenko managed to outwit the KGB back in 1989, assuming it is him."

"He left the facility in the Alps when Wallace and I escaped. What he doesn't realise is that we know he's holed up on an isolated farm in Shropshire. Surveillance teams are watching him twenty-four seven. We suspected that he was somewhere in Shropshire from the maps Wallace found on the memory stick. Information gleaned from the owner of the firm who delivered crated equipment to the farm confirms our suspicions. It's them all right."

Conrad had come into contact with Plushenko on one of his forays over the Wall. He was a handsome, striking-looking devil in those days. That explained why he wore a prosthetic mask – double protection in case he was recognised by Soviet agents. Not even his top aides in the Black Militia knew his real identity.

"Wallace is holding off until I get to Shropshire. He issued a press statement about an armed gang on the loose, warning the public not to try any heroics. We don't want the Generalissimo to know he's been sussed."

"Everything will be on a need-to-know basis for the time being," Pearce interrupted. "Any leaks could spark a major panic all over the country."

Washington was taking the same stance, but IMIC was in the thick of it. They had to stop the situation from escalating.

CHAPTER SEVENTY-ONE

Shropshire, England

Overhead, ominous clouds dominated the sky, obliterating a watery moon. It had been raining steadily all day; dripping off the branches, soaking the ground that was rapidly turning to squelching mud. A low wind moaned through the trees adding to the misery of the men concealed in the copse. Only the faint scurrying of nocturnal animals disturbed the silence.

Conrad crouched low, scanning the distant farmhouse through his night-vision binoculars. Illuminated figures moved between the outbuildings and the huge barn. There was no sense of urgency in their movements.

"Looks fairly quiet," he whispered.

"Too quiet," Wallace replied.

"We have to locate the Generalissimo – Plushenko, if it is Plushenko. Only *he* will have access to Black Crystal. He's too paranoid to entrust it to anyone, not even his closest aides."

They had been watching the farm all day, waiting for the right opportunity. Every hour reports were coming in from all over Europe and the United States. A number of small-scale attacks had been made on nuclear power plants. Los Alamos in New Mexico, Diablo Canyon in California, Sizewell in the United Kingdom and Beznau in Switzerland. Public concern was mounting. Questions were being asked in Westminster,

Brussels and Washington. The Generalissimo had all the trump cards.

Wallace spoke quietly into his two-way radio to the armed response team positioned in the wood.

"We're going in. They'll have security guards and dogs everywhere so the less movement out there the better. Whatever happens, wait until you hear the order. We don't want bullets flying everywhere if we can help it."

"Understood, sir."

"There's an SAS unit and a chopper ready to go in if we don't come out alive," Conrad added. "Okay, move out."

They made their way across the ploughed field to the perimeter fence, stumbling in water-filled ruts. Crouching low beneath the security cameras they reached the fence. Electrified – too high to scale.

Wallace touched Conrad's arm and shook his head. Silently, he gestured for him to follow. He was a Shropshire man and knew the area like the back of his hand. Most farms backed onto each other. Somewhere, there would be a common fence. The Militia would have a hard job installing an electrified fence on adjoining land.

They skirted the fence until they came to a patch of waterlogged ground about half a mile behind the farmhouse. It was just as he thought. The wire fence came to an abrupt end. Instead, a stone wall stretched horizontally into the distance.

"Nice one, Ben," Conrad whispered.

"There may be a fence further in, but I doubt it. Fences within fences, especially electrified, would arouse suspicion. It would soon get around over a pint in the farmer's local. Besides, there's no access for vehicles or any public footpaths."

They scrambled over the wall and dropped down on the other side. Crouching low, they listened for any sound or movement in the darkness. No sound, only the wind whining through some nearby trees. They staggered on through the rain, mud squelching over their boots. Conrad stopped, peering through his night-vision goggles. Suddenly, he jumped on Wallace, pushing him to the ground.

"Over there," he muttered, "CCTV."

Wallace followed his pointing finger towards an enormous pine tree. Partially concealed, halfway up the trunk, a faint red light gleamed in the darkness. The slightest movement would give them away. Slowly, the camera swept the ground in front of them.

"Make a run for it when the camera arcs back again. Get behind the tree and wait for me."

Nanoseconds after the camera swept the ground Wallace jumped up and ran towards cover. Crawling through the mud he rolled down the slope out of sight of the camera.

"That was close," Conrad muttered, hitting the ground. "There must be other cameras out here. Keep your eyes peeled!"

They were about a quarter of a mile away. The farmhouse was partially concealed in a hollow surrounded by trees. Its position afforded good cover from the road, as it couldn't be seen from that angle. There was no sign of light or life.

They slithered along the wet grass on their stomachs. The ground around them had opened out making them more vulnerable, but at least there was nowhere to put surveillance cameras.

"Bloody cows!" Wallace grimaced, wiping his hand on his trouser leg.

"We should have some luck tonight then," Conrad grinned.

They crawled along until the shadowy outline of a large building loomed out of the darkness. In the near distance dim lights glowed in the farmhouse. Suddenly, a figure appeared in their line of vision and headed for the barn. Light poured out as the door opened and closed again.

"That's odd. This type of barn is usually open-sided," Wallace commented. "There's definitely something strange about it. The timber this side looks new and recently painted."

Stealthily, they half crawled, half ran towards the building. Conrad held out a warning hand as another black-clad figure walked towards the barn.

"Let's take a gander in the farmhouse first," he whispered. "The Generalissimo likes his home comforts. He could be billeted in there."

Keeping low, they ran over the cobbled courtyard towards the farmhouse and came up under a large sash window. Both men pressed themselves against the wall, either side of the window, holding their semi-automatic pistols at the ready. A gap in the curtains gave them a good view inside the house. There was no sign of anyone. Conrad moved around the left-hand side of the house while Wallace took the right. A minute later they met at the back door.

"There's nobody downstairs on this side," Wallace whispered.

"Nothing on this side either. There are no lights on upstairs so it's unlikely there's anyone up there."

"Our man could be upstairs sleeping," Wallace suggested. "After you."

Conrad turned the ancient door knob and pushed

open the door. The flag-stoned hall was lit with ornate, old-fashioned wall lamps. The hall ran the length of the farmhouse from front to back. Wallace pushed open a door and peered inside – empty. In the kitchen a kettle slowly boiled on an Aga. One by one, they eliminated each room.

Satisfied, they went out into the hall and started upstairs. Conrad gritted his teeth as a floorboard groaned under his weight. He stopped, waiting for someone to appear. Breathing a sigh of relief, he climbed up to the landing – only four doors. He motioned to Wallace to check the two rooms on the right while he made his way along the landing to the rooms at the rear. The right-hand door revealed a good-sized bedroom: a single bed, wicker basket chair, bedside cabinet, reading lamp, a battered wardrobe and chest of drawers.

Conrad slid open the top drawer – women's underwear, tights and a few pairs of woollen socks. The second drawer contained sweaters and scarves of various hues. But it was the bottom drawer that grabbed his attention. It was crammed full of sweaters and balaclavas – all black. The wardrobe revealed the same. Navy slacks plus three pairs of black trousers and a black parka.

Closing the door behind him, he crept to the right-hand door and waited. No sound came from within. He pushed it open and shone his torch around the room. It was a surprisingly modern bathroom with a large walk-in shower cubicle. Shower gels, shampoo and body lotions were lined up on a chrome stand attached to the shower wall.

Wallace came up to his side and peered in. "Women's things," he whispered. "The other rooms have twin beds:

348

men's militia uniforms in one of the wardrobes. Judging by the armbands they're all senior computer experts."

"There must be other dormitories."

"Maybe they're in the outbuildings," Wallace suggested.

"They've probably dispersed most of the Militia. All they need now are the computer guys."

Stealthily, they moved back across the cobbled courtyard past the four single-story outbuildings. They appeared to be completely deserted. Like the farmhouse, they contained sleeping quarters. Rows of single beds arranged like a military dormitory, with lavatories and showers at the far end.

"Judging by the number of beds there can't be more than about twenty militiamen. Now, let's find their boss. He's probably got security and a handful of his inner circle protecting him."

"Perhaps he bunks up with the women?" Wallace grinned in the shadows.

They backed against the stone wall as the Judas door in the barn opened. Bright light silhouetted a thickset figure emerging into the yard. He trudged towards the farmhouse and disappeared inside. Light flared in one of the bedrooms. A few minutes later the light went out, but the man didn't reappear. Another figure emerged from the barn and walked towards the farmhouse.

"They must be working in shifts," Wallace muttered."

"Well, that's two down," Conrad whispered. "Move out."

They headed back to the house and crept upstairs to the bedrooms. Cautiously, they moved along the landing to the first room. Wallace pushed open the door. It was in complete darkness. A man lay on the bed snoring, his mouth wide open. Wallace put his hand over the man's mouth while

Conrad delved into his pocket and retrieved a syringe. The militiaman's eyes shot open. He tried to sit up, but Wallace pushed him back onto the bed.

"Hurry up!" he muttered.

Conrad plunged the needle into the militiaman's arm and counted. Gradually, he stopped struggling and went limp. Wallace pulled the bedclothes up under his chin.

They waited a few seconds behind the bedroom door. No sound, not even a snore. Conrad stepped inside. The bed was empty. Suddenly, a figure sprang at him from out of the darkness. He dodged to the right, the glint of a knife whizzing past his head. He lunged at the man, bringing him down with a rugby tackle.

Wallace held him down while Conrad injected him with a strong sedative. He wanted both men alive in case the Generalissimo escaped. They hauled him onto the bed and covered him with the duvet.

"They'll be out for hours," Conrad said. He pulled a black balaclava from his pocket. "We'll use their parkas."

"What happens when they wake up?" Wallace asked.

"They won't remember a thing."

"How are we going to get into the barn? They may have rigged up retinal scanners."

"I doubt they've had time for anything elaborate. Don't forget they left Switzerland in a hurry." Conrad searched the militiaman's clothes. "Bingo!" he exclaimed, holding up a plastic key card.

Walking casually towards the barn, Conrad peered at the side of the door. There was nothing there; no key card slot. Carefully, he pushed the door handle down and stepped inside. A guard was stationed beside another door made of solid PVC. At the side of the door he spotted a metal block with a slot for the key card.

"Forgotten something?" the guard queried.

"Couldn't sleep," Conrad muttered, pulling the balaclava up over his mouth.

"Nor him," he added, indicating Wallace. "We'll work for another couple of hours."

The guard nodded and stepped to one side. Conrad inserted the key card and pushed open the door into a small anteroom. It was stacked with straw bales on three sides. Another solid door opened into the barn. He didn't expect to see what was inside. The whole barn was ablaze with lights. It had been subdivided into prefabricated rooms, separated with walls like an open-plan office. A bank of ten computers was set inside the largest of the spaces. The others contained single computers. All were manned except two.

Conrad strolled towards one of the unoccupied units and slid into the swivel chair. Wallace went into the adjoining space. A militiaman, wearing a yellow armband, poked his head into the unit.

"Back already?"

"Couldn't sleep – we both needed a pee," Conrad said without turning around.

The guard grunted and walked away. These computer nerds, they never stopped working. He would give anything for a couple of hours sleep.

Conrad prayed they hadn't changed the password, otherwise they were stuffed. He typed in OPERATION BLACK CRYSTAL in capital letters. The familiar icons popped up onto the screen, but now there were others he hadn't seen before: gas, electricity, water installations, nuclear power stations, banks, hospitals, military establishments. He clicked on the nuclear icon. Immediately, a list of installations popped onto the screen showing which ones had already been targeted with minor attacks. He scrolled down again and again.

It was unbelievable. The Penatgon, GCHQ, MI5, the FSB, Federal Security Service of the Russian Federation. Hundreds of malicious threats were effectively intercepted every day. What was different about Black Crystal? He had to find out and fast. They had to destroy this new installation before the Generalissimo launched his cyber revolution.

Trying to appear calm, Conrad searched for some indication of when the full-scale attack would happen, but there was nothing. Only some information was accessible. The majority of it was in hidden files that required individual passwords. God knows how long it would take to decipher the information, even if he could hack into it. The memory stick they had retrieved from the militiaman in the Alps was only part of the operation.

He got up, yawning loudly, and walked casually by Wallace's unit. Wallace stretched elaborately and cocked his head to listen.

"Stay where you are. Look busy. I'm going to snoop around. If the Generalissimo is here my guess is he's probably in this building somewhere where he has maximum protection."

He started moving down the narrow space between the units, flexing his shoulders and rubbing his neck. A security guard eyed him curiously, watching his every move.

"My shoulders are killing me," he complained, walking up to the guard. "Far too long at the computer. I need to walk to loosen up."

Conrad continued around the barn alternately criss-crossing the facility, searching for some evidence of the Generalissimo's presence. He sauntered back to Wallace's cubicle.

"I'm ready for some shut-eye now."

"Me too," Wallace knuckled his eyes.

"He must be somewhere, but he's not in the barn," Conrad whispered.

Together they retraced their steps towards the outer door, inserted the key card, and stepped into the vestibule.

In the gloom Wallace noticed some of the lower straw bales making up the inner wall were jutting out from the rest.

"They haven't been lined up properly," he said.

"It looks as if they've been pulled out and replaced," Conrad murmured.

"But the whole thing would collapse."

"Exactly – why hasn't it?"

Conrad squeezed his hand between the bales. He shoved his arm in as far as it would go, cursing the sharp bits that scraped his skin. Suddenly, the ends of his fingers touched something hard.

"There's something behind here. It's some kind of metal wall." Puzzled, he looked at Wallace. "It could be a door."

Both men examined the area around the bales searching for some kind of lever or button. Wallace kicked aside the straw littering the large flagstones. The corner of one was broken in three pieces. Underneath was a button set in concrete.

"This could be what activates the door," he whispered.

Conrad took out his Glock and pressed his back against the side of the bales. Wallace depressed the button with his foot then lunged to Conrad's side. A low hum and the bales slowly swung outwards revealing a steel door. The straw bales had been stacked against an inner metal skin.

"It's a whole bloody wall!" Wallace exclaimed. "We're not going to get in there, that's for sure."

Conrad shone his penlight along the gap between the bales. It was about two feet wide, just big enough for him to edge along to the end of the wall.

"It seems like a prefabricated, reinforced unit," he said, sidling back to Wallace. "Come on, let's get out of here."

Keeping close to the sides of the barn, they worked their way around. There were no other openings or doors to be seen. They headed for a small thicket of trees about a hundred yards from the rear of the barn. Throwing themselves onto their stomachs, they donned their night-vision goggles. The barn and surrounding area lit up luminescent-green. The only activity was the illuminated figure of a guard as he walked to and from the edge of the courtyard.

They made their way back over the field, avoiding the CCTV camera they had encountered on the way to the farm. By the time they reached the surveillance unit rain had turned into icy sleet. Conrad spoke briefly with the team leader of the Armed Response Team while Wallace briefed the rest of his men. Their position, elevated on a hill, gave them a distant view of the farm buildings.

"The farm and the barn must be kept under surveillance round the clock. I want everybody on the alert. I need not remind you that the gang is highly dangerous." He glanced at his wristwatch. It was almost 04.00 hours. "It will be light in another few hours so I don't want them getting twitchy. There's a stone wall about half a mile from the farm. If they get the wind up they could try to escape. Stay behind the wall out of sight. Whatever else you may see happening stick to your orders. Is that clear?" Wallace barked.

It could get very rough. He cursed under his breath. His men were putting their lives on the line without knowing the real reason. As far as they were concerned they were dealing with an armed gang of bank robbers.

Conrad got into the passenger side of the unmarked police car next to Wallace. Wearily, he knuckled his eyes. It felt as though someone had thrown sand into them. He spoke urgently into his satellite phone then listened, his face set like concrete. The Generalissimo's drive for power had escalated over the last twentyfour hours. More installations had been targeted; an oil rig in the North Sea and a refinery in Texas.

"Banks right across the country have been targeted, from Edinburgh to Cardiff and Plymouth," Pearce informed him. "ATMs have stopped paying out. Banks have refused withdrawals, because their systems are down."

Customers had started to panic, demanding access to their accounts. It had been a field day for handbag snatchers and muggers, especially when small businesses were paying in their daily takings.

"You're right Jack. This is just the tip of the iceberg. The maniac intends to destabilise the economy before he employs the full force of Black Crystal."

"There must be a way to stop him accessing the banks' computer systems?"

"They've had experts working on it. It's hopeless. As soon as they eliminate the threat, another virus infects the system."

Conrad snapped his phone shut. Why is the Generalissimo stalling? Why are the attacks on installations scattered so far apart? Why hasn't he launched Black Crystal into cyberspace? What is he waiting for?

*

In the temporary incident room, Conrad and Wallace stared intently at a computer screen. Clive Pearce's distorted, troubled image stared back at them.

"We have to strike before the Generalissimo realises we've sussed him out, Clive," Conrad said. "It's the only way."

"The Americans are kicking up a storm. I'm having a hard job keeping them at bay. They already have CIA agents operating covertly in London and other major cities. What they don't know is that we already have the Generalissimo under surveillance. It won't take long for them to sniff it out. I can't keep stalling for much longer. I needn't tell you that the Russians have their spies out too."

"All the more reason we go in as fast as possible."

Pearce stared into the near distance, rubbing his chin thoughtfully. He didn't respond for a full thirty seconds. Finally, he stared back into the screen.

"Okay, Jack. I'll speak with Gilbert immediately. The SAS is already on standby. They'll be waiting for your instructions. All contact will be via satellite phone, unless they are disabled. Washington is a few hours behind us. By the time everything is put in place it will be too late for them to object. If you don't succeed in capturing the Generalissimo… " He didn't finish the sentence. He leaned over his desk, his face close to the camera. "Good luck."

He flicked a switch and his image quickly faded.

CHAPTER SEVENTY-TWO

Shropshire, England

The predicted light falls had turned into heavy snow. Now it was turning into a full-scale blizzard. Already, a howling wind was whipping up deep drifts against tree trunks and fences. Branches heavy with snow drooped under the extra weight. At the edge of the small wood Conrad and Wallace waited.

"Are you okay?" Conrad asked.

"I'm fine," Wallace replied in a surly tone. He was beginning to realise just how out of condition he was after his excursion to the alpine facility.

"This is all we need!" He peered through the curtain of snow to the distant farm. "Trust the bloody Met Office to get it wrong again!"

"Ready… 02:25 hours," Conrad whispered. "Synchronise your watch." Even a few seconds were vital to the success of their operation.

Impeded by swirling snow and deep drifts, it took them longer than they anticipated. Twenty-five minutes later, they crouched behind the wall poised for the slightest sound or movement. The sky was black with storm clouds, but the night was illuminated by the brilliance of the snow. The black clothes they wore would stand out rather than camouflage them.

They made their way across the fields until they reached the crest of the slope. Suddenly, a figure sprang up behind them. Conrad spun round, his Glock at the ready.

"Still quick on the draw, Jack."

"Bloody hell!" Conrad recognised the resonant public school drawl of George Bentley, ex-military intelligence. "You're lucky I didn't clobber you!"

"That's no way to treat an old friend."

"What the hell are you doing here?" Conrad asked, noting the winter camouflage Bentley was wearing.

"SAS, old chap. My men are in place waiting for my instructions," Bentley whispered. "They'll move in as soon as you give the order. You can't see them, but they can see you."

Bentley spoke quietly into his two-way radio. A head popped up above a snowy mound and quickly disappeared.

"We go at 03:00 hours. There may be some Militia asleep in the farmhouse, but most of them are working in the barn. I'm certain that the Generalissimo is in a secure metal room," Conrad said. "We tried to get in, but the door is solid steel. We'll have to blast our way in."

"That won't be a problem," Bentley replied smoothly. "My boys will see to that."

"It's vital that we get him out alive. He's no good to us dead. Once the attack starts he'll know via his computer link with the main facility. I'm sure his personal quarters will be reinforced against attacks like they were in Switzerland. He'll try to escape amid the confusion. That mustn't happen."

"I doubt there are more than twenty there altogether, including two women," Wallace interjected. "Don't be fooled. They're as highly trained as the men and probably just as vicious."

Conrad scanned the farm area through his thermal night-vision goggles. Nothing stirred. The guard was probably sheltering inside the outer door. He glanced at his wristwatch. One minute to 0:300 hours.

"Get ready." Bentley spoke rapidly into his radio as Conrad counted down the seconds.

"Go!"

Jumping up they ploughed through the snow over the crest of the rise. Half crawling, half stumbling, they moved towards the farm that lay like a country Christmas card below them. One by one they dropped to the ground under cover of the copse. There was still no sign of movement anywhere in the vicinity of the farmhouse or the barn.

"Take the farmhouse and the outbuildings," Bentley said to the man closest to him. "The rest of us will take the barn."

Like snow leopards they stalked the farmhouse, moving in and out of the shadows. Splitting into pairs they crept towards the stone buildings. A seasoned SAS sergeant held up his hand and listened at the door of the first dormitory building. Not a sound. He moved from building to building looking through the small sash windows. His infrared imaging goggles immediately told him the first room was vacant. Quickly, he moved to the next dormitory. This time he heard loud snoring coming from within. He ascertained that two of the rooms were unoccupied. The others must be in the barn. That made life a whole lot easier.

Just as I expected, no security men outside the barn, Conrad thought. Cautiously, he opened the door. A guard was lolling against the wall, half asleep. Recognising the uniform he waved them in, his eyes bleary with fatigue. Conrad showed his key card and inserted it into the lock. The guard grunted and turned away. In a split second Conrad chopped him on the back of the neck, caught his limp body and lowered him to the ground.

Bentley and his men charged through the open door into the facility. He slammed a startled security guard with the butt of his rifle. Without a sound he fell unconscious to the ground. Suddenly, pandemonium broke loose. Security men swarmed from various points behind the units. There were more of them than he had anticipated, but they had been taken completely unawares. He threw a tear gas grenade into the nearest computer unit while his men tackled the rest.

At the periphery of his vision, he saw a man raise his gun. Before he could fire Bentley downed him with a single shot. The chatter of machine gun fire filled the air as militiamen fired wildly around the barn. Computer operatives ran towards the open door coughing, tears streaming down their faces. Security men shot them in the back as they ran. They knew their orders. When there was a security breach they shot to kill, even their own.

Taking advantage of the chaos, Conrad and Wallace ran down the corridor to the hidden door. An SAS man wielding an ILAW, a single shot Interim Light Anti-armour Weapon rocket launcher, followed close on their heels.

"The back blast area is clear. Get that door open!" Conrad ordered.

The soldier pulled out the safety tab, placed the rocket launcher on his shoulder and fired. There was hardly any recoil from the launcher as the rocket slammed into the metal door. The entire facing wall was demolished by the blast. Debris fell inwards into the room impeding their progress.

"Just as I thought; it's a single unit bunker!" Ignoring the danger, they scrambled over chunks of metal, stone and shards of wood from wrecked furniture. In the far right-hand corner a smaller steel construction caught Conrad's attention. Kicking aside the debris he revealed an opening about three-feet square. "Over here!" he shouted. "It's a tunnel!"

"He's well away by now," Wallace scowled, lowering himself into the aperture after Conrad.

Storm lanterns, suspended from beams supporting the tunnel roof, hung either side at the foot of a narrow flight of stone steps. Conrad pulled out a powerful flashlight and shone it into the tunnel. The light cast eerie shadows on walls that glistened with moisture.

The roof and walls had been shored up with timber props like the ones used in old mines. They made their way along the tunnel, keeping to the flagstones placed strategically along the floor. A thin film of ice laced the walls, glistened underfoot.

"There's another set of steps," Conrad said over his shoulder. "It must lead… " He stopped mid-sentence holding up a hand. Both men pressed themselves against the wall waiting with bated breath. A scrabbling noise came from the darkness a few yards in front of them. Wallace cursed as something darted across his feet, temporarily unbalancing him.

"Bloody rats!"

At the foot of the steps an icy blast of air blew in from above them. He climbed up and stuck his head through the opening. Snow fell in soft flakes, settling on his face and eyelashes. Hauling himself up, he pressed his body flat on the snow.

"Where the hell are we!"

Wallace scrambled out behind him. They were in a small wooded area; the same thicket they had hidden in before.

Sounds of gunfire and shouting came from the farmhouse. Suddenly, an explosion ripped through the air. The barn was a blazing inferno. Flames shot into the air lighting up the night sky. Illuminated figures dodged among the farm buildings and burning vehicles. A lone figure ran out into the snow, his clothes ablaze.

Frantically, the militiaman rolled on the snow trying to extinguish the flames. Other figures emerged from the stone outbuildings, prodded by SAS men. Overhead, the thunder of a helicopter engine drowned out the noise from the farm.

"How the hell did the SAS get their chopper out in this weather?" Wallace shouted.

Scrambling up the slope they ran towards the stone wall. Suddenly, the chopper loomed out of the snow right in front of them. It hovered about twenty feet off the ground, swaying dangerously from side to side. A single shot rang out, quickly followed by the chatter of a light machine gun.

"Get down!" Conrad yelled. "They're not SAS. They've come for the Generalissimo."

He dropped to the ground and fired his Glock over the head of the illuminated form crouched in the snow. All they could do was try to disable him. It was imperative he was taken alive.

A blurred figure leaned out from the helicopter and threw something out – a harness. The figure on the ground attached it to his waist. His body lurched violently from side to side as he was winched upwards. Seconds later, the chopper rose unsteadily into the curtain of snow and disappeared into the blizzard.

"I can't believe they're flying in these conditions! It's lunacy!" Wallace said. "The chopper must have been camouflaged somewhere on site."

Conrad and Wallace made their way back down to the farm. Bentley's men had rounded up all the survivors. SAS men had pistols aimed at wounded militiamen huddled against the stone outbuildings.

"There's a snow plough on its way clearing the country lanes so we can get this lot out," Bentley said, indicating the prisoners. "They'll be taken to a military hospital under close arrest. The rest will be transported to a secure military installation for interrogation."

CHAPTER SEVENTY-THREE

Shropshire, England

Near the Welsh border, south of Hereford, the helicopter pilot struggled to control his craft. Suddenly, it lurched then spiralled towards the snow-covered field. The Generalissimo teetered towards the open cabin door. They were only about fifteen feet above the ground now. He screamed as a gust of wind sent him hurtling out of the cabin into swirling snow. The pilot struggled to maintain control of the craft, but it was useless. Bucking like a mule it plunged to the ground and burst into flames, the pilot trapped inside the mangled fuselage.

On the ground, the Generalissimo stirred slightly. The breath had been knocked out of him, his leg hurt. He felt as though he had been kicked by a dozen mules, but he was alive. Gingerly, he stood up wincing as he put his weight on his injured ankle. Nothing broken – his fall had been cushioned by a deep snowdrift. Miraculously, his laptop was still slung around his back. In the near distance, sodium lights glimmered through the curtain of snow illuminating the sky with a muted orange glow.

Searing pain shot through his ankle when he tried to stand, but he managed to take a few steps. By the time he reached the main highway, he was exhausted with pain and the effort of ploughing through drifts. Snowploughs had been out clearing the road, but there was very little traffic moving. He straddled the verge, stopping occasionally to rest. He saw nothing for a full ten minutes, then he heard the deep growl of a truck labouring towards him. Headlights cut through the swirling snow, closer and closer, until they were almost upon him. Stepping out into the road, he waved frantically. Startled, the driver swerved then slewed dangerously to a stop.

"What the hell?"

A man limped towards the passenger side of the truck and banged on the windscreen. His head was covered in a fleecy snood like the ones used by skiers. It was pulled right up over the lower part of his face. Denny could only see his eyes. He lowered the window and leaned over.

"You bloody idiot! You could have been killed!"

"My car got stuck over there." He pointed to a barely visible side road. "I've injured my leg. I must get to a hospital!"

The truck driver hesitated slightly then reached over and hauled him up inside the cab. Across the field, lights glimmered from a cluster of isolated homes. He had been on this same run for ten years delivering goods to out-of-town hypermarkets. Why would the man trudge over the fields for help when he could have gone to one of the outlying cottages?

"You should have walked to one of those houses over there," Denny said.

"I'm a stranger to these parts. I panicked thinking I would get lost. The pain seems to be easing off a bit," he said. He rubbed his ankle. "I think perhaps I'll be all right now. Where are you heading?"

"Cardiff."

The Generalissimo started as a disembodied voice crackled from the two-way radio.

"What's it like with you, Denny?"

"Still on the road – slow progress, but at least I'm moving. It's just stopped snowing and the wind is dropping."

"Don't take any chances, Denny. Over and out."

The Generalissimo smiled inwardly. It couldn't have worked out better. Flights would probably be grounded, but the intercity train to London could be running later today.

"What are you doing?" Denny asked curiously when Plushenko booted up his laptop. "You won't get a signal in these parts. Another few miles and you may be in luck."

He couldn't believe his laptop was undamaged. When he finally managed to get online, he booked a seat on the Cardiff to Paddington train. Getting a seat on Eurostar to Paris at the right time was more difficult. His ribs were sore, but the tension in his chest evaporated when he managed to book a last-minute cancellation in business class.

His attacks on computer systems had been selective. Everything had returned to normal, but only until he decided otherwise. Now all he had to do was tolerate this moron Denny for another few hours. Wrapping his scarf round his neck and face, he settled back and closed his eyes. Lulled by the warmth of the cab, and the rhythmic swish of the windscreen wipers, he drifted into a dream-filled sleep.

He was standing at the head of an oval table. Seated around it were the heads of the G20 countries. Silent, fearful, they stared at his masked face waiting for him to speak. He was in command, invincible. Directing his gaze at the Russian President, he felt the hate coursing through his veins. They had betrayed him – ordered his death, but he had come back from the dead to create the Black Militia.

His closest aides, resplendent in their black and gold dress uniforms, stood to attention round the walls of the room. He looked up at the enormous motif set in the wall; a black snow crystal surrounded by solid gold. Slowly, he raised his hand and started to pull up his mask. Before he could pull it off, he felt someone shaking his shoulder, touching him. Nobody touched the Generalissimo! Somewhere between sleep and wakefulness, he heard a voice calling to him.

"Wake up, we're on the A470 heading for Cardiff."

Startled, he sat upright taking in his surroundings.

"I'll drop you off near the Civic Buildings before I go back to the depot. If you go through the underpass at Boulevard de Nantes you'll be near the main shopping area. Hey, are you awake?" Denny gave him a playful shove. "Here," he said cheerfully, handing him a sandwich from the plastic box on his lap.

The Generalissimo shook his head and looked out through the window.

"I feel a bit queasy," he said. His words were muffled by the snood covering his face.

"Why don't you take that thing off for a bit," Denny laughed, tugging at the snood.

Immediately, the Generalissimo pulled it back into place. Too late, Denny had seen his face. Now he would have to die.

"I need a pee. I'll stop here for a minute," Denny said. "There's a lay-by up ahead."

Denny pulled into the lay-by and let the engine idle as he went behind the curtain to the back of the cab. *Thank God for portable loos*, he thought. Closing his eyes he savoured the feeling of emptying his bladder. He couldn't put his finger on it, but there was something very strange about the guy in the cab who called himself Max; something very odd indeed.

He was zipping his flies when the knife slammed between his shoulder blades. He screamed, but it was muffled by the sound of the idling engine and heavy traffic. He felt the knife twist as it plunged deeper and deeper into his flesh. He fell forward onto his face, the knife sticking out of his back.

"*Nobody* sees the face of the Generalissimo."

Those were the last words Denny heard before total blackness engulfed him. The Generalissimo pulled out the knife and jumped out of the cab. Carefully, he washed it in the snow, removing all traces of Denny's blood.

Fingers of grey light streaked the horizon. Soon it would be light. He had to move fast, but his ankle was still too painful to walk far. He jumped back in the truck and managed to put it into gear. *The handbrake – where the hell is it?* After a lot of cursing, he finally juddered out of the lay-by onto the main road. A huge, articulated lorry sped past him catching him with its back draft. He slammed on his brakes. The vehicle wobbled slightly then snaked across the lane, slewed onto the hard shoulder, and scraped along the crash barrier. He backed up, straightened the truck and nosed back out onto the dual carriageway.

There was a road sign coming up. He peered through the windscreen: a slip road to Taffs Well. Where the hell is that? Cardiff and the M4 were straight on. He made a snap decision. They would be watching the roads in that area. No, instead of going into Cardiff he would go down the M4 towards London, abandon the truck near Bristol and catch the intercity train from there. Satisfied, he exited the A470 at the Coryton roundabout and drove up the slip road onto the M4 towards Newport. Two hours later, he was boarding the intercity express to Paddington.

CHAPTER SEVENTY-FOUR

London, England

The lights were back on in London. Twice in forty-eight hours the city had again been plunged into darkness. People were feeling scared and vulnerable. The enormous Norwegian spruce in Trafalgar Square blazed with Christmas lights, but few people were out to admire it. The blackouts had had a devastating effect on the tourist economy. People were staying away from the shows, museums and other attractions.

Conrad had left Wallace to mop up the carnage in Shropshire. At least they had destroyed the facility on the farm. The wrecked helicopter had been found in a field between Hereford and Abergavenny, but the Generalissimo was on the run.

"You look ragged," Pearce remarked, noting Conrad's unshaven face and the dark circles under his eyes. "You need some sleep."

"How can I sleep with that madman out there?" Conrad replied.

"Birmingham, Manchester and Cardiff airports are on high alert, including private air strips. All the main rail stations have been alerted and traffic is being stopped on all major roads. There hasn't been a single reported sighting of him anywhere. He may have slipped out of the country already.

"Pavel Leonid Plushenko," Pearce said pushing a fat file across the desk.

"The trouble is we don't know what he looks like, certainly not like this." Conrad tapped the photographs on the desk in front of him. "He might have had plastic surgery."

"It's possible, but somehow I don't think so," Pearce interjected. "You said yourself, he was a handsome devil – unusual colouring for a Russian. Apparently, he was a womaniser; a very vain man. He had a string of affairs with the wives of high-ranking members of the Politburo and a very senior KGB officer. He made a lot of enemies."

The photograph showed a raven-haired man with piercing, cornflower-blue eyes. There was something haughty and arrogant about his chiselled features and aristocratic nose.

"Sophia Dreher is right. Narcissistic megalomania – it fits."

"We still don't know that the Generalissimo is definitely Plushenko," Pearce stated. "Notice the scar just here." He pointed at a thread-like white scar running across the top of Plushenko's left eyebrow.

"Nobody in the Black Militia has seen his face. If they had they would be dead meat," Conrad added. "Are there any other distinguishing marks?"

"He has a small scar on each buttock. Apparently he got them sliding in the snow on a sheet of metal when he was a boy. The metal cut into him when he came a cropper."

"Well, that's not much help. I haven't seen his face let alone his backside," Conrad chuckled wearily.

"We have a comprehensive file on Plushenko. Family background, education, his rise through the ranks of the

KGB; his personal tastes in music, health records, even his allergies. It seems he was allergic to cows' milk."

Conrad raised his eyebrows quizzically and shrugged his shoulders. Suddenly, it clicked. He sat up, a stunned look on his face.

"That's it!" he exclaimed. "The goats; it's definitely Plushenko! The goats were kept to provide him with milk. That's what I saw in the Swiss facility; a portable pasteurizer and steriliser."

Pearce slapped the manila folder down and rested his elbows on the desk. "I'll be damned!" he exclaimed. "But it won't help us find him."

Wallace's men had questioned everyone living in the isolated areas where the chopper came down. An elderly couple reported that they saw it crash and burst into flames. Only the pilot's charred body was found in the burnt-out wreckage.

"I don't know how he did it, but he wasn't in that chopper when the emergency services arrived. It's possible he could try to get back to the facility in Switzerland."

"He'll know the first place we'll think of is Switzerland," Conrad said. "He may assume we'll discount it, because it's too obvious. On the other hand perhaps that's what he wants us to think."

"The only other way out is by sea. We've got the ferry terminals covered, but I don't think he'll try to get out that way. Hang on," Pearce said, reaching for the telephone. "I told you I didn't want to be disturbed for at least… " He stopped mid-sentence, a frown creasing his lined forehead. "Okay, put him through. It's Ryder," he mouthed at Conrad.

Pearce listened intently for a few minutes then carefully replaced the receiver. He leaned over the desk cradling his chin in his hands.

"Apparently an abandoned truck was found early this morning in an industrial park on the outskirts of Bristol. It was blocking access for other vehicles. A security officer went out to investigate. The keys were still in the ignition so he climbed up to switch off the engine. He spotted a foot sticking out from the curtain drawn across the back of the cab. It was a dead man, or so he thought, covered with blood. Miraculously, it turns out he wasn't dead. He's on life support at the University Hospital of Wales in Cardiff."

"Is that significant?" Conrad asked, raising his eyebrows quizzically.

"Earlier, a guy working in one of the loading bays saw the driver jump out of the cab and run off. He couldn't provide the police with a description, because his face was covered up and he was wearing dark glasses. He thought it odd that he was wearing an expensive overcoat. Not the kind of gear a lorry driver would usually wear. Could it be Plushenko?"

It was more than a possibility. Conrad rubbed his grizzled chin thoughtfully. The police had already traced the truck. It was part of a retail food chain covering the United Kingdom. The driver was on his usual run from Shrewsbury to Cardiff.

"He could have hitched a lift. Most truck drivers would stop if someone was stranded in the snow," he said.

"It makes a lot of sense," Pearce added. "Plushenko could have trekked across the field, south of Hereford where the chopper came down, and flagged down the truck.

"If he wanted to get to an intercity train line it would be easier to go to Cardiff, but I think he deliberately avoided

Cardiff with the intention of getting a train somewhere along the M4 corridor. It's got to be Bristol."

"The intercity train to London runs every hour," Pearce said. He pressed a button on the telephone and spoke into the intercom. "Isobel, get Ryder on the line. I want him covering St. Pancras. There's a possibility Plushenko will try to get out of the country on Eurostar. Jack is on his way over."

Conrad raced out and jumped into an unmarked police car. The driver slammed a blue light on the roof as they zigzagged through traffic at an alarming speed.

"Cut the lights and siren," he ordered, "before we approach the station. We don't want to warn our man."

He had the door open before the police car skewed to a stop at St. Pancras.

CHAPTER SEVENTY-FIVE

Eurostar, St. Pancras to Paris

Plushenko looked up from his laptop and stared pointedly at the plump blonde chattering on her mobile phone. Over the last hour she had talked to her cleaner, ordered party food from Marks & Spencer, booked theatre tickets and had a cosy conversation with a friend. Didn't the bitch know she shouldn't be using a mobile phone in a quiet carriage? Another man, buried behind *The Daily Telegraph*, glanced over the top of his newspaper and glared at her. Completely oblivious to her annoying behaviour, she carried on talking and laughing. He would have tackled her, but he didn't want to draw attention to himself.

Snow-covered fields gave way to a mess of concrete warehouses and office blocks as they passed Slough and headed into Paddington. Passengers poured out of carriages and walked en masse to the automatic barriers at the end of the platform. Plushenko inserted his ticket, but the metal gate didn't open. For a brief second his heart fluttered. The ticket collector held out his hand for the ticket. He let him through without even glancing at him.

Huddled in his heavy overcoat, he made his way to the taxi rank and waited impatiently in the queue. At last! The attendant waved him to a cab covered in advertisements for United Arab Emirates. He had folded up the fleecy snood

375

so it resembled a pea hat, but kept his scarf pulled tightly up over his face.

"Where to, gov?" the taxi driver asked.

"St. Pancras, Eurostar," he mumbled.

The taxi pulled up at the Eurostar drop-off point, halfway along the old Victorian brick-built Barlow shed.

Plushenko had forty-five minutes before boarding. He found a seat in the business class lounge and pretended to work on his laptop. It seemed like an eternity until a disembodied voice announced passengers could board the train. Impatiently, he rode the escalator up to the platform. It seemed to be moving at a snail's pace.

"Welcome to Eurostar." The stewardess smiled the regulation smile. "Have a good journey, sir." Barely acknowledging her, he hurried aboard.

He sat tensely in his seat willing the train to start moving, every sense alert to his surroundings.

*

Conrad charged across the concourse at St. Pancras heading for the Eurostar check-in. A man matching Plushenko's description had been spotted getting into a taxi in Paddington. He had given his destination as the Eurostar terminal. The Railway Police at St. Pancras had been alerted. They confirmed that he was headed for Paris, Gare du Nord.

"The Paris train has boarded, sir," the girl at the check-in counter told him. "It's leaving in two minutes."

Ignoring her protest, Conrad pushed through and raced up the escalator onto the platform, his heart pounding like a drum. If the police, or Gilbert's men, tried to apprehend

Plushenko at Gare du Nord, it could be catastrophic. It could force his hand sending Black Crystal hurtling into cyberspace.

"Ernst," Conrad spoke urgently into his phone as he ran. "If Plushenko is on Eurostar I'm convinced he'll try to get back to the facility in the Alps. He'll probably have a chopper waiting at Geneva."

"Pearce has already contacted me. We'll be ready for him."

"Don't try to arrest him. He's carrying a laptop. I suspect he'll use it to launch Black Crystal. Wallace is already on his way to Geneva."

Conrad flashed his security card and jumped onto the train just as the guard was closing the door. He looked down the carriage – standard class. Plushenko would want access to the Internet so he would more likely be in business class. Before making his way along the carriages, he donned a pair of transition spectacles and pulled a woollen hat over his head. Fortunately, he hadn't shaved for two days. His grizzled chin and darkened glasses helped to disguise his face. Plushenko knew what he looked like from his imprisonment in the Swiss facility. The last thing he wanted was to warn him he was being tracked. Taking out his satellite phone he dialled a number.

"Patricia Bonnet," a cultured voice answered.

"Plushenko may be on his way to Gare du Nord. I don't want him giving me the slip again," Conrad said, after outlining the situation. "If you spot him, try to get his laptop."

"Don't worry, Jack. He won't get off the platform."

*

Plushenko breathed a sigh of relief, but he couldn't relax. His mouth watered when the steward came around with trays of hot food. He hadn't eaten since the day before. Suddenly, he felt very hungry. After tackling the pre-cooked meal and two cups of tepid coffee he felt better. The caffeine recharged his batteries. Smiling inwardly, he settled back in his seat. They wouldn't catch him now.

Conrad worked his way along the train from the last carriage until he came to business class. Every seat in the first compartment was occupied. He spotted a well-known cabinet minister, surrounded by aides, engrossed in bundles of paperwork. Others were busily tapping away at their keyboards. Slowly, he moved across the intersection into the next compartment.

A man with his back to him was working on his laptop, a scarf covering his neck. Conrad sidled past him towards the glass sliding door a few seats in front. The young Asian man looked up briefly and returned to his work. It wasn't Plushenko. Perhaps the police had got it wrong. Could he still be in London?

As he entered the last compartment, he spotted a man sitting facing him in a window seat close to the exit. His hat and scarf covered most of his face. He had his laptop open, completely engrossed in his work. Conrad stopped abruptly and dropped down into the nearest vacant seat. He disciplined himself to breathe evenly and slowly as adrenaline increased his heartbeat. A stewardess pushed her trolley down the aisle in front of him. She stopped near the man in the window seat.

"Would you like more coffee, sir?"

Briefly, the man raised his head and looked at the girl.

There was no mistaking those penetrating, blue eyes. The Generalissimo! Conrad didn't dare approach him. Plushenko could activate Black Crystal from his seat, risking thousands of lives. He had to wait until they reached Paris.

Conrad watched him intently during the whole journey. He seemed completely engrossed in his computer. They were almost out of the tunnel when Plushenko suddenly sprang up. Before Conrad knew what was happening he reached up, yanked the communication cord, and dived through the glass sliding doors.

Wheels screeched on metal as the brakes engaged, bringing the train to a juddering halt. Plastic cups, food cartons and trays shot off tables into the aisle. Passengers lurched forward in their seats. A small boy screamed as his head hit the rim of the table in front of him. The stewardess tried to grab her trolley as it careered down the aisle. A man coming out of the lavatory lurched forward, slamming his face into the opposite wall.

Conrad dived out of his seat and stumbled down the aisle after Plushenko. Suddenly, all the lights went out. Passengers shouted out, their voices edged with fear.

"We've crashed!" a woman yelled. "We've crashed!"

Conrad managed to wedge his foot between the sliding doors before they closed. He squeezed through into the intersection. The external door was wide open. Dropping down at the side of the track, he pressed his body against the wall. In the distance, a shaft of light from the tunnel exit pierced the darkness. Hugging the wall, he edged along until he emerged into wintry sunlight.

Squinting against the harsh light, he scanned the area around the tunnel mouth, but there was no sign of Plushenko.

Damn it! He must be here somewhere! Then he remembered the escape passages. They were placed every 375 metres so that passengers could safely access them from the front or rear of the train. He must have gone through an escape passage into the service tunnel. The only way to go was up the embankment towards the nearby town of Coquelles. Hurriedly, Conrad punched a number into his phone.

"Patricia, I've lost him. He may be heading for Coquelles to get a train to Paris, or even a chopper."

"We have the stations and airports covered. If he comes into Paris we'll be waiting for him."

Conrad crossed over into the service tunnel and walked the full length of the train towards the previous escape route. Plushenko had eluded him again. He shone his flashlight up the tunnel and walked about a hundred metres past the rear of the train. Not a sound or movement.

He made his way back to the train and hauled himself inside. Suddenly, the lights flickered and stabilised. Conrad wasn't sure why the lights had gone off in the first place. That wasn't normal when the emergency cord was pulled. That must have been what Plushenko was up to on his laptop. A white-faced passenger, holding tightly to a woman who had fainted, sighed with relief.

"It's all right," he reassured her. "The lights are back on."

Suddenly, the train manager's voice blared into the compartment. "We'll be on our way in a few minutes. There's nothing to be alarmed about. Someone pulled the emergency cord. If anyone saw the person concerned please report it to the train manager."

In the gloom of the service tunnel Plushenko gave a satisfied smile. He would have been cornered if Conrad had walked to the next escape route. Instead, he had duped him again. They would be waiting for him at Gare du Nord, but he wouldn't arrive. He had arranged to pick up a Hertz rental car in Coquelles under the name of Luc Byard. By tonight, he would holed up in a luxury hotel in Versailles.

CHAPTER SEVENTY-SIX

Versailles, France

Plushenko sipped his glass of wine while he surveyed the elegant dining room. A woman glanced across at the handsome man staring at her. Retrieving her mobile from her handbag, she listened intently for a few seconds. She looked annoyed as though she had been stood up.

Plushenko's eyes roamed over her face and body. He forked a piece of meat into his mouth, his eyes never leaving her face. There was something overtly sexual about the gesture, sending an unexpected thrill coursing through her body. Smiling, he saluted her with his glass. Ignoring his advances, she left the table and wandered into the bar.

"Is everything to your satisfaction, Monsieur Byard? Would you like more wine?" the sommelier asked.

"Champagne; a bottle of Veuve Clicquot. Keep it on ice in the bar."

Rising from his seat, Plushenko followed the attractive brunette, deliberately bumping into her.

"*Je vous demande pardon, mademoiselle,*" he said in perfect French. Clicking his heels he gave a slight bow. He smiled disarmingly. "May I introduce myself – Luc Byard."

"Amélie Prideaux," the woman replied.

Temporarily flustered, a pink bloom blossomed on her

throat rising slowly to her face. The man exuded animal sexuality. He was seducing her with his eyes.

"Please have a glass of champagne to apologise for my clumsiness."

"I'm supposed to be meeting someone," she explained, "but he has been held up at work."

It was a lie of course. This was not the first time that Gerard had left her in the lurch. He had rushed straight home when his wife had rung to say that his little girl was feverish. Their five-year affair was coming to an end. She had not seen him for almost a week, not since a hurried liaison on Christmas Eve.

For a fleeting moment, Amélie hesitated. What was she thinking of letting a strange man pick her up? She noted the expensive suit, the well-manicured fingernails, the startling blue eyes. What was the harm in a glass of champagne? She shivered, a thrill of excitement and apprehension coursed through her. She couldn't resist this man. She knew without doubt he would end up in her bed.

Sipping champagne in her elegant apartment near the Palace of Versailles, Amélie told him all about Gerard. Evidence of him was scattered everywhere. Expensive shirts in the wardrobe, toiletries, an electric razor in the bathroom. It couldn't have worked out better.

He had been gentle with her at first until she started to struggle. As his lovemaking became more and more violent, he put a hand over her mouth to stop her crying out. Stuffing his handkerchief into her mouth, he pinned her shoulders to the bed. He had spiked her drink, but she still had enough strength to claw frantically at his face. He put his hands around her throat, increasing the pressure as his excitement grew.

Amélie's eyes were wide with terror. He liked that; it gave him a feeling of power. He didn't want to kill her, but it was too dangerous to let her live. Plushenko looked down at Amélie sprawled over the bed. The light had gone out of her eyes now, but she was beautiful even in death. A mistress murdered by her wealthy, married lover.

Plushenko slipped out of the apartment and headed for the Metro. Earlier, he had booked a room at the Hilton Hotel on Rue de Courcelles near the Arc de Triomphe. It was possible the police would look for him under the guise of Luc Byard, but he no longer existed. Still, he had to lie low until the heat subsided.

CHAPTER SEVENTY-SEVEN

Paris, France

Conrad settled back on the plush seat of the Bentley. Light flakes of snow danced in front of the windscreen. Sparkling fairy lights twinkled on the trees lining the Champs Élysée. At the far end the Arc de Triomphe was illuminated in golden light. Lamps blazed outside the imposing building as they drew up outside Patricia's apartment. She was waiting for him with a hot toddy. He sipped his drink and sighed.

"I'd forgotten how comforting this is."

"Why don't you take a hot shower and we'll talk later," she suggested.

After dinner, he sat back with a large brandy. Patricia had deliberately given the staff the night off so they could talk freely. He patted his stomach contentedly while he mulled over the state of play.

With her usual efficiency, Patricia had posted lookouts all over Paris. Plushenko seemed to have disappeared into thin air. Where the hell did he go when he left the Eurostar train? They had scoured the areas around Coquelles and Calais. Private airstrips, fields, anywhere a plane or helicopter could land. There hadn't been a glimpse of him anywhere.

Jumping off the train was a brazen move, but that was all part of Plushenko's delusion that he could outwit anybody. He was here somewhere, probably right under their noses.

Patricia wandered in with her gin and tonic and sat beside him on the sofa.

"If he's in Paris he won't get out without our knowing," she said, as if she had read his thoughts. "My guess is he'll travel to some rural area where he can be picked up by chopper from an isolated field."

"He's not going to risk a commercial flight, of that I'm certain." He yawned expansively. "I'm bushed. Let's talk again over breakfast."

*

Conrad devoured delicious hot croissants and steaming coffee while he browsed through the morning paper. Suddenly, he stopped, cup halfway to his mouth.

"What is it, Jack?" Patricia asked, leaning over to replenish his cup.

"A young woman was found murdered in an apartment near the Arc de Triomphe."

"It was in the evening papers yesterday – a lovers' quarrel. They've arrested a man."

"He's been released – gold-plated alibi. His daughter was rushed into hospital that night with suspected meningitis. The nurses verified that he was there all night." Patricia raised a quizzical eyebrow. "The victim had been drugged and raped, the same as Joanne Howard. I'm going to see Jules Laurent, my contact in the Prefecture of Police. I want to find out more about this murder."

CHAPTER SEVENTY-EIGHT

Paris, France

Chief Inspector Jules Laurent tapped a pencil on his desk. Thinning mousy hair, sallow skin, moustache tinted nicotine-brown: a man you would not notice in the street, on a train or anywhere else. He looked like a hundred other French middle-aged men. But his eyes were sharp and knowing. He was notorious for his demanding standards in conducting criminal investigations.

"The woman was drugged, raped and strangled. It was a particularly sadistic assault. A lot of bruising, if you know what I mean." He shifted uncomfortably in his seat. He had investigated dozens of murders over the years, but this kind of brutal crime still made him squeamish. He had two daughters of his own. "We'll get the filth sooner or later, Jack, but why are you so interested?"

"I've been working with your counterpart in Geneva – Ernst Dreher. He tells me you worked with him investigating human trafficking about five years ago." Laurent nodded. "I also need *your* help."

Conrad outlined the events leading up to Plushenko's escape. He raised his hands, palms up, in a futile gesture.

"We're up against a maniac, Jules. We've lost him, but my gut instinct tells me he's hiding out somewhere in the city."

Paris was teeming with tourists from all over the world.

It would be easy for Plushenko to get lost in the crowds. He could be walking along the Champs Élysée at this very moment sticking up two fingers at the police.

"The facility in the Alps was deserted when Wallace and I went up there, but I'm convinced that's where he's headed. If we don't stop him, the consequences will be catastrophic." Conrad's mobile vibrated in his pocket. "It's Ernst."

"Pierre Fournier has ordered another suit." It took a minute for Conrad to register what Dreher was telling him. "From the same tailor in Paris."

"Are you sure that this Fournier and Alex Campbell are the same man?"

"Absolutely sure – the same eyes. Apparently, he ordered the suit two weeks ago over the telephone. Their measurements are also exactly the same. It's being picked up from the store tomorrow night at eleven o'clock."

"What if he decides to turn up today?"

"He won't, the suit isn't quite ready. Unfortunately, the seamstress was off work yesterday. She's working all-out to get it finished by tomorrow night otherwise he'll cancel the order. They agreed to open up especially for him. He must have given them a lot of business to open up late on New Year's Eve."

"We'll be waiting for him," Conrad replied, snapping his phone shut.

*

Conrad watched the entrance to the tailor's from the hotel opposite. He had been sitting there sipping coffee for over an hour. Jules had men watching the area plus a man inside the store posing as an assistant. It was dead on eleven o'clock. His heart thumped in his chest when he spotted a tall man sporting a homburg, a scarf pulled up over the bottom part of his face. The man gazed at the display of men's clothes in the illuminated window for a few moments then walked briskly away.

Further along the street a figure, wearing scruffy jeans and a red anorak with the hood pulled up, walked sloppily along the pavement and stepped into the store. Conrad sighed. Perhaps Plushenko had got wind that they were watching him? Perhaps the tailor had warned him off? Suddenly, his mobile shrilled.

"A kid has come to collect the suit," a voice whispered.

He lunged for the door knocking over his coffee. At the same time Jules and the other agents converged on the store and grabbed the startled youth.

"Who asked you to pick up this suit?"

"Monsieur Fournier… he gave me twenty Euros to pick it up," the terrified boy blurted.

"Why? What do you know about him?"

"I don't know anything. I'm just a student… at the Sorbonne. It was a bit of extra money, that's all."

"If you're lying you'll go down for this," Jules barked. "Take him in for questioning."

"Please, I don't know anything!" the boy cried hysterically. "You can check with the university. Monsieur Fournier approached me in a bar. He gave me the money and promised more when I delivered the suit."

"That's exactly what you're going to do!" Conrad said.

*

Conrad followed the boy making his way towards the south pillar of the Eiffel Tower. New Year's Eve – tourists and Parisians alike were swarming into the Trocadero to see in the New Year. The boy disappeared and reappeared in the throng of merrymakers. He was only thirty metres behind him now.

As the teenager came up to the pillar, Fournier stepped out of the crowd and took the package. Conrad lunged at him. Unable to halt his momentum, he hit the concrete with a jarring thud. By the time he was back on his feet Fournier was disappearing into the crowd.

Conrad threaded his way through the mêlée and caught sight of him backtracking towards the Pont d'Iéna. Instead of crossing the bridge, he turned sharply and ran along Quai Branly. Bypassing Pont de l'Alma, he raced down Quai d'Orsay and turned onto another bridge.

"Jules, he's crossing the Pont des Invalides on to the right bank," Conrad yelled into his satellite phone.

He was way behind him now. They passed the Rond-Point des Champs Élysée and crossed over Rue la Boétie. He strained his eyes trying to keep the ever-distant figure within sight, but it was no use. At the junction of Boulevard Haussmann and Rue de Courcelles he lost sight of him completely.

"Jules, I've lost him. He's got to be holed up somewhere in an apartment or hotel. I'm going to scout around."

In the Purple Bar of the Hilton Hotel, on the Rue de Courcelles, Pierre Fournier sat in a secluded corner watching people coming and going. He smiled to himself relishing the fact that he had outwitted Conrad again. Briefly, he closed his eyes. When he opened them again Conrad was standing near the entrance to the bar talking to the concierge who was shaking his head and gesticulating in the Gallic way.

Calmly, Fournier walked out and took the lift to the executive floor lounge. Taking a glass of champagne he sat down, his eyes never leaving the entrance. He tried to disguise his anxiety when Conrad walked into the bar five minutes later, his eyes sweeping around the room. There was an atmosphere of jollity as midnight approached. A flat-screen television flickered on the wall, panned over the crowds around the Eiffel Tower, then switched to the Champs Élysée.

The countdown began. On the stroke of twelve, champagne corks popped around the room. Most of the inebriated guests were kissing and hugging perfect strangers. An attractive girl flung her arms around Conrad and kissed him on the mouth. He pretended to respond, but he was watching the bespectacled man sitting on his own quietly sipping a drink.

A woman wobbled towards the man and leaned over to kiss him. For some reason she backed off, casting nervous glances over her shoulder. Conrad sidled over to the woman and put his arm around her.

"How about a kiss for me? He doesn't know what he's missing."

Puckering up, she planted a wet kiss on his mouth. Seeing another target in her sights she wandered off.

Conrad pushed through the bodies and sat down opposite the man.

"Happy New Year."

"Happy New Year, Jonathan Landers." The man introduced himself in faultless English.

"Paul Winters," Conrad replied, using his middle name and his mother's maiden name.

Conrad scrutinised the man's reaction, but there wasn't a flicker of recognition or fear in his voice. They exchanged pleasantries for a few minutes.

"Will you have another glass of champagne?" Landers asked amiably.

"Not for me. I've had too much already... acid stomach." Conrad grimaced. He wanted all his wits about him. "Perhaps some hot chocolate to settle my stomach."

"Hot chocolate it is. In fact, I think I'll join you."

The throng of guests had thinned out, heading out to clubs and bars. Landers motioned to the waiter.

"Hot chocolate for both of us and make sure it's *hot*." He turned to Conrad. "They never seem to get it right in hotels."

"Of course, monsieur," the weary waiter replied with a tight smile.

Conrad studied Landers while they chatted. Distinguished, early fifties, silver-haired, pencil moustache, gold-rimmed transition spectacles. Charming, self-assured; a man who demanded deference. Conrad couldn't be certain of his eyes, perhaps greyish blue – it was hard to tell behind the darkened lenses. It was all wrong. Nothing fitted with the description of Campbell or Fournier. So why did he have an uneasy feeling about the man?

"Will there be anything else, Monsieur?"

"Ah yes," Landers said, "I forgot to mention I don't want cow's milk. I'm allergic to it. "Goat's milk is fine, if you have it, otherwise I'll have black coffee."

Conrad froze, struggling to assimilate what he had heard.

Heart thumping painfully in his chest he tried to appear nonchalant. Was this just a coincidence? He had to see the eyes behind the glasses.

"I think I'd better have a leak before I drink anymore," he said. Unsteadily, he stood up almost keeling over. "I feel a bit woozy." Suddenly, he lurched forward. Landers managed to catch him before he crashed into the table, but Conrad's hand caught the side of his face knocking off the spectacles. "I'm so sorry. I'd better sit down."

Landers swiftly picked up his glasses and replaced them; but not before Conrad caught a glimpse of the hard, cornflower blue eyes and the barely discernible thread scar over his left eyebrow. Then it hit him with startling clarity. Campbell, Fournier, Landers, Plushenko; they were one and the same. He was staring straight into the eyes of the Generalissimo. Heart thumping like a piston engine, he struggled to work out what to do next. A rush of adrenaline surged through his chest. He had to appear as normal as possible. He grimaced at Landers.

"Ask the waiter to keep my chocolate warm. I'm going to the loo."

Conrad smiled at the girl sitting behind the desk at the entrance of the executive lounge.

There was no way anyone could leave without passing the desk. He waited a few minutes, but Plushenko didn't appear. He took a deep breath and walked back into the lounge. His smile faded when he spotted the vacant table. Had Plushenko recognised him even with the week's growth of beard? Patricia had persuaded him to keep it saying how different he looked. He raced back to the desk.

"Has anyone left since I spoke to you a few minutes ago?"

"A young couple just left and Mr Landers left a few minutes ago."

"But I would have seen him."

The girl shrugged her shoulders. Cursing under his breath he went back into the lounge.

"When did Mr Landers leave?" he asked the waiter urgently.

"He has left? I thought you wanted the chocolate kept warm? Perhaps he has just gone to the bar."

Conrad cursed under his breath. Why hadn't he thought of it? Plushenko must have gone to the bar concealed at the back of the room and slipped past him when he re-entered the lounge.

He charged to the lift just outside and punched the button. It had stopped on the fourth floor. Was Plushenko in the lift or had he taken the stairs? Suddenly, the lift started to descend again. This time it wasn't stopping on every floor.

He raced to the fire exit, ran down the stairs and burst into the ground floor foyer. It was deserted. Everyone had gone out earlier to enjoy the festivities. Suddenly, a car screeched to a halt outside. He ran out just in time to see a silver Mercedes pull away. Plushenko stared at him through the rear passenger window as the car hurtled away down the Rue de Courcelles. Conrad made a mental note of the number plate then rushed to a waiting taxi and jumped in.

"Follow that Mercedes!"

"But monsieur, the taxi is reserved!" the driver cried.

"Just follow it!" Conrad ordered. He flicked open his phone. "Jules! I've found Plushenko, but he's given me the slip again. He's in a silver Mercedes heading down the Rue de Courcelles!"

They chased the Mercedes towards the junction with Boulevard Haussmann and turned on to Avenue Friedland. It was about a hundred metres in front of them now, nudging its way through the jam of vehicles circumventing the Arc de Triomphe. The taxi gained enough ground for Conrad to see the Mercedes entering Place Charles de Gaulle on to Avenue Foch. They followed it as far as Avenue Victor Hugo then back towards the Arc de Triomphe. They lost him at the Rond-Point des Champs Élysée.

"I've lost them Jules. Can you get a chopper out?"

"There's one already on standby."

"Get the pilot to pick me up at the Heliport de Paris in Issy-les-Molineaux. I should be there in about thirty minutes."

Conrad looked down on the city from the chopper. Vehicle headlights moved below him like strings of Christmas chaser lights. The Eiffel Tower and the bridges of Paris were resplendent in golden light. Even after dark it was one of the world's most beautiful cities, especially this time of year. It was the early hours of the morning, but revellers still swarmed the main streets.

Suddenly, the bright lights below them flickered and died. The city was plunged into darkness. Another power cut. The helicopter's searchlight swept the area below, but there was no sign of the silver Mercedes. By now Plushenko could be anywhere in Paris. On the horizon fingers of silvery light probed the sky above the city. It was past four o'clock in the morning by the time he got back to Patricia's apartment.

*

In the Hotel de Brabazon, Plushenko flipped open his laptop. It was time to declare war. Soon he would be in control of the most powerful countries in the world, but first he would play with them for a little while longer. With sadistic pleasure he tapped a key and waited. He checked his watch. It was midnight in America. Time to see in another New Year?

In New York's Times Square all eyes looked up at the dazzling, illuminated ball waiting for it to drop, heralding the New Year. Suddenly, the square was plunged into darkness. Not a single neon light flickered on the buildings.

"What the hell happened?" a voice yelled in the darkness.

"Don't worry, they'll be back on soon. Grid overload I expect."

But the lights didn't come back on. Panic rippled through the crowd like a fast-moving river. Cigarette lighters flamed, sputtered and died. A rookie cop fired a shot into the air to calm the crowd, but it had the opposite effect. Everyone started to move at the same time. A sea of bodies frantically shoved forward, trying to get out of the claustrophobic mass closing in on every side. The sound of breaking glass, trampling feet and cries of terror echoed in the air. Simultaneously, the lights went out all over Europe for the second time in twenty-four hours. He tapped the keys again sending a message into cyberspace. Washington, London, Beijing, Moscow; all the major governments in the world would receive his message.

'Your cities are in darkness. Soon there will be no water running from your taps, no light, no heating. There is worse to follow. Your business infrastructures

*will grind to a complete halt creating panic and a run
on the banks, but the coup de grâce is yet to come. Your
time is running out – the Generalissimo.'*

In the Commissaire's office Conrad sipped the scalding
espresso. The caffeine surged through his body giving him
the lift he needed. The chaos of the night before was still
being assessed. Good-natured celebrations had turned into
a nightmare. Shops had run out of candles, storm lanterns
and flashlights. Hospitals were operating on emergency
generators. Not a sign had been seen of Plushenko all through
the daylight hours.

Jules sat opposite him, a grim look on his face. Conrad
had crashed out for a couple of hours, but he was exhausted,
barely able to keep his eyes open. Suddenly, his secure mobile
buzzed.

"Regis," he answered.

"Our man has been in contact." Pearce read out the
e-mail Plushenko had sent. "What I don't understand is that
he hasn't given us any ultimatum. What does he want?"

Judging by what they had seen on the memory stick,
retrieved from the crashed helicopter in Switzerland, it was
obvious that Plushenko didn't need money. He had billions
stashed away in Switzerland and the Cayman Islands. He
wanted to destabilise the world economy. That, in turn,
would create tension between countries.

"'The coup de grâce is yet to come'. What does he mean?"

"My God, could it be he really means a conventional
war? Through cyberspace he can infiltrate military and
government installations – GCHQ, the Pentagon, Moscow.
Play on long-standing suspicions; turn country against

country then he'll be in complete control." Conrad heard the gasp at the other end of the line.

"We're still one step ahead of him," Pearce stated. "He doesn't know about the meeting with the G8 countries in Washington and they don't know his real intentions. We must try to limit that knowledge for as long as we can."

"Jules," Conrad said, turning to the Commissaire, "keep the chopper on alert. I think Plushenko will try to get out of Paris tonight. The trouble is he could be in any kind of disguise."

"Airports, railway stations, even boats on the Seine are being watched. Private airfields and heliports are also under surveillance. Anyone looking vaguely suspicious will be stopped and questioned."

"What about private helipads?" Conrad blurted. "How many are there in the city?"

Jules shrugged. "There are none in the centre. A couple of major hospitals have rudimentary facilities for emergencies only. Otherwise there is Issy-les-Moulineaux or JDP heliport outside the city. There used to be a rooftop helipad at the Hotel de Brabazon on Rue Honore de Faubourg, but it's no longer used."

Conrad looked thoughtful. Could Plushenko be brazen enough to make his escape from the street that housed the Élysée Palace, the official residence of the French President of the Republic?

*

Conrad sat silently in the unmarked police car observing the rear of the Hotel de Brabazon. He had been sitting there for two hours watching and waiting. It was crazy. He didn't even know for sure that Plushenko was in the hotel. Jules had made some discreet enquiries at reception, but staff couldn't confirm that anyone matching Plushenko's description had registered.

It was quiet, not a sound to be heard except the muffled noise of traffic that never ceased in Paris. Suddenly, a faint gleam of light on the rooftop caught his attention then disappeared. He strained his eyes to see the light again – nothing. Just when he thought he had imagined it he glimpsed it again, just above the safety barrier on the roof. The light was moving now from side to side.

Heart thumping, Conrad jumped out of the car and raced towards the fire exit door. It was locked from the inside. Using all his weight he charged at it. The impact jarred his shoulder sending him off balance. The door hadn't budged. Then he remembered the handheld ramming device Jules had told him was in the boot of the car. He hauled it out and pounded the door until it flew off its hinges.

Suddenly, he heard a loud roar and a whop, whopping noise. A helicopter! He ran up the stairs and burst through the door on to the roof. The wind created by the chopper almost knocked him off his feet. Out of the darkness a man ran towards it. A hand reached out to haul him aboard. Conrad lunged at his legs. A vicious kick to the head sent him sprawling. With a jarring thud, he dropped face down on the concrete. Gasping in pain, he struggled back onto his feet. In the gloom he caught a last glimpse of Plushenko's face before the chopper flew away into the darkness.

CHAPTER SEVENTY-NINE

Bernese Oberland, Switzerland

The French Airforce scrambled a helicopter and picked Conrad up from Issy-les-Moulineaux Heliport. Wallace was waiting for him. He had been flown to Paris from RAF Shawbury in Shropshire.

"Breakdancer, this is Regis," he yelled over the noise of the chopper. "I'm heading for the slopes with Rookie."

"Don't break your leg again," Pearce replied.

"I'll avoid the black runs."

Conrad snapped his phone shut. Reports had come in that air traffic control was down at Heathrow, Charles de Gaulle, Berlin Tegel Airport, Madrid, Leonardo di Vinci in Rome and Geneva. Tensions mounted as hundreds of disgruntled passengers swarmed the airports after missed flights for business meetings, weddings, funerals, holidays. Fights broke out as the chaos mounted.

Trains had stopped running. Signal systems on major intercity lines had broken down and passengers had been evacuated from the Eurostar tunnel. ATMs were spewing out cash and swallowing cards.

Families lucky enough to have a stock of emergency candles sat in half-light behind closed curtains, huddled together to keep warm. Central heating systems, depending on electricity to spark the boiler, had stopped working. The lucky ones luxuriated in the warmth of log-burning stoves, self-satisfied smiles on their faces. No television, no radio, very little light to read.

Children played in semi-darkness on their Nintendos, but soon that plaything would run out of energy. Yellow candlelight in the restaurants and bars created fantastical shadows lending them a surreal atmosphere. The scent of fear hung in the air as they sipped their drinks and half-heartedly made conversation. This was no ordinary power cut. The lights had gone out all over Europe.

"I can't get through to airport control in Bern!" the pilot shouted over his shoulder.

"Can you fly on to Interlaken?" Conrad yelled over the roar of the engine.

"Yes sir, but I haven't got the authority. Besides, I'll barely have enough fuel to get back to Paris."

"Leave it to me. I'll take responsibility." Conrad punched a number into his satellite phone. "Ernst, I need a chopper to pick us up in Interlaken. There's a golf course between the town and Neuhaus not far from a couple of campsites. We'll come down there."

Dawn had broken by the time they landed on the golf course just outside Interlaken. Battling against a flurry of light snow, they raced towards the Eurocopter EC45 chopper out of Rega's Air Rescue base in Bern, its rotating blades churning up snow into a mini blizzard.

"Are you certain that Plushenko is in Switzerland?" Wallace asked.

"I'm not sure of anything," Conrad replied, "but it's the most likely place. He'll reason we won't expect him to come back there, unless you have any other ideas?"

Wallace exhaled white vapour into the freezing air. He was still angry that Plushenko had got away from them in Shropshire.

Weak rays of sunlight pierced the clouds revealing patches of blue as the chopper circled the facility. Conrad looked down on snow-covered slopes. Only the occasional scrappy pine protruded from the blanket of white. Sweeping his binoculars over the area, he noticed the goats' grazing patch was no longer visible. Nor was there any sign of the concealed doors housing the helipad. Suddenly, he homed in what appeared to be shallow snowdrifts.

"Bloody hell! There's something shining down there."

"Those are the metal helipad doors we saw from inside the facility. Plushenko is here all right and he knows we've found him. He turned to the pilot. "Can you set down on that flat area just above the facility?"

"Only a lunatic would attempt it."

"But could a lunatic do it?"

"If the snow is packed hard enough, but it's extremely risky. If the wind picks up we'll be in big trouble."

*

Perched on the narrow plateau above the dilapidated hotel, they waited for Plushenko's helicopter to emerge. It was their only option, but not for much longer. The weather forecast was grim. Ominous shadows swept across the mountains as light faded into dusk, bringing a lull in the wind and snowfall. Suddenly, the clouds parted revealing mountain peaks that looked as though they had been crafted from icing sugar, glowing surreally white.

"This could be when he makes a break for it," Conrad said.

The pilot nodded and carried out his safety checks in readiness for flight. In the distance another swirl of dark cloud threatened on the horizon. From the facility a flickering light appeared. Peering through his high-powered binoculars Conrad saw the hangar doors slowly open wide. Rapidly, a helicopter rose up out of the gaping hole, its blades revolving in a hot take-off.

"Now!" he shouted.

Snow sucked at the helicopter's skis as it rose into the air and flew up towards the peaks. Conrad fired a volley of shots, but it was useless. The chopper banked and flew off.

"He's probably making for the field near Lauterbrünnen. We have to head him off!"

"The wind is picking up again," the pilot yelled. He was struggling to keep control of the craft. "I'll have to set her down!"

"Not yet!" Conrad shouted back. "Look, he's just in front of us."

The chopper bounced in front of them like a rubber ball on a string. Suddenly, a shot rang out over the whop, whopping of the blades. It pierced the window, grazing Conrad's cheek. Focussing a thermal imaging scope Conrad scoured the chopper cabin. He detected the pilot and another figure huddled in the cockpit.

"Look out!" he shouted. "He's got an AK-47!"

"What the hell are they doing?" Wallace yelled.

They could just make out the dim shape of the cable car line that stretched up to Mürren from Gimmelwald, the precipitous drop into the valley falling away beneath them.

403

As the chopper descended towards Stechelberg the wind caught it, sending it off course.

"They're out of control! They're heading straight for the cable!"

In front of them the pilot struggled to gain height, but it was too late. The helicopter hit it full on, its blades entangled with the steel cable. For a brief moment it hung there, swaying precariously from side to side in the eerie light. Suddenly, a highpitched scream pierced the air. The chopper broke away from the cable and fell like a stone. They followed its progress as it hurtled downwards, its blades tearing away from the fuselage. A ball of orange flame marked the spot where it smashed into the valley floor.

"I'll have to set her down in Mürren," the pilot said, "if we can make it."

They could barely see through the gloom as they lost height. Conrad scanned the area below them searching for the landing pad used to transport skiers from the towns.

He's some pilot Wallace thought admiringly as the skis hit the tarmac.

They trudged to the Hotel Bellevue near the Schilthorn cable car. They would have to wait there until mountain rescue arrived. In the meantime they needed a drink and some hot food inside them.

At daybreak Conrad and Wallace, accompanied by a search party, found the burnt-out aircraft and the remains of two men. The mangled body of the pilot was still strapped in his safety harness. They stared at the remains of the other passenger. His face was unrecognisable; the charred body sprawled in the snow in nightmare fashion. Conrad felt a grim satisfaction. Plushenko was dead.

CHAPTER EIGHTY

London, January 2017

Clive Pearce paced impatiently between his room and Isobel's. After a few days rest Conrad and Wallace had flown back from Switzerland. They were on their way up. Pearce walked back into his office, his face grim.

"Take a pew," he said when they walked in. "Glad to see you both back in one piece." He sat down behind his desk, swinging from side to side without looking at them. Conrad knew that pose. His boss had something on his mind. Finally, Pearce said, "It wasn't Plushenko."

Wallace started to say something, but Conrad held up his hand to stop him.

"What the hell do you mean?" Conrad asked.

"Forensics established that neither of the bodies found at the crash was Plushenko."

"But it must have been him! I saw him get into the chopper on the roof of the Hotel Brabazon in Paris. The facility in Switzerland is the only place he could have gone."

Pearce shrugged his shoulders. He didn't have an answer. His guts churned. They had been outwitted again.

Conrad struggled to assimilate the information. Plushenko must be still in the alpine facility waiting to make his escape. But that wasn't possible now. The blizzard had really closed in making it completely inaccessible. He must have gone somewhere else. Where was he? Why was he still playing games with them? The lights had come back on, but for how long? Sooner or later, banks and industries would be completely destabilised. What could happen next terrified him.

"Apparently, nothing of any significance was found in the burnt-out shell of the helicopter, certainly no laptop, disks or memory sticks," Pearce said.

So this was just a lull to create a false sense of security before the real strike. A strike he could perpetrate entirely on his own, from any country in the world. They had to play him at his own game. Where was the last place anybody would look for him?

"Russia!"

Pearce stared at Conrad incredulously. "Isn't that the last place he'd go?"

Disguise was second nature to Plushenko. That's how he had survived without being sussed out all these years. He was a master manipulator with a devastating ability to employ psychological and cyber warfare. Conrad wanted him; he wanted him badly.

"He's originally from St. Petersburg. He's clever and arrogant enough to try to outwit the Russian Security Services. He would know the best way to avoid detection. It would give him a buzz knowing he was outwitting the FSB. It's counter-psychology. Besides, he's done it before when the KGB organised his 'fatal accident' in Berlin."

Pearce shook his head. "We can't be sure he's in Russia. He could be anywhere – South America, the Far East."

"He probably has forged passports in a dozen different names," Conrad interjected, "and he speaks several languages fluently. I want to go after him."

Pearce pondered the consequences for Conrad if the security services discovered he was military intelligence. Most of his recent assignments had been in the Middle East, but there was always a chance he would be recognised.

"The Ruskies are in complete denial about Plushenko's death. They can't accept that he's duped them, which will be to our benefit. We'll drop the hint that our man wasn't Plushenko after all. A bit of egg on our faces is a small price to pay."

Pearce nodded in agreement. "I hope you're right." With a sigh he walked into the outer office to arrange details for Conrad's false identity papers.

CHAPTER EIGHTY-ONE

St Petersburg, February 2017

Conrad sipped his coffee as he studied the crowds through the window of Cafe Zinger on Nevsky Prospekt opposite Kazan Cathedral. He was travelling as a tourist under the name Gordon Schofield, an accountant from Reading with a passion for Russian architecture.

It was freezing outside, but like most buildings in Russian cities it was sweltering inside. The restaurant had been refurbished since his last covert visit over ten years ago. Now it sported deep green walls and chair covers. Even staff wore matching green and black uniforms. The babble of conversation illustrated the diverse nationalities of tourists to be found in St. Petersburg.

A woman in an expensive fur coat and silver fox fur hat lingered near the entrance. She beamed with delight when she spotted him.

"Darling, how are you?"

He rose, kissed her on both cheeks, and beckoned to a hovering waitress. She ordered an espresso while Conrad helped her take off her coat.

She was married to William Davidson, a wealthy American industrialist, whose great-grandparents left Russia in the late 1800s and settled in New York. On a business trip to Paris he met and fell in love with Ekaterina Merezhkov:

a journalism graduate from St. Petersburg studying modern languages at the Sorbonne. Under the pseudonym Veronique Thierry she wrote scathing political articles about the disappearance of journalists in Russia.

Just days after they married in the American Embassy, William whisked her off to America where she lived a life of luxury as Kate Davidson. With a dual passport she travelled to St. Petersburg several times a year. She visited relatives, toured the art galleries and shopped on Nevsky Prospekt. What her husband didn't know was that she was a conduit for a Russian dissident group with cells in all the major cities.

"What do you know about a man called Pavel Alexei Plushenko?" Conrad asked.

"Didn't he die in a boating accident in East Berlin in the late eighties?"

"That's what the Russians think – they set it up to look like an accident. We believe he's still alive. It's likely he's back in Russia using false papers."

"That's madness. The FSB would pick him up straight away."

"Not if they were certain they had knocked him off. He won't use any of the false identities he's already used, otherwise he would have been nabbed by us already."

"But why St. Petersburg?"

"It's his birthplace. Before he went into the KGB he lived here with his parents. They're long dead – he has no family left. Besides, if he went to Moscow, even heavily disguised, he could be spotted by one of his old cronies. A lot of them would be dead or retired by now, but one or two could still be around."

"You think he'll take on Russian identity?"

"Unlikely, probably French or German. He's fluent in those languages as well as Russian. His English is perfect. He's tall, slim, has startling, icy-blue eyes and is totally unscrupulous. He also has a white scar over his left eyebrow. He's a handsome devil and a womaniser. He's in his fifties, but looks younger. It's possible he may have arrived here during the past week. He's adopted various disguises so I can't tell you anything about hair colour."

"Sounds interesting," Kate replied, raising her eyebrows.

"Don't be fooled, Kate, he's a vicious killer."

Russia hadn't yet been badly affected by Plushenko's cyber attacks. It wouldn't serve his purpose to create chaos in the country where he was hiding out. His plans were breathtaking and frightening in their complexity. There was no doubt he could gain total control of major global economies, defence systems and military personnel, if only for a period of time. Enough time to throw the world into confusion. Set country against country; initiate a war in cyberspace – a war that could spark World War Three.

"Don't worry," Kate said, noting Conrad's grim expression. "I'll get my people on it. If he's here we'll find him."

She finished her coffee, kissed Conrad on the cheek, and walked towards the exit. At the door she turned and smiled back at him. He sighed, *If only she wasn't happily married to Davidson.*

*

An imposing dark-haired man, sporting a neat beard, smiled at the young waitress in Teplo Restaurant just off Bolshaya Morskaya Street. He appeared to be just another tourist crowding the cosy rooms. Natalya, the head waitress, watched him covertly as the girl moved between tables delivering meals. There was something about him that gave her the creeps. He was staring at the waitress with a half smile on his face; a look that suggested something more than another coffee. When Sonya brought the bottle of Malbec he had ordered, he smiled and whispered in her ear. There was no mistaking his intent. He wanted to spend the evening with her.

A plain girl, Sonia had never been very successful with men. Her heart fluttered unbearably when he suggested dinner that night in a very expensive restaurant. He took her hand gently in his and looked deep into her eyes. Sonya was vulnerable, lonely and completely mesmerised by his attentions.

They arranged to meet in the lobby bar of the Grand Hotel Europe at seven thirty. He had finished his potato and salmon pancakes with caviar, followed by a generous helping of beef stroganoff. Swallowing the last mouthful of Malbec, he paid his bill and headed for the Hermitage Museum.

Under the name Helmut Schroeder he had booked into the Renaissance St. Petersburg Baltic Hotel, which gave access to the Hermitage via the room key. It meant he could avoid the enormous queues that trailed down the pavement. After showing his passport he joined a guided tour visiting displays in five interconnected buildings. He was in no hurry; he had a whole week to kill, so why not enjoy it? After two hours he had had enough and walked back to the hotel.

At six-thirty, he made his way to the Grand Hotel Europe where he had booked a room for one night. When Sonya walked shyly into the lobby he took her hand, led her to a quiet corner and ordered champagne. Overwhelmed by the opulence of their surroundings, she quickly succumbed to his advances. When he suggested they should take the remainder of the champagne to his room, she didn't object.

As soon as he closed the door, he pushed her onto the bed and started ripping off her clothing. Befuddled by the alcohol, she lay back without attempting to push him off. This was not what he liked. He wanted the bitch to fight, to claw at him, plead with him, but Sonya was too tired. She closed her eyes and started to drift into sleep.

Suddenly, a violent slap brought her back to full consciousness. Through the alcoholic haze she saw his fist coming at her. The blow broke her nose. Terrified, she tried to push him away, but he rained punches at her, slamming her back onto the pillow. Blood trickled from her nose and seeped down the back of her throat. Bruises bloomed on her cheeks and under her eyes. Now she was ready for him. Now he could take her.

She was barely alive when he had finished with her: his face would be the last one she would see before she died. When his hands gripped her neck, a kind of peace settled over her. She slipped into death with the same acceptance she had lived her life. This was all there was for Sonya.

He stuffed his soiled clothes into a bin bag and tucked Sonya up as though she were sleeping. Grabbing the bag, he carried it to the fire exit and raced down the stairs. He threw it into a large waste container before hurrying back to his room in the Renaissance Hotel. After washing the colour out of his hair, he shaved off the beard and took a hot shower to eliminate any signs of blood. He put on the fresh suit he had left there earlier that day and slipped out of the hotel, luxuriating in the knowledge that he had dispensed with another whore. She hadn't even asked his name. They were all the same except his beautiful mother.

*

From the sixth-floor restaurant of the Renaissance Helmut watched fat flakes of snow falling past St. Isaac's Cathedral, so close he could almost touch it. In winter, snow covered the faded grandeur and shabbiness of the buildings, turning the city into a fairy tale of glistening white reminiscent of its pre-Bolshevik past. Since Gorbachov's Glasnost and Perestroika the decadent West had found its way into the very heart of St. Petersburg. He shuddered at the image of McDonald's on Nevsky Prospekt.

His thoughts were interrupted by the arrival of an elegantly dressed woman accompanied by an elderly man. They sat down at the adjoining table. His eyes roamed discreetly over her body. She was a stunner; just his type. His scrutiny of the woman hadn't passed unnoticed. Giving her full attention to her companion, she controlled the sudden thrill of anticipation.

Just as their drinks arrived the old man's mobile rang. Apologising profusely for the interruption, he went outside to take the call. The woman looked over the top of her glass and smiled provocatively. Helmut stood, bowed slightly, and clicked his heels.

"Allow me to introduce myself – Helmut Schroeder from Leipzig," he said in Russian.

"Ekaterina Merezhkov," she replied, using her Russian name. "You are German? I must compliment you. Your Russian is perfect."

"I am something of a linguist." He smiled modestly. "I am on vacation in your beautiful city."

"Uncle Piotr, is something wrong?" she asked, as her companion approached the table.

"I'm so sorry, my dear. I know how much you were looking forward to this evening. Those clowns in the warehouse have messed up an urgent shipment. I'll have to go and sort it out immediately. Perhaps we can rearrange for tomorrow evening."

He kissed her on both cheeks and hurried out towards the lift.

"I am staying here at the hotel. Perhaps you would care to join me for dinner," Helmut suggested.

"Thank you, but you are a total stranger. I think I'll have an early night instead."

"Please, we may as well enjoy dinner together and a glass of champagne," Helmut pleaded. "By the time the evening is over you will know all about me."

"I suppose it will be all right," she said tentatively. "We're both staying here at the hotel. It would be nice to have company, but I have to go to reception first to check on my tickets for the ballet."

*

Conrad walked into the hotel foyer wrapped in a fur coat and Cossack hat, his collar pulled up over his face so that only his eyes could be seen. He stood behind Helmut at reception while Kate enquired about her tickets for the Kirov. When they turned to leave Conrad took a good look at the man who took her arm. He took out his handkerchief, wiped his

414

nose, and inclined his head slightly towards a couple sitting in reception. They followed Helmut and his companion into the Canvas dining room.

Kate smiled over the top of her glass straight into Plushenko's ice-blue eyes. He didn't look anything like the description she had been given, but she knew it was him, even though he had tried to disguise the scar over his left eyebrow with make-up. Women noticed that kind of thing.

Natalya from the Teplo was a member of Kate's dissident group. She had contacted Piotr who put a man on his tail. After trailing Plushenko through the Hermitage and back to the Renaissance Hotel, he waited in the lobby. Plushenko knew he was being followed. It was the same man who had followed him around the Hermitage. Giving him the slip before he went to meet Sonya in the Grand Hotel Europe would be child's play.

His meeting with Kate Davidson was no accident. It was set up knowing his weakness for beautiful women. The perfect honey trap, but would Plushenko fall for it? Kate glanced briefly at the couple a few tables away seemingly engrossed in conversation. They would be watching out for her throughout the meal. Piotr's people were discreetly placed in the foyer and near the lifts.

Plushenko was charming throughout the meal, but she knew he had other things on his mind. He plied her with wine, topping up her glass after a few sips. She reached out for a chocolate and deliberately knocked over her glass. The wine spilled in a crimson pool over the pristine white tablecloth and dripped down onto her skirt.

"Oh, how clumsy of me! This will stain!" she cried, dabbing frantically at her skirt. "I'll never get it out. I'll have to go up to my room and sponge it."

"Shall I come with you?"

"No!" Kate replied hastily. "I'll meet you down here for a nightcap in twenty minutes."

Plushenko picked up his laptop and went up to fetch his coat and hat. *Time for a short walk to clear his head, then that tantalising bitch will get what she deserves.*

The cold air hit him in the face when he stepped out of the hotel and walked the short distance to St. Isaac's Cathedral on Isaakievskaya Sobor. It was snowing heavily. A freezing wind swept across the square. Snow swirled all round him, blurring his vision. Behind him Conrad was keeping a safe distance. He didn't want Plushenko doing one of his disappearing acts.

The magnificent golden dome of the cathedral, over a hundred metres high, loomed over them. *What the hell?* Plushenko walked swiftly across the snow-covered grass, leapt over the railings and ran up the steps. By the time Conrad reached the entrance he had disappeared between the columns. His stomach lurched. *Had Plushenko sussed that he was being tailed?*

Trying to keep in the shadows, he circumvented the enormous Byzantine-style building watching Plushenko dodge between the pillars. He peered into the semi-darkness of the portico, straining his eyes for the slightest movement. *Where the hell was he? The façade was illuminated. He would spot him if he tried to run for it.* Pressing himself against a pillar, he listened for any sign of movement.

Suddenly, Plushenko sprang from behind a column and ran down the massive granite steps. Conrad lunged at him, bringing him to the ground. The laptop fell into the snow. He grabbed at it, but Plushenko aimed a sickening kick to his diaphragm. Winded, he sank to his knees gasping for air. Plushenko was on his feet running down the steps in the light illuminating the cathedral.

Suddenly, a figure ran from behind one of the pillars, his shadow falling on the snow.

"Nobeca!" he shouted. The man moved into the light. "You will not escape this time."

"Morozov!" Plushenko froze long enough for Conrad to stand up. "You'll never capture me, Morozov! I fooled you once and I'll do it again!" he screamed.

Before Conrad realised what was happening Morozov lunged at Plushenko. Still clutching his laptop, he pushed him off and ran towards the corner of Admiraltyeskiy Prospect. Conrad chased after them along Ulitsa Yakubochiva.

Dodging traffic, he followed them onto Blagoveshchensky Bridge. About twenty metres ahead, Morozov caught up with Plushenko and pushed him to the ground. Something gleamed in his hand. Conrad went for Morozov's legs. Lashing out with a vicious kick to his knee Morozov ran towards a waiting car. Seconds later, it had disappeared from sight.

Sirens wailing in the distance, Conrad stumbled to Plushenko's prostrate figure. His dead eyes were wide open, his mouth distorted with shock. The laptop was still strapped firmly to his shoulder. A hypodermic needle jutted out of his neck.

Swiftly, he searched Plushenko's pockets and retrieved two memory sticks. He wrenched off the laptop and smashed it violently against the balustrade until the outer casing fell apart. Now, he had to destroy the hard drive. He finished it off with the butt of his Glock and threw it over the side with the laptop.

He had to work fast before the FSB agents caught up with him. Struggling to maintain his balance on the icy ground, he hauled Plushenko's body up over the parapet and pushed it into the night. A sharp crack came out of the darkness as the body hit thin ice and disappeared into the freezing waters of the River Neva. Nobeca had come home.